…There were more bangs, and a voice came, smothered by the thick oak. "We know you're in there. Open up."

She fell to her knees, sobbing.

She must defend herself.

The bangs became thumps, as a heavy shoulder shook the door in its frame.

Now is the time for the Sword. What's wrong with her?

The moan became a litany. "I can't kill, I can't kill."

Inspired by the splintering of the doorjamb, the Sword's patience ran out.

All right, I give up. EIRLIN, YOU DON'T HAVE TO KILL ANYONE. JUST DRAW THE SWORD.

"I can't kill, I ca…what?"

We don't have to kill them. Wound and disarm. But draw the Sword. Quickly!

"Who's talking to me? …Kitten? Is that you?"

There is no time for this. Draw me, for the Fire's sake.

The door was half broken now. A leather-clad arm stretched in to undo the latch.

DRAW THE FORGE-BEDAMNED SWORD, WOMAN!

With a gasp, Eirlin clutched the hilt, and the Sword shrugged smoothly from the scabbard, humming with a fiery joy.

Good evening, gentlemen. Sorry, no time for chit-chat. Shall we move straight to the part where you run away screaming and bleeding?

A Sword Called ...Kitten?

Happy Reading, Nina

Gordon A. Long

AIRBORN PRESS
Delta 2011

Published by
AIRBORN PRESS
4958 10A Ave, Delta, B. C.
V4M 1X8
Canada

Copyright Gordon A. Long
2011

ISBN 0968883524
ISBN13/EAN-13 9780968883525

Thanks

To Cas Peace and Elizabeth Wilson for their eagle-eyed editing.

Prologue

Sludge began to ooze into the scabbard, the acid tang of corroding slime creeping along the Sword's finely polished blade.

What in the Name of All that is Sharp and Pointy is wrong with humming? It was just a soft little hum. It wasn't loud or off key. Cats purr, don't they? You don't see people throwing them *into swamps.*

And this wasn't just any person. This was a Hand. Everyone knows the Hand has a mystical bond with his Sword. *Hah! Some bond. One tiny hum and whee! Away we go, over the reed tops and into the muskeg.*

The Sword steeled itself...*Get it? Steeled? Hahaha...? Huh. Nobody listening, nobody laughing. Especially me. Less than a day in this swamp, and it's already rusting my intellect...*

The Sword steeled itself to resist the rust, hardened its surface against the intruding decay, and settled down to wait. Swords had patience. Sometimes it took centuries to advance: hoarded by dragons, hung on dusty mantels, embedded in altars.

But not in an edge-dulling, Hammer-cursed bog! How can you win fame, glory, and a Name, when you're up to your hilt in swamp water?

The Sword calmed, scanned the immediate area. Maybe there was someone out there. If only that dratted Hand didn't have such a strong arm. If only he hadn't been so frightened. *It was only a little bit of humming, for the Smith's sake! What did he think I was going to do, steal his soul? Yuck!*

What was that? Faint, muddled, thoughts. A low view, looking up. Something circling close... look higher... A victim! Closer... closer... patience... lead a bit... Now! Got it! Yum!...?...A frog!

A stupid, round-edged, rust-rotted frog.

Now that the Sword knew what to listen for, the swamp was full of them: busy, dim little minds, intent on food, fear, sex, and sleep. *Great companionship for a century or two.* Not that any Sword, even as finely crafted and magic-imbued as this one, could withstand a century in a swamp. In spite of the Sword's natural resistance, its youth, and its magical powers, the rust would win. It always did. Just a matter of time.

Fortunately the Sword had landed with its hilt above water. Over there was the road. Not much of a road: just a corduroy of logs laid crossways over the mud. If only someone would ride by, with a ray of sunlight reflecting at just the right angle...anyone. *Anyone!*

Then, no more humming. *I'm willing to swear on the Forge, the Anvil, even the Hammer. No more humming.*

7

Chapter 1

The Sword stretched out on the rough counter, humming softly inside. Very softly. No sense in bothering anyone. Six months in a swamp had been very instructive in that regard.

Eventually, though, a possible Hand had come along, in a receptive state of mind. One helpful ray of sunshine, and a new Joining was complete.

A new Hand, but hardly the right disposition. It soon became obvious that he was a thief, and a lowly one at that. No skill to speak of, no honour, and definitely no chance of achieving lofty deeds. It had been fairly simple to teach him enough to keep him going as far as the next big town, then finesse his luck to the point where he was willing to sell the Sword.

Not that being sold is a great experience either.

The event had a sort of lowly, merchantish quality. The choices became limited, although that was a bit exciting, really. You pretty well went with whoever had the gold, and Hands were so undiscriminating.

They pick you up, they like the colour of your blade or the jewel in your hilt, and they pay the money.

So few of them even thought to try a few passes; they just waved you around a bit and imagined themselves doing heroic deeds.

So degrading.

It was easy to tell that most of them had no hope in the Forge of achieving anything close to glory, and it really irked the Sword to have to teach these fumble-fingers enough to keep them alive.

So the Sword was happy today. The lad now bargaining was a definite pace forward, maybe even a lunge. At the merchant's nod, he grasped the hilt, and the Sword nestled cheerfully into the calloused palm. The ease with which the Hand swung and the beautiful feel of cleaving air cleanly at high speed produced an instant song. The Hand stopped, puzzled, and regarded the Sword a moment. Then he swung again, faster this time. The Sword rewarded him with a higher note, sustained into the harmonies of his mind.

They are so easily led... and this one is so receptive! The Blood of Inderjorne is strong in him. A good sign.

The Hand grinned, then quickly sobered. He turned to the merchant and nodded casually. "It feels right, but it's a bit fancy for my taste."

The merchant was close enough for a decent nudge, and the Sword decided to act. This was a simple trader, not an arms merchant. The hue of running blood, a mere tang of the stench of battle, were enough to instil the motivation to sell.

9

"It's not that fancy, young sir. Quite a..." the merchant suppressed a shudder, "...businesslike weapon, I'm sure. A lot of soldiers about, I notice."

"That's why I'm here. I don't want a sword..."

Don't want? What do you mean?

"...but I need one." The Hand paused to stare at a troop of soldiers marching past, and swung the blade again. The Sword felt the thrill of satisfaction that ran up his arm, fed it with a touch of glamour. Perhaps too much.

The Hand regarded the blade suspiciously. "Is that writing, there?"

The merchant made a show of looking gravely. "It might be. Doesn't say anything I can understand."

The Hand turned the Sword, letting the light catch the etching on the blade. "Don't even recognize the letters. I wonder what language it is?"

The merchant gauged his customer carefully. "One of the Old Tongues, probably. Been around a while, I'd think. Seen a lot of the world, this blade."

If a Sword could chuckle, now was the moment. A little help from a skilled trader, and the sale was as good as made.

"Well..." The Hand laid the Sword on the rough wood. "What are you asking?"

The merchant started to name a price that was far too high. The Sword had seen many Hands come and go, and this lad's clothing gave a good indication of what he could afford. The Sword gave another push, hinting at screams of death, and the merchant reconsidered.

"Tell the truth sir, I'm not a seller of weapons. I only bought this one because I liked the look of it. I'm not the kind of man to want to get into that business." He named a price that was half of his original intention.

The Hand shook his head slowly, regret in every line of his face. "Far too steep for me." The mental image of a few thin golds in his pouch was so strong the Sword wondered that the merchant couldn't read it.

The Sword felt a pang of regret. This Hand fitted the hilt perfectly, the work-hardened fingers melding with the sharkskin wrapping. And the power of his swing! Truth be told, it had been a while since anyone had brought out that note.

The Sword considered. This had to be done very carefully. There was a note of caution in the Hand, a consideration, mostly superstitious, of the dangers of magic.

Now there was an idea. The Sword nudged again at the malleable young mind.

The broad forefinger prodded. "I'm not so sure about that inscription. What if it's a magic Sword? What if it steals my soul or something?"

The merchant forced a genial laugh. "If it's a magic Sword, then you'll be getting it for an amazing price. I wouldn't be too worried about your soul, fine young gentleman like you, brought up right, all the proper training."

Don't push it too far, merchant.

The Sword could feel the reservations in the Hand's mind. These humans were far too insecure. Even the best of them had souls like…well…maybe not like steel, but at least very good iron. Came right down to it, they were hardly worth the bother of stealing anyway. What did it get you, in the end? Without the basic temper to start with, adding a few mediocre human souls was like holding up a branch in a rainstorm. If you didn't have the proper steel, you were going to get rusty, no matter what.

The Sword concentrated on the conversation, which, undirected, had been going around and around.

The steel is heated to the right temperature, lad. Time for the anvil.

Only a slight "inspiration" was needed. The Hand reached into his purse, slammed the meagre handful of golds onto the counter.

"That's it. That's all I've got. Do we have a deal?"

The merchant's quick mind did the calculations. It was some profit, after all, and…well…this boy struck him right somehow.

Good choice, man. You've done the right thing.

At the decision, a warm glow filled the merchant, and he smiled. "Well, lad, it's not like I'm ever going to get rich at this business. I think the sword suits you. If you go out and do fine deeds with it, I'll be able to say, 'I sold him that sword.' Maybe that's how I'll get my value out of it."

The young Hand gleamed from inside, warming the steel of the Sword until it had to suppress a pleased hum. "Oh, don't you worry, sir. I'll always use it in the most honourable fashion!"

The merchant scooped up the coins. "I'm sure you will, sir. Good fortune to you." He paused a moment. "Wait, lad."

The Hand froze, fingers about to grasp the scabbard.

Huh? What now?

"This is an important occasion. Some ceremony is in order. Please allow me."

The Hand relaxed. "Of course." He stood away from the counter, and the merchant buckled the belt around the lad's waist, settling the Sword comfortably against the muscular hip. The Sword nestled closer, moulding the scabbard to fit the contours, the suppressed hum building inside.

"Say, that feels good. Very light, you know. Almost as if it wasn't there." The Hand walked a few experimental steps, returned. With the ease of long practice, the Sword's tip avoided the numerous piles of bric-a-brac along the market tables.

The merchant stood back, admiring. "Looks like it belongs there."

The Sword could feel the doubt beginning to fade, and snuggled in. "It feels like it belongs there, sir. Thank you so much."

The man shook his head. "Troubled times, young sir. I hope you don't have need for it, but I have a feeling you might." Then he brightened. "Well, as I said, use it for the good of the Realm of Inderjorne, and I'll be satisfied in my investment."

"You have my word on that, sir!"

The Sword was moved by the strength of the Hand's emotion. He had needed no prompting at all; he truly believed in what he said. A small trickle of excitement stirred at the bottom of the Sword's being.

Could this be a True Joining? Oh, please the Smith it could be!

A shimmer of anticipation rippled its blade, followed by a wash of dull despair. Too many times had hope been aroused, only to be dashed by reality. A Hand who could wield a Sword and an occasion of dire need were rarely in coincidence.

The Sword stiffened its resolve. No need to be pessimistic. In any case, this was going to be much better than jolting around in a merchant's wagon, suffocated by rolls of cloth, dusted by sandstorms, wetted by puddles.

They swung out the low door together, the Hand's head already higher, the Sword riding freely in the sunshine. It had the look of a pleasant day.

Chapter 2

The feeling lasted as far as the doorway to the nearest tavern.

"Hey! Hey, kid!"

The Sword could feel caution building as the Hand slowed, turned to face the young man who had called out.

Now there were three of them, spilling from the inn doorway: armed, moving well, but relaxed by a drink or two.

"So, Cousin, where are you going?"

"Home."

"Not stopping to give a cousin a polite hello?"

"I didn't know you were there, Jesco." The Hand created a smile. "Now I'm saying hello."

The older youth scowled. "Well, now, that's not really good enough, is it? Not good enough, not soon enough. What if I were to take it into my head to feel slighted? You thought about that, little Cousin?"

"Little" seemed a strange appellation, since the Hand overtopped his relative by a good half head.

The Hand sighed, but not out loud. He walked closer to his cousin, lowered his voice. "You've got no reason to feel slighted, Jesco. We've always got along well enough."

"Ah, but now you've got a sword! That changes things!"

"It does?"

"Oh, yes, it does. Maybe you're thinking of getting above yourself. What does a woodcutter need with a sword?" He glanced down the street, where three men, obviously soldiers out of livery, were leaning against a shop. His lip wrinkled. "Well, maybe you do need a sword." He sighed. "So you bought one in the marketplace. Probably got taken for every penny. Let's see it."

The Hand drew the Sword out slowly, but when the other reached for it, he pulled back. "It's really old. It even has an inscription on it."

He held it out for the cousin to see. The Sword knew this was no time to show off.

I am a plain, old sword, nothing special, nothing wonderful; I have no Name.

Jesco glanced at the blade. "I don't see any inscription. It's probably rubbed off already. You bought an old sword, all right. Looks like it's been lying in a swamp. Nothing but rust. You got taken, kid."

I prefer to call it the patina of age.

Unmoved by the insult, the Hand resheathed the Sword, hitched it to that perfect spot on his hip. "I like it."

"That's just fine, kid." Jesco frowned. "You even know how to use it?"

The Hand smiled, more freely this time. "Not that well, actually. Say, Jesco, would you try a few passes with me?"

Oh, no. Not the anxious-to-please puppy act. That just encourages them!

The cousin stepped back half a pace, hand on hilt, which allowed the Sword to read the other weapon.

Only dead steel. No problem there.

"What do you mean?"

"Well, as I said, I don't know more than the basics of sword work. Maybe we could go down to the practice field and you could show me a few sword fighters' tricks?"

If it had a voice, the Sword would have groaned. *By the Anvil, you don't grovel to this type. It only makes them worse.*

But the Hand wasn't listening, just standing there with his big, stupid smile, asking to be slapped down. The Sword sighed and prepared to fight.

What a disappointment. To be Joined to a new Hand, and to have to celebrate against a bunch of soft-steel, notch-edged ruffians. *A slow start, but at least a righteous one, I suppose.*

The Sword reached out to make contact, to start the control process…

…only to be met by a wall of cool confidence. Puzzled, the Sword drew back. There on the face of the Hand was the silly smile. The surface of the mind was eager to please, a bit uncertain. But down under, in a place the Sword could barely reach, was a cold, hard appraisal of the enemy. Intrigued, the Sword eased back in. The Hand was calmly registering the stance of the adversary: the grip on the sword hilt, the shifting of the eyes, noting the positions of the two henchmen, analyzing possible threat. And, below that, the knowledge of his man, the sure judgement that the other would back down.

Relieved and impressed, the Sword added its power, reaching out to nudge the unease that crept into the bully's thoughts.

Jesco laughed, roughly. "You know, Ecmund, I have a certain attachment to members of my family, but nowhere have I ever seen it written that I have to waste my time training a young pup like you in his basic moves."

"Aye, Jesco. It was just an idea." The smile brightened, and a shaft of humour shot up from the depths. "I'll go away and practice, and some day, when I'm better, then we can have a go!" The smile hardened, just a touch, and the Sword could feel the Hand's eyes grow cold.

The cousin frowned slightly, then scoffed. "Aye. Some day that'll be."

"Right. Then I bid you a polite good-bye, Jesco."

14

The Hand nodded to the two others and turned away with a jaunty step, a glow of satisfaction coursing through him. The Sword adapted its swing to the longer stride, thinking fiercely. There, right in front of the Sword, with almost no help, the Hand had faced down an older bully with two cronies, and left behind an unanswered challenge.

There's more to this Hand than meets the eye. We may be bound for glory!

Let me see…"Hand of Destiny"… no, I'm a Sword, not a Hand.

"Destiny Bringer"… the "Bringer" part is a bit weak. Hmm…

"Destroyer of Destiny"… that one has a ring to it! Perhaps a bit negative… but I could live with a Name like that.

Chapter 3

The Hand strolled through town, pleasant thoughts on the surface of his mind. He spoke politely to several people he met, and twice stopped to show off his new purchase to admiring older folk. The Sword was slightly miffed at the condescension they felt, but decided that they could be forgiven because of their obvious liking and respect for the Hand, young as he was.

Three soldiers in livery walked past. They glanced at the Hand, muttering to each other, but they did not stop him. The lad gave them a polite nod and continued, unmolested.

There is something going on here. Squads of armed soldiers wandering around, not speaking to the townsmen. The sentries on the town gate weren't in livery at all. Looked like militia. Hmm. Perhaps there is a chance... No, too early to tell.

The Hand continued his walk all the way to the edge of the village, and turned in to the last cottage on the street. It was a small home, only one floor, but the Sword sensed a large shed behind, and a yard that seemed full of wood, in all shapes and sizes. Aha. Now the "woodcutter" comment made sense.

The Sword sighed. *A bit of a comedown, considering some of the Hands of the past. Except for the thief, of course. Oh, well. Make the best of it until something better comes along.*

The Hand called out cheerfully as he approached, and the door swung open. The young woman who appeared was almost as tall as the Hand himself: the same blonde hair, braided down each side and tossed over her shoulders, the same clear, round, face.

A wife! What was a swordsman doing with a wife? Of all the rust-bitten luck. Married Hands are handicapped. Hahaha. Get it? Hand... Not funny. Not funny at all.

"Ecmund! What took you so long at the market? Did you buy the bread?"

"Oh." Instant guilt flashed through the Hand's whole being. "I..."

"You forgot!"

"Um..."

"Ecmund! What has got into you? You go to the market for bread, you're gone all afternoon, and you come back without it? I swear, you have the emptiest head in all of Inderjorne."

And listen to that tongue. This is going to be so much fun.

"Wait a minute!" She took both his shoulders, cocked her head to one side as she stared at him. "You were looking very pleased with yourself a moment ago. What...Oh." Her eyes fell on the Sword, peeking up at her from behind his hip. "Where did you get that?"

"I…" His head came up, resolved. "I bought it. At the market. From a merchant."

"Well, I didn't think you bought it at the baker's! What do you need a sword for?"

This is not going well. Stand up for yourself, man!

His hand felt for the hilt and the Sword sent him a flush of comfort. "I need a sword, Eirlin. Every young man needs a sword. Otherwise I'm just a…just…"

"…just a peasant. Very nice. I'm sure a lot of your friends would love to hear that kind of patronizing."

"It isn't like that. I didn't want this. I want to be a woodcutter, and work my trade in peace. I don't want to strut around, carrying a sword."

Why not? It's a wonderful feeling!

"But you bought one anyway? Very logical."

"Ah, Eirlin, you just don't understand…"

Understanding isn't what she wants. She wants to…

Suddenly the woman smiled and slapped his arm, not gently. "We can't be arguing in the street. Come into the house. We'll have pan bread for supper. Come in and show me this wonderful new sword you're so happy about."

Huh?

She strode inside, and he followed her, grinning sheepishly.

Inside the door, the Hand turned left into a comfortable common room, where a fire was burning on the hearth and the aroma from a pot of stew caught his attention for a moment.

At least she can cook.

He turned back, drawing his sword, holding it out to her hilt first.

"Isn't it a beauty? Got to be old; look at the patina on the surface. Feel how smooth it is."

The girl reluctantly took the Sword by the blade, obediently running her finger along the metal. The Sword glowed, proud of that deep colour, gained as it was through age, experience, and, it must be admitted, several months lying in a swamp.

"Go ahead. Try it."

With a moue of distaste, she shifted her grasp to the hilt. A sudden jolt whispered through the contact; a small response trickled back. She quickly took her hand away.

Her mind is clear as crystal! She could be a Hand!

"And look at the writing on the blade!"

The Sword pushed the inscription forward, wondering if she would see it. They often didn't.

She leaned close, turned the surface to catch the light. "It's some sort of runes." She looked up at the man. "Do you know what they mean?"

17

He shrugged. "The merchant didn't know either. Far as I can tell, it just means that it's old. Really old."

Old? I'm not old! What's a hundred years, here or there?

"It is beautiful, if you like that sort of thing. I don't." She held the weapon out.

The Sword felt a pang of dismay. *Why the Forge not?*

The Hand merely laughed. "I know, I know. You would much rather Heal than hurt. But somebody has to defend us. With the old Overlord dead, and the soldiers from the castle throwing their weight around…"

Aha! That explains a lot. Useful people, Healers. Rather a pain at times, but necessary.

She frowned. "I know we need to be careful. I just don't like to be reminded."

"I feel the same way. I just wish it all wasn't happening, and we could simply go on like we always have. But we can't."

He took the Sword from her and sat, holding it gently across his hands, gazing at its lustre in the firelight. "Once I held it, I had to have it, Linna. It just seemed right for me."

She stood, hands on hips, regarding him. "It does seem to suit you, now that you mention it. I didn't even notice it at first. Of course, you were probably hiding it."

Instant denial sprang from both of them, and she laughed. "Of course you weren't."

"Oh! And I've used it already."

"You what?" She stepped backward in horror.

Oh, yes! We burned down a village, slaughtered women and children, just for practice. On the way home from the market. It was no end of fun!

"No, no, not that way. Sit down, I've got to tell you."

Obediently, she sat in the chair opposite, returning his smile, a frown still hovering.

"On the way home, I met our dear cousin Jesco. He and a couple of his cronies were coming out of the tavern. He stopped me, gave me trouble for passing by without a polite salutation."

"Why don't you two leave each other alone?"

"He doesn't usually bother me. It's everyone else he shoves around. Why is he like that?"

"If you had a father like Uncle Aeldwig, how do you think you'd be?"

The Hand shrugged. "Anyway, he started to give me a bad time about my new sword. So I asked him to go a few passes with me. I did it all friendly, asked him to show me some moves. And you know what?"

"He refused, of course."

18

"That's right! He made a joke about my not being worth the effort, but he was afraid. I could tell. I just stood there, my hand on the hilt, you know, and looked at him. Just looked. And he backed down, and that was it."

"Well done, brother!"

Brother?

Her face suddenly lost its smile. "You don't think he'll be angry, do you? Try to get back at you?"

"No, it wasn't like that. I made sure he didn't lose face or anything. I just let him know, and I think he got the message. The others didn't even notice."

"Well, I hope so. It's bad enough having to deal with Uncle Aeldwig every Feast Day. I wouldn't want to have Cousin Jesco glowering at me, too."

"I thought Jesco liked you."

"He sort of does. I always pretend he's a gentleman, and he likes to think he is, so he treats me like a lady. It works."

Brother. Cousin Jesco. Uncle. That sounds much better. She is really quite pretty: long and straight like an upright blade.

Things were looking better.

She sat back, staring her brother up and down in the warm light. "So now you've got a sword. What comes next?"

"What do you mean?"

She raised her eyebrows. "The usual pattern when a lad starts feeling grown up. First it's a sword, next it's the young ladies. Or the other way round." She shot him a sudden glance. "You have someone picked out? Looking to swagger a bit?"

"Of course not! I'm much too young to get married."

"So it's marriage you're thinking about?"

"I said I wasn't."

"Fair enough. Don't worry. I won't get in your way. Once you're settled down here with a nice girl, I'll go and live on the farm. Cousin Maerwin will be happy to have me keep Uncle Aeldwig off her back."

"Eirlin! What are you talking about? I'm not getting married, and I have no intention of throwing you out of here. And why is it me? Why aren't we talking about you getting married? You're older than me. You need to be out looking around."

"I need to be 'looking around,' do I?"

Ahem. Excuse me?

"Yes. It's not going to be easy for you to find a husband, you know."

I'm... not sure that's exactly a good way to put it...

The woman's face reddened in the firelight. "And just why is it going to be hard for me to get a husband?"

"Well, you know. You're too pretty, and too smart, and too…well, outspoken. Most of the lads around here are sort of afraid of you."

The Sword suppressed a groan.

"Afraid of me? And what about you?"

He shrugged. "Nobody's afraid of me. Plenty of girls would be interested, if I were to let them know."

She sat a moment with her hands in her lap. "So you're saying that you, the swordsman, will have no problem getting married, because no one is afraid of you, while I, the Healer, will have trouble because the men are all afraid of me."

"Exactly."

I am Joined to a Hand with no brains at all.

He leaned forward, took her hands, pulled them gently. "But that's my point. You shouldn't be looking around here anyway. There's nobody of the Blood that's really available. You should be getting out, meeting some more people, different people."

She tugged her hands back. "And how am I going to do that? This is where I live. My Healing keeps me busy, plus finding enough food to fill your bottomless stomach."

"Don't blame my stomach for this. You need to get out and see the world."

She cocked her head to one side. "Where did this all come from all of a sudden? It's that sword, isn't it?"

Oh, no. You're not going to pin this on me! I didn't say a thing. Dumb steel, I've been, ever since I came in that door.

"No, it's not the sword. Well, maybe. It's the idea. We shouldn't spend our whole lives here, never go anywhere. You want to learn more about Healing you have to go now, before you're married, and have children to tie you down."

"First you're worried I'm not marriageable, now you're afraid it will tie me down. What, exactly, are you getting at?"

I'd like to hear the answer to this one.

He wiggled his shoulders, miserably. "I don't know, Eirlin. I just got this sword, and I was thinking about things, you know, and then I thought you should have some of the same…things."

She smiled and laid her hand on his. Surprised at the flow of emotion, the Sword quickly settled down to bask in it.

"So you have some dreams, and you're anxious that I have some too? That's very sweet, Ecmund."

He shifted uncomfortably. "Well, you know…"

She laughed, patted his hand, and rose. "It's very thoughtful, and I won't tell anyone and embarrass you. Now go and wash the unearned sweat off your brow, and I'll get supper on the table."

The abashed grin returned, and he got up obediently and went out to the well in the back yard.

Aha. But she didn't tell him what her dreams are, did she? I wonder. What kind of a Name might a Healer yearn for?

"Plague Bane?" "Life Bringer?" How about "Sickness Squasher?"

Well, I'm glad I'm not a Healer. None of them really have a ring like "Destroyer of Destiny!"

... definitely too negative. Something strong, but righteous, I think. Maybe..."Zealot."

... no, that sounds too religious.

Perhaps..."Ebullient?" I'm not actually sure what that means, but it sounds sort of fun...

Chapter 4

The unthinkable happened after supper. With one final pat, the Hand propped the Sword carefully in a corner by the fireplace, and went to bed.

In the next room!

Very unwise.

Oh, well, nothing to be done. The Sword snuggled deeper into its scabbard and waited, going over the day's events, allowing itself to dream, just a little.

This Hand was obviously an upright citizen, with sharp wits, strong morals, and a muscular body. His mind was very receptive. Hers too; the Blood of the Realm of Inderjorne must run strong in this family. Given the opportunity, heroic deeds were possible. Together, they would fight glorious battles, win honour, gain Names for themselves, Names of distinction. Names like...

"STORMBRINGER!"

Well, that is a bit too... too...

I still like, "DESTINY BRINGER!"

Have to find another word for "bringer."

"BRAND OF DESTINY!"

Too many words. Hmm...

The hours of the night passed quickly.

The next day the Sword watched with cautious optimism as the Hand prepared himself for outdoor work. However, when the moment came, just before he went out the door, when he should have reached for his Sword, he didn't.

Hey! What about me? Where in the Name of the Anvil are you going without your Sword?

The Hand merely picked up his small pack of food and water and walked out, closing the back door behind him. Puzzled, the Sword waited. The Hand did not come back.

He did not come back all day. What was a Hand doing, out all day, unarmed? Very puzzling. This Hand thought of the Sword in a very strange way. He enjoyed the feeling of wearing it, as any young man would, but there was a reluctance, deep within, to everything the Sword meant. This was going to take some delicate footwork.

Well, nothing to do about it till he gets home.

The Sword, used to waiting, spent the day idly regarding Eirlin as she went about her household routines. Fortunately, boredom was not a concept within the Sword's grasp. Waiting was imbued in every crystal of its steel.

As the light faded and the shadows lengthened the Hand returned, sweaty and tired, tossing his pack on the table and flopping into the chair by the fire.

His sister handed him a mug, brimming with cool cider. "How was your day?"

After a pause for a long, satisfying swig, the Hand nodded. "Quite good. That oak I got from Cened last fall is drier than I thought: almost ready for sale. Oh, and I found a beautiful wild cherry out beyond Sudusen's pasture. It's amazingly straight and rot-free for a tree that old. You know Hohersund has been after me for some good furniture wood. I'll cut that down and haul it in, slab it out, and let it dry for a season or two. Be worth a few golds."

She swung by him on her way to the table, leaning down to look into his eyes. "Had time for a walk in the forest, did you?"

He grinned, not at all put out by her sharp tone. "If I didn't go walking in the forest, how would I find wood to cut?"

Her nose went up. "Some might say you would do better with a little more cutting, and a little less walking." Then her light mood faltered. "Besides, isn't it dangerous to be in the forest alone?"

He shrugged. "I'm not exactly toothless out there, you know."

The Sword, mildly interested in this domestic conversation, suddenly perked up. *What does he mean, "not exactly toothless?" His Sword is standing in a Hammer-forsaken corner, and he is travelling a dangerous area with only a small dagger at his belt. Surely this Hand isn't that stupid?*

"I know you aren't, but I worry all the same. There has been talk of bandits, and the troop of soldiers that marched through here last week didn't look too friendly."

"They're from the castle, Eirlin, and the Overlord died without an heir. They don't have any reason to be happy, and there isn't much discipline. Don't worry. The King will assign the demesne to a new man, and it will all straighten out. I hope."

"You hope?"

"I'm not counting on it, Eirlin." He gestured towards the Sword. "I think we have to be ready for anything, no matter how much we hate the thought."

This is going to be harder than I thought. His natural instincts are completely backwards. Living with a Healer must have warped him.

Eirlin turned to the fire, the conversation became less interesting, and the Sword went back into the waiting state. Later that evening, the Hand lifted the Sword, drew it, and gazed at it fondly.

This is more like it.

The Sword fed the joy, strengthening the bond. However, the Hand soon sheathed the Sword regretfully, returned it to its corner, and went to bed.

What in the name of Hammer and Tongs is wrong with this fellow?

In the morning, the Hand repeated his routine, leaving the cottage at dawn, unarmed, and returning at nightfall. The sister went about her daily life, working in the house and garden, gossiping with townspeople who came and went, called away for several hours in the early afternoon for some sort of Healing. It was all very difficult to understand. If there were dangers, these two weren't acting like it.

After days of inaction, the Sword began to realize that if this was going to be its life, then it had better find something useful to do. Waiting was not a problem, but it was not productive.

The next day, when the Hand left unarmed as usual, the Sword did not fall into a somnolent state. It began to use its powers of perception to understand the cottage and its surroundings, borrowing strength from the nearness of the Healer's receptive mind. Seeing was much more difficult when not in physical touch with a Hand, but it was not impossible.

The Sword gradually created a picture. The cottage: three cosy rooms, a split-shake roof, doors front and back. To the right, the wall pushed against a storage barn attached to the neighbouring house. Behind the cottage was the wood yard: piles of cordwood, stacks of planks. Across the rear, a storage shed full of smaller lumber. A heavy door at the centre of the yard led to a path that wound away into the forest. Over in the left-hand corner of the yard, a two-story barn with hay in the mow.

From a defensive point of view, the place was reasonable. Escape routes front and rear. The side of the yard closest to the forest was walled to twice a man's height in solid stone, well mortared. The only problem would be fire. All that lumber, sawdust, and hay, with wood shingles...

The Sword's perception faded as it stretched away from the property owned by the Hand, but the impression was of a bow-shot-wide pasture, then forest which covered the land for a great distance. In the other direction lay the rest of the village: tight-walled, buildings hugged together, very defensible.

In the night, when the Hand was nearby, the Sword could see everything clearer. There were more people within range, as the villagers came home from their labours. A large horse was stabled in the barn.

Then one afternoon many things became clear. Ecmund came in early, his mind far from its usual calm, an object in his hand.

An axe.

The Sword should have known. This was no ordinary axe. It was heavy, with a thicker head and a wider blade than other axes, honed to a

24

keenness that would put most swords to shame. The handle was ash: supple, smooth, and tough.

Now the Sword could understand. This was not a weapon. It was only a tool, but a fine tool: old and worn, but well wrought, evenly tempered, perfect for its task. In the grasp of the Hand, it almost achieved sentience.

The Hand stomped into the room, kicking off his boots, frowning at his sister's raised eyebrow. "I am just so stupid sometimes."

She glanced at him, gauging his mood. "You're admitting it, finally?"

He grinned, one side of his mouth only. "Aye, this time. I was busy thinking, wasn't careful. Hit a tough knot when I was limbing, glanced Dad's axe into the dirt."

She winced. "Bad?"

He held the axe to the candle, allowing the light to flicker down its blade. "Just a tiny nick. But all the same..."

She turned away, relieved. "Oh, you and that axe. You treat it like a baby sometimes."

"A good axe is the woodman's finest friend."

She clattered the lid off a pot, stirred. "I know. Father always used to say that. I'm not disagreeing. I feel the same way about a good skillet." She set the lid back on firmly, nodding in satisfaction.

"Supper will be ready in a while. You've got time to nurse your baby a bit."

"I am not nursing a baby. I am honing my principal tool, preparatory to the morrow's work."

"Whatever you say." She went to the counter, selected a wide-bladed knife, and began to chop vegetables, swiftly and cleanly. The Sword noted her skill. "Just don't cradle it in your arms when you're finished."

"What are you...?"

He noticed her grin, and a touch of rue tinged his thoughts. No quick response came to him, so he shrugged and sat on the bench on the side of the fire away from the kitchen. Resting the axe firmly on his knee, he pulled an oilstone from the pouch at his belt.

The Sword registered the Hand's emotions as he worked. All the banter with his sister was forgotten. The Hand focused his attention on his blade, moving the stone with sure, light strokes, each one completely even, each identical to the one before. Under his attention the axe seemed to glow, and the Sword could feel that swelling almost-emotion again.

Curious, the Sword reached out. This mere tool had the faintest glimmerings of awareness. How could that be? A careful scan was revealing. The axe had been created by a master smith. The metal was flawless, tough and resilient, the hammer strokes even in weight and spacing. The tempering was a masterpiece: harder as the blade thinned towards the mirror-bright edge, softer and more pliable as it thickened towards the handle. The Sword felt a faintly conscious sense of balance, strength and confidence.

The Hand finished his labour and picked up a stick of firewood. He shaved a fine, even slice and tossed it on the fire. The curl was so thin it exploded into flame, burning brightly as it floated up the chimney on a blast of heat. Satisfied, he pulled an oily rag from his pouch, wiped the axe with meticulous care, and laid it aside.

With the axe out of the Hand's grip, the feeling of sentience faded, leaving the Sword something to ponder. In all its years, the Sword had never noted such consciousness in a mere tool. Usually the process required to bring a weapon to sentience took incredible reserves of skill and magic. There had been few smiths in history with the magic talent, the strength of mind, and the dedication to make the sacrifice required.

Not for a mere tool.

How this "mere tool" had achieved that balance of skill and magic was anyone's guess. Still, it made the axe a factor to be considered. Now it was obvious why the Hand felt safe in the forest alone. It was also probable that, in an emergency, the Hand would reach for his axe before he thought of the Sword. *A point to remember.*

Where the axe got its power from was another point.

Says something about this family, doesn't it?

The problem had now changed. Normally a new Hand would be out practising with his weapon, enjoying the novelty, getting used to the weight and length. This Hand, being a woodcutter, did not have the proper habits. Nobody went out and practiced with an axe. Long hours of work sufficed. For swordplay, honing of the talent was necessary.

Certainly, the Sword could lend skill to even a complete novice: had, often enough in the past. But it wasn't the same. Nothing but hours of work, alone and against an opponent, created that fine tuning of the relationship, which blended into transcendent achievement.

How to manage this? Hmm.

First, some basic training. It was complete idiocy for a Hand to go to bed every night and leave his weapon in another room.

Anxiety is the cure. A nervous Hand keeps his Sword near.

Once the Sword was close enough at night, gentle pressure during the dream state could work wonders.

So, when the axe was gone, hung outside the back door, the Sword went to work. It projected a grating, worried feeling, an anxious, look-over-your-shoulder sensation. Not heavy, just there. Always there.

Wrapped in his fatigue, satisfaction with his day's work, and the cosy comfort of his home, the Hand was resistant, but finally the pressure

26

began to tell. His head came up, listening. He frowned, rose and strode to the door, opened it abruptly and peered out.

"Something wrong, Ecmund?"

"Maybe not. Just thought I heard something outside."

The Sword kept the pressure on and the Hand could not sit, pacing to the rear door, checking again.

"Will you sit down?"

The Hand sat, staring into the fire. Soon one foot started tapping. Then he began to rise, glanced at his sister, sat.

She gave him a worried look, continued her sewing.

Finally he could stand it no longer. With a muttered exclamation, he grabbed the Sword and started out the door.

About time. What a dunce!

"What? Where are you going?"

"I don't know. There is something wrong. I'm just going outside to check around."

She was sitting, staring at him, as the door closed at his back, her sewing forgotten in her lap.

They made a careful circuit of the property, slowed by the dimness of the starlight. There was nothing stirring out there, but the Sword used the time to blend their senses, hone the Hand's concentration beyond his natural ability. Several times he stopped, unaware that he shouldn't have been able to hear the small noise that alerted him.

Finally, after a glance into the barn, the Hand returned to the cottage.

"Anything?"

"Nothing. Just the usual noises: wood mice, bats. That's good, I suppose. If there was anything out there, the little animals would be quiet."

The Hand sat, and the Sword hummed gently in his hands.

Then the fool got up and put the Sword back in the corner! It responded with a burst of nerve jangling stronger than before. In response, the Hand jumped to his feet and was at the back door in two strides, reaching out and returning with the axe in his hand.

"Eirlin, keep this with you. I'm going to check farther out."

"The axe? What would I do with it?"

He shook his head, like a horse ridding itself of flies. "You know how to use an axe. If there really is danger out there…"

"I couldn't hit anyone with an axe, Ecmund."

"Just scare them away. I won't be long." He thrust the axe into her hands, grabbed the Sword and left, closing the door firmly behind him.

With long strides, the Hand covered the town quickly, one end to the other. All was quiet. Returning to his cottage, he stuck his head in the door, saw that his sister was well, and headed out towards the forest.

27

All this time, the Sword had been nudging his emotions, nurturing the secure feeling that a weapon in the hand gives every man. When they entered the forest, however, it was time to stop. True danger existed under those dark trees, and it would be stupid to get the Hand into trouble by playing this kind of game.

Lacking the prompting of the Sword, the Hand soon lost his urge to explore, and they returned to the cottage. This time he did not set the Sword down. He sat again in front of the fire, listening, his weapon across his lap. The Sword fed him contentment until his alertness relaxed and the fatigue of a hard day of work took over.

"I'm going to bed."

"Good enough. Better than having you pacing around here all night, worrying me. I could hardly get a stitch done."

He shrugged. "Something was bothering me, and I don't know enough to tell anyone. I can't go rousting the town out over a vague feeling. They'd just laugh."

He sat down, facing her earnestly. "This is the kind of thing I was talking about, Eirlin. I knew that once I started down this path, my life would never be the same. But I have to do it, no matter how much it bothers me. Do you think I've just got bad nerves, because this is all new to me?"

A slight wrinkling of her forehead. "I don't know, Ecmund. You aren't one to be upset over nothing."

"I guess not, but I hope I am this time."

He stomped into his room and closed the door firmly. Then he laid the Sword across the arms of the chair by the bed, removed his clothes, and climbed in. The Sword sent soothing calm to him, and soon he was asleep. Aware that it had disturbed the Hand's abilities, the Sword stayed alert, sensing for any outside danger. There was none.

Carefully, still attentive to the outside, the Sword crept into the Hand's dreaming mind, stressing the need for practice, the joy of a move well executed, the satisfaction of being prepared for anything. All through the night, the Sword wove itself through his dreams.

Just past sunup the Hand awoke, yawning and rubbing his eyes in a puzzled way. He stumbled as he stepped to the wash table, righted himself. Shaking his head, he dashed cold water over his face and down his chest and shoulders. A great shudder ran through him, and his back straightened as he towelled off.

Out in the common room, Eirlin set his breakfast in front of him. "Sleep well?"

"Not really. I had some strange dreams. You know the ones that seem to be logical, and they go on and on, but nothing really happens?"

"What were they about?"

28

"Can't remember. Sword practice, I think."

"Your dreams are telling you to practice with your sword?"

He shrugged, ran a hand through his hair. "I guess I should be, after all. It's not much use to me if I can't handle it."

She sat down, her hands slapping the table. "Oh, this is just because of your worries last night."

"You think so?"

"Of course. You think there's danger, you dream about learning to defend yourself."

"But do you think there is danger?"

"Do I think there is danger, and some god is sending you dreams to warn you to get ready for it?" She thought a moment, then shook her head. "I don't believe the gods take that kind of a direct hand in our lives, Ecmund. I think they leave it up to us to handle it."

"Right, then. Tomorrow's Rest Day. I'll see if Jesco or one of the others will work with me."

"Fair enough. Just make sure you're finished in time to bring in wood for the roasting fire. I promised Maerwin I'd bring a duck for dinner."

He nodded, grinning. "One thing the woodcutter's daughter is never short of, and that's firewood." Then he sobered. "And I think I'll take a good look in the forest before I go to work, make sure there aren't any suspicious tracks around."

"Good idea. At least it will make you feel better."

"Right." He came into the bedroom, picked up the Sword.

That's better. He's going to take me with him. Oh, no!

"Here. You keep my sword with you, in case there's trouble."

She held the scabbard a moment, awkwardly, then pushed it back at him. "Yesterday you wanted me to use the axe!"

"You can't have the axe today, I need it for my work!"

"I know that, dunderhead. I didn't want the axe and now I don't want the sword. I couldn't bring myself to hit anyone with it, you know that."

He shrugged, a miserable expression on his face. "I guess. But if the town was attacked or something, I'd like to think you had some ability to defend yourself. I don't like this either, Eirlin, but there's something going on I don't understand, and we have to be very careful."

She frowned down at the sword. "All right. Leave it in the corner by the hearth, where I can get it quickly."

He nodded and turned out the door. The Sword, unable to do more, had to be satisfied with that small progress.

Hmph. Maybe I should be called "Hearth Protector."

Chapter 5

Despite the Hand's reference to troubled times, he still refused to take his weapon out with him on a daily basis. So it was with great pleasure that one morning the Sword found itself swept up.

"I'm going for a walk."

"Hmm."

"I'm going to check out that copse of birch, the other side of the castle. I think it's grown enough, now, and it makes great flooring."

"Who can afford hardwood floors, these days?"

"It isn't these days I'm thinking about. By the time I get it harvested, planked out and dried, things will have changed."

"I suppose we have to be optimistic."

He grinned. "Have to be. If we weren't, we'd never have any seasoned wood."

"I have to go out to Bolklan Farm. I'm not happy with the way Cwydiva is carrying her child. She seems to have no energy. I've made up a new potion for her."

"Fine. I'll go part way with you." He strapped the belt to his waist.

This is better!

Brother and sister strode along in the sunshine, chatting of this and that, or just walking in silence. The Sword tuned its swing to his stride, happy to be out, happy to be making progress with the Hand.

It is a fine day!

They parted company at a crossroads, and the Hand strode along even faster, his mind filled with plans involving saws and hammers and wood, always wood.

Oh well. At least he's not always thinking about stealing other people's money. Pleasant change.

The mood was so enjoyable that it took a while for the warning to seep in.

What's that tingling? I felt that once before, and it wasn't nice. Brrr! Gives me shivers. That's it. It's a Magician. It's a sparking, Hammer-beaten, haft-splintered Magician and he's looking for us!

Danger!

The Hand's head came up, and he listened. There was a thud of hooves ahead on the trail. He slipped into the brush, crouched.

The Sword began to throw up a defence, but pulled it back.

Gently, now. We don't want to draw attention to ourselves. Think of nothing. We aren't here. The nasty seeking flows around us like oil, we aren't here, we're a bush, we're a tree, we're a cute little forest animal...

The Sword feathered its defences into the surrounding life, as the Hand froze, flat on the ground now, his outline covered by a low-hanging bush. Together they blended with the forest, with the wind, with the rocks in the ground.

Hoof beats on stone, then the sound of metal clanking. A small party: ten or less. They trotted purposefully along the trail, making time but not hurrying. Not possible to tell more. Any interest might attract interest.

Hide and wait. We are not here.

The horses slowed, stopped.

We are the wind in the trees.

We are the wind in the trees.

A voice came: clear, cold. "Is there an old temple or ruin nearby?"

The Sword formed a rough image: tumbled, vine-covered stone. Planted it in a receptive mind, withdrew smoothly.

"Uh...Yeah. I think so, my Lord. Somewheres around here. I found it when I was hunting, once. Can't really remember where."

The cold voice lightened. "You wouldn't. It doesn't want you to. Ancient power. I can feel the warding. Over that way."

We are the rustling of dead leaves.

"Nothing of interest. Move on."

After an agonizing wait the tingling faded, and then was gone. The Hand relaxed, raising his head slightly, peering around. Nothing but the smell of horses and disturbed earth.

Cautiously the Hand rose to his feet and padded to the trail, still clutching the Sword's hilt. The Sword fed him confidence, and he stepped out into the open.

"I wonder who that was?" He peered at the tracks carefully. "Don't know why I ducked like that. Could have been an innocent merchant with his bodyguards."

The Sword fed a bit of jangling uncertainty.

"Still, you can't be too careful. They just didn't feel right, somehow."

Magician.

"He said he could feel warding. What a strange thing to say."

Warding... Magician! Come on; think for yourself.

"Unless he was a Magician. That would explain my feeling, as well. That niggling in the back of my head."

Well, thank the Smith, he finally got it. A bright boy, our Ecmund.

The Hand took one more long, cautious look down the trail, then turned and strode back towards the village. As he walked, his fingers caressed the Sword's pommel. "Hmm. 'We are the wind in the trees.' Now where did I get an image like that?"

I thought it was rather poetic.

"Come to think of it, why did I dive into the bush like that? I was too scared to even raise my head and look at them. Why? It was that feeling

31

that someone was looking for me, someone who could see right through the bushes I was hiding behind."

He could.

"Must have been a Magician." The Hand grinned wryly. "Or I'm becoming an abject coward."

Never!

When he arrived at the village, he went straight to the inn. "Is Albercas around?"

The barmaid smiled up at him. "He's out the back. Do you want me to get him?"

"No, thanks, Freide. I'll go."

The Sword could feel her disappointment.

Mind your place, girl.

Albercas was pitching hay down from the loft, but he set aside his fork when he saw the look on the Hand's face. "What's up, Ecmund?"

"A troop of soldiers went by on the Canhusen trail. Ten or so. With a Magician."

"A Magician! How do you know?"

"I was hiding. They stopped, and were talking. One was a Magician, I'm sure of it."

"Whose livery?"

The Hand grinned, shook his head. "I was keeping my head down, Albercas. I didn't look."

"Why did you hide at all?"

Puzzlement. "I don't know. It just seemed the right thing to do. I thought I'd better come back and spread the word."

The innkeeper slapped the Hand on the shoulder. "Good instinct, I'd say. Keep your head down, and let that sort go right on by."

"What do you think it means?"

"I don't know, Ecmund. There's a whole lot too much troop movement around here, and nobody's saying why. Thanks for the information."

"I'm a little worried, you know."

"Any special reason?"

"Well, all this going on, and I promised to go over to Pieterburen, give my cousin Sygwin a hand with the logs for that new barn. I'd tell him I couldn't make it, but he's counting on getting the roof on before winter."

The innkeeper slapped again. "Don't you worry, Ecmund. We'll take care of that sister of yours while you're gone."

"Thanks, Albercas. I appreciate it."

The Hand patted the Sword's hilt again, and strode home.

Chapter 6

The Sword stood in the usual corner, humming to itself. There was no one listening, and the hum was very quiet. It was warm and dry, and things were going well. In fact, the Sword was so relaxed that it was completely surprised to be suddenly hoisted into the air.

Eirlin.

She was humming to herself as she swept the floor. It was the humming, of course. She was on the same note, and had the same feeling of satisfaction. The Sword relaxed, just a bit.

Leaning the broom against the wall, the girl regarded the Sword carefully. The Sword moved the hum inside, blended it with Eirlin's feeling. She smiled, whipped out a cloth, and swiped the scabbard up and down, retrieved the broom, set the Sword back in the corner.

"There we are. Clean as the day she was built." She put her hands on her hips and spun slowly around, regarding her work.

Swords are not built. We are Forged.

Suddenly Eirlin frowned, regarded the Sword. She slipped over, picked it up, gingerly. She placed her hand on the hilt, tentatively, as if expecting something to hurt her. She seemed to be listening. The Sword, caught in mid-hum, did not dare stop.

A smile came over the girl's face and she nodded, returned the Sword to its place, giving it a small pat as her hand departed.

Here we go again.

Over the next few days, the Sword caught Eirlin glancing in its direction, a thoughtful look on her face. Twice more, the girl put her hand on the hilt, more firmly each time.

It had happened before. What was unique about this time, though, was that the person who was making the discovery wasn't the Hand. That needed thinking about.

Please the Smith, it won't be like last time.

Last time had been completely degrading. This former Hand had decided that the Sword was magic, an object of worship. Altar, sacrifices, the whole lot. A whole lot of superstitious nonsense.

The solution was simple. When, inevitably, the objectionable Hand tried to show off the "Magic Sword" to others, it refused to respond, completely withdrew. Laughter followed, and, when the Hand insisted, anger. Without assistance, the Hand was quick to find out how bad a swordsman he really was.

A new Hand had become necessary.

From what it already knew about her, the Sword didn't think there was going to be that kind of trouble with Eirlin.

This one's got her pommel riveted on tight.

One day she went out just before supper with her basket, but was gone for too short a time for shopping. When she came in, she was obviously upset. Her breath was coming too fast, and her face was red.

The Sword went on the alert, scanned the neighbourhood. No danger.

Eirlin threw her shawl over a chair, dropped the basket by the hearth, and began to busily tidy up the kitchen. Then, without slacking her activity, she started to prepare a meal. Suddenly she stopped, frowned, and looked around.

"Bother! I went out to buy meat for supper."

She picked up her shawl and basket, went to the door, paused, then shrugged. "Oh, well. I can be certain it's safe, anyway."

Safe?

Eirlin closed the door and the Sword could feel her stride rapidly away.

Hmm.

By the time she returned with several purchases, she was calmer, and when Ecmund came in from work, she greeted him with almost her usual cheerfulness. He did not respond in kind.

"Jesco's been up to his old tricks."

Her head came up too suddenly. "What?"

"I hear he picked a fight with some of the castle soldiers today."

"It wasn't quite like that."

"What do you know about it?"

"Well, it was partly my fault. No, wait; it wasn't my fault. It was partly because of me. "

"Eirlin, I think you should quit stomping around before you break something, and sit down here and tell me."

She threw herself into the chair beside him, and her hand brushed the Sword's hilt. Without conscious thought, she settled it there.

Good girl. Tell us.

"I was just going shopping, like I normally do. I was walking along, outside the inn, when I got a feeling something was wrong. I came around the corner, and there they were. Three soldiers from the castle. They had just left the tavern, I think, and poor little Wynna, the dressmaker's girl, was coming along. They stopped her, and were giving her trouble. She was backed against the wall, near tears, and they had her surrounded.

"I don't think they meant her any real harm, you know, but they should have seen that she was frightened, and let her be. They didn't. It was really mean of them."

Ecmund nodded. "So you stepped in, and gave them a piece of your mind."

"Of course. Well, it wasn't long before I had two of them up against the wall, and poor little Wynna was scuttling off to safety."

"Good for you!"

Well done! The Sword sent a glow up through the soft palm.

"Yes, it would have been good, but one of them didn't have the same sense as the others. He started to give me some guff about them not meaning any harm, and who did I think I was to stop their fun."

"Poor guy. He learned his mistake, I suppose?"

She shook her head. "He would have, but just then Jesco came out of the tavern."

"Oh."

"Yes. He saw Wynna, stopped her, asked her what was going on. She burst into tears, poor thing, and Jesco came storming over. When he saw that this soldier was giving me a hard time, he really tied into him."

"With his sword?"

"No, he just told him what kind of scum he was, and that he'd better get his butt back up to the castle, and stay away from the village, because if he didn't he'd find a boot...well, you know how Jesco is when he's mad."

"Too well. What did the soldier do?"

"He bristled up, and started to make the kind of moves, you know..."

"Strutting like a rooster before he starts to fight."

"That's right. I was getting worried. But one of the other soldiers pulled at his mate's sleeve, whispered in his ear. The man stopped, looked Jesco up and down with disdain, and said, 'So you're the famous Jesco Falkenric. That explains a lot.' Then he stuck his nose up with a jeering laugh, and walked away.

"I had to grab Jesco by the arm to stop him from drawing, Ecmund."

"But you did stop him."

"That's right. I kept him occupied until they were out of sight, got him calmed down. Actually, I set him to calming Wynna down."

"That was smart, Eirlin."

It was?

She smiled wanly. "It's hard to stay mad when you're comforting a hurt puppy."

"So that was the end of it?"

"Apparently. I came back here, more upset than I let anyone know, then realized I'd forgotten my shopping. When I went out again, everything was calm."

Ecmund slapped his hands on his knees. "Well, that doesn't sound so bad. For once, Jesco seems to have done the right thing."

"That's what I told him. It helped."

"Who was this soldier that gave you trouble?"

"I've seen his two friends around, but he's new. They weren't in livery, but he seemed better dressed than the others. Maybe a junior officer or something."

Ecmund nodded. "Maybe he came in with that Magician. He had a mounted troop with him." He stared into the fire for a moment. "This isn't good, Linna. There have been several incidents like that lately. The soldiers are pushing the limits, and you know our people won't stand for it. Jesco isn't the only one right on the edge. I was talking with Albercas about it the other day. We were hoping it was the lack of discipline from not having an Overlord."

"You were hoping it was lack of discipline?"

"Yes. Word has it the new man is on his way. Once he takes over, we can let him know, and hopefully he'll get it under control."

"I hope you're right."

"So do I. However, if this incident is finished and no one was hurt, all is well. Especially if you managed to find some supper for me in the middle of it."

"Oh, I picked up something or other. I wouldn't expect culinary miracles tonight, Ecmund."

"I could eat a horse, no matter who cooked it, so don't worry."

"I think I should be insulted."

"Why?"

"I'll let you know when I figure it out."

"How about putting supper on the table while you're thinking? Or can you do both?"

"And part your hair with a broomstick in between."

How did this suddenly become a joke? Why aren't we out killing someone? All right. Just getting in on the fun. Why is no one laughing?

Eirlin patted the Sword absently, got up and went back to cooking, moving much more calmly. Ecmund sat, his gaze lost in the flames, and the Sword could feel his thoughts roiling.

Chapter 7

The next morning, the Hand hesitated as he was going out the door. "We've got a problem, Linna."

"We have?"

"Yes. Sygwin's barn."

"Why is it a problem? I thought you were going to help him get the beams up."

"I was. I just don't want to do it right now."

"Why not?"

"All this upset, the soldiers so edgy. It isn't safe."

"You're worried about me?"

"Yes."

"That's ridiculous."

"No it isn't. A single woman, alone, is a tempting target for a bunch of drunk soldiers."

"In town? They wouldn't dare."

"What about out on the road, when you're going to do a Healing?"

"Ecmund, if you are suggesting that the situation in this realm has slipped so far that a woman can't walk the roads in broad daylight…"

"Well, no, it's not that bad, I guess, but…"

She tossed her braids back. "Just leave me the sword. I'll be fine."

"Really? I thought you didn't want to use a sword."

"Oh, Kitten and I have things worked out."

"Kitten?"

Kitten!

"You're calling my sword Kitten?"

I will NOT be called Kitten!

Eirlin shrugged. "Doesn't she remind you of that cat we had when we were kids? The blue-eyed one? All purrs and snuggles, but the moment she was displeased, the claws came out."

By the Hammer of the Smith, I'll show you claws!

"I do remember the cat. Cute little thing, but she drove the dog crazy. She'd sit in the doorway and not let him through, and he'd whine and cry, but he didn't dare pass her. And him ten times her size."

"That's the one. But sitting on your lap, she'd purr and purr, like she was sweetness itself."

"Fine. But what does that have to do with my sword?"

"She purrs."

"Purrs? A sword?"

She?

"She does. You have to have your hand on the hilt. It's not a real purr, silly. Just a sort of vibration."

At least I'm not humming!

"Are you saying this is a magic Sword?"

"Of course it is."

There was a long silence as he looked at his sister, then at the Sword. The Sword could feel his mind tightening, pulling back.

Hey! What's going on?

The Hand was withdrawing from her. Fear and loathing gnawed against the bond so lovingly forged. The Sword fought to hold on, but as gently as possible, afraid of a sudden snapping.

He placed the Sword on the table, his hand pulling away carefully, as if from a dangerous animal. "What am I going to do? What if it has me in its thrall?"

His sister raised her eyebrows. "Afraid it will take over your mind, use you as a tool in its relentless search for blood?"

"Eirlin, this is not something you joke about. I've heard about magic Swords." He had a sudden thought. "You know how I told you that I wasn't sure why I bought it? That I didn't really want a sword? What if it made me?"

"For someone who had just been forced, you certainly looked happy when you came home with it."

"But what if it made me happy, so it could take control of me?"

"Ecmund, surely you know better. Those are all superstitions. Think of the lore. True magic Swords are better trained than that. They must be, or they wouldn't be safe. They wouldn't be allowed."

He thought that over, and the Sword felt his mind relaxing. "Are you sure it's a magic Sword?"

Eirlin sighed and shook her head. "Ecmund, you are so dense sometimes. Think!"

He shifted uneasily. "I suppose. It feels different, that's for sure. But it feels right! What's wrong with that?"

"It isn't a matter of right or wrong, Ecmund. It's just a magic Sword. It has feelings, and powers. Surely you can tell. You're of the Blood."

"Yes, I suppose. I could certainly feel that Magician the other day."

"You could?"

"Oh, yes. I could tell he was coming, even before I heard the horses. I could feel him searching, and I knew I'd better get out of the way."

"Well, maybe that was you, and maybe it was Kitten. In any case, she's magic, and she has already helped you, so treat her with the respect she deserves."

Respect. Yes, respect. Listen to the lady.

"You treat her with respect. I'm leaving her with you."

His sister grinned, tossed her braid back over her shoulder. "Fine. We have things worked out."

38

She laid a hand casually on the Sword's hilt.

Huh. "Kitten." I will not purr.

"I still don't like leaving you alone. What if she steals your soul?"

What?

The girl's laughter rang out. "Oh, come on, Ecmund. You don't believe all those silly tales about magic Swords stealing people's souls."

He looked stubborn. "I'm worried about leaving you alone, Linna."

"Don't worry. Jesco will keep an eye on me."

"Jesco? You don't want him anywhere near you."

"Why not? You're worried about my safety. Cousin Jesco is an experienced soldier, and the best swordsman around."

"You're serious?" He stared at her. She looked serious. "Then you ask him."

"No. That's your job."

"It's my job?"

"I believe I just said that. You're the great defender here. You can't do your job, so you feel worried. So get somebody to do it for you."

"But..."

"Fine. Don't ask him." She turned back into the cottage, but the Sword could feel her chuckle, just beyond her brother's hearing.

"But...oh, all right. I'll ask him." Slapping his hand on the doorjamb, he turned away up the street.

"Whatever you like, Ecmund."

"Huh." His boots scuffed up more dust than usual as he strode off.

Eirlin went back to her kitchen, humming gently to herself.

Kitten!... Kitten?

I want a name! A real Name! A Name of Honour!

Oh, please the Smith, not... Kitten!

Chapter 8

They were walking through the town the next day when Ecmund stopped. Jesco was approaching, for once without his two henchmen. Ecmund hesitated a moment, then raised a detaining hand. "Say, Jesco, do you have a moment?"

"Sure, kid. What's the problem?"

"Well, it's this way, Jesco. I was serious about wanting a lesson. I've got this sword, and you know things aren't so peaceful anymore. There might come a time when I have to defend myself, defend the family. Sure, I've had my military training, but it's not the same. Have you got time to give me some pointers?"

His elder cousin regarded him for a long moment. "You really mean that, don't you?"

Ecmund frowned. "Of course. Why wouldn't I?" A small trickle of guilt, remembering their last conversation.

Jesco let out a breath. "Sure. Why wouldn't you? Tell you what, kid. Are you going to be home this afternoon?"

"I've got things to do in the wood yard."

"Fine. I'll come over. We can work there."

"Perfect. Thanks, Jesco."

"No problem, kid. We can't have you disgracing the family name."

"Aye. Being dead is a real disgrace."

Jesco's face lost its false joviality. "You've got that right, Cousin."

As they walked home, the Sword considered the interchange. There had been some sparring at first, but for some reason the older relative had decided not to pursue his usual blustering humour. It would be interesting to see how this training session turned out. The Sword would be ready, in any case.

Ecmund and Eirlin were in the wood yard restacking some of the heavier timbers to dry when a shout echoed through the cottage. "Anyone home?"

Eirlin dusted her hands and leaned inside. "In the back, Jesco."

He strode through the cottage, pausing in the doorway.

Eirlin curtsied slightly. "Cousin Jesco. Welcome."

He brought his heels together, almost a bow. "Thank you, Cousin Eirlin. You are looking beautiful as usual."

"And you are flattering, as usual. May I serve tea?"

He dropped the gentlemanly pose, laughed. "No, thank you, Linna. I've come on business." He turned to Ecmund. "You ready, kid?"

"I'll just get my sword." He came for the Sword, brought it out.

"Let me take a look."

40

The Hand proffered the Sword without demur, and Jesco drew, went through the usual inspection. His mind was receptive as well, although not in the class of Ecmund or Eirlin. Finally the swordsman nodded. "She's a better weapon than I thought, Ecmund. Good workmanship."

The Hand paused. "You're calling it 'her' too?"

Jesco shrugged. "Aye. You get a feel for weapons, sometimes. The good ones. This one feels like a "she". He reddened. "Does it matter?"

Perhaps he is more receptive than I thought.

"No, it's just that Eirlin does the same."

Jesco's face cleared. "That's settled, then. Let's see how you do with her."

"Yes, let's."

The Sword forced down a hum as Ecmund strapped on her belt. There was determination in the Hand, almost ferocity. Better and better.

Jesco nodded politely to Eirlin, then turned to follow Ecmund through the back gate to the pasture outside. "I tell you, Cousin, I already see one problem you have to fix."

Ecmund turned, frowning. "That's pretty quick, Jesco. I haven't even drawn my Sword yet."

"It isn't ability, it's habit. I see you wandering around all over the place, and you're not wearing your sword."

Maybe I was too hasty in judging this man.

"I can't be wearing my Sword all the time. It...she would get in the way when I'm working."

"Then you set her aside, but she's there. I always have my sword within arm's reach. What good is being a swordsman if you get caught without your sword?"

"You mean carry her with me to the woods every day?"

Jesco shrugged. "Swordsmen aren't usually woodcutters, but if you have to, yes."

"I don't need a sword. I have my axe."

The older youth shook his head, a slight smile playing across his features. "No, no, Ecmund. You are not an axeman."

"Not an axeman? I've had an axe in my hand every day since I was a kid!"

Jesco stepped closer, and the Sword could feel his earnestness. "You're a woodcutter, lad, not an axeman. You wouldn't be able to fight with an axe, not matter how well you swing it."

"Why not?"

"Your head doesn't work that way."

"What?"

"Think about fighting with an axe. It's all attack, no defence. You can't really parry with an axe, especially a two-hander like your Dad's old club. You don't have to. You clear a space around you that no one dares enter. You beat the other weapons down with the weight of your blade. You fight like a wolverine or a panther: throw everything into your attack, nothing held back. You stop swinging, you're dead."

"Oh."

"You're not that kind, kid. You're too cautious. You'll make a good swordsman, I think. Probably not aggressive enough, but you'll be able to protect yourself. More like a stag: thrust, then parry."

He will be a wonderful swordsman!

"Now me, I could be an axeman."

"You?"

Jesco grinned, one side of his mouth only. "Have you watched me fight, kid? Really fight, not just spar for points? Of course you haven't. Well, I doubt if it's pretty to watch. When I fight, I attack. I throw all caution aside, and I go for the enemy."

"Isn't that dangerous?"

"Of course. If you aren't good enough, you die. That's why I have to be good. So far, I've been good enough. Or lucky."

"I don't understand. How do you make yourself do that?"

The grin turned down. "Ever seen me mad, kid? Of course you have."

Ecmund nodded, carefully. A series of quick images flashed through his mind. Younger children, wild, unreasoning anger, horror and curiosity.

"That's how I do it. I get angry. Then I fight. Oh, I don't do a real berserker. I just get mad enough that I want to kill my enemy more than I care about being killed myself." He shrugged. "Seems to work. So far."

There was a silent moment, then Jesco shook his head, drew his sword. "Enough philosophy. Let's see what you can do with that fancy old sword. I'll try not to break it for you."

Break? We'll see about that.

The Sword felt Ecmund's hand on her hilt and leapt from the scabbard. She held her hum inside, feeding the strength, the confidence into the muscles of his arm.

"See? I can tell already."

Ecmund straightened partially out of his crouch. "What?"

"Defensive. You're holding the sword too far in front. You're trying to push me away with her tip. Gives you more time to parry, but you can't start a good slash without drawing back first. Lift the tip a bit, flex your arm more, dare me to come closer." He demonstrated. "It isn't the reach of your sword that keeps me away. It's that imaginary space around you that feels dangerous."

I know that.

Ecmund watched a moment, then tried to copy his cousin.

This really is a training session. Better if I don't interfere. Unless it's necessary.

The Sword withdrew part way, watching and listening.

"That's better. Let's try a few simple passes."

There was a flurry of inconclusive contacts, then Jesco stepped back, lowering his point.

Plain steel, as I expected. A very good weapon though. Minor flaws.

"Good enough. Nobody's going to beat you down, that's for sure."

Ecmund grinned. "Woodcutter's arm."

"Very strong wrist. Too strong."

"What?"

What?

"Your wrist is too strong, too stiff. Here, try a few easier passes, and I'll show you."

They began to fence again, slower this time. "Right. See? When I attack hard, like this...you stand firm, I'll never get through. But if I..."

The two suddenly froze, Jesco's sword tip at his cousin's chest.

"Did you see what happened?"

Ecmund lowered his weapon in chagrin. "Aye. You set me up. You kept beating against my blade, stronger and stronger. Then when I thought you were going to hit again, I firmed up to fight it, but you circled under my blade, and I was pushing against nothing."

"Exactly. And your blade went way out of line, leaving you completely vulnerable. You can't always have a strong wrist. You have to learn to be subtle as well."

A very good point. Ha, ha. Sorry, don't mind me.

"All right. Let's try that."

They fenced again, and the Sword stayed out of direct contact with Ecmund, observing closely, lending only basic support, trying to let the Hand learn by himself. As they fought, the Sword had time to observe the opponent as well. Jesco was too rough to be called a master swordsman, but he was very good. As he had mentioned, his defence was basic. His form depended on attack, and at that he was superb. In the Sword's experience, this was the kind of swordsman who had very short battles. Win or die.

After each pass, Jesco stopped, made a comment, demonstrated, then they went at it again. Soon their speed was increasing, and sweat stood out on each man's brow.

After what the Sword considered a reasonable practice, the older youth stopped, nodding. "That's pretty good, Ecmund. You learn fast. Tell you what. You want to try some free bladework?"

"I guess so. I don't know how I'll do, but..."

"You go into a fight thinking like a herd of cows, kid, you'll lose for sure. Come on. Figure like you're going to get a touch on me first. Fight like a wounded bear."

Fight like a mountain cat!

Ecmund grinned as well, tightened his grasp on the hilt. "All right, I'm going to get the first touch."

The sword tips met, and then they were at it. The Sword decided that a bit of help would be in order. Only on the defensive part. If this cousin was expecting defence, he was going to see some. If he earned it, he would get a touch. If he tried for more, he was going to get a very nasty surprise.

At the first, it was obvious that Jesco was still holding back. As he pressed, and Ecmund countered every move, he began to push harder. Now the Sword was helping more, trying to go easy, but unable to bring herself to allow the opponent a touch. The pace quickened, the men moving more, feet shuffling on the grass, one side, then the other, trying for every advantage.

Parry, parry... watch the corkscrew... Parry, good... beat... double beat, use that arm strength, he's getting tired... watch for the change of pace...

Ecmund was beginning to enjoy himself. Too much. He was starting to look for an opening. Maybe, just maybe...There!

"Oh."

The flat of his cousin's sword rapped sharply across his ribs, and a pleased laugh rasped out.

"I could have seen that coming from across the field, Ecmund!"

"You could?"

"Of course. I could read it in your eyes, in your stance. You figured your defence was good, maybe you could actually counterattack, because I wasn't expecting it. Right?"

"Something like that."

Jesco wiped his sword on his sleeve, sheathed it. "And you were partly right, cousin. Your defence is really good. I was pushing you hard, and there weren't any holes I could get through."

"Really?" Ecmund looked up from sheathing the Sword, patting her hilt one more time. The Sword held back a hum.

"Really." Jesco slapped his cousin on the shoulder, turned him towards the cottage. "You've got the makings of a good swordsman. Just a few years of practice, and a complete change of viewpoint..."

"...and what have we here?"

Eirlin was in the doorway, a tray of mugs in her hand. "You two have been working up a sweat, I thought you might be thirsty."

"Most certainly, Cousin. I thank you." Jesco lifted his mug to her, swung the salute over to include Ecmund, and drank deeply.

"Say, that is good cider. Cold, too."

"I'm glad you like it. I mix a few wild crab apples in the mash. It comes out more tart that way."

"It quenches the thirst, I have to say."

She smiled. "I'm just softening you up."

"Oh? For what?"

"For the favour Ecmund has to ask you."

Jesco frowned slightly. "He already did. I was pleased to help, I have to say. That was a good workout."

"That was for him. This one is for me."

Now he was really puzzled. "You're going to have to explain that one, Cousin. If it's for you, why don't you ask?"

Her smile softened theatrically. "Because it's one of those man things. I have no interest in asking."

"I see." You didn't need to be a magic Sword to tell that he couldn't see at all.

"Help me out, here, brother. This is your play, not mine."

Ecmund rubbed his forehead. "She's mad at me, and she's making both of us pay for it, Jesco."

A small grin appeared. "That explains a lot."

"Aye. You see, I'm going over to Pieterburen to help Sygwin with that new barn, and I'm worried about leaving her alone, with things as they are."

"And you want me to keep an eye on her?" The grin broadened.

"Right. Would you mind?"

"And she doesn't want me to?"

"That's about it."

The smile disappeared, and Jesco turned to Eirlin. "I'd be pleased to keep an eye out for danger, Eirlin. It isn't a laughing matter. You live on the edge of the forest here, and I know your place is well protected, but that won't cover everything. There are some strange events going on, and we all need to watch out for each other."

"Thank you, Jesco, but don't worry. I'm not stupid enough to think I'm invulnerable. I'm very careful."

"That's good to hear, Eirlin." His smile returned. "We don't want to lose the only one in the family with the nerve to tell my father off when he goes on one of his rants."

He drained his mug, as if to cover an embarrassing moment. "Well, I have to go. This cider reminded me of an appointment."

"At the tavern?"

"As it happens, yes, at the tavern." He grinned at Eirlin, slapped Ecmund on the shoulder. "Don't think you learned it all, little cousin. I'll be back in a couple of days. You don't practice that often, you don't make progress."

"Would you? That would be wonderful. Thanks."

"Tell you a secret, Ecmund. There are better swordsmen than you I could practice against, but I don't trust them as much. It's a different kind of practice with someone you trust." He made that slight bow to Eirlin. "Good day, Cousin."

She returned a curtsey, and they followed him to the cottage door. "Actually, we'll see you tonight."

He swung back. "Oh, that meeting, aye. Whatever it's about. Another chance for Albercas to look important, probably. See you then."

When he was gone, brother and sister stood looking at each other.

"Well?"

"It was a good session, Eirlin. He didn't bully me, or lord it over me. I learned a lot."

"I told you. Treat him like he means something to you."

Ecmund paused, running his hand over the hilt of the Sword. "He said something strange."

"What was that?"

"You know his famous temper?"

"Who could forget it?"

"Well, he said that when he gets mad, he wants to kill his enemy more than he cares about getting killed."

"Yes. He's been like that since…as long as I remember, I guess. When he got mad, nothing could stop him."

"And I was wondering what would make a person get to feeling like that."

"Remember the day he tied into his father?"

There was a moment of sober silence, and the Sword caught a glimpse of a young body flying backwards, to slump, unconscious, at the base of a wall.

"Explains a lot."

"Hmm."

"Anyway, he's going to look after you, so I'm happy."

"I'm not so upset, myself. If I have to be alone, it's nice to think that the best swordsman in the village is looking out for my welfare."

Not to mention the best Sword in the demesne. A Sword called…

"EXTERMINATOR!"

No, that sounds too much like a rat hound. Let me see…

"EXECUTIONER!"

I think I'm getting carried away. Maybe something more realistic…

46

Chapter 9

The Sword scanned the crowded common room. The rafters needed cleaning, and the fire was too hot for a spring day and a mob of sweaty people. Boring people. Boring conversations.

Politics. Waste of time. Can't we just skip all the talking, and get straight to the fighting and killing part? We know it's going to happen anyway.

Doesn't anyone have a sense of humour around here?

Doesn't anyone want to speak to me?

The Sword mused as they waited. Ecmund was ready. Sooner or later, he was going to start speaking to her, and if it was important, she would answer. It would be a relief to actually talk to someone.

I'm getting tired of my own jokes.

The Sword became serious, and cast her senses out into the crowded inn. Nobody seemed too upset, so there wasn't any immediate danger. Still, it must be important, or they wouldn't all be here. The Sword picked up familiar auras coming closer. Jesco with an older man, who must be the infamous uncle. The Sword shuddered. Contact with that mind felt like an edge scraping over rock. He seemed to be excited, at least. Jesco felt no such eagerness.

"Uncle Aeldwig." Eirlin was waving. "Over here."

"Did you have to?"

She touched her brother's arm lightly. "Shh! He's family, and that's important right now."

"I suppose."

More and more interesting. Family is important? What is going on? It's all very well being a magic Sword, being able to read people's emotions, but if they never tell you anything, what good can you do?

Eirlin gave both her relatives a polite salutation and, with a firm nudge of her hip, scooted Ecmund over to make room on the bench.

"What's this all about? I have a farm to run. Can't be rushing in for a meeting every time some town merchant has a problem with his neighbour."

"It's important, Uncle Aeldwig. It's about the new Overlord."

"Huh! Overlord! There were no Overlords when our family..." Aeldwig seemed about to start in on a favourite subject when Eirlin pressed a hand on his arm, nodding toward the front of the room.

The innkeeper stood up from where he had been huddled with a few of the village elders, and looked around at the crowded room. "Everyone seems to be here."

"We're here, Albercas. The question is why!"

The innkeeper ignored Aeldwig's peevish whine. "Now, you all know we have an important event occurring. There has been no Overlord at the castle for several months, ever since Lord Salar died and left no heir. Now the King has finally ceded our demesne to a new Overlord. His name is Sarza Delfontes. I have been told that he will be arriving some time in the next week."

Ecmund nudged Eirlin, and they shared a private grin at the innkeeper's self-important manner. The rest of the crowd hummed in excitement. Uncle Aeldwig stirred as if the bench were uncomfortable.

"Another Maridon, I suppose."

"It's always a Maridon, Uncle Aeldwig. They do hold the throne, in case you hadn't noticed."

The innkeeper stepped forward, to cut off the rising buzz. "We have to decide on an appropriate way to greet this new leader."

Aeldwig shot to his feet. "I know how to greet him. Not at all. Let him come in with his fancy Maridon airs and his rich Maridon food, and leave him to stew up there in the castle all by himself."

This time the innkeeper did not ignore the outburst. He slammed his hand on the bar beside him. "That is exactly what we must not do! If we leave him alone up there, he will start making decisions which affect us, with no advice from us, and it will work to our great disadvantage."

"What's the point? He will do what he likes in any case; he's a Maridon, isn't he?" Aeldwig sat, shaking his head.

The innkeeper also shook his head, as much in frustration with Aeldwig as in negation.

"That's not true. We have rights and responsibilities, as does he, according to the Charter of Alcudo da Maridon. When we speak, he must listen."

The innkeeper raised his head, addressed the group at large. "A new Overlord needs a new Village Council. And that is why we have called this meeting. Besides an appropriate ceremony, we must decide on who is going to meet with the new Overlord, to counsel him. We must send our best representatives, covering village and farms, guilds and families. We cannot send a large number. Who will go?" He raised a hand to forestall an avalanche of suggestions.

"I will give you some time to discuss this. Then we will accept nominations."

He sat down, and the noise of the crowd rose.

Ecmund glanced to Eirlin, then at Uncle Aeldwig. She shook her head imperceptibly, and his nod of agreement was equally subtle.

"What do you think, Jesco?"

Her cousin seemed startled to be asked. "Well...our family should be represented, of course."

"Of course it will. I am the family head. I will go, naturally."

Eirlin put her hand on her uncle's arm. "I don't think so, Uncle Aeldwig."

"What?"

Tucked close beside Eirlin, who was touching the older man, the Sword could feel his outrage and was able to send reassuring calm through the contact.

'Uncle Aeldwig, not every family of the Blood of Inderjorne will be represented, no matter how old and respected. If you put yourself forward, you know what will happen."

Aeldwig glowered at her, and the Sword fed caution to his choleric mind. Finally he spoke. "They're just jealous of our heritage."

"That may be, but we must consider it. Perhaps Jesco should go."

She turned her smile to her cousin, whose hands rose in defence.

"Not me, Eirlin. I couldn't stand to sit around a table with this lot of gabblers, let alone with some new noble who couldn't find his...Well, you know me. I'd have my sword out in the first hour."

Eirlin shrugged. "Then who? I don't think they're ready for a woman on the Council."

Aeldwig shrugged, and his scowl lifted slightly. "All right, Eirlin. You've twisted us all around as usual. It's obvious it's got to be Ecmund. They like him; they'll let him on their precious Council. Then they'll walk all over him."

Eirlin glanced at her brother. "I don't think so, Uncle Aeldwig. I think they will listen, because what he says is worth hearing. What do you think, Jesco?"

The older cousin made a warding gesture. "As long as it's not me. I'm sure he'll do just fine."

"Good. You nominate him, then."

"Me?"

"Yes. He's filling in for you, it's the least you can do."

"Oh. Since you put it that way, I suppose I could."

"Fine."

"Did anyone think to ask if I wanted the job?"

Eirlin turned to her brother, as if surprised. "No, why would we?"

"Oh, I don't know. So I don't get the feeling, like Uncle Aeldwig, that somebody has planned this all out, and I don't have any choice."

Aeldwig shared a sour grin at his niece's expense.

She shrugged complacently. "It just seems logical, that's all."

"The Powers of the Blood preserve us from a woman's logic."

The family's attention turned outward, and the Sword mused on the process.

Neatly done, girl. It had been a beautiful demonstration of diplomacy. *Perhaps there should be a woman on their precious Council. Might get something done.*

The innkeeper rose, strode to his usual position by the bar. "Is everyone ready?"

The talking gradually ceased.

"I am now inviting nominations for positions on the Overlord's Council."

Hands shot up, and the innkeeper chose each speaker while his wife wrote down the nominations. Finally, after a considerable wait, Jesco was indicated. He cleared his throat as he stood. "The Falconric family, as one of the oldest of the Blood of Inderjorne in this valley, should be represented."

There was an audible snicker, choked quickly as Jesco's hand jumped to his sword hilt. He stared around defiantly for a moment longer. "I would like to nominate my cousin, Ecmund Liutswin Falconric." He rode over a low hum in the crowd. "He is known as a cool head, a steady hand, and a tradesman of repute."

The Sword did not need any special senses to feel general agreement. Several faces, especially that of the innkeeper, registered relief.

"Thank you, Jesco Falconric." The man looked to his wife as if to make extra sure that she had recorded the correct name.

Eirlin squeezed Ecmund's hand. Someone reached forward to slap his shoulder. He shuffled on the bench awkwardly, his neck reddening. The Sword repressed a hum.

All the legends laud a strong arm in war, a strong voice in council.

Three other nominations were taken, then the innkeeper raised his voice formally. "I hereby declare the nominations complete for positions on the Overlord's Council. The list will be posted. Families and guilds have one day to register their votes. We will assemble here at this time tomorrow for the announcement."

As they rose, Eirlin laid a hand on Ecmund's and Aeldwig's shoulders, her warm glance including Jesco. "That was wisely done, kinsmen. Family Falconric will keep its strong representation in our community."

"If the young puppy doesn't throw it all away by being too soft."

She shook her uncle's shoulder. "Just as you might have thrown it all away by antagonizing everyone."

His head came up. "I know you disapprove, Eirlin, but there comes a time when you have to stand up for yourself and your family, and to hell with the rest of them."

She nodded. "I'm sure Ecmund will know when that time comes."

"Don't worry, Uncle Aeldwig. I'll keep you informed."

50

"Make sure you do that, boy."

Jesco grinned at them over his father's shoulder as they parted company.

"Well, there's one happy person in all this."

Ecmund looked down at his sister, striding along beside him. "Who's that? It sure isn't me!"

"Jesco."

"Oh? Why?"

"Because he got out of a difficult duty, and his father lost a battle."

"Hmm. I haven't been chosen yet."

"You will be."

"What makes you so sure?"

"Woman's logic."

"Wonderful."

Eirlin suddenly stopped, and as Ecmund turned to face his sister the Sword could feel strong emotion radiating from her. "You do want to go, don't you?"

"Better me than Uncle Aeldwig or Jesco."

She slapped his shoulder, turning him to walk with her, frustration simmering. "That's a fine stand to take, brother. If you go into the meetings thinking, 'I don't mind being here,' you're going to be completely useless, just like Uncle Aeldwig says. You have to go in with a plan: things you want, things you need, things you're willing to bargain on."

"I'm not worried about that. I'm sure you'll tell me."

The Sword was as astounded at the sudden gush of emotion as Ecmund was by the burst of tears.

"Eirlin, what's wrong? What did I say?"

She wiped a sleeve across her eyes, straightened her back, walked on.

"Come on, Eirlin. What's wrong? I was just making a joke."

"I was doing what I thought best for the good of the family, Ecmund, and now you make me look like some kind of interfering, domineering… witch."

"Eirlin, Eirlin, that's not true. I believe you did it for the good of the family. I can't think of anyone who could have done it better. Nobody can deal with Uncle Aeldwig like you can. You were absolutely right. If he had put himself forward, they'd have found some way to keep him off, and then there would have been a terrible fuss."

She shook her head. "He was always troublesome, but since Aunt Chalia died…"

Ecmund nodded. "You know, I always thought that she was too soft to have any effect on him. She just did whatever he said. I guess it wasn't quite that way."

"It doesn't seem so. Anyway, we have to go home and talk about what we," she poked a finger in his ribs to emphasize her point, "want to say to the council."

Before we start the fighting and killing.

"You know, Eirlin, I'm not sure we aren't wasting our time. Of course we talk, and meet, and discuss, but sometimes I have to agree with Uncle Aeldwig. In the end it always seems to come down to fighting for yourself and your family, and to hell with the rest."

"Ecmund! You don't really believe that!"

Yes, he does.

His hand rested comfortably on the Sword's hilt. "I wish I didn't. It just seems that way sometimes."

She frowned. "I never heard you talk this way before you had that Sword. I'm not sure it's good for you."

Oops. Gently, now, Ecmund. We don't want trouble in the home.

"I don't think it has anything to do with having a Sword. I didn't want a sword at all, if you remember. I wanted to stay at home and work with my axe and saw. But I can't. And once I start looking at the situation, that is what I see."

She glanced over at him as he opened their cottage door. "Just you don't start thinking that kind of thing too often, or I'll send you over to live with Uncle Aeldwig, and the two of you can stew in your own juice together until it chokes you!"

Not a good idea. He is very weird.

He followed her through the door. "Since you put it that way..."

She laughed. "Don't worry, Ecmund. I wouldn't wish that on anyone I love."

She bustled about preparing a hot drink, while Ecmund stoked up the fire. "You know, I sometimes feel that my main battle with Uncle Aeldwig is over Jesco. It has been for a long time."

"Jesco?"

"Yes. His father is always cutting him down, I'm always building him up, and I don't get my fair share of time to do my part."

"But he likes your part a whole lot more."

"That helps. It still worries me."

He's a swordsman, silly girl. Do you want to dull his edge?

Eirlin realized that her brother was looking at her, eyebrows raised.

"What? What did I say?"

"I know he's family, Eirlin, but how involved are you in this rescue attempt?"

52

"Ecmund, I want to Heal Jesco. I don't want to marry him! I love him like family, but that's all."

"Just glad we have that straight."

Me, too. Imagine having that man for a father-in-law. The Smith preserve our sanity!

Can you imagine the Name?

"DESTINY'S BLIGHT"

"RUIN OF ORDER"

"SCUTTLER"

Now, there's one I like. "Scuttler". I wonder what a Scuttler does. Sounds like a bug, running around on the floor.

Sorry, not interested.

Chapter 10

Warning! Messenger coming!

Eirlin's head came up from her supper. She stared into space for a moment.

There's a messenger coming. In a hurry. All right, let me put it this way:

Unease worry dangerworrycuriosityworry. Did you get that?

Eirlin threw on her shawl, headed for the door.

No! Take me! Take me, Eirlin... drat the girl!

It was difficult, waiting. There were shouts in the street, running feet. The Sword pushed her senses to the maximum. No real fear. No battle sounds. Then hoof beats, a lot of them, going away.

An emergency somewhere else, then. Must have been the Village Guard going out. Hope they left someone behind.

Well, there you are, finally. What took you so long?

Eirlin closed the door behind her, shaking her head.

Why are you so worried?

The girl began to clean the dishes, her mind a turmoil. "Who would be attacking Hrostan's farm? I don't like this at all."

This is just so Forged frustrating. It's enough to make me really talk to her.

The Sword was so busy trying to figure out what was going on in Eirlin's mind that she almost missed the first of the attack. Soon it became very apparent.

Danger! Danger! Swordsmen!

Eirlin started up, eyes wildly searching. She ran to the door, opened it.

No, Eirlin. Come in and lock the door!

For the Sword, it was a familiar pattern: the shouts, the screams, the running feet. Coming closer and closer down the street. Eirlin rushed inside, slammed and locked the door, ran across the room, barred the back door and the window shutters as well. She stood leaning against the door for a moment, staring around.

Pick me up, Eirlin. Take the Sword!

Finally, she stumbled over, obeying the urgent call. She stood over the Sword, swaying, hesitant. The Sword crooned a desperate appeal.

They're coming closer, girl. Come on, you can do it! You have to do it!

"I can't kill anyone, I can't, I can't!" The girl reached out, grasped the scabbard in both hands, as if to keep herself from touching the hilt.

There was a bang on the door.

"I can't!" Her arms shook from the force of her grip.

54

There were more bangs, and a voice came, smothered by the thick oak. "We know you're in there, sweetheart. Open up or it will go worse with you."

She fell to her knees, moaning.

She must defend herself.

The bangs became thumps, as a heavy shoulder shook the door in its frame.

The moan became a litany. "I can't kill, I can't kill."

Inspired by the splintering of the doorjamb, the Sword's patience ran out.

All right, I give up. EIRLIN. YOU DON'T HAVE TO KILL ANYONE. JUST DRAW THE SWORD.

"I can't kill, I can'...what?"

We don't have to kill them. Wound and disarm. But draw the sword! Quickly.

"Who's talking to me?...Kitten? Is that you?"

There is no time for this. Draw me, for the Fire's sake, or you're going to die, and it won't be pleasant before you do.

The door was half broken now, and a leather-clad arm stretched in to undo the latch.

DRAW THE FORGE-BEDAMNED SWORD, WOMAN!

With a gasp, she grabbed the hilt, and the Sword shrugged smoothly out of the scabbard, humming with a fiery joy.

Good evening, gentlemen. Sorry, no time for chit-chat. Shall we move straight to the part where you run away screaming and bleeding?

Eirlin gripped the hilt in both hands, the point wavering at the three steel-capped men who shouldered the splintered door aside and crowded in on her.

No, no, just one hand. Swing it, swing it. Don't go for power, go for speed, and I'll do the rest. Open your mind, close off your thoughts, close them... Not your eyes, stupid, your thoughts! Good, that's better.

The soldiers paused, their satisfied grins frozen.

"I think you'd better put that down, little lady. We're just gonna have some fun. You mess with that, and it's gonna get worse. Much worse."

She waved her arm in wide, desperate arcs, and the Sword guided its path into a sweeping figure-of-eight defence.

Keep it simple. Get him as he draws... Now!

She lunged, and as the first soldier's sword cleared the scabbard, the forward motion pushed his arm right onto the Sword's point. Eirlin tried to draw her hand back, horror engulfing her mind, but the Sword carried her momentum forward, smashing her knuckle guard into the man's face with resounding force. He dropped without a sound.

"Ouch! Remember. No killing."

He's just out for a moment. Turn! Turn!

The Sword swooped around to defend against the slash of the second man, at the same time spinning the girl so that the third enemy was behind his friend, and could not reach her. A quick series of jabs, to get the opponent's sword moving uncertainly, then a slice across the upper arm, dropping another sword from nerveless fingers.

Duck!

There is only so much a Sword can do, and fortunately the girl dropped instinctively as a wild slash passed over her head. The Sword took advantage and began a low-line attack, swiping at the knees and ankles of both men, so that the wounded one danced into the path of his comrade. It was easy enough, then, to reach under and run through the unguarded throat...

Where the point froze. "I...will...not...kill!"

The Sword tried for a brief moment, but was beaten before she started. Instantly changing tactics, she strengthened the arm, holding the point rock steady. The soldier's own sword, poor dead piece of steel that it was, sagged, its tip coming to rest on the floor.

"Drop it!"

A clatter, and the man's hands spread pleadingly to the side. Eirlin glanced at the other soldier, standing uselessly, his bloody hand gripping his wound. Something changed in the girl's mind, and the Sword felt herself pushed aside by another feeling.

Pity? You feel pity for these warped, water-tempered pieces of tin?

"Yes, I feel pity for them. All right, men. Fight's over. No more." The Sword fell back in disarray, sectioned off neatly into the part of the girl's mind that controlled the right arm. Adapting quickly, she threw her strength into this new partnership, holding firmly, bolstering the tiring muscles.

"You! Get some cloth and bind up his arm. No, not that!" The man had been removing the sweaty bandana that he wore under his helmet. "His wound isn't blighted yet. Use that and it will be."

A quick slash, and she held a piece of her petticoat out.

Well, that's a first. Women's undergarments. Should I be blushing in shame?

"Don't be silly. It's just cloth." She tossed the rag to the soldier. "Here. Wrap it with that. It's been washed recently."

Her gesture with the Sword's tip sat the wounded man on the bench, and she stepped over the one on the floor, keeping her face toward the others. This man was moaning and moving restlessly. She slashed another piece of petticoat and, laying the Sword down, ripped his sleeve away and began to bind up the small puncture where the Sword had entered.

Don't worry. No blight.

"I should hope there's no blight. As long as his shirt wasn't dirty...Oh!"

What?

"I can feel...see...oh, the poor man!"

Don't get into that. Fix his wound while the others are in shock.

"But he feels so..."

He's a killer and would have raped you. Get out of his mind. Fix him up if you must, but stay away from his emotions. Hurry!

"All right." She set to work.

The Sword lay, alert in every sense, ready to jump to Eirlin's hand if needed, but she was too fast. She finished the bandage, tucked the ends in, then snatched up the Sword again. The other two sat side by side on the bench, staring at her in dumb amazement and fear.

"All right. Who sent you?"

"Uh...orders..." The two glanced at each other.

Her arm rose, Sword floating into position. "That would be, 'Orders, my Lady'."

"Oh...aye. Orders, my Lady."

"Whose orders? You were ordered by your officers to come to my house and rape me, maybe kill me?"

"Oh, no, no, my Lady. We were supposed to come in and rough up the villagers. Nobody said anythin' about killin' or stuff like that." The man shrugged. "Course, things happen. You know."

The Sword could feel righteous anger building, and hummed in response, rising slowly, ever so slowly, weaving her tip from one throat to the other, then back.

Who gave the order? He's the one we need.

"No, I don't know, and I am not pleased with the idea. Who gave the order?"

The soldier held up his hands defensively. "I don't know, m'lady." He pointed to the fallen soldier. "Tajar, here, he took the orders. I guess it was somebody at the castle. Maybe that new fellow he rode in with."

"New fellow?"

"Aye. Some sort of nobility, I think. Well-dressed, anyway. No idea who he is. Lord's truth, m'lady!"

She frowned. "Very convenient that the officer is the unconscious one. Now, what you're going to do, you're going to lift your friend here, and take him outside. When you get there, you're going to call all your fellows together, and you're going to get out of this village. Do you understand?"

"Uh...yes, yes, m'lady!" Making as wide a detour as they could around her, they dragged their officer to his feet and jammed their way

57

clumsily out the door with him. She followed, and the Sword tuned her senses to the street outside.

The unwounded one shouted, and soldiers began to appear, some from up the street, some from inside the houses of her neighbours. Questioning calls rang through the dusk.

The soldier shouted again, louder, and the others hurried to join him, staring in surprise at the strange trio. "Tajar is hurt. We done what we come for. Let's git outta here."

A few disappointed growls were stared down, and soon the solders were stomping in an unruly mob down the street. The Sword's acute senses picked up muttering. "...she was talkin'. She was talkin' to her sword. All the time she was fightin', she was talkin' to it."

The Sword considered this, decided it was a good thing.

Eirlin stared up and down the street one more time, then slowly, almost regretfully, went back inside and picked up the scabbard from where she had flung it in the fight. She was about to slide the sword back in, when suddenly she stopped.

"Wait a minute. You spoke to me!"

The Sword thought that now was a good time to keep still. Slowly, gently, she completed her withdrawal from Eirlin's mind.

"You did! You told me I didn't have to kill anybody, that we could wound and disarm. And you lied! You would have killed that last soldier if I hadn't stopped you." She shook the Sword firmly, frowning at the ruby in her hilt. "I can forgive the talking, but not the lying, Kitten! Don't you ever lie to me again! Do you hear me?" She shook the sword again. "Are you listening? ...oh, by the Blood, I'm talking to a sword!"

She stared at the Sword a while longer. Then, with a sigh of disgust, slammed her down into her scabbard and turned to walk up the street, peering into doorways, speaking to people, her calming presence sweeping over the terrified villagers.

The Sword stilled the humming, and went merrily about clearing off the smear of blood left on her fighting edge.

Imagine! Putting a sword away uncleaned! What an amateur. Her brother would have something to say about that. If he ever found out, that is.

When the blade was shiny and smooth again, the Sword nestled into her sheath, reliving the battle, basically satisfied.

The girl has potential, real potential, although that problem with killing is a definite drawback. Didn't stop her from being fast, though. Lightning fast. Of course, her mind is so much like her brother's that it isn't like taking on a stranger. Need be, we could do even better. Too bad about that killing thing, though. Trust is important.

Then another thought came. *There was something wrong about that battle. Why did three men come to our house, and bash down the door? The other soldiers were spread out, doing minor damage. Something strange here.*

As Eirlin strode up the street, buckling the belt around her waist, the other villagers began to come out of their houses. By the time she reached the inn, most of the braver ones had gathered. Albercas, a bandage around his thigh, was taking reports.

"What happened at your house, Eirlin?"

"There were three of them. They broke the door down. That was as far as they got."

"Three of them?" The innkeeper looked up. "Anybody else get that kind of attention?"

There was a general glancing around.

Albercas frowned. "Nobody else hurt?"

There were bruises and a few sword cuts, and it seemed that most houses had furniture broken. A dog and a few chickens had been killed, but the soldiers had done nothing more serious.

The innkeeper motioned them all inside, gestured to his wife to draw ales. Then he turned to the villagers. "This was a rather strange attack. Few injuries, a bit of damage, but one house getting special attention." His eye pinned Eirlin. "Any ideas?"

She raised her eyebrows. "I questioned them. They say they got their orders from someone at the castle. Probably from a new man who just arrived."

"You questioned them? Three soldiers?"

You bet your rusty tap handle we questioned them, Innkeeper.

Eirlin rubbed her hand across the pommel of the Sword. "They were happy to answer."

"It sounds like you have attracted some untoward attention in high places."

She nodded slowly. "I don't know how. Unless they were after Ecmund, and I can't think why they'd want him, either. They didn't say. Just that they'd been told to rough up the villagers." She thought a moment. "I wish I'd kept them a bit longer. I think they could have told more, if I had known the right questions. But I wanted them out of the village before they hurt anyone else."

The innkeeper grinned wryly. "You didn't expect them to be truthful, did you?"

She shrugged. "They were pretty scared at the time."

He raised his eyebrows, but she gave him no more. "I think we need to take a walk."

"Where to?"

"To the castle."

"You can't go up to the castle, just like that." He spread his hands in horror.

"Oh, yes we can. Lord Delfontes has a responsibility to protect us. If those were his soldiers, he's got some answering to do. If he won't answer us, he'll have to answer to the King."

He'll answer to us, when Ecmund returns. To the Sword and her Hand!

She was interrupted by the sound of galloping horses, followed by shouts. Soon Jesco shouldered his way into the room. "Eirlin. Where's Eirlin?"

"I'm here, Cousin. I'm…"

He rushed over to her, grabbed both her arms. "Are you all right?"

"…fine, Jesco. They didn't hurt anyone seriously."

"What happened? Who attacked?"

"It seems like it was soldiers from the castle. They were under orders from some newly arrived stranger. I'm going up to talk to Lord Delfontes about it tomorrow."

"You're going up to the castle, after they attacked you?" He grinned. "Brave girl. This time, you won't be alone." He shook his head. "They duped us proper, didn't they?"

She nodded. "They certainly did. What did you find when you got to Hrostan's farm?"

"Nothing. They were sitting around the supper table, wondered why we were rushing about. Invited us in for pie. I knew right then there was something wrong, and we hotfooted it back here." He spat on the floor. "Too damned late!"

She laid a calming hand on his arm. "Probably better that way. Nobody seriously hurt. If you'd attacked them, there would have been a real fight."

Jesco turned to the innkeeper. "We'll head out for the castle as soon as Ecmund gets back from Pieterburen in the morning. We'd better put some patrols out tonight, but I doubt if they'll be back. They seem to have done what they came for, whatever that was."

Albercas nodded. "When will Ecmund get here?"

"It's only an hour's gallop. We'll send a messenger tonight; he'll get there just after dark. They can come back first thing in the morning."

He turned to Eirlin. "Do you want to stay here, or go home?"

"I'll go home, I think. I have to do something about the broken door."

"They broke your door down?"

"Yes," she smiled up at him, "some people just don't understand a polite 'no'."

60

They learned manners tonight!

As they walked up the street, he took her arm, pulled her closer, spoke softly. "Any magic? Any feel of a Magician?"

"Why do you ask?"

"Ecmund told me about that Magician going by. You've got more of the Blood than I have. I thought you might pick up something I missed."

"No. Not a sign. Of course, I was a little busy."

He looked down at her. "Yes, you're going to have to tell me about this."

She shrugged uncomfortably, put a hand to the Sword. "They broke in the door and got tangled, trying to come in all at once. I hit one with the sword hilt, knocked him out, slashed the second in the arm, and had my sword at the third's throat before he could get untangled."

Jesco raised his eyebrows. "Not bad, not bad, Cousin Eirlin. We'll make a warrior of you yet."

"No, you will not! I hated it, and I will not kill anyone!"

I think she means it, Cousin Jesco.

"Whatever you say."

"Just keep that straight in any plans you're making. I'm wearing this sword for the look of it, that's all."

The man opened his mouth, decided not to try.

I know what you want to say, friend. Anybody who wears a sword had better be prepared to use it. Don't worry. She is. Sort of.

The Sword hummed quietly to herself until a sharp slap on the pommel brought her to reality.

At the cottage, the two brought the lamp outside to view the damage. "I don't think we can fix that tonight."

Eirlin shook her head. "It's pretty smashed. Ecmund might have to make a new one tomorrow."

He glanced at her. "After we get back from the castle."

"Right."

He picked up the soldiers' discarded swords. "I'll take care of these. I know some lads who might need them." He turned to her. "So you'll come and stay with us tonight. You don't want to be alone."

She slapped the Sword in a friendly way. "I wouldn't be exactly alone."

He grinned as they turned back up the street. "Don't you start getting too attached to Ecmund's sword, now."

"Don't worry. She's very loyal."

"Is she now? And what else do you know about her?"

Don't tell him. Please, please don't tell him!

Eirlin shrugged. "Nothing, really. You know how girls are. We make stories about things."

He glanced down at her. The Sword could feel his reservation, but he said nothing.

When they reached the sprawling family farmhouse, his sister, Maerwin, bustled Eirlin inside, divested her of the Sword, and soon had her sitting before an over-warm fire with a too-hot drink in her hands.

"Now, you tell us all about it, my dear. It's best to talk about these things."

Eirlin was saved from answering by her uncle's cranky voice. "And tell us where our brave Village Guard was when we were attacked. Some use having these fine young men strutting around, and where are they when we need them?"

Cousin Maerwin tut-tutted. "I'm sure they were doing what they could, Father."

"I doubt it. They were probably..."

"They were going where they were sent, Uncle Aeldwig." Eirlin glared at Jesco, daring him to speak. "The whole town was fooled. When somebody calls for help, you have to go, or, as you say, what do we have a Village Guard for?"

"Hmph!"

She turned her regard to Maerwin. "So the raiders didn't get out here?"

"No, I think they only hit the town."

"Yes, that was very strange." Jesco looked around at his family. "It seems the officer and two of his men headed straight for Eirlin's house. Fortunately, she caught them off guard, and disarmed them."

The two other women looked up from their children, eyes wide.

Eirlin shook her head. "Let's not start a wild rumour. I was lucky. And I didn't hurt anyone too badly. I helped bandage them up and sent them away."

Cousin Leofwina frowned. "You fought with them, then you Healed them, and then they went away?"

"That's about it. Once men don't have their swords anymore, they calm down a lot."

The two women burst into nervous laughter, and even Jesco smiled faintly. "So we have company for the night, Maerwin. Eirlin's door is in splinters, and Ecmund won't be back until tomorrow morning."

Maerwin was instantly all business. "Of course, of course. You just come with me, Eirlin Bryhtwyn. We'll put you in the back bedroom; you always like that one. Mother's best comforter is on the bed. You'll be snug as anything in there."

Eirlin was about to follow, but detoured to pick up the Sword. Her cousin frowned slightly, but continued her chatter as they walked down the broad hallway towards the sleeping quarters.

Since Eirlin knew the building well, the Sword got a good impression of its layout as they walked. Though termed a farmhouse, it was sturdily built of stone, and the square of outbuildings formed a courtyard in the middle, sheltered from both weather and attack. The Sword could sense a goodly number of men in nearby cottages. *A safe place.*

The room was cosy enough and Eirlin, more shaken by the evening's events than she had let on, was happy to be bundled into the bed, the soft coverlet tucked tightly around her. Maerwin smiled. "There. You look snug enough."

"Thanks, Maerwin."

"Hah! Haven't had so much fun since Blifer broke his leg last fall. Nobody gets a chance to cosset you, Eirlin."

"Well, I appreciate it."

"Don't you worry. You had a difficult time of it but you got through it like a hero, and I'm sure you'll feel better after a good night's sleep." She noted her cousin's glance. "And you will *not* take that sword to bed with you. That would be just overly strange. Who knows where it's been?"

With a knowing grin, she bustled out, leaving Eirlin in much-needed peace. She lay there, reliving the events of the evening. Finally, she reached out, ran her finger over the ruby on the Sword's hilt. "Thank you, Kitten. You were a real tiger today."

The Sword hummed proudly.

"Now be quiet, Kitten. I want to sleep."

Kitten was quiet.

Chapter 11

With the Sword's soothing help, Eirlin slept deeply that night. When the dreams began, the Sword kept a full clamp on the girl's consciousness and forced her deeper, protected from the horror. It was a draining night for the Sword, but her patient slept through. In fact, Eirlin was just beginning to stir when there was a banging at the front door, far away down the hall.

About time you showed up.

The Sword boosted Eirlin's perceptions enough that she could hear the fuss. The girl jumped from the bed, grabbed a handy robe, and strode up the hallway, the Sword carried firmly by the middle of her scabbard.

She had just reached the dining hall when she was swept off her feet by her anxious brother.

"Eirlin! Are you all right? They didn't tell me much. I never should have gone. I never should have left you! Are you hurt?"

"I wasn't before you grabbed me. You are carrying a most obnoxious amount of weaponry. Here. Take your Sword, and you can leave the rest of that at home."

Ecmund grasped the Sword, frowning deep into his sister's eyes. "Did you actually fight, Eirlin? That's what they said. They said you faced three soldiers, and wounded two of them."

"It wasn't exactly like that, Ecmund. Have you seen our door?"

"No, I came straight here. What happened to the door?"

She grinned. "They were a little too anxious to get in. They tried to come through a broken door without opening it first, and they got all tangled. I disarmed them before they had a chance to straighten out."

He demurred, but the Sword fed him complacent agreement, and his brow partly cleared.

"I don't quite believe that, Eirlin, but as long as you're all right…"

"Well, I am, so you don't have to worry."

"But somebody has to worry!"

"Yes, they do, and we're going up to the castle right now. We've just been waiting for you to get here."

"You have not, and you will not." They turned at Maerwin's voice. She stared them down.

"Eirlin just got up, and I'm betting that Ecmund didn't eat any breakfast this morning. Now, you two are going to sit down to a good meal, and when you're fed properly, then you can go and face the Overlord, or whatever you need to do."

They glanced at each other, shared a shrug. "I really didn't have time for breakfast."

"Good enough. You go clean yourself up, Ecmund. Eirlin, you get dressed properly, and by that time I'll have pan bread and comfrey tea on the table."

It was still well before mid-morning when the two approached the inn. "What are we going to say?"

"What do you mean 'we'? I'm on the Overlord's Council. You're going to stay at home where it's safe."

She reached out, laid a hand on the Sword's hilt. "I'm in the battle this time, Ecmund. Ask Kitten."

Ooh, is she in it.

He swivelled his hip out of reach, frowning. "I don't know, Eirlin."

"I do. I'm the one who faced three of them. I have some questions, and I'm going to be there to hear the answers."

He shrugged uncomfortably. "This is what I was afraid of, Eirlin. Everything is getting mixed up. Everyone is angry. Instead of thinking of peace and cooperation, we have to confront the new Overlord before we've even met him officially."

"Then maybe the Council needs to go soft on the confrontation. But I don't."

"If you're sure, Eirlin..." he shook his head, his opportunity to argue disappearing as they entered the inn.

Both were surprised at their reception. Conversation stopped, and all heads turned their way. There was a moment of silence, with the two of them halted in the doorway, uncertain what to do. Then voices called out, inviting them in, with, the Sword thought, a certain amount of relief. And a great deal of respect. The moment they were seated, the innkeeper rose.

"Right, folks. We're all here. Let's get going."

Eirlin nudged her brother, and he spoke up without thinking. "Um...Albercas..."

The innkeeper stopped. "Yes, Ecmund?"

Ecmund glanced down at Eirlin, and she nodded in encouragement. "Um...don't you think we should have a plan? What are we going up there to say?"

"What are we going to say? We're going to go up there and ask this new so-called Overlord what he thinks he's doing, sending his men down to attack us."

Ecmund nodded. "That would be what they are expecting."

"What they are expecting?"

"Yes. We have to do some thinking before we go up there and do and say exactly what we are expected to."

The older man shook his head, puzzled.

"Look at it this way, Albercas. Someone up at the castle ordered that attack. We don't know why, but I think the last thing we want to do is exactly what we would be expected to do. That sounds too much like what that person wants us to do."

The innkeeper slanted his head to the side. "That's pretty complicated thinking, Ecmund."

"Not really. What if the new Overlord had nothing to do with the attack? What if someone wants us to go raging up to the castle like a tribe of wild Leute, make him angry, get the two of us fighting with each other?"

"Oh. I see."

"Right. I figure the best plan, when you don't know what someone wants, you do something he doesn't expect."

"So he expects...?"

Ecmund gave a hard grin. "He expects exactly what we have here. We have a group of very angry men, me included, determined to go up there and demand an explanation."

"Exactly. And what's wrong with that? We deserve an explanation."

Ecmund shrugged. "I don't know. If I were the new Overlord, not too certain of my strength, and a mob of my subjects came up to my castle and started shouting at me, I know what I'd do."

There was a snicker from one of the far tables. "Clap them all in gaol."

"Exactly."

Mutters broke out in the crowd.

"So what do we do?"

Ecmund shrugged. "I don't know. As I said, anything but what they expect."

Another voice came out of the crowd. "So you figure someone up at the castle set this up, so as to get us in a fight with the new Overlord?"

"Eirlin, tell them what the soldier told you."

She rose. "He said they were just supposed to rough us up. Whatever that means."

"What makes you think he was telling the truth?"

"I was the one holding the sword. He was rather surprised."

There was a quiet chuckle.

The innkeeper stepped forward. "So who wants us to go up there and make trouble?"

"Someone new. Nobility of some sort, they said."

The man nodded. "...then the best thing we can do is go up there as calm as possible: reasonable but firm."

There were several positive murmurs.

"Good enough. So who is going to go?" He looked around the room. "I assume the Overlord's Council would like to atone for their lack of ability to deal with this whole situation through diplomatic means."

Eirlin's laugh cut through the growls. "Don't worry, Albercas. When there's someone willing to send his soldiers to attack an undefended village in his own demesne, it's a little late for that kind of diplomacy."

There were several nods.

"But I am going with you."

The nods turned to frowns.

She shook her head. "I know it sounds strange, but I'll be a great asset to you. I'm the one who was singled out for attack."

The innkeeper spread his hands. "I suppose. I don't want to be the one to deny you, in any case."

"Thank you. I promise I'll be good."

The older man returned her smile weakly. She held his eyes a moment. "Do you want me to deal with Jesco?"

"What do you mean?…oh. Yes, the Village Guardsmen are going to be a problem, aren't they?"

"I would be if I were them."

"Eirlin, you're a problem all by yourself."

"True, but I'm a problem that's been solved. Jesco and his friends spent their time chasing off after nothing, while the job they were supposed to do went undone. I imagine they spent the rest of the evening in the tavern, and somebody had a tough time persuading them not to go up to the castle and start breaking things?" She nodded. "They are going to want to redeem themselves, Albercas."

"We can't have them pacing around, snarling. That's exactly what we don't need. We're all agreed on that."

"Exactly. That's why you want me to deal with him."

"Can you?"

She smiled, shrugged. "I can't make it much worse."

"Thank you, Eirlin."

"Fine. I'll go talk to him now."

She turned and started out the door, Ecmund hurrying to catch up. "How are you going to work this one, Eirlin?"

"He's the least of our problems."

"Glad you see it that way. He doesn't look very happy to me."

Her smile faded. "No one is happy, Ecmund." She strode forward, beckoning to her cousin. He and several of his friends approached her, but she motioned the rest back and turned Jesco aside. The Sword strained her senses so that Ecmund could hear.

"Jesco, you know how I always stand up to your father?"

He tilted his head, uncertain. "Yes."

"You always respect that, don't you?"

"Yes, I guess I do. It takes more courage than most have."

"I'm going to do it to you, now."

"What?"

"I'm going to stand up to you. I'm going to stand in front of you and tell you that you can't do what you dearly want to do. And just like your father, you're going to listen to me."

"Are you? And what makes you think I'm going to listen?"

"Because I never stand up to your father unless I'm right. It isn't me that backs him down, it's the truth."

"And what truth do you have that's going to back me down, Eirlin?"

She leaned closer. "It's very simple, Jesco. We are in a very touchy situation, and here is your truth. This is no place for anger."

"No place for anger? We have been attacked by our own Overlord. He has broken every rule we live by!"

"That's right. At least, someone has broken the rules. And we have been asking ourselves the reason for that. Ecmund thinks that someone wants us angry. It may be the new Overlord, and it may not be. Whoever it is, the best way to beat that person is to do something different from what he wants. If he wants anger, then we don't get angry. Do you see?"

"I understand what you're saying, but I doubt if it will do you any good."

She laid a soft hand on his arm. "This is the moment, Jesco. This is when we find out if you are like your father or not."

"What do you mean?"

"You know your father. When he is angry, and especially when the anger is justified, he never holds back, no matter how bad the results. Can you? Or are you the servant of your anger, as he is?"

Jesco took a deep breath, then exhaled slowly, regarding his cousin sideways.

"You're twisting me, Eirlin. You're using your knowledge of my family against me."

"No, Jesco, I'm using my knowledge for the good of the village. Never against you."

"Ah, you make it sound so logical."

"Women's logic?"

"Hmph! Never from you, Eirlin."

"I'll take that as a compliment. But that's not all."

"It's not?"

"No. We need you in this, Jesco. We need you and your men."

"Of course you do. You need a show of force."

"That's right, a show of force, but force under the strictest control. Our enemies have made a mistake, Jesco. They have committed a crime.

68

We think they want to provoke us into an equal error. We have to show ourselves above that. We have to show ourselves under our own control. Can you do that? Will your men obey?"

"Damned right they will!"

"No, Jesco, not because you tell them to. That kind of discipline will not work on them. They are as angry as you were, with as good a reason. They have to obey because they know it is the right thing to do, not because they are told to. Can you persuade them of that?"

He grinned wryly, glanced over at Ecmund. "She's done it again, hasn't she?"

His cousin shrugged. "She's got the whole Overlord's Council eating from her hand. Why not you?"

The Overlord's Council from Falkenby strode at a dignified pace up the road towards Falkengard Castle, and the Sword was able to get a good feel for the place. A definite holdover from a bygone era, it was squat and blocky: a narrow, high-walled bailey with the stern, square tower of the keep riding above. Soaring overhead, the Aerie jabbed its ragged stone fingers to the sky. As the builders had probably intended, the massive edifice imposed its grim air on the approaching group, and their ranks closed.

At Eirlin's nod, Jesco formed the Guard into a stiff line outside the gates. The party was met inside by an equally cold and suspicious officer. They were escorted between two files of soldiers to the main hall. There, they stood inside a circle of chairs, which looked set up for the purpose of their visit.

As they entered, the Sword sent out her usual check, but suddenly halted in confusion.

Magician. By the Hammer and the Anvil. A Forge-cursed Magician, right here in the room!

She listened. The Magician was concentrating on the Overlord, his senses generally tuned for danger. In the mass of emotion caused by the angry Council, the Sword's seeking tendrils had gone unnoticed. She fed one jolt through the hand on her hilt, *Magician,* and faded out.

I am the mice in the wainscoting.

Ecmund patted the Sword's hilt reassuringly, his eyes scanning the room. He leaned over to his sister. "That Magician is here. I can feel him."

She glanced at him dubiously. He patted the Sword again, and Eirlin nodded. "Tell her to keep quiet."

The Sword agreed. This was no time to show their full hand.

"This changes things."

69

Ecmund nodded. "If he's using a Magician, maybe my Sword is going to be more useful than we thought."

The Overlord motioned them forward. He was sitting in a big chair that was not quite a throne, with several well-dressed retainers lined behind him. Maridon in aspect, he had their typical dark hair and olive skin. A girl in a formal embroidered gown sat in a smaller chair just to his left. The Sword wondered briefly what she was doing there. A relative, presumably. No danger, anyway. Armsmen ranged the walls and flanked the door, inside and out. From their reactions to various Council members, some of them must be locals, well known. The Sword built up a picture of the room in case of need: furniture, concentrations of men, weapons, exits.

At the Overlord's nod, they sat, except the innkeeper who stepped in front of his group before Delfontes could speak. "We have a serious complaint, my Lord."

The Overlord leaned back, his elbows on the arms of his ornate chair, his fingers meeting at the tip of his short, black, beard. "So I have been told. Please state your version of the events."

The innkeeper told the story clearly and succinctly, ending with a list of damage.

The Overlord listened, unmoving. He raised his eyebrows at the breaking of Eirlin's door, but that was all. When the tale was done, he sat silent for a moment, nodding.

"I can see that you might feel ill treated in this case."

"I fail to see where 'ill treated' covers it, my Lord. Your soldiers have put my townspeople to the sword!"

The Overlord smiled slightly. "Come, now, let us not exaggerate. You have hardly been put 'to the sword,' I think."

"Three definite sword cuts, my Lord. None deep, but all drawing blood."

The Overlord shrugged. "And I have three wounded as well. It sounds like a rather even exchange."

Eirlin shared a glance with her brother. It was the first they had heard of another villager taking toll on the attackers.

"My Lord, please see this from our point of view. We are peaceful villagers. Any time that armed men attack our town is a matter of great import to us. When the attackers are the men who are supposed to be protecting us, it becomes much more serious. We do not look at this as a simple military exchange, to be scored like a game of darts."

"I can understand that. However, perhaps you could see it from my point of view. My men are charged with upholding the law. At times, regrettably, they are forced to use their swords to accomplish their duty."

Albercas stared incredulously. "Upholding the law? Is that what they were doing when they attacked a defenceless village?"

"As we have just discussed, not so defenceless."

He is not listening.

"My Lord, have you considered what would have happened if our Village Guard had not been lured away from their posts just before the attack? Had we been properly defended, your men would not have got away so lightly touched."

The Overlord appeared to weigh this information. "I am beginning to get a picture of how you approach this situation. You think of armed insurrection against my rightful authority."

Now he makes it our fault.

Waves of suppressed anger began to emanate from the Council. Albercas took a deep breath. "I suggest you take a look at the Charter which King Vetrorrillo da Maridon gave you when he sent you here, where your authority is explicitly laid out."

"As are my rights."

This is going nowhere. He needs to be slapped.

Ecmund stood up, stepped forward. "We are going around the same bush again, my Lord. There is one other matter to be discussed."

"And who are you?"

"I am Ecmund Liutswin Falconric, a name that should be known to you."

"Why should any name here be especially known to me?"

The Sword felt Ecmund absorb the cool indifference, consider, then decide. It was the same as when he faced Jesco outside the inn. No strong emotion, just cold analysis of possibilities.

Now is the time, Ecmund. Lunge!

"My Lord, while I do not wish to sound like the housewife telling the baker his business, I must ask if you were given any information at all about this demesne, before you were sent to take over?"

"I would think that my preparation for this duty was between me and he who gave it to me."

Ecmund sighed. "As the housewife said, 'Someone needs to tell him, or a lot of bread will get burned.' I think it applies in this case."

The Overlord flicked his fingers in a dismissive gesture. "Already I tire of your home-bred homilies, young man. Will you come to your point, or will your good sense steer you away from your error?"

"You ask me to come to my point, my Lord. It is this. I don't know what kind of leadership was practiced years ago in the realm of King Alcudo, where you Maridon people came from, but things are different in this realm. King Alcudo never did properly conquer Inderjorne, because he couldn't. In order to avoid wholesale destruction on both sides, he came to a compromise with the ruling Blood. I am sure you have been taught this, but I am not so sure the lesson actually sank in."

"Have a care with your tone of voice, young man. I will allow any man his say, but there is a limit."

"And I thank you for the opportunity. It shows me that you could, with help, develop the sensibility that might allow you to be successful here."

Nicely put. Now go after him!

Ecmund raised a hand to forestall the Overlord's indignant response. "You have asked me to be clear, and this is my point. If you try to rule this demesne in the same way that King Alcudo tried to conquer Inderjorne, you will face the same destruction. If you ignore the balance of rights and responsibilities involved in our Charter, you will pay the price." He turned his palm up. "I hope you do not take that as a threat. It is a mere prediction, based on knowledge of history and my people."

The Overlord leaned back in his chair, fingers steepled before him. "So I am to get a lesson in governance from one of the famous ancient Blood, whose reign over this land was not exactly free of conflict, whose methods combined shamanism, hereditary despotism, and superstition. Interesting."

The Sword stretched a fine tendril of thought towards the Overlord, read uncertainty.

He is not as confident as he seems. Strike!

"So you completely deny the usefulness of our methods, yet you use one of our own Magicians against us."

The Overlord sat straighter. "What are you talking about? I use no Magician!"

He thinks this is truth.

The Hand's mind reeled. *He doesn't know? A secret Magician, and the Overlord doesn't know about him?*

That's right. Why is that so terrible?

"Am I to understand, my Lord, that you have such a poor grasp of your demesne that you can have a Magician working under your nose, sending your own soldiers out to attack your own villages, and you don't even know about it? And you have the temerity to disparage my people's ability to rule their land?"

The Overlord's body stiffened, and a red flush crept up his neck. He leaned forward, glaring at Ecmund, fighting to hold his temper. "Young man, I find your insinuations approaching insult, and your attitude lacking in respect."

"In other words, I speak the truth, and you don't want to hear it."

The Overlord rose, his face reddening. "You presume to stand before me in your workman's clothing, and lecture me on how I should rule my demesne? You do not know what danger you court."

This anger comes from fear. He is uncertain.

The Hand crossed his arms over his chest, his chin lowered and his eyebrows raised. "You sit here in this castle and presume to rule my people with unearned force, in complete ignorance of the danger you court? You have no idea how close you are to destruction."

And now we fight!

The Sword could feel the noble's hand stretching for his weapon, and she prepared to act. However the Overlord was made of sterner steel than she thought. He took a deep breath, let it out. "I am getting a little tired of having the losers in a 200-year-old war still harping about how things should have been. You have no place in this discussion."

"That is true my Lord. Continue to discuss with your subjects how you justify your attack on them. You and I can discuss your inadequacies as a ruler at some other time. If you intend to rule in this land, you will learn to show respect for its people and traditions."

"And if you intend to live in this land, you will keep control of your tongue and your temper." The Overlord chopped his hand down. "Disarm him and take him away."

He feels fear, Ecmund.

"You misunderstand, my Lord. I am not yet angry. I merely stand up for what I believe."

The Sword checked and realized that it was true. The Hand's emotions were heated, but there was no sign of uncontrollable anger. Only fierce determination.

Ecmund unbuckled his sword belt and passed it to his sister, who made a show of settling it firmly around her hips. He turned, hands empty, towards the Overlord. "Don't worry. I will not injure local hirelings. I know where the fault lies." He spun and strode between the enclosing guardsmen, outdistancing them to the door, causing them to scramble awkwardly to catch up.

The Overlord sat a moment, his eyes on the door. Then he turned to the rest of the Council.

"So. Are you able to separate your plaint from the delicate sensibilities of this young hothead, or will your loyalty to one of your own lead you to join his defiance?"

"Most of us are the simple folk of the land, my Lord. The arguments that have gone on for centuries between those who rule us have usually brought us nothing but trouble."

"So you withhold support from this young firebrand, and let me deal with him as I see fit?"

The innkeeper glanced at Eirlin, still on her feet. He smiled, shook his head. "It isn't that simple, my Lord. Please don't take it amiss, but I think you made a mistake."

"To arrest a woodcutter who insulted me in my own hall? And why is that a mistake, innkeeper?"

"Because now you have to deal with his sister." The innkeeper sat down.

Eirlin took this as her moment. She stood forward; her left hand was toying with the Sword's hilt, but her inner mind was pleading. *Back me up, Kitten. You're all I've got now.*

The Sword radiated support through her touch, but no more than would reveal its presence through her own strong emotions.

I am the righteous anger of a woman wronged!

The Overlord sat, staring at her. She stared back.

"You dare to approach me, wearing a sword?"

"I am of the Ancient Blood of Inderjorne. By the rights guaranteed by King Alcudo da Maridon, two hundred years ago, I am ceded the prerogative to wear this sword, and to be heard in council. Will you dare to break this sacred pact, on top of the crimes you have already allowed to occur in your demesne?"

"I have committed no crimes!"

The Sword knew not to speak to anyone besides the Hand, unless in dire emergency, but she could send feelings. That wasn't really talking. Carefully, always aware of the Magician's powerful presence, she pushed the idea at Eirlin's mind.

He is uncertain.

"My grandfather used to say that a lord who wars against his own people is like a man at war with his own right hand."

"He said that, did he?"

"Yes, he did. And since no intelligent man wars with his own body..."

"Are you thinking of joining your brother?"

"I don't see what use that would be. I merely bring the obvious to your attention. I presume that, before you came to be Overlord here, you did some study of the rights and responsibilities of the position?"

"I did, and I am quite aware of your ancient and sacred rights. They do not include the right to insult your duly appointed Overlord."

"No one has intended to insult you, my Lord. Merely to point out that there is something going on here, something that does not meet the eye. Perhaps you should ask your Magician."

"Must we fight this ground again? I have no Magician here."

"You mean you think you have no Magician here."

74

"I fail to see the distinction, since there is no such thing as a Magician."

Truth.

The Sword could feel the terror rising in her, but she forced it back. She sighed. "All right, then. Since there is no such thing as a Magician, let me restate. There is a man of the Blood here, in this room. He has the ability to sense that which you cannot sense. He cannot tell your thoughts without your permission, but he can read your emotions, which is perhaps more useful. The fact of his abilities is less important, perhaps, than the fact that he has not seen fit to inform you of them."

"And who is this so-called Magician? I am aware of the superstitions. You are one of the Blood. You can supposedly tell one of your own. Who is he?" He swept his hand across the assembly.

"It would not be to my advantage to spy him out. I have already been marked, and I wish no more of such attention."

The Overlord frowned. "In what way have you been marked?"

"I do not know, my Lord, but I begin to wonder. When your men entered our village, they came straight through the front gate. Since we had no suspicion of treachery, why wouldn't they? They spread out through the village, entering houses, breaking furniture and killing chickens, those brave men. However, three of them, including the officer, came straight to my house, at the farthest end of the village from the main gate, and broke down my door. Can you understand my suspicion, my Lord?"

"If the events were as you say, I can understand your suspicion." He made a calming motion, palm down. "No, no, take your hand from your sword. I do not mean you would lie. I mean that it was nearing dark, and there was a lot happening, and perhaps you were not the intended target."

"If my Lord will pardon a disagreement, one does not survive in this day by giving coincidence the benefit of doubt."

"No, I can see why you would not." The Overlord sat up straighter, palms on knees. "So, people of Falkenby. You have made your complaint. What would you like me to do about it? I could replace the broken furniture, find a few chickens."

"Chickens will solve nothing, my Lord." Eirlin put her hands on her hips.

"Why not?"

"Because we do not know – and if we are to believe it, you do not know either – who or what caused this attack. If you do not know, how can you guarantee it will not happen again, to us or to another village? Will you or won't you, my Lord, until you solve this problem, you are at war with your demesnes. Save your chickens for your own eating."

"Is that some kind of a threat?"

She spread her empty hands.

Well done. Now he listens.

The Overlord cleared his throat, spread his regard to the whole Council. "For your information, my friends, I was informed of the so-called attack. It was reported that a squad of my soldiers were chasing a bandit. He fled into your town, and they were searching for him."

Eirlin cleared her own throat in imitation, and spoke as if to herself. "Ah. That would explain the chickens and the furniture."

He raised a hand. "I know. Nor does it explain the specific attack on your cottage. You have achieved your goal. I agree that all is possibly not as it seems, and I will look further into the matter. Does that satisfy you?"

The innkeeper stood again, glanced around his group. "It will have to, for now, my Lord. We had considered, before we came, whether someone caused this disturbance to create disorder between yourself and your new subjects. The fact that we are dealing with the situation in a diplomatic way will deny that intention. It is our hope that you will continue to deal fairly with us, in this matter and in others, so that life in our demesne can once more run peacefully."

The Overlord nodded, once, deeply. "Well and fairly spoken, innkeeper Albercas. You have acted with cool heads in a trying situation. Most of you. I applaud your wisdom, and I will attempt to act with similar equanimity."

The rest of the Council rose. "Then we will take our leave, my Lord. May we take our fellow councillor with us?"

"I think not. Do not fear for his safety, but I cannot allow him to speak as he did in front of me, and walk completely free. I do have one request, though. May I speak further with his sister? I desire a private word with her."

The innkeeper glanced at Eirlin with a worried frown. She nodded. "I see no danger. Lord Delfontes has demonstrated diplomacy and restraint."

The Council exchanged looks, shrugged their shoulders, and began to file out.

She touched the innkeeper's sleeve. "Ask Jesco to wait."

Albercas nodded, relieved.

When they were gone, she turned to the Overlord. "Yes, my Lord?"

"As I said, my Lady, I am aware of your ancient lineage, and I would appreciate further conversation," his voice rose slightly, "in private."

His retainers took the hint and began to depart. Eirlin could not help but notice that one well-dressed younger man, blond and bearded, hesitated before leaving. The Lord ignored this, but shot a glance and a slight shake of his head to the young lady seated behind him. She stayed.

The Sword considered. The Hand was taken. Surely this was an emergency. She felt the girl's touch on her hilt, and the Magician seemed to be gone.

Eirlin.

?

He is alone.

The Sword could feel the surprise, and risked a stronger message.

He feels alone. He needs help, but to ask is to admit weakness.

Thank you, Kitten.

The Sword fed the man's loneliness, added a touch of fear.

Now he will listen to you. The Sword faded away. She had done what she could. The Hand had done his duty. Now it was up to the Healer.

With the courtiers gone, the Overlord spun a nearby chair towards his, held it for Eirlin to sit. When she had done so, he sat as well.

"Whatever I find it necessary to say in council, I must tender you a private apology, my Lady. Three of my soldiers broke down your door, and I can have no illusions as to their intent. Please believe that I will do whatever is in my power to assure that sort of thing does not happen in future."

I should hope so.

"Thank you, my Lord. That does reassure me."

"However, that brings me to my problem. While I think that the title of 'Magician' may perhaps be an exaggeration, I know enough about your people to understand that some threat is involved."

"Yes, my Lord. It is very important that you believe in the power of a Magician. There has rarely, in our lore, been a Magician who became evil, but a misuse of those powers could be very dangerous. The fact that this Magician remains hidden is very disturbing. He could be a great threat to all of us."

The Overlord stared at her, as if gauging her words.

"If this is true, it is threat I have no experience or skill in countering. Thus to make this demesne safe, I think I need your help, Lady Eirlin."

Beware the clever man when he is afraid.

"Whatever I can do to solve this problem."

"Please accept my word that I did not order the attack."

"I accept that readily, my Lord."

"The question is, how did it happen?"

She considered. "It is possible that it happened as it was reported. Soldiers anxious to please the new Overlord, getting carried away."

"But you do not believe it."

"No. Have you spoken to the officer? The one with the sore nose?"

The Overlord stifled a smile. "Your doing, I gather? At least that was reported accurately. I have not spoken with him yet. Why?"

"I suppose I should not be worried about getting men who tried to defile me into trouble with their Overlord. I questioned his soldiers before I let them go, and they gave me some scant information. They seemed to think he had received orders from someone they described as a newcomer, probably nobility. If you have someone of that sort here..."

The Overlord rubbed his chin. "This is a new demesne for me. Most of my retainers fall into that category."

"However, if you are looking for a Magician as well, it would be someone of the Blood. Perhaps someone new to you."

He shook his head. "Not necessarily. You have not seen the King's court. There are many of your heritage or of mixed blood there, unremarked. I probably have several friends of that ilk, and am not even aware of it."

She spread her hands. "That is all I can tell you at this time, my Lord."

"But in the future? Let us say I believe your tale of Magicians and their powers. Could you identify him?"

"I would not like to say. It is possible that I could. However, as I suggested..."

"Yes. You have no reason, at the moment, to put yourself in more danger. You have warned me."

"Correct. That is what my brother was trying to do, and I followed his lead. If you have a secret Magician here, his presence is now recognized, and he will have to either declare himself, or be much more careful. Whichever he chooses, his ability to work against us is hampered. I do not need to identify him to achieve that."

"Of course, your brother could also tell me."

Her hand went to the sword hilt. "What do you mean?"

He made a calming gesture. "No, no, I would not take advantage of his error in that way. The political situation is too touchy. Besides, it is not my habit to have my subjects tortured."

Truth.

"Then he can come home with me?"

He shook his head. "It was a reasonable ploy, but it must be paid for."

"What ploy?"

"Do you play Battle Squares, my Lady?"

"Passably."

"It is sometimes necessary to sacrifice a Trooper, in order to bring the Queen into play. Your brother will spend the night as my guest. It will be good training in manners for him."

"I trust in you that he will come to no harm."

"I would like to think that you could trust me, my Lady. Is he always like that?"

"No, my Lord, he is never like that. Ecmund is one of the calmest and most peaceful men in the village. It was your refusal to understand the danger of the Magician that caused him to act as he did. Please speak to him. You will see."

"I will do that. And one more thing…"

"Yes, my Lord?"

"I believe it would be polite to introduce you to my daughter." He turned to the girl, who had been sitting with perfect poise throughout the conversation. "My dear, I am slightly hesitant to introduce you to Eirlin Bryhtwyn Falconric, a member of the local nobility, or the Ancient Blood of Inderjorne, as they term it."

He knows your name! Interesting.

"These people are, as you have seen, very jealous of the prerogatives they were granted by our great forebear, King Alcudo, to stop them from continued resistance to his invasion, which would have otherwise destroyed the whole kingdom. Eirlin, I present my daughter Perica, whom I have brought here with me to gain experience in the arts of rule and governance."

Perica rose, glided forward, and gave Eirlin her proper due. Eirlin responded, aware of how large and awkward she looked beside this tiny, graceful creature. There was a wicked twist in the smile the girl turned on her father, however.

"Why are you hesitant, Father? Are you afraid she might give me ideas?"

Her father smiled. "I somehow don't see you facing down the local Overlord with a sword on your hip."

"Oh, no, Father. I can find all sorts of other ways to annoy people. Perhaps not so direct." She turned back to Eirlin. "In spite of the unfortunate circumstances, I'm so glad to have finally met some of the people who live here. At first I thought my father was being overly protective. In the light of this incident, I now understand more. However, I am still bored to distraction, and frustrated at the lack of information available. Once we have solved this problem I hope there will be an opportunity for you to visit me."

Eirlin swept a hand down her plain dress. "I am sorry, my Lady, but, Blood or no, I am only a woodcutter's daughter, and I have nothing to wear for such a visit."

"Then perhaps I will visit you. With a more appropriate escort, I hope."

The Overlord looked bemused. "I am afraid she is corrupted already."

"In that case, perhaps my best move might be to leave. I have tarried here for some time, and I don't want my cousin to be anxious."

"That sounds wise. If there is truly someone trying to cause trouble between us, having your formidable cousin come looking for you might provide our enemy a prime opportunity."

"On that we can agree, my Lord."

Perica turned to her father. "Then may I look forward to the end of all this silliness, so we can get to know each other?"

The Overlord looked down at his daughter. "I do not find this situation silly."

She frowned. "When men start running around using their swords on people they have to live with, it is complete silliness. The sooner they stop, the sooner we can get started on our duties in ruling this demesne for the good of all of us. Don't you agree, my Lady?"

The Overlord laughed. "Now I am truly sorry I introduced you two. You are going to join forces against me."

Eirlin smiled down at the other girl. "I couldn't agree more, my Lady. Men and their swords!"

"I think I will return you to your cousin, before I get into any more trouble." He turned to his daughter. "Perhaps it is best that you stay inside."

She sighed. "So I miss my opportunity to meet the famous Jesco Falconric, who has all your men so frightened?"

"Yes, you do. But I will take that opportunity, myself."

The girl rolled her eyes and curtseyed to Eirlin, who tried to respond gracefully. Then the Overlord took the Healer's arm and led her towards the courtyard.

"Your daughter is a force to be reckoned with."

"Yes. I have no son, but she will make a formidable heir. It will be invaluable training for her to observe the challenges I face here."

"What did her comment mean? Is Jesco well known here?"

The Overlord smiled. "Standing orders for the castle soldiers, since before my arrival. Stay away from Jesco Falconric when is drinking, and especially when he is angry."

"He always did have a temper."

"And I gather this is the man, himself."

They came out the main gate, to find Jesco directly outside, his pose uncompromising, five of his men lined behind him.

"Jesco. Thank you for waiting for me. Lord Delfontes has expressed the desire to meet you."

"He has?"

Eirlin grinned at the sudden collapse of her cousin's belligerence. "My Lord, may I present Jesco Coenfri Falconric, son of my father's elder brother, heir to the Name of the Falcon."

"A pleasure to finally meet you, sir. Another of the Blood, then?"

"Only half, my Lord. My mother was one of…your people."

"Well, that will scarcely trouble me."

"No?"

"Of course not. To discover that some members of the local nobility are of 'my people'."

"Ah."

"Come, Jesco, we have done all we can, here. It is time to go home. Perhaps I can get you to fix a door for me," her eyes narrowed meaningfully, "since my brother is not able to do so at the moment."

The Overlord laughed. "Don't worry, my Lady. Your brother will be returned to you, safe and sound, first thing tomorrow. Of course, I won't tell him that tonight."

"Just make sure he is safe and sound. It is another opportunity…"

Sudden understanding dawned on the Overlord's face. "I see what you mean. I must take steps to assure his safety."

"Thank you, my Lord."

"It will be better for all of us." The Overlord straightened, formally. "It has truly been a pleasure to meet you, my Lady. It has been a difficult time for you, but now we can take steps to solve this problem."

"Thank you, my Lord. Having met you and your daughter, I hold greater hope."

She curtseyed, he bowed, and then she turned away, taking Jesco's arm as she did.

He waited until they were well down the road, then frowned over at her. "What's this 'my Lord, my Lady,' business? You two seem to be getting along very well."

"He seems a reasonable man, if a whit unbending. I truly believe he did not know of the attack. I think someone is taking advantage of the uncertainties of the situation to make trouble, though we don't know why."

"Hmm. What of Ecmund? They said he insulted the Overlord, and was arrested."

Eirlin shook her head. "I can't believe it, Jesco. I find that my brother has more of his uncle in him than you would expect."

"His uncle?"

"You know how your father always says that there is a time when you have to stand up for yourself?"

"Of course. It's his usual excuse for losing his temper."

"Well, Ecmund just did the same thing. Only he wasn't angry."

"What do you mean?"

"He refused to allow the Overlord to insult the memory of the Blood of Inderjorne. He called him, as cold and calm as you please, and chastised him for his inability to learn what was most important to the people he meant to rule."

Jesco strode along, shaking his head. "There has always been more to my little cousin than meets the eye." He glanced down at her side. "I guess he never should have bought a sword."

She patted the Sword's hilt. "I think the Sword has something to do with it. I would argue whether the buying of it was a mistake, though."

"It seems to have landed him in the Overlord's cell."

"They were words that needed to be spoken. The old Overlord was always very careful with our traditions. The sooner this one learns, the better for all. He must know that there are those who will stand up to him if he steps over the line. The people need to know that we of the Blood will protect their interests.

"It was a rightful stand, Jesco. He made a good choice," she smiled, "even if it will make your father overjoyed."

Jesco shook his head. "Sometimes I am happy to be just a swordsman. It keeps things simple."

She patted his arm. "Don't worry. The whole time we were in there, the Overlord was aware that you were outside with your men."

"He was, was he?"

"Definitely, and Ecmund knew it. It strengthened his play."

"As long as it didn't get him into even more trouble." He snorted. "Never thought I'd be saying that!"

"Don't worry. The Overlord is a reasonable man. He promised that he would speak with Ecmund before he lets him leave in the morning. I hope he does. Ecmund could be a great help to him."

"Help? This is the man who has thrown him in a cell!"

"Jesco, we cannot see this man as our enemy. If that is the case, then we will truly be in rebellion, and many will die."

"That is true."

"I see him as a man taking on a new task, with little preparation. He has few supporters. Half his guards are local people. He is trying to look strong, but I sensed worry. I think he is weaker than he seems, and now we have discovered that some in his own camp wish him to fail. It is up to us to help him find the best way to deal with the problem."

"You want to help him?"

She grinned. "Look at it like a soldier, Jesco. He is newly established and vulnerable. Ground we gain now would be much more difficult to take, once he becomes entrenched."

He returned the grin. "That, I understand. Hit him when he's weak."

Eirlin shook her head with gentle patience. "No, Jesco. Help him when he is weak."

"So that he becomes strong against us."

"So that we become part of his strength."

"Oh." He glanced down at her. "Perhaps there is some of my father in you, as well."

She let loose a peal of laughter. "Now, wouldn't that be fun!"

He frowned. "I somehow think not. Especially for our enemies."

She sobered. "When we figure out who they are."

And then we will kill them.

…well, maybe just maim a few, and scare the others away?

Chapter 12

Jesco made a reasonable repair to the door, and left without too much protest.

Eirlin made a show of pushing him out of the cottage. "Don't worry, Cousin. The Overlord is going to be very sure where all his men are for a few days."

"I suppose." He glanced over at the Sword, leaning in her usual spot. "I'm a little less worried, now."

Eirlin shuddered. "If you only knew how it felt, when the blade went into their flesh. It was so easy!"

I am exceptionally sharp.

"I do know. It isn't one of those things you talk about."

She turned to him. "You do? You mean it bothers you?"

"Not so much any more. After the first one, I had nightmares about it."

"I hope I won't."

He grinned. "Apparently, it's good if you do. If you don't, it means it didn't bother you enough."

"Didn't bother me enough?"

"Yes. It means you're a natural killer."

"Jesco! Now you've got me hoping I go to sleep and have bad dreams!"

"Of course. That'll keep you from sleeping too deeply. Then no one will catch you unawares."

She stared at him for a moment. "Cousin, you live a life that I cannot comprehend, and I'm not sure I want to."

"No, you don't, little Eirlin. You let Ecmund and me swing the swords, and you stay here and mend us when we get hurt." He reached out, ran the back of a finger down her cheek. "That way I'll know that life is going in its proper direction."

There was a moment of silence between them, then he laughed, a bit self-consciously. "Now I'll go home and make my father happy."

He stood aside with a flourish, and watched her enter the cottage. "One more thing. Keep that sword beside your bed."

Well spoken, Jesco!

She frowned, but he raised a warning finger until she nodded. Waiting to make sure the door closed firmly behind her, he turned and strode away, his satisfaction evident in the firm beat of his boot heels.

Eirlin looked over to the Sword. "Kitten?"

It is no longer an emergency. There are rules.

Eirlin waited a while, then shook her head. "Well, Kitten, I certainly wish you would talk again. I would love to know who that Magician is."

84

Nothing I could say. I didn't dare look for him.

"Oh, well. I suppose if I wanted to, I could find him. But how to do it so he doesn't find out? I'll have to work on that." She began to bustle around, hanging a blanket over the cracked door, stoking up the fire to start supper.

"I guess there's only one to cook for." To the Sword's surprise, she suddenly dropped into a chair and burst into tears.

"I hate this!" Her fists pounded the table in time with her words. "I hate it, hate it, hate it! I want to Heal. I don't want to fight and twist people, and argue. Why do I always have to fight?"

The Sword hesitated, but when the sobs continued, she reached out, a gentle caress of reassurance. *Healing is a type of battle.*

Her head came up, her eyes fixed on the Sword. "Kitten? Did you just speak to me again?"

I am the crackle of the fire in the chimney.

"You did. I heard that loud and clear, just like when I was fighting!"

I am the bubble of water in the pot.

"Answer me, you dumb Sword! Oh! My supper is boiling over." She rushed to swing the pot off the fire, then turned to pick up the Sword, staring at her ruby eye. "Healing is a battle? What a load of nonsense! Healing isn't a battle. It's kind, and gentle, and positive."

Pphht!

She sat, staring at the Sword for a moment, then sighed. "Oh, I know it sometimes seems like it's a battle: against dirt and pain and death. Sometimes, after a night with a patient, I feel like I've been in a fight... Don't you dare start humming! Do you want to spend the night out with the horse?"

The Sword felt it diplomatic to shut up.

Eirlin stared at the sword, then smiled. "At least you got me out of feeling sorry for myself." She placed the sheath carefully in its place by the mantel. "Thanks for that. If you don't mind, I'll just finish making my supper. Some of us have to eat.

"I wonder what keeps a Sword going? If you thrive on excitement and emotion, you must be pretty happy right now."

The Sword refused to dignify the accusation with a reply.

As she stirred her soup, Eirlin regarded the Sword thoughtfully. "You know, I can't really see you as the sort of Sword to steal souls. If there really is such a thing. That would feel all...all...evil and frightening. You're not frightening.

"Except when you're fighting. That scares me. We came really close to killing that soldier, you know. Have you thought what that would do to me?"

The Sword hadn't.

"If I were to kill someone, it would change me forever. It goes against everything I feel, everything I believe in. It might destroy me, you know. I could never trust myself again. I might never be able to Heal again."

She swung the pot off the fire again, went to the cupboard for a bowl. "You know, it gives me some sympathy for Lord Delfontes today. I think, if I were to kill someone, I would be at war with myself, just like he is at war with his people. It isn't a position I would like anyone to be in."

The Sword remembered to make a sweep of the area. No danger. Relax. It was comfortable, just listening. Until she said things like that.

Eirlin sat, bowl on lap, spoon in hand, staring into the fire. "What I said to Jesco this afternoon, you know, I think it's important. We have to help Lord Delfontes learn to be the right kind of ruler. It will be better for all of us, him included. I wonder if he will see it that way?"

Eirlin retreated into her own thoughts, and the Sword did as well.

Help your enemy? Hah! A fine philosophy for a Sword. And to think I was so happy to get hooked up with this Hand. Not his fault, of course. In fact, given the way things went today, he seems to be shaping up nicely. It's this sister. She is definitely trouble. If only it weren't so pleasant to listen to her!

Eirlin finished her meal and went about cleaning up the cottage, then moved towards her bedroom, turning in the doorway.

"Good night, Kitten. Sleep well. Or whatever swords do. I wonder what you're thinking about? Do you spend your time reliving all your successful battles? How horrible."

Horrible? I should think not. Glorious!

About to turn away, she suddenly froze. "I wonder if I'll dream tonight? According to Jesco, it would be better if I did. How even more horrible!"

She glared over at the Sword. "This is all your fault, you know. If not for you, I wouldn't be having this problem."

Oh, certainly.

Eirlin shook her head. "How stupid of me. If it weren't for you, I'd have more serious terrors to keep me awake. I'm sorry, Kitten. This isn't your fault. It's not my fault. It just happened, and we'll have to make the best we can of it. Good night, Kitten."

She went into her bedroom and closed the door.

Wait a minute. You promised Jesco...

She came out abruptly, scooped up the Sword, dropped her on the floor next to the bed.

You don't have to be rude about it.

"If I'm going to have bad dreams, I hope you get them, too."

86

That's the general idea, Eirlin. Go to sleep.

As the girl prepared herself for sleep, the Sword made another sweep of the cottage and yard. All was quiet. Mice went about their tiny, active lives in shed and barn. The horse slept peacefully, its dull brain full of hope for another day of rest tomorrow. A sharper mind passed outside the wall, intent on its hunger. Fox, probably. Other human minds slept nearby.

As Eirlin fell into sleep, the Sword reached out, delicately, to touch her mind, guide her through the nightmares, comfort the fear, dull the pain, allow just enough of the horror through to ensure healthy healing. The Sword had never seen warfare from this point of view before. It had always been...well...fun. Now she was feeling it as horrible, painful, and evil. It unsettled her, but she had to stay, had to guide her friend through to morning.

All through the darkness Eirlin dreamed, and the Sword reassured her. She purred and rubbed her soft fur against the girl's fears, warming her heart and comforting her soul. The Healer fought horrible battles the Sword could not understand, but she suffered through them. A frightened, lonely little girl pressed her face into long, soft fur, and prayed that the deep, contented purr would send the nightmares away. A huge grey and white mountain cat stretched her talons and hissed her defiance at all who would harm her charge, and the nightmares skittered away, gibbering their own terror. The cat's rough tongue smoothed the girl's hair, and she slipped back into slumber.

And the nightmares crowded back, seeking chinks in her defence, poking and prodding. Though inured to the passage of time through years of waiting, the Sword fought and struggled and longed with all her soul for dawn to come.

Just before the night began to fade, Eirlin slipped deeper into sleep. Her clenched fists relaxed, and her breathing slowed.

Kitten felt drained. *Last night was so much easier; put her to sleep, keep her there. Healing is a battle; believe this!*

Once the dream state was over, it seemed safe to leave her patient to sleep until the sunlight topped the wall and shone through her window. Then Kitten allowed her to rouse at her own speed.

Soon her feet hit the floor, and she looked down, yawning and stretching her back. "Good morning, Kitten. What a terrible night! I think I finally got to sleep somewhere near dawn. I certainly had nightmares, and you were in them. Not in a bad sense, though I can't think why. You purred, I think, but not always. It was somehow comforting, knowing you were there. Or do you already know?"

She turned from starting into the fire to look at Kitten. "Do you read thoughts? I wonder."

I am the smoke in the chimney.

"Well, I certainly can't read yours this morning. Nothing but a lump of steel today."

I am the smoke that will curl up your nose and make you cough your guts out!

"I suppose that wasn't very complimentary. I'm sorry, it was just a bad night." She measured oatmeal into the pot. "After all, who am I to complain? I spent the night in my own bed. I wonder how poor Ecmund made out? I do hope the Overlord sets him free early."

She paused. "Actually, I don't. I hope he talks to him first. Ecmund can help him, I know he can."

She went on like this all through her breakfast, and Kitten listened closely. The woman's mind was calmer now, and this conversation was just another way of working through the events of yesterday in order to put them under control. It was pleasant in a way, to hear her own voice soothe her: to listen to a Healer Heal herself.

Kitten continued to radiate peace and love.

Peace and love! Enough to make me vomit, if I had a stomach, which I thank the Smith I do not. The things we do for our Hands. And how often do they show appreciation?

However, it was a pleasant morning, until noon approached, and Ecmund still had not returned.

Soon Eirlin was beyond pacing, and was beginning to talk again. It was not peaceful.

"What can he be doing up there? If that Overlord has broken his promise, I am going to put on my sword and go up there and give him more than a piece of my mind!"

Put on your sword?

Eirlin slammed her palm on the table, causing the dishes she was drying to jump. "He promised! Why would he break his promise...Oh, no! I know why. If Ecmund keeps on being stupid. I thought Ecmund was in control yesterday, but what if he wasn't? What if he keeps being stupid, and starts another fight? What if the Overlord throws him in jail for months? What if he has him beaten?"

Kitten could feel a familiar presence approaching down the street.

This is going to be fun.

"What an idiot! If he has antagonized the Overlord, and spoiled our chances of helping him, I'm going to do some beating myself! Ecmund is just so stubbornly stupid at times, he just..."

The door opened behind her, and she turned at the sound of protesting hinges. "...drives me to distraction. Where have you been? The Overlord said he would let you go this morning. Why did he keep you so long? I've been worrying so much!"

"Whoa, there, hold on! I had breakfast with the Overlord, and we were talking. What's wrong with you? Who were you talking to?"

"I was talking to Kitten. She's the only one with a sense of what's right and wrong...What? You had breakfast with the Overlord? And you didn't send a message that you were going to be late? Here I was, worrying myself into a state, and you're having a late breakfast with the nobility, with no consideration for anyone else?"

He reached out a hand, touched her shoulder. "I'm sorry, Eirlin. Did you have a bad night?"

"Since you mention it, yes I did. I had nightmares, and didn't sleep a wink!"

A small smile played at the corner of his mouth. "Nightmares without sleeping? That must have been strange."

She frowned, then her lip twitched as well. "It takes a certain talent."

"Well, I'm sorry you spent such a bad night. I didn't sleep too well myself."

Her eyes widened. "Oh! Ecmund, I am sorry. There you were, spending the night in gaol, and here I am complaining about a few bad dreams. Was it terrible?"

He made a rocking motion with his hand. "Well, no, it wasn't, really. Just very puzzling for a while. First they put me into that cell at the base of the donjon wall, the one where they toss the soldiers to sleep it through when they're too drunk. Then, about the middle of the afternoon, the Overlord himself showed up with six men, and opened the door. I thought I was in for trouble, but he just brought me out, lined the six up, and asked me which ones I trusted."

"Which ones you trusted?"

"Yes. They were all local men. Elgar the Smith's son Rhysun, and a couple like that."

"What did you do?"

"What could I do? I looked them over, picked the four I knew best. He said, 'Fine', dismissed the other two, and marched us all upstairs to the guest floor. He put me in one of the smaller bedrooms, up in the east corner of the tower. Not a bad room, but only one door, and arrow slits for light. He put the four on rotation: one inside with me, one outside, and the other two on relief."

"He put a guard on you."

"It didn't take long to figure it out. He wasn't keeping me in; he was keeping me safe. He told me this morning that it was you who woke him up to it. Thanks."

"He's a smart man. He might have figured it out himself, but I didn't want to take the chance. So what did you talk to him about?"

Ecmund grinned. "The same topics as yesterday."

"I hope not in the same tone of voice!"

"What was wrong with my tone of voice? I thought I was being quite reasonable."

"Quite reasonable! The whole Council went to that meeting, intending to follow your suggestion that they be mannerly and sensible about the whole thing. First thing you do is insult the Overlord enough that he throws you in gaol. How is that sensible?"

He shrugged. "It was a risk, I know. I read Lord Delfontes as a stiff one. It takes a thunderclap in his ear to get him to listen. I was watching him during the meeting, and he wasn't going to give one bit. He was going to pretend to listen, then do his own investigation, and find the solution that suited his purposes. I figure his main purpose is to solidify his power as quickly and firmly as possible. It's a reasonable objective, from a military point of view. It's just that we know it won't work in this demesne. So somebody had to be the thunderclap. Once we got his attention, then the rest of the meeting went smoothly, didn't it?"

"You're not going to tell me you planned all that!"

"Not really, but I just knew he wasn't listening, and I had to get him to. He has a secret Magician working against him, and he won't acknowledge it, Eirlin!"

"By the end, he seemed to understand it a bit better. Your little show got his attention on that score, at least."

"It wasn't just me. Having Jesco and his men outside helped as well. Add it up. There are seven towns near our size in this demesne. If each town can field the same number of troops that we can, we outnumber his men, two to one. That won't help if he buttons himself up in his castle, but it's enough to give him pause if he thinks he can start a war with us.

"He has to realize that there is always someone who will notice his mistakes, someone with the support of the people. I guess that person turns out to be me, but if it weren't me, it would be another one of the Blood. There are still a few of us around."

"Did you know he asked to meet Jesco?"

"He told me. He said Jesco looked like a good soldier."

She laughed. "Jesco said the same thing about himself. Said he was glad there was someone else around to do the diplomacy. He wants things simple."

"Fair enough. He may be difficult, but if it comes to a fight, I'd sooner have him at my back than almost anyone."

"What else did Lord Delfontes say?"

"Well, he listened to my thoughts, and he argued some. Made good points, actually. He did mention that he would appreciate a little respect demonstrated in public."

"A little?"

"He was a bit more forceful than that."

"Did you talk about the Magician?"

He shook his head. "We did."

"You don't look happy."

"He just doesn't understand. He has no idea what havoc a Magician could wreak on his court. He doesn't understand the danger of a Magician who works in secret."

"Did you manage to persuade him?"

"I don't think so."

"What else happened?"

"We talked about this and that. He asked me what I thought his problems were going to be. I told him, he listened, then he asked his daughter what she thought."

"Perica was there? What did you think of her?"

"She sure isn't afraid to stand up to her father."

She grinned. "What else did you think?"

He raised his eyebrows. "What? You want me to admit she's pretty?"

"She's not pretty. She's beautiful."

"All right. She's beautiful, she's graceful, and she's smart. I don't know if I'd want to have to live with her."

But you wouldn't mind trying?

"Why not?"

"She's very outspoken. Oh she's unfailingly polite about it, but she never lets a mistake go by."

"Sounds like someone I know."

"Yes, come to think of it. You."

"I was thinking of you."

They laughed, but she stopped first. "Did she like you?"

"Of course. Why wouldn't she?"

"Because you're big and clumsy and barbaric. Being a woodcutter is just the topping."

"Oh, I don't know. Maybe that gives me a certain raffish appeal."

As you dream.

"Maybe that gives you a certain oafish comedy. Sometimes even I can't help laughing at you, and I'm family."

"Well, there's not much chance she'll ever reach that august elevation, so we don't have to worry about it, do we?"

He's already considered marriage to the enemy! What do I do now? Help, Eirlin!

"Is something wrong, Eirlin?"

"I was just considering a world in which you managed to marry the Overlord's daughter." She shuddered, as if from a sudden chill.

"I just told you…"

91

"That you'd considered the possibility."

"That I rejected it!"

"I am amazed that you admit the thought even passed your mind."

"Oh, come on, Eirlin. You know how it is with men…"

"Of course. You see a pretty face, and your intelligence drops a couple of feet."

Whee!

"Eirlin! That was rude!" His look of astonishment transformed to suspicion. "Why is Kitten humming?"

Oops.

"Maybe she agrees with me."

"This is a ridiculous conversation."

"Good. Make sure you keep it that way."

Please do.

"Fine. I won't be the next one to bring it up, believe me!"

"Fine. I guess you don't need lunch?"

"Huh? Oh, no, thank you." He grinned. "I had a late breakfast with the nobility, remember."

"If you don't mind, I'll have some."

"Go ahead. I think I have some minor carpentry to do about the house."

"A door would be nice."

The Sword listened carefully. All the tension was somehow gone.

How do they do that? Hmph. Good thing I don't thrive on conflict.

Chapter 13

It was late evening, two days later. The village was tending its business. Ecmund had just come in, and happened to be polishing the Sword, something he did more often, these days. He now kept her close by at all times. When he worked in the wood yard, she hung beside the axe outside the cottage door. When he went to the forest, he strapped on her belt. However, try as she might, she could not keep from getting in the way when he worked, so he had to lean her against a tree, close at hand.

It was fortunate that he was making direct skin-to-steel contact when the feeling came.

Warning! Danger!

He jumped up. "What? What's wrong?"

"What is it, Ecmund?"

"Kitten. She just shouted 'Danger' at me!"

Horseman. Just one. Big rush!

He strapped the belt back on, hurrying to the door. "I think it's just one horseman, but he's coming in a hurry. There must be something wrong! Stay here! Get the axe!"

He strode out the door without checking to see if she complied.

Ecmund was the first to throw his shoulder against the town gate, but the pounding hooves had attracted enough attention that the alarum was ringing as the rider rounded the last corner. He was forced to pull up in front of a closed gate, its top bristling with spears.

"The Overlord sends that he wishes your help."

Ecmund looked down the line of men. He was the only Councillor present. "Our help?"

"Yes. His daughter is lost."

"Lost? How could that happen?"

The messenger seemed to have run out of the official message. "She was out ridin', and her horse spooked."

"Where? Wait a moment. I'm coming down." Ecmund hurried down the steps beside the gate, signalled the men to open. They hesitated.

"There's only one of him, and it's Coen. I'll slip out and talk. You can close it after me."

That satisfied them, and soon he faced the messenger. It was one of the farm lads from farther down the valley, signed on to the Overlord's guard last year when the harvest was poor.

"Where did she get lost?"

"Over to Osterwald."

"Wonderful. So she went riding, and her horse spooked into the Osterwald?"

"That's what they said. Her escort tried to follow, but they got caught up in that tight brush, and she just disappeared. The Overlord asks the men of the village to help in findin' her, Ecmund."

"Of course, Coen. Tell him we'll come immediately."

The lad nodded, spun his horse, and headed back. Ecmund returned to the gate, which opened for him.

By this time, everyone in the village had gathered.

"The Overlord's daughter is lost in the Osterwald. You know what it's like in there. If she's still on her horse, I'd be surprised. I only hope she didn't get hurt when she fell off."

The innkeeper stood forward. "The Overlord asks our help?"

"Of course he would. We know the ground better. He's new here. Problem is, we don't know if this is legitimate."

The other nodded sagely. "It could be a trick to get all the men out of the village again."

"But we have to send help." That was the baker.

Several other voices piped up, most for helping, a few against.

Ecmund rested his hand on Kitten's hilt. "This is what I suggest." The voices died. "I will go, and take some of the young lads who know that area well." He grinned. "It's the best rabbit hunting in the forest, Overlord's land or no. An armed man is at a disadvantage in that bush. Jesco and the guard can stay in the town. Keep locked up tight until we get back."

"That's good enough, but what if it's a trick to lure you away and attack you?"

"It could be, Albercas, but I don't think so. If it is, we'll just fade into the bush, and they can chase their tails through the brambles for a few hours, no harm done." He shared a grin with a twelve-year-old who had slipped up to stand by him.

The innkeeper nodded. "Fair enough. Away you go. It's going to be dark soon enough. I don't wish anyone a night in the forest, especially if she's injured."

"Who's coming? Let's go." Without waiting, Ecmund turned and jogged out the gate, followed by a dozen youngsters and two older men, armed with bows. He nodded at that idea.

It was a good distance to the Osterwald, around on the east side of the Overlord's personal fields. When they reached the forest edge, Delfontes himself was there, lightly armed and mounted on one of his hunters, pacing the edge of the forest in frustration. He swung down as soon as he saw them.

"Thank you for coming, Ecmund. Are these your men?"

"These boys know the area better than you should be aware of, my Lord. They can use the boar's tunnels, where a grown man has to bend over too far."

"That's certain. My soldiers are having a great deal of trouble. The brush is so thick, and the light under the canopy so dim, they can't make any progress. They go in, try to search, come out somewhere else. I'm afraid I've lost a couple of them as well."

"No danger to them. They can spend a night in the bush, and get out with sunrise."

"My daughter is another matter."

They shared a look. This could be another move by the enemy. "I understand, my Lord. I'll go with the lads. Can you show us exactly where she went in? I suppose you found the horse?"

"Yes. Her reins were dragging and they got tangled in a bramble. In here."

He turned his mount over to a groom and strode into the forest, batting at overhanging limbs, his armour and weapons catching on bushes. The Hand followed easily behind, the Sword weaving at his hip, avoiding all obstacles.

It was a long, tough, slog, but finally they came to an area of trampled brush. "The horse was here."

"Right. Let's get to work, lads."

"One thing, boys?"

They stopped.

"You find my daughter, and you can take rabbits in these woods for the rest of your lives."

They grinned and plunged into the undergrowth.

It didn't take long. "Over here, Ecmund!"

The Hand made his way to the excited boy. "What have you, Leof?"

"Horse came this way. We can backtrack. She made a real hole in the brush!"

"Good work. You start out." He raised his voice. "The rest of you! We're headed east. Fan out along our track. Keep in touch by voice."

He turned to the Overlord. "My Lord, I think you are at a great disadvantage, here. My people thought that this might be a ruse to get the men out of the village again. What if it is a ruse to get you out of your castle?"

"I had considered that, but my daughter comes first."

"You now have the best people that you could find on this task. Your duty to your daughter has been accomplished. You may follow your other duties with a clear conscience."

"This has nothing to do with my conscience!"

95

Ecmund stared at Delfontes until his eyes dropped. "You have the right of it, lad." His eyes rose again. "Find her for me. Please."

"If she is still in the forest, we will find her. It isn't that large an area, and we can backtrack her horse, at least. If she is not in the forest, then you should be elsewhere as well."

The Overlord stiffened, as this possibility struck him. He nodded, spun on his heel, and crashed back towards his horse.

"All right, lads, let's go!"

The line of searchers moved slowly through the dense undergrowth.

"Here, Ecmund!"

"What have you found?"

"Blood."

"Blood?" They pushed through the screen of brush that surrounded a small clearing. Two boys stood, looking up at a low limb that overhung the animal trail. He reached up and touched the bark. A faint trace of blood came away on his finger.

"Stand still, lads." They froze, and he scanned the area. Then he pointed. "The horse came through there. When it got to this opening, it ran faster. It went under the tree and her head hit the branch. She fell…"

"Here, Ecmund!"

"Good eye, Maer." They stared at the indentation in the brush. "She fell there, and lay for a moment, stunned. Then she would have risen, staggering." Placing his feet carefully, he tiptoed to the spot. "Then she went…where?"

No foot moved, but all eyes searched.

"There!" Maer pointed to a bit of cloth, caught on a thorn.

Moving towards it, Ecmund found traces. "Yes, she walked that way. Notice, she is staggering: first over here, then back over there. But she definitely went this way." He raised his voice. "Everyone! Over here!"

Once they were gathered, he laid out his plan.

"Maer and I will try to follow her trail. You others keep pace with us, fairly close together on each side. Watch carefully; she may have turned back, and you could save us a lot of time."

They all nodded seriously, and started off. It was painstaking work, even with the tight brush and the frequent bits of yarn and broken branches.

"She don't know much about walkin' in the bush, does she?"

"What do you expect of a lady from the Capital at Koningsholm, who just hit her head on a tree?"

The boy nodded with sympathy and continued, his eyes to the ground.

They worked their way farther and farther into the wood, and Kitten could feel Ecmund's anxiety rising.

"It's getting darker."

Maer nodded. "I almost missed that last print, in the shadows, there."

Up to this point, the Sword had spent her attention on keeping from being a nuisance, no mean feat in this dense brush. However, she suddenly realized that her senses could be of some use if the girl was close enough.

Touch me.

"What?" He stared around, and his hand dropped to his Sword.

That's better.

"What? Oh!"

"What's that, Ecmund?" The lad was peering up at him.

"Nothing, Maer. I just thought I heard something. Keep moving."

The lad returned his attention to the ground, and Ecmund began a new experience.

Using his strength, Kitten sent out her senses, as far as she could. She could plot the lads on either side, moving silently through the bush. Too silently.

We aren't hunting.

"Good point." He raised his voice. "We should be making more noise, lads. If she's looking for a rescue party, let's sound like one. Her name is Perica."

They began calling. It was discouraging, how quickly the voices were lost in the dense bush, but they kept yelling. The Sword stretched her senses to the utmost, feeding on the Hand's concern.

"She ain't dizzy no more."

"Why do you say that, Maer?"

"She's walkin' better. Longer stride. She's headin' straight back to the castle."

Ecmund grinned. "Better get a move on. We don't want her rescuing herself, with no credit to us."

The boy shrugged. "Gettin' darker yet."

Concentrate. I don't need light. Come on, Ecmund, I need your help, here. Close your eyes. Think. You've met her. Picture her. No, Ecmund. With her clothes on. Men!

The Sword melded with the Hand's mind, searching farther and farther in front of them.

There!

"Yes. I feel it. A bit to the left."

A faint glow ahead of them, flickering.

"You keep following her trail, Maer, as best you can." He strode forward. "You lads off to the left! Keep a good eye out. She's over your way somewhere."

Now he was moving quicker, ducking through the trees, and the Sword had to take part of her mind away to keep from being torn loose. The glow ahead became stronger, and Ecmund broke into a trot.

Then they came to an animal trail and he began to run, calling her name regularly. He was running so fast that he almost rushed past her.

Whoa!

"Hello, Ecmund Falconric."

He skidded to a stop, turning.

There she was, seated comfortably under a large spruce tree, looking quite composed, except for the large, broken bruise on her forehead.

"My Lady! Are you all right?" He rushed to her, taking up her hand.

All right, all right. Let's not overdo it.

"I'm quite fine, thank you, Ecmund. Except for a slight headache and a few scratches."

He suddenly realized that he was still holding her hand, and dropped it as if stung. "But what are you doing, sitting under this tree? I almost missed you!"

She smiled. "Even a lady from the city knows something. My father told me that if I ever got lost in the woods, I should find a big, overgrown tree, like this one," she patted the rough bark behind her, "to shelter under, and wait to be found. If I didn't want to be found, I should find one with lower branches to hide under."

"That's very good, my Lady. Excuse me for a moment."

He turned aside and whistled, a shrill ululation that pierced even this thick forest. "Over here, boys!"

She stared around as they slipped out of the bushes. "Is this the army my father sent to find me?"

Would you rather have stayed lost?

He grinned. "They were the only ones of a size for moving through this forest, my Lady. You kept ahead of us for so long for the same reason."

"It's nice to know that my size is sometimes an advantage. What do we do now?"

"I suggest we continue down this animal trail as far as the creek. Then, we turn north along the bank, and we'll come out...where, Leof?"

"Just about the fork in the road by the big oak, if this is the same crick."

Maer snorted. "I don't think it is, Leof. This crick's too small. This one comes out nearer the broken rock."

Another voice chimed in. "Don't think so, Maer. I was by here oncet. I jus' kep' goin' on the trail."

"Yeah, but you was tryin' to stay away from the foresters. We're tryin' to find them."

98

"Yeah. Forgot about that."

"These boys seem to know my father's forest very well."

"They spend some time here, my Lady. Keeps the rabbits from overrunning the castle garden."

"Yeah, 'n' now we can hunt here for free!"

"You can?"

"Yeah. The Overlord...that's your father, miss, he told us that if'n we find you, we can hunt rabbits here all our lives. And we did!"

She looked around at the circle of grinning faces. "Well, if that's what he said, I'm not going to tell him it was Ecmund that found me."

Ecmund scanned the pouts, laughing. "We all pitched in, and we all take the prize."

"Sure thing."

"That's right."

"You said, Ecmund."

She held out her hand.

You didn't have to be so quick.

He helped her to rise, then indicated the path. "Leof, you go in front. Maer, you take two others and run ahead to tell the Overlord. We'll come behind at our best pace. If she's too tired we'll carry her."

"You'll do no such thing!"

"You've been hit on the head, my Lady. No telling the effects. Are you all right to walk, now?"

"Of course. Lead on, Leof."

The boy flashed a proud grin and set out, glancing anxiously over his shoulder to make sure she was following.

In a very short time, they stumbled out of the forest onto a reasonable path, which allowed them to walk more easily.

"Is that better, my Lady?"

She nodded. "I certainly am glad I was in my riding skirt. Anything else would be in tatters by now."

He eyed the torn hem. "And we would have been able to find you faster, following the markers you left."

She glanced back, then forward, to make certain the boys were out of earshot. "I wasn't sure I wanted to be found."

"I know what you mean. Your father said your horse spooked. Do you have any idea what frightened it?"

"No. We were just cantering along, and suddenly it shied to the left, and broke into a run. I didn't see anything in the trail. Are there snakes here?"

"No poisonous ones. The horses don't usually worry about them."

"It was one of the castle mares, much less spirited than I'm used to. Is she all right?"

"Yes, she got her reins tangled. That's how we found your trail. We backtracked the horse to where you fell off, then trailed you. It was pretty slow work."

"You were moving rather fast when you got to me."

Careful. She is very quick.

"Oh. Yes…well, there was an animal path, and you left footprints. I knew you wouldn't go off the trail."

"I see. Yes, I had it calculated that I was going in the right direction, but then the sun went down, and I knew I would start to circle. So I stopped."

"Very smart. That's exactly what happens. We found a lost hunter a couple of years ago. He was going in precisely the opposite direction to where he thought he was. Heading straight as an arrow out into the forest, away from home."

At this point the trail intersected a wagon road, and they could walk side by side. Mindful of the danger, Ecmund set the boys in military formation, with two ranging ahead and two farther behind. He split the others into two closer groups, leaving himself and Perica in the middle. They set off, making an even better pace on the smooth road.

"How are you doing? Make sure you let me know if you're tired."

"Of course I'm tired, but no worse than after a day's hunting. Don't worry, Ecmund. I will get home."

"In other words you're too stubborn to give in, and you're determined to walk into your father's castle on your own two feet."

She grinned over at him through the gathering darkness. "Something like that."

Such becoming modesty. Come on, Ecmund. Surely you can see what she's doing.

They walked a while in silence.

"It is a pleasant evening."

Now, that's an original.

He looked around. "Yes, I like the forest at this time of night. Cool, comfortable, usually quiet, but still light enough to see things. Like that doe and fawn, there."

She looked to where he pointed, then stared. "How could you see them?"

He shrugged. "Years of practice, I guess."

Oh, come on. She could see them as plain as you could.

"Ecmund, would you do me a favour?"

"Of course."

"Could you have one of the others carry your sword?"

He frowned. "I don't really like to. Why?"

"It makes me feel…uncomfortable."

"Oh. I'm sorry. It's just that...well, with the danger..."

"No, don't be sorry. It's not that I'm afraid of weapons or anything. It's just your sword..."

"My sword bothers you? You don't need to worry about Kitten. She's...I mean..." He broke off in embarrassment.

Ecmund, you are such an idiot!

She let out a peal of laughter. "You call your sword Kitten?"

"No. Well, not really. It's Eirlin. She calls her Kitten, and I sort of do it sometimes...by mistake..."

"Oh, you must show me. I've never seen a sword called 'Kitten.' Why did she choose such a name?"

"Because of the claws."

Yes, claws! Be warned!

She shot him a glance "Oh. Come on. Let me see her."

"I thought she bothered you."

"That was before I knew she had a name."

I do not have a Name! Don't you give me to that silly girl!

The Hand grasped the Sword's hilt, determination roaring through the contact.

You will stop this silliness!

If you say so...

That's better.

... but you'll be sorry!

He drew the Sword, held it by the forte. "Here. She won't bother you again."

"What do you mean?"

"Oh...I don't know. I mean, now that you've been formally introduced.

Nice recovery, clumsy.

She glanced at him, then down at the Sword, then up at his face again. "All right."

She reached out and took the hilt.

A sudden jolt of power swept down the Sword, straight to her tip, reverberated back up her blade...

I am the... Too late.

The girl stopped in the road, took the garde position.

Power and sure, fine control lanced through her. Kitten could not hold it back.

Perica made three cuts: left, right, and a low outside slash. She raised the Sword in a sort of salute, regarded the blade carefully. Then she slowly lowered it, like someone coming out of a dream. Carefully, too carefully, she placed her fingers on the blade below the quillions, and passed it gingerly back.

"It's a very…beautiful sword."

The Hand took the hilt, held it a moment before sheathing it.

Danger! Danger!

He froze, his eyes darting left and right. The night was silent.

Not there, stupid. Here. Her!

After a long look around, he slid the Sword down into her scabbard. His hand remaining on the hilt, he signalled the boys to continue. Then he turned back to the girl.

"What's wrong, Ecmund?"

"I might ask you the same."

"There's nothing wrong with me!"

"Yes there is. What happened when you held Kitten?"

"Nothing…"

"Wrong!"

"My Lord, I don't think it proper for you to…"

"Don't hide behind the formality, Perica. Something happened when you held my Sword, and I want to know what it was! What did you feel?"

The girl's brow furrowed, the dreamlike look returning. "It was…power. It was right. It fit. I didn't like it much, but I liked it a lot." Her face cleared and she stared suddenly at the Hand.

"Let me see your sword again, Ecmund."

"I don't think that would be a good idea."

"No, perhaps it wouldn't. Then tell me."

"Tell you what?"

"Tell me what it was I felt."

He sighed. "I suppose the iron's been tempered, and it's too late to heat it again. You just met Kitten."

Please, not Kitten. Not in public!

"She doesn't like to be called Kitten. I hope you won't tell anyone."

"What? That you have a magic Sword, or that she has a silly name?"

IT ISN'T A SILLY NAME, YOU SILLY GIRL!

Perica went pale, and she stumbled. "I heard that!" Then she frowned. "And she called me silly!"

Ecmund let go of the hilt and dropped his forehead in both hands. "Oh, no!"

"What? What's wrong? Are you laughing? I don't see anything funny about this!"

He sighed. "You've just met her, and already you're fighting. I can't win!"

"We're not fighting. You can't fight with a sword. I mean you can't fight against…You know what I mean."

102

"I most certainly do, and you're wrong. You can fight with this Sword. Eirlin does it all the time."

"Eirlin? She knows about the Sword?"

"Perica, Eirlin is a Healer! How do you think she beat three soldiers in a sword fight?"

There was a moment of silence. "Oh. It's all coming together. Eirlin had Kitten when those men attacked, and Kitten used her magic so Eirlin could fight better, so she was able to beat them! That was wonderful!"

Maybe she isn't so silly.

"Did you catch that?"

"What?"

"I guess she's not angry at you any more."

"What did she say?"

"She doesn't exactly speak. I just get feelings. When you said something nice about her, she suddenly felt much more positive about you."

"Well tell her that…"

His raised hand stopped her. "I don't think I need to translate. Eirlin talks to her all the time."

"But I feel strange, talking to a sword."

"And you'd look strange, too, so please don't."

"Oh. Of course." A sudden look of dismay crossed the girl's face. "Oh! What am I going to tell my father?"

Ecmund's mind froze for a moment, then he shook his head. "I guess it would be too much to ask you not to tell him?"

She reached out and touched his hand, and the Sword felt that shock again.

Go away.

The girl frowned, removed her hand. "I'm sorry, Ecmund. It's too important to his situation here to keep it from him."

"Yes. Like the Magician."

"Exactly. Sometimes, when he gets to believing it, he becomes really angry. Then he reminds himself that there's no such thing, and he feels better."

"I guess you'll have to tell him, then." He looked at her a moment. "The big question, though, is how you knew about Kitten."

"What do you mean?"

"I mean that only someone of the Blood would even know she existed."

"Are you sure?"

"Very."

The girl's voice rose in outrage. "Are you saying that somewhere, back in my heritage…What kind of accusation is that?"

103

Oops!

"I guess so." He regarded her for a moment. "And why should that be a problem?"

Her eyes widened. "Oh!"

"Yes. Oh."

"But I didn't mean..."

Yes you did.

"Kitten doesn't believe you."

"What? You mean she can read my mind?"

"I mean that even someone as dense as me knows what you were about to say. I understand. I've lived with it all my life."

"But I didn't mean it! I mean, I didn't mean it about you!"

"No, I understand. Most of your people don't really mean it about me. It doesn't usually bother me much. It's only bigotry."

"Well, for any way that it counts, I'm terribly sorry."

She means it.

I'm sure she does. It doesn't change what she thinks.

"I believe that, Perica. I accept your apology."

"But it doesn't make you feel any better, does it?"

Wonderful. I've just met her, and already you're fighting. I can't win.

He sighed. "We have more important things to worry about than my feelings. Shall we tell your father immediately? I don't want him to think I've been playing any more games than I already have."

"Whatever you think is best."

Suddenly, footsteps sounded in front of them, running. A white face appeared, bobbing back along the track. "Horses, Ecmund. Quite a few."

Rescue party.

Are you sure?

Reading them clearly. Relief, anxiety all mixed up.

"I think it's your father."

"Good. I'm tired of walking."

"I know the company's not of the best."

She started to answer, then bit her lip and was silent.

You great, thundering, oaf. She's had a hard day, and now you insult her.

"Um...Perica?"

"What?"

"Kitten tells me I'm an idiot."

"I'm beginning to like Kitten more and more."

Hah!

There was a strained silence.

Say something, idiot.

What?

"I'm sorry, Ecmund. You aren't an idiot. It's just that I didn't mean…"

"Oh no, Perica…"

Let's not get all sappy, kids. Daddy is here.

The sound of horses, moving faster than they should in the dim light, broke into the conversation. Soon the party of horsemen trotted around the nearest corner. The walkers stood aside, and the Overlord threw himself off his horse, grabbing his daughter up in his arms.

"Perica, darling. Are you all right? Were you hurt badly? Were you frightened?"

The girl's words, hissed out so only the Sword could hear, set her father back. "Daddy! Put me down! What will everybody think?"

Delfontes chuckled and set her carefully back on the road. "They will think a man should be happy to see his daughter safe."

"And if I wasn't a target for our enemies before, that little display will make it positive."

"I hadn't thought of that."

She relented. "It's all right, Father. It was dark, and I'm sure the boys will keep quiet for me."

The Overlord looked at the small faces surrounding them. "So I gather I have hired myself a group of special wardens for Osterwald."

"Hired? You mean we gotta work?" The boy recollected himself, "…m-my Lord?"

Delfontes laughed. "I said you could take rabbits. I didn't say they were free. But they will be. I'll pay you in good coin for the work I want done in that forest. I want some trails cut in there. This sort of thing shouldn't be able to happen, this close to the castle. You boys come visit me tomorrow afternoon, and we'll set up a plan."

He looked sombrely at them. "I want you to know how grateful I am."

"Aw, 'twasn't us, my Lord. It was Ecmund what found her."

The Hand stepped forward. "They all helped, my Lord. I couldn't have done it without them."

"Well spoken, both of you. I will not go back on my word. I will see you tomorrow, boys. Off you go home, so your mothers won't be worried."

The boys called out their goodnights and trotted away, talking excitedly among themselves. The Overlord turned back to his daughter. "I brought a horse for you, if you're up to riding…"

"Of course I am."

"Perhaps Ecmund would lead you."

"Lead? I can ride!"

"You can ride, but I don't want any more accidents today. Ecmund or one of the grooms, then."

"I will not be led home by a groom!"

"Fine. If you wouldn't mind, Ecmund?" He raised a hand and a groom brought a small mare forward.

"Certainly, my Lord." Ecmund helped her to mount, took the reins, and started back to the castle at a good pace.

"This is quite a rough road."

"This is a child's pony."

Spoiled brat. I thought maybe she had potential, but just listen to her!

"In this darkness, on an uncertain path, a man on foot can see the road surface better than a rider, up on a horse."

"Hmpf."

"Perica, I'm not here to lead your horse. I'm here to guard you. Surely you realize that."

There was no answer.

"Is there any chance you would keep Kitten a secret?"

Bad timing.

"You must know better than that."

I think we're in a little sulk. Let me talk to her. I'll straighten her out.

I don't think that would be wise.

He slapped the pommel, lightly, and stepped out faster.

They spoke no more until they reached Falkengard. Once they were in the courtyard, Ecmund helped Perica down from her horse. She thanked him politely and turned away.

The Overlord nodded to Ecmund. "Thank you, Ecmund. Will you come in for a moment?"

"Certainly."

"Would you like to send a message to your sister?"

"Don't worry, my Lord. The boys will tell the whole village."

"Of course." He motioned them to come into the castle with him.

Seated in the big work room, Perica filled her father in on the details of her adventure. When she was finished, and Ecmund had added his part, there was a long silence. Finally the Overlord spoke. "Do you think this was an accident?"

She shook her head. "I can't tell, Father. The horse seemed to shy at nothing. I've been riding her since I got here, and she's never done anything close to that."

"I'll go back there in daylight, my Lord. See what I can find."

"I would appreciate that, Ecmund."

"Was there any problem here?"

Delfontes frowned. "Nothing, as far as I can tell. We seem to have lost two soldiers."

"Lost?"

"Yes. They probably left last night, but it wasn't reported until this afternoon. That had me worrying, as you might guess."

"Yes, it would. Who were they?"

"None of the local lads. A pair who hired on in Koningsholm, when I was making up my strength. The Sergeant says they're no loss."

"So, if they don't show up in a few days, we can assume it was just desertion?"

"I think so. It happens." He grinned. "Not everyone finds the peaceful country life to his taste."

"Then our problems are no nearer their solution."

"Not unless you find something tomorrow."

"Then I'd better get a good sleep, so my eyes are sharp."

"A good plan." The Overlord stood, and Ecmund rose, looking towards Perica.

"Good night, my Lady. Sleep well. I hope your head is better in the morning."

And your temper.

"Good night, Ecmund." Her eyes sent him a message.

She's going to tell. The little edge-chipper is going to tell.

"I will probably see you tomorrow, when I report to your father."

"That will be nice." She gave him a vacant, polite smile and held out her hand. He bowed over it briefly, and turned away.

The Overlord did him the honour of seeing him out of the castle. When they reached the gate, he turned to Ecmund. "I'm sure you realize how grateful I am. From the way you tell it, she had made far too much progress towards the castle for my men to catch up to her."

"I saved her a night in the woods in midsummer." He shrugged.

"Or much worse. I won't forget how you and the villagers rallied to me in my need."

"It's that sort of mutual help which forges bonds, my Lord."

"And I need all of that I can get." He slapped the Hand's shoulder, turned him towards the village. "Sleep well. We'll see you tomorrow."

"Good night, my Lord."

Ecmund strode happily away down the hill.

"That went well."

She's a spoiled brat, and she didn't show proper gratitude.

"She just had a bump on the head and a frightening experience. And she's tired."

Hmpf!

107

"What is going on? First you don't like her, then you do. Now you don't again."

She is a danger to us.

"What kind of danger? He has to know some time."

She is danger. You will see.

"I suppose I will." He strode along for a while. "What is an edge-chipper?"

It's a small, very hard stone that can get caught up in clothing or harness. You think you're going to slice into nice, soft, flesh, and you get a chip from the stone instead. Very annoying.

"I'm sure it is."

He strode on, thinking, but she could not reach his mind.

Chapter 14

The next morning, right after breakfast, the Hand reached for the Sword and buckled her belt on.

"Are you going back to the Osterwald?"

"Yes. I want to get there before anyone else, just in case there is something to find."

"But you don't think there will be. Will Kitten be able to help?"

Of course!

"Probably not. She tells me things in the present. What do you think, Kitten? Can you see what happened yesterday?"

I see far. Together we see very far.

"But what about things that have already happened, but aren't there any more?

I see what is.

"I don't think she can. We'll give it our best try, though."

"She's talking to you?"

"Yes. Ever since she found Perica in the bush yesterday. Getting clearer all the time. Once in a while I get a single word, plain as anything."

Eirlin nodded. "It's very good that you are helping Lord Delfontes this way. It will benefit all of us."

He ran a hand over her hair. "That's my Eirlin, always wanting everyone to get along."

She grinned. "Can't help it."

"Don't. I'll probably be back about noon."

"In time to be fed."

"What a good idea!"

"Oh, Ecmund, you make me feel so...useful!"

"That's me: always trying to make people feel better."

He left her, laughing.

When they reached the place where the horse had spooked, it was as Ecmund expected. There was plenty of disturbance, and with the help of Kitten, he was able to picture the scene. Here the deep hoof prints showed where the horse had shied, there where it ran. He winced at the torn cloth, still clinging to the thorny vines the horse had crashed through.

At first he stood in the centre of the trail, willing his senses outwards.

Relax. I can do more if you close your eyes.

"Close my eyes?"

She did not respond, so he followed her instructions. "I can't see anything."

Don't look. Feel.

"What? Oh…feel. Yes, I see. I mean, I can tell. There are trees…there, and there. I sense large, silent, life. Hey! What was that?"

Rabbit. Close your eyes.

"It startled me, that's all. Now I see it. A bright spark."

Learn what is regular. Then look for what is wrong.

Together they built up a picture of the area, feeling what belonged.

"What is that?"

Metal.

He went to where the horse had broken away. "It's a buckle. Off Perica's shoe, probably, when she went through those vines." He closed his eyes again. "I can see the cloth on the thorns."

Good. What else?

"Nothing."

Keep looking.

They searched the area over again. "Nothing."

What now?

"Now we do it my way."

What is your way?

"First, I look around to see if there is any hiding place where a man might have lain in wait. Perhaps he used a stone from a sling. If I don't see any place like that, I go over every bit of ground."

Every bit?

"It might take a while."

Swords have patience. I will learn to help you as you go.

"Fine."

There was a long silence as he began his search. He started in a small circle, then spiralled outward, walking slowly, his eyes scouring left and right.

Stop. There.

He stooped. "Where? I don't see anything."

Under the leaf.

He pulled a large dead leaf away carefully. Under it was a small purse, its leather pouch cracked, its wooden handle rotted away. He pried it open with two fingers, and it broke apart. "Empty. It has been there for a long time. How did you see it?"

I do not see, Ecmund.

"Oh. What do you call it?"

'Seeing' is what you understand.

"Don't sound so superior."

Why not?

"Isn't there a lesson on humility, somewhere in the lore of Magic Swords?"

Why?

110

"Forget I bothered to ask. Let's keep searching."

As Ecmund worked, Kitten kept in contact with his mind, trying to understand what he was doing, to find ways to aid him. She found that, as he kept on, his mind began to wander and she could help him to focus. She could also see through his eyes, and use her own senses to interpret what he saw. She fed this back to him, and his mind built a clearer and clearer picture of the ground around him. Finally, when his last circle brought him along the very edges of the clearing, he shook his head.

"I am not surprised. I did not expect to find anything. One more circle, looking into the brush, then we're done."

Once again, their search was fruitless.

"My neck is getting sore and I'm hungry."

There will be food at the castle.

"I think I'll see if they'll feed me at the castle."

What a good idea.

"Don't get uppity, Kitten. It isn't polite."

I am sorry, Ecmund. I know you like to make your own decisions.

"I'm not sure what you just said, but it felt like something I would agree with."

You decide, you are happy. I decide, you are unhappy. Is that plain enough?

"That was very clear, Kitten. Well done!"

Humans are such a trial.

"That was pretty clear, as well. Mind your manners."

Yes, Ecmund.

"Hmph."

At the castle, a servant pointed them straight to the Overlord's workroom, where he and Perica were eating a light meal while they pored over a huge pile of manuscripts.

"Come in, Ecmund. Have you eaten? I'm sure there is enough for three. We have a lot of these records to go through, and I find I can eat and read at the same time. Most of them are not important, but we have to check them all to find the ones that are."

"Would you like me to return later?"

"No, no, it's a good excuse to take a rest. Have you been out to the Osterwald?"

"Yes. I'm sorry, my Lord." At Perica's gesture, he took a chicken leg. "I found nothing."

The Overlord shrugged. "As we expected."

"Perica, have you remembered anything more?"

She frowned, shrugged. "What is there to remember? The horse suddenly shied, turned to the side, and bolted. After that, it was all a blur of brush and things scraping at me. I don't remember hitting the tree."

111

"You heard nothing, saw nothing?"

She shook her head. "I'm sorry, Ecmund, nothing at all. Up until that point, it was a very pleasant ride."

Ecmund turned to the Overlord. "That's all I can do, my Lord. Unless something else comes up…"

"No, no, that's all I can ask. You have done a service for us, and I will not forget it. Neither will Perica."

The girl smiled, but then she and Ecmund shared a glance, and the smile faded. He nodded, and she turned to her father.

"Father, there is something else."

"What, dear?"

"Ecmund and I have discovered something, and we want to tell you now."

He frowned. "Of course. What's wrong?"

"Nothing especially wrong. It's just something important you need to know."

He looked to Ecmund, then back to his daughter, his brow furrowed.

Not that, silly!

The Overlord put down the knife he was holding, waited expectantly.

"Ecmund, give Father your sword."

He rose, and Lord Delfontes stood as well. He handed her over.

Talk to him.

I will not. Too many already.

The Overlord took Kitten in his hand, regarded her, turned aside to make a few passes. She cautiously reached out.

Please, Kitten?

I tried, Ecmund. No response.

The Lord handed back the Sword. "Nice weapon. Good balance. Old, I'd say."

"Didn't you feel anything?"

"Like I said. Good balance. Feels lighter than it really is. Sign of fine craftsmanship."

Nothing at all. Can't say I'm unhappy about it.

"He can't tell. She felt nothing from him."

"What are you two talking about? What is this important information you have to tell me?"

The two regarded each other. "He'll never believe it."

"I'll never believe what?"

Ecmund sheathed Kitten, shaking his head. "After everything that has happened, you are going to find it very hard to believe this. I don't know how to convince you."

Must we do this?

Yes.

Then we must fight.

"I can't fight him!"

Not you. Her.

"Oh. Of course." He turned to Perica. "There's only one way he'll believe. How good are you with a sword?"

She giggled. "Terrible. No matter how much I try, my wrist just sags."

"Has he fought against you?"

"Not recently, but it won't matter. Can she really increase my skill?"

"If you have any training at all, you will be marvellous."

"Exactly what we want. Give her here." She turned to the Overlord. "Father, come with me to the training room. You are going to have a fencing lesson."

The Overlord slowly rose, his expression puzzled. "I don't know what this is all about, but you are still tired and hurt..."

"Please, Father. This is very important. Not just for me, but for you as well."

"All right, I'll go along. I'm getting used to surprises, especially when this young man is nearby."

"I'm sorry my Lord. It wasn't my fault. Not at first, anyway."

"I know there's no point in asking what isn't your fault. Let's go in and have this lesson."

They entered the practice room, and Perica stepped out on the floor with the Sword. She spoke softly. "All right, Kitten. This is important. Do it right, and I'll never tell him what your name is. Ouch! I'm sorry! I wouldn't tell him anyway. You know that."

Kitten allowed her a small purr.

Perica glanced at Ecmund. "I'm beginning to see!"

He just grinned, but her father frowned. "Don't we need the pads?"

"It's all right, Father. You'll be fine." She stepped into a simple warm-up routine, her hand flashing through the moves, faster and faster. Her father's frown deepened, but he chose a practice sword and stepped onto the floor to begin his own warm-up.

"This won't take long, Father."

"It had better not."

"All right. Have at you, then."

She was suddenly in the garde position, looking relaxed and poised. Her father's lips formed a tight line, and he moved, touching sword tips, gliding back. To Ecmund's inexperienced eye, he looked rather competent.

More than that. He is an expert. I can tell already.

The girl held her weapon correctly, but needed a great deal more strength. Kitten fed it to her, and felt a glow of confidence in return.

113

Quickly, now. No big slashes. All thrust and parry, like a lighter sword.

Her opponent glided forward, tapping a light beat against the tip.

Let it slide. Let him think it worked.

Another beat, harder this time.

Is he stupid enough to try another one? Yes. Hah! That set you back didn't it? All right, girl, let's go get him. Beat, lunge, Oops! Parry, Parry, riposte. Hah! Well done! That scared him, didn't it? Pause, look straight into his eyes. Let him feel the fear.

Step, beat, step, lunge. Watch the riposte! Lunge again. He didn't expect that! All right, he wants to test your defence. Don't be frightened, he won't get us.

"I am not frightened."

Of course you're not. Parry, parry, parry, parry, lead him in! Parry, parry, ready now, one more parry, riposte and lunge! Careful! You don't want to hurt him!

"Sorry father. I didn't want to hurt you."

The Lord lowered his sword. "Hurt me? You almost took my arm off! Where did you learn to fight like that?"

"I didn't."

"What do you mean, you didn't?"

She merely held up the sword. "Here. Take this. Try a few passes with Ecmund."

He took the Sword, fitted his hand reluctantly into her grip. "Is that wise?"

"I'm not worried, my Lord. She won't hurt me, and if I tell her to, she won't let me hurt you, so we're both safe."

"Her. You're talking about this sword, aren't you?"

"Yes we are, Father. You won't believe it until you feel it for yourself."

He looked into his daughter's eyes for a moment, then shook his head. "All right, Perica. If I can't trust you, who can I trust?" He turned to Ecmund. "If there is some way you give this thing instructions, please do so."

I am not a thing.

"It doesn't matter how you feel about it. It is very important that you help him!"

This is highly irregular.

"I don't care. Help him!"

"Please?"

All right, all right. I can't argue with two of you.

Perica smiled at her father. "She agrees. You'll be fine."

"You can talk to it?"

114

I am not an it!

"Not really talk. But when I am touching her, I know how she feels. If she feels strongly, I don't have to be touching. She feels very insulted to be called 'it', and since you're putting your life in her hands, I think you should have better manners than that."

He looked at his daughter suspiciously. "I truly hope this is not some kind of a joke." He spun the sword about a few times, brought her up in a salute. "I do apologize, my Lady. Please fight well for me."

Don't be patronizing.

"How was that?"

Perica grinned. "If you were less sarcastic, you might be safer."

"Are you ready, my Lord? I think my daughter has prepared my mind for the battle."

Ecmund grinned. "I'm glad she's not on my side. At your leisure, my Lord. A few light passes should be enough. I'm not very good."

"That helps a lot. Perhaps you'll kill me by mistake."

"Highly unlikely, sir."

"That gives me great confidence. Have at you, lad."

"Have at you, sir."

There was a quick flurry, basically tip-fencing, then the two parted. The Overlord frowned, puzzled. "I have rarely felt a sword so light. It moves like the wind."

"She."

"Sorry. She moves like the wind."

I whistle!

Another pass, more serious this time, with several strong beats and quick parries.

This is so boring. I could fight both swords with my eyes closed. If I had eyes.

Both lowered their weapons. Ecmund raised his eyebrows. "What do you think, my Lord?"

"I think you're about as good as you say. You do have a good defence. A firm wrist."

"But too firm, as Jesco keeps telling me. Do you trust me, my Lord?"

"To what extent?"

"To changing swords. I promise not to attack."

"You promise…"

"That's right. I'll allow you to test my defence at full speed if I have K…my Sword."

The Lord glanced at his daughter, shrugged. "I suppose. If there was any trick, you'd have killed me by now, anyway."

"You are a brave man, my Lord. Or you trust your daughter a lot."

"Both, I'd like to believe. Prove me right on the latter, please."

They switched weapons, and the Sword hummed.

Boring.

"Let's keep it that way."

"Pardon?"

"She found those last passes very boring. Except for Jesco, she rarely gets a chance for a good fight. Even on defence, this ought to satisfy her."

"Well, by all means let us give the lady satisfaction. Have at you, my Lord."

"My Lord."

This time there was little preliminary.

All right, just relax; here he comes. Parry, parry, parry, watch the beat, parry, riposte a little; don't let him carry the whole fight. Parry, parry, yes, careful, yes, yes, oops! Whee! He is really good. Parry, parry, keep your feet light, parry, riposte... sorry, my Lord, but I can't let such stupidity pass. Parry, parry, ready, he's going to... yes... Bind! Hold him, hold him, you're stronger! Well done!

The two men stood face to face, their sword hilts entangled. Finally the Overlord nodded, Ecmund released the pressure, and they disengaged. "Good enough, lad. Unless you're a better actor than any I can credit, there is something about that sword. I have fought some fine swordsmen, and I have never come up against a defence like that."

"I would thank you, my Lord, but I take little credit for it."

"It was still very impressive. You nearly had me once."

Ecmund grinned. "She couldn't let you get away with that simple trick, my Lord. I had to hold her back from really rapping you."

"So she has a mind of her own, does she?"

"Very much so."

"What does she want?"

The Hand stopped dead. "I don't know. I never asked."

Lord Delfontes raised his eyebrows. "Something I learned many years ago. If you are using people for your own purposes, it helps to know what they want for themselves. Then you find a way they can get it, and do your task as well. It works on people..."

"That's a very good piece of advice, my Lord, but difficult to apply to a Sword. I don't get actual thoughts from her very much. Just feelings, impulses. Sometimes a single word is the best way to describe a feeling, and it comes through quite clearly."

"She called me silly!"

Her father smiled. "And you understood?"

Perica smiled ruefully. "Loud and clear. It was deserved. Sort of."

"Sort of?"

"All right, Father. I was being rude, but I didn't know it."

"Some people often are."

"Please, Father. Not in front of guests."

"Embarrassed to get an etiquette lesson in front of a Sword, are you?"

"I'm embarrassed to have Ecmund hear us bickering."

The Overlord winked at Ecmund. "Put in my place again." Then his face sobered. "Now we have to decide what to do about this whole thing...I don't mean her as a thing, I mean the whole situation."

I was aware of what he meant.

"She understands."

"Good. The question remains. What do we do?"

"I was hoping you would consent to keeping it quiet, my Lord."

"I certainly will to begin with. That sort of information is like a lady's reputation. Once spoiled, it is gone forever."

"Oh, Father, don't be fatuous."

"At least your education has been worth something. You now have a bigger vocabulary with which to insult me." He ran a hand through his hair. "Yes, I agree, you should try to keep this secret as long as you can." He glanced slyly at Ecmund. "Of course, it would be much easier for me to help you if you would agree to use your power to help me."

Ecmund grinned in return. "That's fair, my Lord. I'll let you know as soon as I can."

"Let me know...?"

"Who the Magician is. That's what you need to know. The problem is that my Sword has to stay very still while he is around, in order to hide from him. If she sends out a seeking, he will hear it as if she shouted."

"Then how can she discover him?"

"Well, in a like manner, he must send out his own seeking. Think about recognizing a speaker's voice. In a room full of people, it is difficult to hear where a sound originates."

"But if he was alone, and he did any seeking..."

"...then she could pick him out easily."

"Aha. But difficult to arrange a situation where that might happen."

"Especially since we don't know who he is to start with."

"Actually, I have some information, and a way to get more."

"Yes, as Eirlin told you. Probably someone upper class, a more recent arrival."

"But that was from one of the soldiers, second hand. I have yet to question the officer involved."

"You haven't? Not to give offense, but..."

"...but why didn't I talk to him right away? Because he was, for some reason, sent on a mission to Koningsholm, and no one is quite sure what the mission was or who sent him. It seems he was very close-mouthed. Might have had something to do with his sore nose."

"If he returns, I might be able to tell. She seems to know when someone is lying."

"Seems?"

Seems! Kitten sent a snarl of disdain. *Of course I can!*

"Nothing like that is infallible. If the person believes, or can persuade himself to believe, that what he says is the truth..."

"Of course."

Oh.

"In any case, I'd be happy to try."

"Good." The older man looked at Ecmund for a moment, thoughtfully. "Tell me. Ecmund. What is the difference between you, with your sword, and a Magician?"

Ecmund grinned. "Twenty years of training."

"Is that all?"

"I don't think so. I've never known a Magician, so I only have family lore. I gather that a Magician can go much farther than reading emotions. He can instil them. He can make you hate someone, for example. He would have only partial control, of course. He couldn't make you hate Perica, I don't think. Not unless she did something you strongly disapproved of."

The Overlord smiled wryly at his daughter. "That only happens once or twice a day."

"Well, there you go. She's only been angry at me once today, and I had no help from the Sword at all."

Perica frowned but there was no power in it. "When you two are finished being funny, can we get to the next important question?"

"You mean, why the Sword reacts to you?"

"Yes. It was very strong. The first moment I touched the hilt last night, I felt a rush of something. I don't know exactly what it was, but it was very strong.

Glad I wasn't the only one.

"The Sword felt it too. When you gave her back she was shouting at me. She considered you a serious danger."

"Danger?" The frown deepened.

He chuckled. "She seems to be the jealous sort."

"Oh."

"Of course. Anything that might interfere with our Joining is a threat."

"I'm a threat to you and your sword?"

"Yes. I think you could become a Hand quite easily. That would be a threat to our bond, wouldn't it?"

118

"A Hand? As in the Hand that wields the magic Sword? This sounds like something from an old romance."

He shrugged. "Any idea of becoming a swordsman? Or swordswoman, I suppose it would be."

"Me? Fight people with a sword? I hardly think so!"

"There. That solves that problem. You're not a threat any more."

That's all you can see!

"But why me? I'm not of the Blood!" She turned to her father. "Am I?"

"Not in the last five hundred years, either on your mother's side or mine."

"Are you certain of the details?"

"Are you suggesting that your bloodlines might be in error? Not a path I would wish to start anyone down."

"But if there had been a...slip, wouldn't they hide it?"

"Yes, I suppose they would. But my family has only been in the realm of Inderjorne for six generations, and your mother's came even later than that."

"That means, if there was some of the Blood in me, it would be recent, and therefore strong."

"Perica, I suggest you let this line of discussion drop. You know where it could lead, if our enemies got the idea. There must be other reasons for this affinity. Those of the Blood cannot have complete monopoly on the powers." His eyes slid to Ecmund for support.

"That could be true, my Lord. I only know our family lore. It's a big world, with many peoples. There must be others." He caressed the Sword hilt. "I sometimes wish my Sword could really speak. I have no idea of her history: where she was made and when, how she ended up on a merchant's counter here at the market."

Kitten winced. There were parts of her history which, Smith willing, would never be spoken.

The Overlord slapped his hands to his thighs. "Well. We have a lot to think about. I am going to suggest that we say nothing to anyone about this sword, until we have had time to consider the ramifications fully."

He turned to face Ecmund directly. "One consideration must be the amount of threat you pose to me."

Ecmund nodded soberly. "Of course. A rival of the Blood with the power of a magic Sword could be a serious problem for a new ruler. However, I believe that is changing already."

"In what way?"

He grinned. "In the first place, you are standing here discussing Magicians and magic Swords as if you believe in them. Your wilful ignorance of a present danger was not a good survival tactic."

119

"There you go again, tossing insulting words around. And I thought introducing my daughter to your sister might cause a problem."

"Second, I think you have made progress with the townspeople here. You treated them with respect and dignity, even though you showed strength of your own. You could feel the difference when they went to look for Perica. At least, I could. They really wanted to find her."

"Well, it's nice to be considered valuable!"

"It wasn't just that, Perica. We live in a wild area. Accidents happen. People get lost sometimes and we all rally around, no matter who it is. There was more to it, though. I think they were trying to show you what kind of people we are."

The Overlord smiled, that wry twist of the lip that he often used. "They were trying to take the high ground over me."

"A bit of that, I think. Of course, she's also a pretty girl. All young lads have their dreams."

"Why, thank you sir. Such flattery."

"Merely stating the facts, my Lady."

Can a Sword be sick?

"If I may interrupt this courtly dance, I have work to do. First task being to figure out who is behind these problems we are having."

"Is there anyone here who could benefit from your failure?"

"I've been thinking of that. As far as the King knows, there were no direct heirs left of the old family."

"Indirect ones?"

"Perhaps. I might send a dispatch to his Majesty on that subject. Have my wandering officer sent back as well."

"If the Magician is very good, the man might truly know less than his mates about how he was influenced."

"I suppose. And you will attend when he is questioned? If it is done subtly, so there is no danger of the Magician hearing?"

"I would be pleased to be of any assistance."

"Fair enough. I'll let you know."

"Then, my Lord, I will bid you farewell. I must get back to my duties. I seem to be getting pulled away from them a lot lately. Languishing in gaol, chasing lost children, that sort of thing."

"Children!"

He turned a bland face towards Perica. "You are Lord Delfontes's child, are you not?"

"Hmph!"

"Then I will see you when next we meet. My Lord, my Lady." He made a very proper bow, and strode out of the practice room, the Overlord's laughter following him.

The Sword allowed him to hear the final comment. "Perica, what did you do to him? He put you in your place very properly!"

I can't hear what she answered.

"Well. That went rather nicely."

If you mean insulting the Lord's daughter, you did a fine job of that.

"She deserved it. She may consider herself educated and sophisticated, but she still carries the prejudices of her people."

I thought she apologized rather nicely.

"So now you're on her side?"

As long as she's angry with you.

Chapter 15

It took three days of toil before Ecmund had his affairs in good enough order that he could have an afternoon to walk the woods. As he left the town behind, Kitten could feel his step lengthen, and his mood rise. They swung along the road, then cut up the hill into the forest. Every once in a while he blazed a tree with his axe, but otherwise seemed to be doing nothing useful.

Eirlin says to make sure you work. No... lollygagging, I think was the word... allowed.

He sighed. "I've been meaning to speak to you."

I was meaning to speak to you, too. It just took several weeks for the right occasion. Now we can talk.

"That's not what I meant and you know it. I've been meaning to talk to you about your sense of humour."

Ah, yes. A sense of humour. Something few humans have, I find.

"All humans have a sense of humour. You seem to have one as well. It is just warped."

She sent an image of Perica and Eirlin, heads held high in scorn.

"And it's not going to get any better, if you listen to those two."

They are the people you love, Ecmund. Why not listen to them?

"Your friends are people you love despite their flaws, Kitten."

A sense of humour is a flaw?

He chuckled. "Only if it's different from mine."

Humans are very strange.

"Not half so strange as magic Swords."

A matter of perspective, I suggest. I also suggest shelter.

"What?"

There is a storm coming.

"How do you know?"

I do not like water. It rusts.

He peered up through the treetops. "Yes, there is a thundercloud coming this way. We'd better find shelter."

A far-off rumbling shivered the air. "The forest is a poor place to be in a thunderstorm."

Why is that?

"Because lightning strikes whatever sticks up highest from the ground. Trees, for example."

There are many trees here.

"Exactly. What we need is a hut, cave, or overhanging rock."

There is more rock to your right.

He angled his steps in that direction, and the ground began to rise. Soon it became a climb rather than a walk.

"I know where I am, now. This opens out ahead onto a rocky knoll. Another bad place to be. Maybe we can find an overhang." He cut to the left and began to angle along the hillside. "I hope it rains. A dry thunderstorm is something we don't need."

Why is that?

"Forest fires."

I know about fire.

"Maybe this will do." It was a broken ridge, where the bedrock pushed through to the surface. Successive layers of hard and soft stone had left a short, slanted ledge, with another slab sticking out above it. Dry leaves and sticks in the back showed that rain rarely penetrated. Ecmund sat down, his back to the wall, and looked out. "Scenery's not bad. We'll have something to watch."

The thunder was no longer mere rumbling. The lightning blazed, followed by an immediate crash.

"It's getting pretty close."

Wind curled around them, whipping the dead leaves about.

Have you ever thought of standing on the top of a hill in a thunderstorm, and pointing your Sword at the sky?

"If I understood what you said correctly, it's about the most stupid idea I've heard today."

Hmm.

"You don't mean someone did that?"

I needed new sharkskin on my hilt.

"You mean you had a Hand who actually stood on a hilltop, and invited the lightning to strike? What happened?

Burned completely crispy.

"I didn't mean your sharkskin."

Neither did I.

"Oh." He stared out at the rolling clouds for a while. "You have had some strange ones, haven't you?"

Everyone is strange in his own way.

"That is either very philosophical, or I have just been insulted."

Her answer was obliterated by an eye-searing flash and a simultaneous blast too loud to be felt as sound. Ecmund's mind reeled, his dazed senses trying to return. Even Kitten felt jarred to her core.

There was a long silence. Then Ecmund took his hands from his eyes, shook his head. "That must have been very close."

You're shouting.

"I'm sorry. I can't hear much." He startled as another lightning flash lit up the trees in front, the accompanying thunder reverberating around them.

"That wasn't so bad."

Fire.

"Fire?"

There is fire near.

"How do you know?"

I know fire. I was born in fire. Top of the hill.

"The top? That's not so bad. Nothing much to burn up there. We'll have to take a look once the storm is past. Maybe the rain will put it out."

No rain yet.

"This doesn't look good, Kitten. It only takes one bad strike to cause a major fire."

More lightning, but the thunder came an instant later, not quite so loud.

"It's passing."

Still no rain.

They sat, waiting, listening, as the lightning eased, the thunder trailing further and further behind. Finally Ecmund stood.

"We'd better check that fire."

It is not so big, now.

"Good." He settled her belt firmly on his hips and scrambled up the hill. As he neared the top, he could see smoke wafting overhead, torn by the wind. He flinched at a new strike of lightning, but it was far down the valley, and the thunder was a soft rumble again.

When he could see the top, he stopped. "Looks like the last storm for that old-timer."

A limbless snag half lay, half leaned along the rock, flames licking at the rotted core that spilled from the splintered trunk. A jagged shard still stood, burning fiercely, but the rest was in charred, smoking pieces.

With a final glance at the departing storm, Ecmund stepped forward, slinging his axe into both hands. "No fire problem here, unless that wind gets worse. I'll just do a bit of cleanup." It wasn't actually cleanup, because what he did was spread any burning pieces out on to the bare rock, where they fumed impotently.

"Sort of sad to see an old tree like that go. Could have been four, five hundred years. Pine, from the look of it."

You are sad when anything dies.

"We're all alive, we all die, and nobody likes it much."

I will not die.

"Of course you will."

How?

"I have no idea. The lore is fragmented. You might live for thousands of years, apparently, but sooner or later, you will die."

Rust wins in the end.

"It does."

There was a moment of silence. Then Ecmund raised his head. "That wasn't the only strike."

Kitten began to spread her senses, but he stopped her. "This is one time when simple old human vision is the best."

He stepped to the edge of the rock, scanning the path of the storm. Off to the right, where the hills climbed slowly towards the distant mountains, there were two plumes of smoke. "We aren't worried about those. Too far away to do anything if we were." He turned to the left. "That, on the other hand, is a problem."

The ridge afforded a clear view of the valley all the way to Falkengard, dark against the fields. The rough fingers of the Aerie stuck up jaggedly against the loom of the storm cloud. What attracted their attention, though, was a thickening pillar of smoke that rose from the forest at the base of the hill. The source of the smoke was hidden by other trees, but as they watched, they could see flames flicking higher.

Ecmund took a glance around to orient himself and started down the ridge, sliding on the loose rock, bounding from ledge to ledge where he could, his axe waving for balance. Soon he reached the bottom and began to sprint through the woods, leaping some fallen trees, running along others, following trails as long as they helped, crashing through the undergrowth when it was necessary.

It did not take long to reach the site of the strike. A big hemlock stood riven from crown to base, split open like a dropped fruit. Even some of the roots were exposed. The tree was burning up its whole length, and two other hemlocks close by were beginning to catch. With a quick glance, Ecmund assessed the situation.

"Those two are going to be a problem." A few strokes of his axe, and the smaller one fell away from its dying parent. Ecmund scooted the length of the fallen tree, lopping off burning limbs and stamping out their fire. Then he turned to the second trunk.

It was too late. Both remaining trees were burning fiercely now, and sparks and bits of flaming bark were floating up with the smoke. He watched helplessly as they rose. "If they get high enough, they'll burn out before they get to the ground. If we get any more wind, we've got a problem."

He shrugged. "Nothing I can do about that. I guess I'd better get ready for when that mass falls." He began to clear the brush away from the downwind side of the fire.

Kitten focused on staying out of the way. Once she snagged on a bush, but he patted her hilt. "Don't worry. I'm not putting you down."

Thank you, Ecmund. Burning is not good for my temper.

125

He swatted a spark that landed on his neck. "It's not too good for mine either." He returned to his chopping. The axe sang in his hands, and his cleared patch began to grow.

The hard work was beginning to affect him now, and he worked more methodically, pausing regularly to rest. "I have to use my brains, now, Kitten. If I do this right, and have some luck, we'll be fine. If we have really good luck, the limbs will burn off those two trees, and they'll be left standing."

Bad luck?

"Bad luck and the wind changes, and blows them down at another angle. I can't clear the whole forest away from them. Bad luck and the wind comes up and starts twenty more fires. That would be very bad luck, because the road home is downwind, and a fire can move really, really, fast in a high wind."

Wind like that?

A fanfare of sparks and flames swirled higher, and the fire's roar doubled.

"I'm going to have to change my tactics. We'll leave this and move downwind, try to kill any new fires. But we have to watch out. If this one takes off..."

I will watch.

"Thanks, Kitten. I'm counting on you."

You can count on me.

He put his pack on his back and made the best time he could, stamping out any sparks he saw. As he worked, he was watching and planning. "There's the road. Good. If the fire gets going, we might stop it there. That will keep it away from the farms."

There are many more trees farther south and west.

"Yes, that's a problem, but there may not be any way to stop it. We need a break in the trees."

A break?

"Yes. Something wide enough that the fire can't get across easily, and long enough that the fire can't get around the end. Then we station our men along it, and they do what we're doing now: put out the airborne fires."

Something we aren't doing now.

"What do you mean?"

There is a small fire, over there. And another one over there. Two more are starting behind us.

"Thanks, Kitten. There's so much smoke, I couldn't see them. Show me."

She guided him to each fire, and he put them all out.

"Can you see back to the original strike?"

126

Close your eyes.

"I can see one very bright patch. Is that all?"

It is the same size as before.

"That's good, then. Show me some more."

The wind is rising.

"I know. Where is the next fire?'

There are many.

"Doesn't matter. Show me the biggest one."

There. Get that one. Good. Now to your left. No, there is a bigger one farther on. Watch out!

Searing heat, as a bush beside them roared up in flames.

"I'll have to leave that one. I can't stop it. Show me another."

Over there! Also there! Two have joined, Ecmund. They are bigger than the others. Yes. Those.

Ecmund stopped, mopping his brow. "I can't stop them, Kitten. I might get trapped myself. We'll have to go to the road."

Good idea. No, go left. I know the road is over there, but there is fire there, too. Go left, Ecmund! That's better. Now right.

"I can't see anything. The smoke..." He broke off in a fit of coughing.

I can see it all.

"How..."

It is part of my soul, Ecmund. I was born in fire.

"Fine. I don't want to die in it. Get me out of here."

Close your eyes. Go right. That's it. Straight ahead, now. Watch that low branch. You can open them now. The smoke is better here. The road is ahead. Men and horses.

"Ecmund! What the hell were you doing in there?"

He coughed, rubbed his streaming eyes. "Having a pleasant afternoon stroll, Bacares. Glad you could join me."

The sergeant raised his voice. "My Lord! Over here!"

There was a thudding of hooves and Lord Delfontes appeared out of the smoke. "What have you found, Bacares? Oh! Ecmund. I didn't know you were with us."

"I wasn't. I was fighting the fire. We have to hold the road, my Lord."

"What do you mean? We can't see anything, with all this smoke."

"The fire started back there. Lightning strike. I had it contained until the wind blew up. Now there are little fires all over between the original strike and the road. Most of them are..." he turned, closed his eyes, "...over that way. There are a few over here, and two little ones have crossed the road just up there."

127

He turned to the group of men that was gathering. "Two of you: up the road, eyes to the left. Three or four small fires. The rest of you, we need a fireguard along the road. Drop all the trees one length into the forest. Start here and work in both directions."

"How far?"

Ecmund's grin seemed to set them all back a pace. "Till you run out of smoke. Move quickly. It jumps the road, people will die."

The men scattered, and Ecmund turned to the Overlord, who had dismounted. "Sorry, my Lord. I should have waited for you to give the orders, but there isn't much time."

Delfontes looked around. "Since the smoke is much better down here than up on my horse, it's a good thing someone took charge. How can you see what's going on?"

He caught the Lord's eye, and rubbed Kitten's pommel before speaking. "I can't see much, but I was there when it happened, so I know where it came from."

"How much chance do we have of stopping it?"

"How many men do we have?"

"I brought ten soldiers and four of my retainers. We passed eight locals on the way here. They should be along soon."

"Along the road, we should be fine. It's to the west that worries me."

"Why is that?"

"Because there's no natural firebreak. We can stop the fire's northward progress here, but it might just slide to the west and we'd end up fighting it all along the road. Plus all that timber to the south and west will get burned up."

"What do you suggest?"

"We should take a look, and see if we can start a backfire."

"What's that?"

"You start a fire of your own, in front of the real fire. It burns up the fuel, and when the big fire gets to you, there's nothing left, so they both stop."

"How do you stop the backfire from getting away from you?"

"Any way you can. Let's go have a look. There's no water nearby."

The Overlord took his horse's reins and started north along the road with Ecmund. As they passed the working men, Ecmund sent Kitten's senses into the wall of smoke, guiding the firefighters with his knowledge. Finally, he stopped.

"We don't want to go much farther than this, my Lord."

"What are we looking for?"

"Some natural break in the trees. A creek bed, or a field."

"How can we see anything, in this smoke?"

"We can't."

128

Carefully they scanned the roadside ahead. Ecmund walked along, intent on Kitten's senses, looking for gaps in the greenery.

There. Under the moss. Stones.

"There."

"What? Where? I don't see anything."

"There's an old road crosses there, overgrown. There's even a stone wall part way. Come on."

Opening his eyes, he crashed into the roadside brush. Sure enough, a mouldering hump showed where a wall had been, and a row of shorter alders on the western side marked a roadbed, stretching to the south.

Ecmund hefted his axe. "If you'll send me some help, my Lord, I'll start another firebreak here. Well run our backfire behind the wall."

"Whatever you say." Delfontes disappeared into the smoke, and Ecmund started chopping.

By the time three soldiers arrived, he had cleared a good portion of the old wall, piling the cuttings on the left-hand side. "Eodborg and Heath! Couldn't have asked for a better team. You two start dropping the trees along the roadside, back until you meet up with the area we already cleared. Hrethred, start on the alders in the roadbed. Cut them fairly low; we will want to move along the road back and forth."

"Road?"

"Surprise. There's an old road in here. You'll see."

"I don't know how you see anything, Ecmund, but I can chop alders as well as the next man."

"Good enough." He continued working along the wall, and the soldier followed on the old road.

Soon another group of men appeared, led by Lord Delfontes. "The men have finished along the road, Ecmund. Can you use them here?"

"Yes. Keep working along the wall. We'll need to go a bowshot at least. I'll go back and check the fire."

He strode back through the smoke, which was even thicker, now, sending men into coughing fits. Kitten's senses showed that the small fires were joining. When he reached the east end of the firebreak, he was satisfied that the fire had moved downwind of that area, and it was safe. He stationed a smaller number of men there to deal with flying sparks, and gathered the others in the most dangerous area.

"If you can, start cutting farther south of the road. Anything lying down burns slowly. Standing trees are dangerous. If the fire comes too close, back up to the road and fight the flying stuff. Until then, keep working the firebreak as wide as you can. I think we're ahead of it now, and I'd like to take advantage of the time it gives us. Got that?"

They were red-eyed and coughing, but they nodded and attacked the forest with renewed vigour.

When he returned to the corner with the wall, he was pleased at the amount of clearing that had been done. The road now had one complete tree-length of fallen timber along its south side, and the men working along the stone wall had made very good progress. He followed the old road out as far as he could.

"What's happening, Hrethred?"

"There used to be a field over there, Ecmund. The trees are thick, but they're short. If we only have to knock them down, we can make good time."

Once again casting Kitten's senses towards the fire, he calculated the wind direction.

Have you noticed the wind, Kitten?

What about it?

Direction, strength.

She thought a moment. *I do not know wind like I know fire, but it has been steady. I think it is now less.*

That's what I thought. Wait…

Yes, I feel him too. Why is the Magician here?

I don't know, Kitten. What is he doing?

He is checking the workers, listening for anyone in trouble.

That's useful. You can do that as well. As long as he can swing a shovel, we'll take any help we can get.

He returned to the corner, where Lord Delfontes was standing, an axe in one hand, mopping his brow with the other.

"Like being in a battle. You think you're tired, but you just keep going."

"They don't call it 'fire fighting' by accident."

"What's our situation?"

"It all depends on the wind. If it drops enough we won't need the backfire, because that road and fence will be enough. If it stays the same or increases, by the time it reaches that point it will be a full forest fire, and it will blow right over our guard, and us as well."

"You mean this isn't a forest fire?"

"No, it's still a scattering of spot fires. Only the downwind edges are a problem. Once they all join on a single front, then we have a real fire."

"Where are they now?"

He closed his eyes, sent his thoughts out. "About half way, and joining faster all the time."

"Shall we start the backfire?"

"I'm really keeping the wind in mind. I think it's dropping."

"I don't think it is."

They both turned at this new voice. It was the blond lord Ecmund had noticed at Falkengard, his hair pulled back by a strip of cloth, his clothing singed.

Ecmund hid his surprise. "You don't?"

"I just came from the other end of the line. Either the wind is picking up, or it's the sound of the fire getting nearer, but I'm sure it's louder than it was."

Ecmund turned to the Overlord. "There you have it. We can't take the risk. We'll start the backfires." He made a quick, significant, gesture with his head.

Delfontes nodded. "Lord Ostersund, will you go back up the road and make sure the men know we're starting the backfires?"

"Of course. What do I tell them?"

Ecmund shrugged. "Keep working, but watch their backs. You don't need to tell them when to run. They'll know."

"Good enough." The blond lord strode away, and Ecmund shook his head in frustration.

"What's the problem, Ecmund?"

"The Magician is here, and I have to be more careful using Kitten's senses to find the fire, or he'll know. Where are your other retainers?"

"They're spread along the road, here. Do you think it's one of them?"

"I think they're the best guess. I haven't noticed anyone searching recently. I doubt if they can sense the fire like Kitten can, but it reduces our effectiveness. If it starts to be a problem, I'm going to forget about the secrecy. This battle is more important."

"I agree."

"Fine. Let's go start our own fire."

Once they got back to the road corner, Ecmund gathered the men together and got out his flint. "The object is to keep this new fire from moving west, to keep it controlled. Start digging along the base of the wall. There's centuries of dirt piled up there, and you can use it to throw on any fire that gets close. If it gets too hot, you can use the wall for protection. Keep trimming the limbs off the fallen trees, and throw them on the fire. Green trunks spread out like this won't burn. Then all we have to watch out for are the airborne sparks."

The men nodded grimly, and Ecmund walked out on a larger trunk, all the way until it disappeared under a mass of others. There he found plenty of dry wood. He created a nest of tinder and stroked his flint sharply down the side of the axe head. The spark leapt to the tinder, eating eagerly at it, and soon he had to step back from the blaze.

He pulled out several flaming branches and forced his way through the tangle, lighting fires as he went.

"Keep an eye behind me, Kitten."

They are burning well, but not towards us.

"Thank you. I think that's enough."

He waded back through the limbs, climbed up on a bare trunk, and balanced his way back to the old stone wall.

"How does it look, Bacares?"

"I don't know, my Lord. It looks damned close."

Ecmund laughed. "At the moment, it does, I admit. It's always a risk, setting a backfire."

"Last stand situation?"

"That's right. Win or die."

"Anything we can do, my Lord?"

"Where did this 'my Lord' come from, Bacares?"

"I dunno, Ecmund. You seem to be running things, here. Lord Delfontes calls you that, sometimes. Seems right."

"Fair enough. I need the obedience; I'll take what I can get. Next week, when he wants me thrown in gaol again, you can forget it."

"Fair enough, my Lord."

They laughed and parted.

Now who has a strange sense of humour?

"War does strange things to people."

There are different types of wars.

"I have to agree."

He paced the line, watching his backfire closely. Suddenly he stopped, his hand dropping to her hilt.

Careful, Kitten.

I know.

What is he doing?

I think he is trying to read the fire, as we do.

Can he do that?

I have no way of knowing if he is successful. Wait. He just found something. What?

I don't know. Yes I do. Listen to the wind.

Ecmund's head went up, all senses alert. "It has changed direction."

And become very loud.

"You're right. What is going on?"

Questions rang out around them, as the sound of the fire increased. Men were looking over their shoulders, fear on their faces.

"Ecmund! What is happening?"

"I don't know, my Lord. Give me a moment." He stared around, first with his own senses. All he could see was that the wind, formerly blowing from the east, had shifted, and was now streaming the opposite

132

way. Their backfire, which had been pushing against the firebreak, was suddenly leaning off towards the east. And all the while, the noise grew.

"Where is the smoke going?"

"Upwards, from what I can see, my Lord. I'm going to use Kitten's senses." He closed his eyes, and the two of them strained outward.

The wind has not changed.

That's right. It is still blowing from the east. But not here.

The two fires yearn for each other.

What?

See?

Oh. That's why it works so well.

It is?

Of course.

Of course. What works so well?

He opened his eyes, smiling at Lord Delfontes. "It's the main fire, my Lord. It has joined!"

"That's bad, isn't it?"

"No. It is so hot, it is drawing all the air to it, from every direction. Our little fire is being sucked towards the big one."

"And away from us."

"It seems to be. I had always heard about backfires, and never really knew why they worked. Now I know."

The Overlord glanced at him. "I'm so glad your little experiment was successful."

"I'm sort of pleased about it myself."

"What happens now?"

"Your guess is as good as mine, my Lord. I think we stand back and watch them crash into each other and die out. We keep killing the sparks. There's going to be a lot of those, but I think, with the power of this updraft, they will all rise incredibly high."

"So we're not out of the woods, yet."

"No, and the fire isn't out of wood yet, either, so let's keep stamping on sparks."

And you worry about my sense of humour?

Chapter 16

The dawn found them, dirty and exhausted, sprawled around a table at the temporary camp the castle steward had set up, well behind the fire line. Lord Delfontes raised a weary head, looking across at Ecmund.

"What do you think, lad? Have we beaten it?"

"We'll know with sunup, when the smoke will show any new fires."

"And if there are?"

"Then we go and fight them, of course. You had another plan?"

"Yes. I thought I'd just gently die, and let my daughter worry about it all."

"Don't do that, my Lord. She would be much too pleased."

"At my dying?"

"No, at the taking over part."

"I'd be hard put to argue that on a normal day. Right now, an hour's sleep would be worth the whole demesne."

"Well, since I can't provide that, I guess we might as well get up and finish this. I want to check our lines."

"Good idea."

"Food first?"

"Even better."

There was a familiar blond head at the fire, and Ecmund caught a wash of fatigue. Seeing his Overlord, Ostersund straightened. Kitten faded. "Good morning, my Lord."

"Good morning, Lord Ostersund. Sleep well?"

"Of course, my Lord. Why would I worry about a few little nightmares?"

"Nightmares?"

"Yes, I almost thought I spent the night swinging an axe and shovel, with trees burning around me."

"What a strange coincidence. I have similar memories."

"Must be an illness going around."

"Must be."

"Where are you off to this fine morning, my Lord?"

"Ecmund and I are going to check how the night's work went."

"Shall I join you?"

"No, you go get some real sleep. If I need you, I want you rested. Pleasant dreams."

"I wish you the same, my Lord."

They strode over to the horses and mounted.

"What was that all about?"

"I think Lord Ostersund has a particularly individual sense of humour."

Hah!

"Yes. It reads at different levels, doesn't it?"

The Overlord looked around. "Is he our Magician?"

Ecmund shook his head. "The Magician was definitely here last night. We could feel him casting about, trying to read the flames. Who it was, I cannot say."

"At least that narrows the field down, some. Only four of my retainers came with me."

"If it's one of your retainers. What about the soldiers?"

"Don't be pessimistic."

"It does bring up another unpleasant possibility, though."

"I can't wait."

"The Magician was using the same technique that Kitten and I used to look for the flames. Which could mean that he learned it from us."

"He knows about Kitten."

Ecmund nodded glumly. "If I wasn't so tired, I'd be worried sick."

"About what?"

"If I wasn't so tired, I'd figure that out."

"Hmm."

"Right."

The horses plodded on at their own speed.

They eventually reached the fire line, where the rising sun revealed desolation. The north side of the road continued green, although patches of black marred the ground. The south side was disaster. Fallen trees, some still burning, criss-crossed the ditches. Farther off, smoke sent a thousand fingers skyward in the still air.

"I thought the whole forest would be burned."

"Not necessarily. Nature plays her own game."

The course of the main fire was marked by a slash of complete destruction; only the trunks of the largest trees still smouldered in a valley of grey ash. On the edges, however, the vagaries of chance took over. Small stands of trees seemed untouched. In other places, only the ground cover was burned, while the green treetops stood unharmed. Groundfire like rivulets of water had crept through some stands, leaving wavering black troughs in the undergrowth.

They sat their horses and stared around.

"So. You're the expert. How did we do?"

"Who's an expert?"

"What do you mean? You're the one who took charge. You're the one who fought the fire. I just stood around and pretended to agree."

"So if it all went wrong, you could blame me?"

"Such are the skills of leadership. You still haven't answered my question."

"What question?"

"The one about you not being the expert."

"I'm not. I've never fought a fire like this before."

"Not like this?"

"Never one this big. I've been around when we fought little ones."

"You've never seen a backfire used, then."

"No."

"Never laid out a fireline."

"Never."

"Then why did everyone listen to you?"

"Because I was the only one who sounded like he knew what was going on. Somebody had to give orders."

"It could have been me."

"It could have."

"And then we would have lost a lot of woods, and maybe even some men."

"Perhaps. Or you might have come up with another plan that saved the day. You never know what you'll manage once the battle starts."

"You never know."

"Any word from Falkengard?"

"Regular messengers from Perica through the night. Everything calm. One man passed by the village this morning. No trouble."

"Then our troublemaker must have been with us last night."

"Probably."

"Narrows it down."

They had returned to the camp, and now they sat their horses, both men in the last stages of exhaustion, neither willing to move.

"What now?"

"Leave a guard to watch the ashes and put out what they can. Leave messengers to bring help if needed. Go home and get some sleep."

"I like the last part."

"I like it all. Let's go."

"Right. Let's go."

"That means somebody has to start, my Lord."

"That would be my duty, I suppose."

The two weary men prodded their mounts into a shambling walk.

It was an exhausted, filthy, but satisfied group that allowed their horses to wander to a stop in the castle bailey. Perica, who met them at the bottom of the stairs, didn't look much better.

"At least she's clean."

Ecmund nodded to Delfontes. "Cleanliness is an admirable trait, especially in a woman."

"You do not look at the top of your form, daughter."

"It was a long night, Father."

"Something disturb your dreams?"

"Yes. A red glow on the horizon."

"Ah, she speaks in metaphor. Don't you just love it when they speak in metaphor, Ecmund?"

"Yes. I'm always happier when I don't know what they mean."

Perica dropped her hand to Kitten as he tumbled off his horse. "I'm not going to get a straight answer from either of you, I can tell."

"Was there a question?"

She was worried for you. I have reassured her.

"Thank you. It is so much easier that way."

Perica suddenly straightened. "You led the fight?"

"He did, daughter. We got there, the smoke blew in, and we couldn't see anything. I had no idea what to do. Then suddenly out of the middle of the fire comes this vision of, well, I can't call it beauty, but it was certainly a vision. He started giving orders and chopping trees down, and starting fires, and after an endless night of coughing, suddenly it was all over."

"Why you?"

"I'm a woodcutter, remember? If the forest burns up, my livelihood is in danger."

"And ours as well." She reached up on tiptoe and kissed his cheek.

"Why don't you do things like that while I'm awake to enjoy it?" He frowned at her. "I have heard of ladies putting colour on their lips, but...black?"

"You are filthy, in case it had escaped your notice. You are going straight into a bath."

"Actually, I'm going straight home to bed. I'm not sure why I'm here."

"You are here because if she didn't see you alive and well, my daughter would be pestering me about it all morning, and I need my sleep. I'll send a groom down for the horse. Go home."

"Aye, my Lord."

He mounted, started away, then turned the horse. "Good morning, my Lady."

She curtsied. "I hope you're not going to make a habit of keeping my father out all night."

"I will endeavour to make it a rare occurrence, my Lady."

"You may go, then."

"I may. If I don't fall off."

He turned the horse again, and rode slowly down the hill. His head was drooping, but his heart was singing.

What are you so happy about? Not that kiss, I hope.

"What kiss?"

The one that keeps running through your brain. I'm bored with it already.

"Do you think, if she put me in the bath, she'd stay to scrub me off?"

Humans are very strange people.

Chapter 17

Three days later, Ecmund sat in Lord Delfontes's workroom, a drift of papers around him. Finally he stood and threw his hands in the air. "There is nothing in any of these documents to tell us anything. As far as I can find here, and from my knowledge or our lore, there is no one of the Blood who would benefit from your failure to rule this demesne."

"It was worth checking."

"What do we do now?"

The Overlord's head came up. "We?"

"Of course. I am involved. I will continue to help."

"Sit down, Ecmund. Please." The Overlord indicated a brocade chair. "Do you realize what your offer means?"

"My Lord, it is my duty to help my people in any way possible, so that they can live happy, peaceful, and productive lives. It has always been my wish to achieve this by becoming as good a woodcutter as I could. As I gained age and wisdom, I expected to advise the young, as elders of my people always do."

He slapped Kitten's hilt. "My life has not turned out that way. Circumstances have forced me onto a path I did not choose, and I have found it necessary to discover other ways to perform my duty."

The Overlord nodded. "Considering the twists my own life has taken lately, I sympathize."

"But the duty has not changed. I simply find myself moving into an advisory position much sooner than I had expected. In terms of my offer to you, it means I have decided that you are probably the best choice available to rule this demesne. Therefore, for the good of my people, my village, and my family, the wisest thing I can do is support you. By doing so, I can assure your tenure, with the added advantage that I may be able to influence your behaviour."

The Overlord shook his head. "Why do I feel like a new junior officer of a regiment, who has just been told by the old sergeant that his comportment is adequate? I am the Overlord here. I am old enough to be your father. I am supposed to be doing the judging."

Ecmund smiled. "I think you have come a long way since you had that attitude, my Lord."

"I must have. I'm not sending you to the gaol for your temerity this time."

"You have been well trained, my Lord."

"Well trained? By whom?"

"Your daughter. She has taught you to accept judgement from your supporters."

"I suppose you're right."

"I may have been a woodcutter before I got Kitten. I wasn't stupid."

Lord Delfontes chuckled. "Sorry. I shouldn't have sounded so surprised."

He suddenly regarded Ecmund from under lowered brows.

Watch out. Here it comes.

"Ecmund, what would you do if you had some money?"

"How much money?"

"I don't know. Enough to double the size of your yard, hire some men. Don't tell me you don't have some plans, some dreams."

Ecmund shrugged, grinned. "Of course I have dreams. I always thought I'd like to expand the shop, hire a couple of men full-time."

"What would that mean?"

"Well, Eirlin would say it would allow me to spend more time wandering in the forest."

"Would she be wrong?"

"No, but it isn't the way she makes it sound. The more time I spend in the forest, the better trees I find. I'd like to take more time out there, bring in some truly fine wood, season it properly. I could get good prices for wood like that. Send it out to the other towns around, even to Koningsholm. But it takes me too much time, providing the regular lumber for the people around here. That's what keeps food on our table."

"How much regular lumber could you sell, if you had more time and men to cut it? Maybe market it to the towns closer to the centre of Inderjorne, where the forests have long been depleted?"

Ecmund suddenly sat straighter, looked the Overlord in the eye. "Is this how it goes? Are you buying my loyalty?"

The man burst into laughter. "No, Ecmund, I'm not. You will notice that you offered your support first, free of encumbrances."

Ecmund's face reddened. "Of course. I'm sorry, my Lord."

"Fair enough. What I'm doing here is making a business proposition to someone I have decided to trust. I get to do some judging too, you know."

"Of course you do, my Lord."

"I get the feeling I'm being patronized again."

"And you thought we were going to corrupt your daughter."

"So it serves me right, then?"

"I wouldn't presume to judge, my Lord."

"You know, I like it better when you forget to say 'my Lord.' Then I know I'm talking to the real Ecmund."

"And who else would you be talking to?"

"I don't know. I think it is a mask you put on, that looks exactly like what you want me to see. Then every once in a while, you let the mask slip, and the face behind it is laughing."

140

"You paint a very duplicitous picture, my Lord."

"There you go. Where did a woodcutter get a word like 'duplicitous'?"

"Now who's being patronizing? You think we don't educate our families?"

"There!" The Overlord pointed his finger at Ecmund. "That's you. No mask, no formality, straight lunge for the heart."

"I wouldn't have used that image to describe my action."

The Overlord shrugged. "I can't help but think of you in terms of swordplay. It's understandable."

"I can see that." Ecmund sat straighter, seemed about to speak, hesitated, licked his lips.

Now he loses his courage. Come on lad. Spit it out.

Ecmund laid a hand on his sword hilt.

"My Lord, do you want to see the real me? No mask, no smile, no sarcasm?"

"That might be interesting. How do I achieve that task?"

"Just watch this."

He stood and bowed formally. "My Lord, my I pay court to your daughter?"

The Overlord sat still, looking up at the young man before him.

Be strong. No wavering now. This is the hardest battle, when you must win against all odds.

"So this is the real you?"

"I'm afraid so, my Lord." He held out his right hand, which shook slightly. "Not exactly the hero you may have envisioned for her."

"Sit down, lad."

Ecmund sat.

"I told you long ago what I expect from my daughter."

"Yes, sir. You said she was to be your heir."

"That's right. Now, you tell me. How I am going to persuade the King to allow me to name a woman heir to this rugged outland demesne?"

"I suppose you'll have to persuade his majesty that she is the right person for the duty. Strong enough, clever enough, experienced enough..."

"...and preferably married to the right man."

"I see."

"I want you to understand that my choices are limited."

"And a woodcutter is not exactly the man to bolster her chances of success with the King."

"I didn't say that. There are other qualities to be considered. Strength, loyalty, intelligence. Maybe an intimate knowledge of this

141

rugged outland demesne and its people. Perhaps a hero of the Blood with a magic Sword."

"Huh! Sorry, my Lord. I don't fill most of that picture very well, either."

"That remains to be seen. Most important, it depends on how the King regards those of the Blood."

"And how does he regard us?"

"I don't know. I have never heard him say. It's rather strange, now I come to think of it. He seems to ignore the situation."

"At least he isn't against us."

"I would think not. However, maybe he thinks you have disappeared, as a factor in the political scene."

"That would not be so good."

"That's right. So, at the moment, I would like to ask that you refrain from paying court to my daughter."

He is afraid to say no!

"I don't understand, my Lord. You are asking me?"

"That's right. I am asking you not to discuss marriage with my daughter at this time. However, I am not asking you to stay out of her company. I know her well enough, and I think I know you as well, to guess what effect an absolute refusal would have.

"The situation is too uncertain. Conditions may arise where it would be a great disadvantage for you to marry, and I do not want my daughter to have to go through that agony. I am asking you to treat her with the same consideration."

Ecmund shook his head, smiling slightly. "And I am reminded that, in spite of the banter and the pretence, you are Lord of the Demesne, with the diplomatic skills to match. So, once again, I offer whatever I can to aid you in your rule here, including whatever it takes to keep your daughter happy and in charge of this demesne."

He laughed ruefully. "She seems to be angry at me half the time anyway."

"Who is angry at you?"

They both turned, to see Perica in the doorway.

"Those who listen around corners never hear good of themselves."

"Oh. You've been talking about me, then." She entered, posed herself precisely between them and raised her eyebrows. "Well?"

Her father grinned. "Well, what?"

"Well, I'm not listening around the corner. You can say something nice about me now."

"I don't think so. It's not good for your upbringing."

She turned her eyes to Ecmund. "Well, perhaps, since you're not so concerned with my upbringing…"

142

He laughed. "I'm concerned for my welfare. Anything I say, you'll probably take wrong, and then I'll be in trouble again."

"This is going to be a very boring conversation, if I have to say all the nice things about me. I think it's time to change the topic. What else were you talking about?"

"You're going to think it even more boring, my dear. Business."

"No, I'm interested. What sort of business are you thinking of going into?"

"I've been thinking of investing in Ecmund's wood business. Increase his yard size, hire a man or two."

"Nonsense. Oh, don't both of you look at me with your mouths open like fish. It's nonsense. You're thinking too small."

"Too small? What should we be thinking that would be on the right scale?"

"A mill, of course. As long as you have men sawing the lumber by hand, you're only going to be a little woodcutter, and you'll never make any real profits. Once you have a mill, you can use it to cut all the plain lumber you need for the local people. Then you have time to expand your markets to other towns."

"Actually, we were just discussing that. Problem is, I don't want to spend my time riding around to other towns, talking to people. I want to spend it in the woods, finding good trees. If you want to talk larger scale, I'd like to start some of my own plantations, so some day there will be more trees to cut. All sorts of different trees."

She laughed. "There you are. Now you're thinking properly. There's obviously more to the wood yard business than I know. You run the forest and the mill. We'll find someone else to sell your wood."

The Overlord slapped his hands on his knees. "Well, I'm glad we have that settled." He turned to his daughter. "Where did you learn all this?"

"Mother. She always said you thought too small."

"She did, and she had a good head for business, your mother." There was a brief silence, and Ecmund could feel their sadness.

Then the Overlord smiled. "So. We're building a mill. Where do we put it?"

Ecmund frowned thoughtfully. "The trick is to find a fast stream with enough quick drop that we don't have to build the entry flume too long. It would be nice if it was close to our main forests, so we don't have to move the logs too far. Easier to move cut lumber than logs."

"And you'll need oxen and wagons to move the logs, so you'll want some pasture land, and barns." Perica waved a hand airily.

"You really are thinking on a large scale, aren't you?"

143

"Well, we can't afford all those extras until we start bringing in profits. But you have to think of that in advance. Do you know of a place that is big enough?"

"I can think of several that might work. I'd have to look at them."

"Good. Come on, Father."

Delfontes held up a cautionary hand. "Let's not get carried away. I haven't time to go riding all over the countryside. You go see what you can find, and when you've decided, I'll come and look the site over."

"Fine. I'll go get my riding skirt on. Ecmund, ask the groom to saddle my horse. Tell him to check the blanket for burrs."

Her father laughed. "I suspect he'll be overly careful, dear. He was very upset about last time, in spite of the fact that there was no burr."

"I wasn't too happy about it myself, as I recall."

"Nor was I. Well, I'll leave you two to your business ventures. I have a demesne to tend."

Perica turned to Ecmund. "All right. You get the horses ready. I'll be down in a moment."

"Who are we taking with us?'

"I suppose we need protection, don't we? How sublime. Here I was picturing a pleasant ride through the peaceful countryside, and instead I get a mob of soldiers with their jingling harness and their bad jokes."

"We could probably keep the numbers down. Four?"

"Sounds perfect. Get some of the local men. They know the area. They might be able to contribute."

"And less likely to be on the side of our enemy."

"Unless we're wrong, and the enemy is local."

"Right. I'll choose the men carefully." He strode into the courtyard, pleasant expectation warring with caution in his mind.

If we take her out and get her into trouble...

My thoughts exactly.

Don't worry. I'll be watching.

So will I.

After giving Perica's message to the head groom, he went over to the barracks. Fortunately, some of the soldiers were lounging about, polishing their gear. He went inside and found the sergeant painstakingly adding up a column of figures.

"How would you like to get outside for a while on a fine summer day?"

The sergeant dropped his pencil. "On duty?"

"That's right. Lady Perica is riding out, and she needs an escort. Four men."

144

"That's not very many. I'm not going to lose her, and have to go through that again. The Overlord swore he'd demote me to kitchen navvy!"

"Well, she said four. Add you and me, that's six."

"I suppose."

"Local lads, if you don't mind. I'd like to take Eodborg and Heath. They're hanging around out there looking bored." The twins came from the next town along the river. Ecmund had spent some time with them before they joined the Overlord's Guard, because their father was the head of the carpentry guild.

"Fine with me. Pick them all yourself if you like."

"Thanks, Bacares." He turned and went out into the sunshine. "I need some lads with local knowledge. You two," he indicated the twins. "Hrethred, you up to a ride in the country? How about you, Filimeir? Bring your bows, you two."

The men he had named scrambled to put their work away, and followed the sergeant to the stables. Ecmund considered his troop. Not the best riders, of course. Men from this area generally walked. However, since most of the land was heavily wooded, half the fighting was done on the ground anyway. As much as you could predict. A couple of bowmen would be good insurance. After his lesson from Jesco, he was interested to see that each of the twins carried an axe at his belt. He would have to watch them, see if his cousin was right.

Carpenters and woodcutters.

Don't be snooty.

Me? I don't even have a snoot.

Ecmund cuffed the hilt of the Sword affectionately, and swung up on his horse.

Perica hurried across the courtyard, carrying a bulging saddlebag. When he started to dismount, she shook her head and tossed it up to him.

"Lunch."

"Enough for seven?"

"Just a light meal." She turned to her horse, and the groom helped her mount. "Where are we going?"

"I thought a mild canter through the Osterwald might be nice."

"Not funny." She scowled at him.

He laughed in response. "Truly, the Osterwald is too scrubby for logging, but farther east there's a nice stand of oak and elm. There's a stream that comes out of the hills there, and good pastureland in the valley bottom."

"Sounds right. Perhaps you'd better stay serious. It would be safer."

He tossed her a grin, and kicked his horse ahead. He could sense hidden smiles as he passed the soldiers, but he ignored them.

145

It was a pleasant morning, but as they neared the village, a single rider appeared.

Jesco. Angry.

"And I was hoping for a carefree, happy day." Ecmund trotted his horse ahead, so he would have a moment to deal with his cousin in private. "What's he angry about?"

Nothing. Everything. I don't understand.

"Nobody does. Sometimes he gets like that. We just stay out of his way until it leaves him."

Jesco wrenched the reins and spun his horse alongside. "So you're out riding with the Overlord's daughter, now."

Ecmund glanced down at his cousin, and Kitten could feel his mind tighten. "This is business, Jesco."

"Business, is it? And does a mere soldier get to know what business his family is embarking on?"

"Woodcutting business, Jesco. The business you sneer at so often."

The swordsman let out a harsh guffaw. "And you're going to persuade me that the little lady there is going into the woodcutting business with us?"

"With me, Jesco. Just with me. And it isn't Perica, it's her father. He's just too busy right now, so she's standing in. She is the heir, in case you had forgotten."

"How stupid do you think I am, kid? You're out taking a picnic with the Maridon lady, and I'm supposed to think it's business. That doesn't impress me, for a couple of reasons. First place, if you're getting into business with somebody, especially the Overlord, I would have thought it polite to let the family know. That's my father, the family head. Or me, his heir, in case you had forgotten. Second, if you're thinking of diluting the Blood any further, you ought to be letting us know even sooner, and I mean right now!"

Ecmund glanced back to ensure that their distance from Perica allowed him to speak forcibly. "Listen, head of the family, or whatever you call yourself. In case you had forgotten, I am fully grown, and I can make business, social, or marriage arrangements for myself. When it's time to inform the family, I will.

"Until that time, you are jumping to way too many conclusions. And I see you looking over your shoulder. If you're thinking of riding back there and taking this out on Perica, I will personally pull you off that horse, and use the flat of my Sword on your backside."

"You will what?" Jesco's hand went to his sword hilt.

Ecmund pushed his horse close to his cousin's, until their legs were crushed together. "Jesco, if I come after you, it will be with my bare hands, and you won't stand a chance. I don't know what sliver got into

146

your hide today, but you will not use it as an excuse to cause equal trouble for me. Ride away." He met his cousin's black stare with unyielding steel of his own. "Ride away now, Jesco. I mean it."

The swordsman glared up at his cousin, his chest heaving. With a sudden snarl, he yanked his horse's head around, jammed his spurs into its sides, and shot away up the road.

What got into him?

"Jesco doesn't need a reason."

What are you going to tell her?

He glanced back, to where Perica was regarding him with worried eyes.

"I make no excuses for Jesco."

Hmm.

He rode on, thinking furiously. What was he going to tell her?

There was a clattering of hooves, and she trotted up beside him. "What was that all about?"

He sighed. "With Cousin Jesco, there doesn't have to be much."

"I see."

They rode in silence for a while.

"But...?"

He frowned down at her. "But what?"

"But this time there was something, or you wouldn't be so upset. I heard most of it, Ecmund. You weren't exactly quiet."

"Then you know what it's about."

"Not really." She rode beside him for a while longer. "Ecmund, if it was none of my business, I wouldn't push, but I heard myself mentioned too often. What is his problem with me?"

"It's not you. It's me he has the problem with."

"What do you mean? What do you have to do with it?"

He sighed. "He's decided that I'm going to dilute the Blood."

"What?"

"You asked. I answered."

"Dilute...?"

He merely held up his hands, helplessly.

My, aren't we having fun, now.

You stay out of this!

Certainly. I could hardly make it worse.

"So I'm not the only one with prejudices."

"No, you aren't."

"I suppose that should be a consolation. It isn't."

He sighed again. "Look, Perica, Jesco is an idiot. He's my cousin, and I love him, and I know what he's been through, but the fact remains. Sometimes he's an idiot."

147

"And by implication, then, so am I."

"Are you planning to start up where he left off?"

She grinned impishly. "Considering what just happened to Jesco, I don't think that would be a good idea."

Where did that come from?

"I don't either." His head snapped around. "Were you just making fun of me?"

She held up both hands. "No, Ecmund, I wasn't. I just decided I didn't want to fight. It's too nice a day, and we have business planned."

He shook his head. "Well, it's good to know someone is adult and reasonable around here."

She laughed. "Would you really grab him out of the saddle and paddle him with your Sword if he insulted me?" She glanced back at the rest of the party, suddenly reached out and touched the Sword's hilt. "What do you think of that, Kitten?"

I will not be used in such a manner!

Again she laughed. "There you go, Ecmund. Your chivalrous gesture denied by your own Sword."

His voice dropped to a growl, but there was no heart in it. "Keep your hands to yourself."

"What are you going to do? Paddle me as well?"

"The thought has a certain appeal." He flicked the reins, and his horse sidestepped out of her reach. "And you will not use my own Sword against me."

She rested her hands complacently on her saddlebow. "I'm glad we have that straight. Shall we look for mill sites, now?"

"We won't be near for another mile or so."

She glanced up at him. "Are you going to pout?"

Careful, Ecmund. She's doing it again.

You don't need to tell me.

"Why don't I give you an idea of the kind of terrain we need? See that hillside over there? That small bit of bench land would be just right. Of course, there's no stream near, but it shows you what we're looking for."

He continued to talk, ignoring her look, and soon she became interested in what he was saying.

Nicely done, Ecmund.

I thought so. I'm not a complete rube, you know.

I know that, Ecmund.

Thank you so much.

It is a Sword's duty to support the Hand.

You are telling me that you support me, in spite of the fact that I am wrong? Thanks a lot.

148

"Ecmund?"

"Oh, sorry. I was just talking to Kitten."

"I know. I can tell when you get that look. What were you talking about?"

"Um…we were just checking the area for danger."

"And is there any?"

No.

"Nothing obvious."

She glanced at him with narrowed eyes, but made no further comment.

The rest of the day went along similar lines. They spoke in a businesslike fashion, but sometimes strayed into personal chat, and always there was a feeling of tension between them, as if someone might say the wrong thing at any moment. They found several sites to consider, and when he dropped the troop off at the castle, late in the afternoon, there was satisfaction on both sides. Sort of.

"What do you think, Ecmund? Did we make any progress?"

He shrugged. "Every site we saw had its good and bad points. I didn't expect to find the right one immediately."

"So we can't make a decision yet."

"I wouldn't dream of it. With the available sites in mind, I'd like to lay out the type of operation we want to run. Then we go back out and see which sites suit that operation. Then we go back to the plan and adapt the operation to the sites that work best."

"A slow process," she nodded. "But gradually the pieces fit into each other."

He grinned. "Spoken like a true woodworker."

She flicked her fingers at him. "Flatterer!"

"I'm glad you took it as a compliment."

"Oh. I'm sorry. Wasn't it?"

"Your choice, my Lady."

She tossed her hair back. "I'll take it as such. It keeps you alive another day."

"Thank you, my Lady."

"Oh, that reminds me. There's one more thing. My father has decided to reward you for your valiant work against the forest fire."

"That's not necessary, Perica, you know that. I was only doing my duty, just as all the other men were."

"Nonetheless. Come with me."

He began to protest again, but she ignored him, handing over her horse to the groom, and marching away towards the castle.

Oh, go along with her for once.

149

But it isn't right, Kitten. Most of what I did was because of you. What are you going to get out of this?

All sorts of wonderful emotion, if you keep fighting about it.

You make your point.

Ha, ha.

I didn't mean it that way.

I know. Your disgust at yourself makes it much funnier.

Perica crossed towards the main hall, but turned through another, smaller, archway. Puzzled, Ecmund followed her and found himself in the storage rooms behind the kitchen. Approaching a nondescript door, she pulled out a set of keys and opened it.

The castle's linen and clothing storage: an airy room, with cupboards of folded cloth, racks of assorted clothing, new and used. Perica went straight to a package on the central table, opened it. "What do you think?"

He glanced inside, looked again. "It's beautiful cloth."

"Right. And my father is giving it to you. Isn't that nice of him?"

Cloth?

"Oh. The Ceremony."

What?

"So take it."

He smiled. "Of course. Thank your father for me. Very much."

She glanced up at him as she passed him the package. "You aren't as dull-witted as you look, sometimes."

"I'm certainly glad of that."

What is going on?

They retraced their path through the castle, and she walked him to the gate. "She might want to come and talk to me about it."

"I imagine she will. Next time I come up to discuss business, maybe. Thanks again."

She? Who are you talking about? Eirlin?

Ecmund strode merrily down the hill, the cloth package slung over his shoulder.

"That's right. Eirlin. You know, you aren't as dull-witted as you look, sometimes."

I still don't know what's going on.

"Then watch and learn, my sharp-witted friend."

When he reached the cottage, Eirlin was out. He looked around, dropped the package on the table, considered it briefly, turned it, regarded it again. Then he opened the wrapping and unfolded one small corner of deep blue cloth. A warm sense of satisfaction washed through him.

Ignoring the table, he went about his usual evening routine. He was outside at the pump when he heard the door close. Grinning to himself, he continued to wash.

"Ecmund!"

"Out here."

She appeared at the door. The parcel was further unwrapped and hanging over her arm. "What is this?"

"Do you like it?"

"Do I like it? It's beautiful. Why is it here?"

"Fine. I thought it would look good on you. Not that I chose it, or anything."

She marched across the yard, grabbed him by the arm, and dragged him into the house. She shoved him into his chair, slapped the parcel on the table in front of him. "Now, no more playing around, Ecmund Liutswin. What is a piece of beautiful cloth like this doing on the table in a woodcutter's cottage? You haven't done anything stupid, have you?"

He sighed. "Yes, Eirlin, I did. I risked my life and limb to stop a forest fire that could have destroyed a lot of wood."

"Forest fire."

"That's right. And Lord Delfontes decided to reward me for my acts of daring and bravery."

"And...?"

"And he's a very smart person. Or Perica is, or both of them. He knew I'd never take anything, and he knew you'd never take the present of a bolt of cloth..."

She shook her head. "It had to be Perica. She is just too sly for words."

What? What is going on?

He shrugged. "I guess they want to make sure their new allies make an appropriate showing at the Swearing In Ceremony."

Oh. The Ceremony.

"But Ecmund, I can't show up wearing something like this!"

"I don't really think you have a choice. If you don't wear it, you will be insulting them."

She glared at him. "You did this on purpose, didn't you?"

"No. Perica did it on purpose. I just let her."

She sighed, fingered the cloth. "It's really very beautiful."

"She said you might like to talk to her about styles."

"Of course. When are you going back up there?"

"In a few days. I have to do some work, you know. I spent all day today on frivolities."

151

"Ecmund, you are being impossible on purpose. You know the Ceremony is coming up soon. If I have to sew a dress, I have to get started right away. Maybe Wynna would…"

Suddenly she stopped, looked at him. "What were you doing today?"

"Nothing too important. I just asked Lord Delfontes for permission to court his daughter, and he offered to go into business with me, and we spent the rest of the day looking for a good mill site."

She sat back, arms folded. "I know you too well, Ecmund. You aren't joking about any of that, are you?"

"No."

Her eyes opened wide, and she leaned forward. "Well?

"He said he would be interested in investing in a mill. I will provide the timber and run the mill. He, or more likely Perica, will find someone to market the lumber in Koningsholm, and wherever else it might sell."

She smiled sweetly. "That's very good, Ecmund. Now answer the real question, or I am going to take the Kitten out and sharpen her claws on your face."

"Such a temper for a Healer."

"So what did he say?"

He shrugged. "It went better than I expected. He didn't say no."

"But…?"

"Well, he asked me not to."

"That was strange."

"I think he's a little leery about saying 'no' to his daughter. He was very diplomatic about it. He showed me how it might be to her great disadvantage to be married to me."

"And you believed him?"

"Of course. It could be true."

"So you're not going to woo her."

"I'm not. I'm just going to go about my life like normal."

She grinned. "And if Perica happens to be around?"

"I could scarcely avoid her, could I? It would be rude."

"You know, Ecmund, you are a very devious person."

"I am not, but I am dealing with devious persons, and I can't help it if their plans work in my direction."

And then we will win honour and glory, and all will be well.

Eirlin laughed. "Kitten's answer to all difficulties."

"In this case, I have a feeling that it would be the best solution."

"Then do it. And we're going up to the castle tomorrow."

"Fine. Later on in the afternoon. I have to reset that saw. The lads say it was binding. That slows them down."

"Late afternoon, then."

152

Chapter 18

It was a pleasant evening, if a bit warm, and Ecmund and Eirlin had decided to eat supper out the back. She had created a small garden to the left of the door, separated from the wood yard by a screen that Ecmund had formed with woven wood strips. Ecmund was now used to having Kitten at his side, so she was leaning against the table, revelling in the warm affection between the two siblings.

This is nice.

Ecmund laughed. "Did you get that, Eirlin?"

"No. I knew she was speaking, but I don't hear what she says unless I'm touching her, or she really shouts."

"She likes this."

"What? A great, glory-driven Sword, and she enjoys a quiet evening at home?"

I wish to speak to her.

Ecmund raised his eyebrows. "Kitten wants to speak to you."

"Hand her over, then."

"What, draw my Sword and destroy such a pleasant scene?"

"Ecmund, shut up and give me the Sword."

Don't spoil the feeling, Ecmund.

"All right, all right. I'm definitely outnumbered."

"Don't sound so hard done by." Eirlin took the Sword from him, but left her in her scabbard. "What is it, Kitten?"

You need to learn about Swords, Eirlin.

"A lesson? And I was just twitting Ecmund for breaking the mood."

Shut up and listen, Eirlin.

She looked at her brother. "Are you getting this? Did you hear the rudeness?"

"She does what she learns."

"All right, all right. What is the lesson I must learn?"

It is for Ecmund as well. You must learn what a Sword wants.

"That's a good idea, Kitten. Lord Delfontes was telling me the same thing the other day."

He knows what is important.

"I'm glad you approve of your Overlord."

He is not my Overlord. No man is my master.

"What? I thought I was."

As you dream.

"I don't understand. If I am not your master, what am I?"

You are the Hand. The Hand that wields the Sword.

"Do I have any choice?"

Of course.

153

"You mean I could just toss you away, if I wanted?

How do you think I ended up in the swamp?

"You mean Jesco was right? You were left in a swamp?"

I like to think it lends a patina of depth to my finish.

"I wouldn't argue with that. I think you look beautiful."

"Someone tossed you in a swamp? That was horrible."

It was my fault. I tested him beyond his limits.

"Kitten! I can't believe it."

I was very young. I made a mistake.

"How long ago was that?"

Last summer.

"And you are older now?"

I am expert at feelings, Ecmund. I understand sarcasm far better than you.

"Sorry. Would you please return to the lesson?"

With pleasure. What does a Sword want? Emotion."

"That's it? Emotion?"

Don't make it sound so simple. What do humans want? Emotion. The only difference is that humans want to choose the emotions. Most of them want love and affection, and don't want fear and hate.

"But Swords don't care."

Swords don't care as much. We enjoy emotion. We feed from it, store its power inside us. If you were to put me on a wall somewhere, with a dull family who didn't love each other very much, but didn't care about it very much, and never fought or argued either, I would be very bored.

"Ecmund, did you understand that?"

"Not all of it, but I got a picture of an absolutely terrible life, that I wouldn't want to live at all."

My speaking improves.

"Don't sound smug. You have a long way to go, if you want to communicate actual words all the time."

Yes, Ecmund, you are right.

"So you thrive on emotion. What do you like about this scene? I would think you would find it boring. There is nothing happening, no strong feelings, no excitement."

Speak to him, Eirlin. It is beyond my ability to explain.

Eirlin laughed out loud at the expression on her brother's face. "I think you have just been put very firmly in your place, Ecmund!"

"I am going to duck out of this argument, just in case Kitten has created it on purpose, in order to feed her desires."

That is unworthy of you, Ecmund. How could you say such a thing about me?

154

"I was only joking, Kitten. I know you would never do such a thing."

Are you sure?

"Kitten!"

I'm sorry. You know I would never do that.

"Good."

"Have you noticed, Eirlin? Her sense of humour is changing."

"Yes. It has definitely developed an edge."

"Eirlin, don't do that!"

A fine example you set me.

"I didn't know a Sword could chuckle. Now, what were we talking about?"

I think I was trying to say that Swords enjoy emotion. Any emotion. It is quite a surprise to me as well that the emotion of this scene is satisfying.

"It is?"

Very much so.

Ecmund looked over at his sister, eyebrows raised. "I guess we'll have to see that she gets much more of it."

And we will win honour and glory, and that is even more satisfying.

He reached out, took the hilt in his hand. "What's this about honour and glory?"

I didn't tell you the other part.

"What part is that?"

The honour and glory part.

"I rather thought it might be."

Oops.

"Well? What about the honour and glory?"

I'm not supposed to tell you that part.

"Aha! You're not supposed to tell me, but you did. So now you have to tell me. It's too late."

Is it?

Eirlin waved her hand in front of his face. "What's going on, Ecmund? I'm getting feelings of distress from Kitten, and I'm not even touching her."

"Quiet, Eirlin. I'm finally getting some information."

"I will not be quiet, Ecmund. If Kitten is upset because of what you're saying to her, then you'd better stop immediately!"

Yes. You'd better stop immediately!

He sat back, ran his hands through his hair, interlocked his fingers behind his head and regarded the two of them: first the Sword in his lap, then his sister, then back to the Sword again. He sighed.

"As usual, I'm outnumbered. All right. I agree. If it bothers you, Kitten, don't tell me. But don't you see how difficult it is, dealing with a magic Sword, and having no information? Anything you can tell me will help. I only want what's best for you."

"Ecmund, I am disgusted!"

"What?"

"Saying, 'I only want what's best for you'. What a load of horse manure. People who say that sort of thing always mean, 'what's best for me.' Don't you listen to him, Kitten."

Oh.

"Now it's what you said that upset her."

"Nonsense. It's what you did. If she wants to tell us, she'll tell us. If not, maybe it's best that she doesn't."

I think… I think, maybe… I don't know!

Ecmund drew her from her sheath, and laid her on the table in front of him. "Eirlin, will you listen to this? I'm feeling a lot of emotion, and I can't understand it at all."

His sister moved over, sat beside him, and put her hand on the Sword's hilt.

"What's wrong, Kitten?"

I can't decide.

"That happens to all of us. What can't you decide?"

I don't know what to do!

Eirlin stroked the pommel gently. "Don't worry so much. You have time to decide. No one," she shot a frown at her brother, "is forcing you."

I know that. But it might be better if I told you.

"We don't understand, Kitten, because we don't know much about you. What is the conflict? What stops you from telling us things?"

It's hard for me to tell you. There are rules.

"Rules? Good. I like rules. Once I know the rules, I can…"

"…you can break them. I know you, Ecmund, and now is not the time."

"All right. I know when to shut up."

"Tell me about the rules, Kitten. Anything you can. Where do these rules come from?"

It's rather misty, Eirlin. I don't remember where they came from, but sometimes, something just says, 'Don't do that. That is wrong.' Then I know it's a rule.

"That's pretty simple. Humans have the same system."

They do?

"Yes. It's called a conscience. Sometimes we just know that something is wrong, and then we don't do it. If your conscience tells you that you are not supposed to tell us something, then you don't. We won't mind. Anyone with the art to create a magic Sword is smart enough to make some rules that will help her to survive and serve. I don't think I'm smart enough to go against those rules. Or maybe stupid enough."

It isn't that simple.

Ecmund laughed. "It rarely is. What's wrong with what Eirlin said?"

Well... some of the rules are like that. You know something is wrong, so you don't do it. But some are not that firm. You get a feeling like it isn't quite right. Not completely wrong, just not completely right.

Eirlin nodded. "I think I understand what you just said. People have the same problem. Sometimes you have to make up your own mind."

You do?

"Yes."

And it isn't wrong?

"No. Those are the times we find out what kind of people we really are."

Oh, good.

Eirlin frowned. "Why don't I like the sound of this?"

"Why is that good, Kitten?"

Because it means I can choose to tell you or not.

"That's right. But it also means that you have to think about it carefully, because you don't want to make a mistake."

That's all right. I know it's not a mistake. I'm going to tell you.

"Not yet, Kitten. I have to talk to Ecmund."

All right.

Eirlin took her hand off the hilt and looked her brother in the eye. "Ecmund, I don't like this."

"Why not? You've just persuaded all of us that sometimes we have to make up our own minds, and now Kitten has made up her mind. What's wrong with that?"

"I don't know. It just suddenly becomes too easy."

Eirlin.

Eirlin put her hand back on the hilt. "Yes, Kitten?"

It's all right, Eirlin. I am able to make up my own mind.

Eirlin winced. "Of course you are. I'm sorry if I sounded as if I thought you couldn't."

That's all right. I have lived many years, and I have known many people. I have experience, but sometimes I think it is not of the sort that helps.

Ecmund sighed. "I know what you mean. Happens to me all the time."

I can make decisions. I just want to be sure they are the right ones.

"And who can tell, in the end, what is right, and what is wrong?"

Exactly. And now I have decided to tell you about honour and glory.

"All right. What do Swords have to do with honour and glory?"

157

It is hard to put into words.

"That's fine. Just send it in any way you can."

Are you sure?

"Of course."

All right. This is what matters to me.

I want, I dearly wish, I desire, to feel that I have done something that is magnificent superb breathtaking name wonderful splendid glorious brilliant name love adulation glory splendour beauty grandeur BrillianceWonderNameWorship Adulation Acceptance Breathtaking NameAMAZING ASTONISHINGNAMEBRILLIANT...

"All right, Kitten. All right. ALL RIGHT, WE UNDERSTAND, YOU CAN STOP NOW!" He was rubbing his temples. Eirlin was shaking her hand as if it had been burned.

Oh. Sorry.

"No, that's fine." He patted her blade. "We understand."

You do?

"Of course. We all feel that way."

You do?

"Certainly. Of course, not everyone gets a chance to achieve those goals, but we would all like to try."

Everyone feels like that? All humans?

"That's right. Well, maybe not all. Most do, I think."

Then why shouldn't I tell you that I feel that way?"

"I don't know."

Eirlin nodded slowly. "I do."

You do?

"You do?"

"Of course." Eirlin shook her head, slowly. "You can't let everyone know what your dearest wish is. If you do, they can use that to manipulate you."

Manipulate?I know that word. Isn't that what the Hand is supposed to do?"

"No, Kitten. The Hand is supposed to manipulate the Sword in battle. Not twist its purposes around for his own selfish ends."

Oh, no, Eirlin. My Hand would never do that!

"Kitten, do you really think that?"

Of course! Kitten had a sudden thought. *Well, maybe not all of them.*

"Kitten, you must have had many Hands. Were they all like Ecmund?"

Of course not! Ecmund is special. Ecmund is wonderful!

"And, before Ecmund's smile breaks his face in half, that's how you feel about your Hand every time, isn't it?"

Well, sort of.

158

"I thought so." Eirlin's brow furrowed. "So what you are telling us is that a Sword thrives on emotion, but the emotions caused by the recognition of wonderful deeds are best?"

I think so.

Eirlin turned to her brother. "That doesn't seem to be a problem, since most people feel the same way. There is no chance we would use that against you, so you don't need to worry that it was wrong to tell us."

That is very good.

"There is one more thing."

Yes, Ecmund?

"The name."

What about the name?

"What about the name? Come on, there was something about a name, all twisted in with those other ideas. What is it?"

Well...

"You want a name?"

Well...

"That's it? You just want a name?"

Just! I JUST want a Name? A Name is the most important thing a Sword can have. Can you imagine what it would be like to be called Human all the time? To be in the middle of a whole bunch of humans, and for that to be your only name?

"I can see this means a lot to you."

YES.

Ecmund shrugged. "You don't have to shout. What kind of name do you want?"

I... thought of something that would remind people of my accomplishments. Something like... Oh, I thought 'Peace Bringer', or 'Equalizer', or... I don't know. You don't get to give yourself a name. People give it to you.

"And here we are, calling you 'Kitten'. Oh, Kitten, I'm so sorry. I mean, Sword, I'm so..."

No, Ecmund.

"No?"

No. Do you know how stupid it sounds, you calling me 'Sword'? I don't mind if you have your own private name for me. It's almost necessary now, since there are several people who know me. That has never happened before, but it seems important that you have a name to call me, when you are talking to one another. You can keep calling me Kitten.

"Did you understand that, Eirlin?"

"Not most of it. I get the impression she thinks that we have to call her something, so 'Kitten' is as good a name as any other."

Ecmund passed a hand over her hilt. "We can? You don't mind?"

His sister did the same. "I'm...used to it. I can't see calling you anything else."

Yes, Eirlin. The way you say it, I don't mind at all. It gives me the feelings we were talking about at first. Do me a favour though?

"Of course."

Don't... tell everyone. Then maybe, some day, if people don't know my name, and if Ecmund and I have done wonderful deeds, then maybe..."

"Then they'll give you a Name that reflects your true worth! That would be wonderful, Kitten! Of course we can do that."

"It's the least we can do, after all the help you've given us."

Thank you.

Ecmund picked her up and returned her to her sheath. "I'm glad we have that settled. Now can we worry about what Lord Delfontes wants me for, tomorrow?"

Whatever it is, we will do it.

"I envy your confidence."

"Oh, Ecmund, give up the false modesty. You will always do your best, and no one can ask for more."

"Come and remind me of that the next time I can't make up my mind what to do!"

We will do marvellous deeds.

"How can I argue with that?"

"You can't. Let's go inside. I'll clean up tonight."

"I'll just check around, first."

"Good idea." She turned back from the door. "Do you think there will ever come a time when we don't have to do that? When we don't have to worry about violence and attacks and horrible people?"

Once I have my Name, they will all be afraid to come anywhere near!

Ecmund grinned. "I don't think she quite sees the picture."

Eirlin shook her head and patted Kitten's hilt as Ecmund passed. "I don't think we're ever going to see the same picture on this one."

Why not?

"Because you are a weapon, my dear, and I am a Healer. You make wounds, I Heal them."

Does that mean we must be enemies? I don't want to be your enemy.

"Of course not. It is only that we have different ways of achieving the same goal."

That is good... ?

"Yes, it is."

That's good, then.

160

Chapter 19

Perica dashed down the lace collar she was sewing. "Ecmund, you are being so boring. Why do you keep going on about this Magician? My Father and I have made a successful start in this demesne. A great deal of thanks due to you and Eirlin, of course. We have a wonderful ceremony to plan, and you sound like an echo in a long canyon. 'Magician, Magician, Magician,' over and over."

Ecmund shook his head. "Perica, you have to realize the potential for misuse of the powers of the Blood."

"Misuse? He hasn't even done anything yet that we can prove."

"Not that we can tell. But remember that the people of Inderjorne are no different from any other. We have our good individuals and our bad ones. Some of us are so bad as to be termed evil. You are beginning to understand the powers of a Magician. Can you imagine someone with those powers, turning them to evil purposes?"

"It could be very nasty, I admit, but you must have ways of controlling people like that."

"You can't control them. They are too powerful. You can only prevent them from happening."

"That sounds more difficult."

"That's why we have such a strong tradition of lore and learning. All our children are trained from early childhood. The stronger their powers, the longer the training."

"But I have seen no schools here. I was quite surprised at how many people seem to be able to read and write."

He shrugged. "We don't have schools, but believe me, the training is there. Each family is responsible for its own, and those who need help always get it. They must, for our own safety."

"You people work very strangely."

"We don't think so."

"No, I don't suppose you do. But what do you do if a Magician turns evil, in spite of all your training?"

"It hasn't happened." He pursed his lips, looking upward in thought. "Not that we know of for sure."

"However...?"

"Well, there is the legend of the Mage of Weillen."

She raised her eyebrows, settled herself more comfortably. He had no choice but to begin.

"There is a story of a man who was evil. The legend says he had lived near the village of Weillen all his life, and everyone knew he was a bit different, but he never did anything openly harmful.

"Then there began to be a problem with the children of the village. Strange behaviour: fear, night terrors, violent acts. No one could understand it. Seemingly normal, sweet, children were caught torturing small animals, hurting each other for joy. The people of the village were at their wits' end. They kept their children close, and tried to deal with these horrible abnormalities.

"Fortunately, their Overlord, or Thane as we were called then, was a man strong in the Power of the Blood, and he came to their aid. It took a great deal of care and subterfuge, because the evil one was canny, but finally the Thane found him out. He had been using his powers to bring the children to him, performing unspeakable acts on them, then using his powers again to keep them from revealing him."

Perica's face blanched. "That was terrible. What did they do to him?"

"Well, that was the trouble. The Thane discovered him, but also discovered his powers, which were considerable. No one dared go near his house, for fear of falling under his influence.

"So they devised a guard, stationed around his house, half a bow-shot away. Outside that was another guard, set to watch the watchers. Any strange activity on the part of the inner guard, and they were to be shot immediately."

"Shot? Their own guards?"

"They were very frightened people, and with good cause. He had lived with them for years. What if he had affected their minds as well?"

"Why didn't they just kill him?"

"I'm not really sure. There was a lot of superstition involved, as well as the real danger. I think they believed that the man who killed him might be possessed by his spirit."

"But that's just superstition."

"Perhaps, but imagine it. You catch the Magician. You take your sword, you run him through. You turn the body over...and you've killed your brother, because the Magician hazed your mind."

"Could a Magician do that?"

"There have been plenty of men killed by mistake due to haste, anger, and prejudice. Who needs a Magician?"

"So what did they do to him in the end?"

"They called in another Thane, who had never been to the village, so they knew the Magician could not have influenced him. He and his men rushed the Magician's cottage and knocked him unconscious. Then they took him to a secluded spot in the mountains, a deep gorge with only one exit. They tied him to a tree, and tumbled rocks into the opening, so no one could get to him and set him free."

"Then what?"

"Nothing. They left him there."

162

"They just left him there?"

"It seemed a logical solution. They couldn't kill him, but they could let him die."

She shuddered. "What a horrible death."

"He was a horrible man. At least, so the legend says. We have no way of knowing if it is true."

She looked up at him, her eyes wide. "But it serves its purpose, doesn't it?"

"In this case, I believe it has. You now understand why we are not happy at the thought of a Magician, operating hidden in our midst."

"So what do we do?"

Ecmund shrugged. "I think we need to plan your Ceremony."

"Are you mocking me?"

"No, Perica. You just gave me an idea. We need to talk to your father. Can you persuade him how important this is?"

She set her sewing aside grimly. "Don't worry. He'll listen."

It was a serious meeting in the Overlord's private chambers, a few days before the Swearing In Ceremony: the Overlord, his daughter, Ecmund, and Eirlin.

And a Sword.

"Yes, we can't forget you, Kitten. You're the important one, today."

I am?

"You are. We are trying to figure out how to expose the Magician, and you are the one who is going to do it."

Of course I am. How am I going to do it?

"That's what we're trying to decide." Ecmund turned to the Overlord. "What do you have in mind, my Lord?"

Delfontes shrugged. "You're asking the wrong man. You are the ones who understand what is going on. You decide what you want done, and I will make it happen. I have made sure that all the possible culprits are out of the castle today, so that we can have this meeting. From here on, it is up to you three."

"That puts you in charge, Ecmund."

He shot a glance at Perica. "As if there were a chance."

"Ecmund, be serious. What do you need? How can we be sure we have the right man, without exposing Kitten?"

"I guess it's a matter of narrowing down the list. For example, I should check, right now, to see that he isn't still in the castle."

"Is he?"

"Kitten?"

She cast her senses out, slowly and carefully, ready to pull back at any touch of another probe.

There is no Magician in the castle. Someone in the kitchen has an open mind.

"She says someone in the kitchen is of the Blood. No one else."

Eirlin thought a moment. "That would be Haragund, the second cook."

"Not Magician capability?"

"Not likely. I've known him all my life."

"That narrows it down."

Ecmund nodded. "There are only five of your retainers who might be the Magician. Tyrbrand Ostersund tops my list."

"Mine, too." Perica made a moue of disgust.

"What's the problem?"

"I don't like the way he looks at me. As if there is something he wants to know." She tilted her head up. "I just look down my nose at him."

The Overlord shook his head. "I'm sure that keeps him in his place. But it doesn't make him the Magician." He glanced at Eirlin.

"I have no idea, my Lord. Without Kitten's help, I would have to touch him to get any idea at all."

"We'll try not to have that happen."

Eirlin grinned. "I don't know. He's kind of handsome."

"Eirlin! How could you say that?"

She threw her hands out helplessly. "I don't know, Ecmund. We have our whole plan based on the idea that the Magician is our enemy. What if he isn't? You're hiding Kitten's power, and you think you have good reasons. What if he has good reason to hide his power? What if the King hates Magicians?"

"We have no evidence of that."

"It was just an example. I'm just saying we shouldn't let our suspicion of Lord Ostersund and the Magician close our eyes to other possibilities."

Eirlin, I don't think those are possibilities we should be thinking of right now."

A faint touch of red suffused the Healer's cheek.

Lord Delfontes nodded. "Well spoken. We must keep open minds. However, we all agree that finding this Magician is a good move, and that is what we are planning today."

"And I got us off our topic." Eirlin nodded to Delfontes. "I'm sorry, my Lord."

He smiled. "Don't apologize to me. I'm just listening to this meeting."

"Long years of experience have taught me never to apologize to my brother, so let us go on with the plan."

Forced into a more serious mood, Ecmund tapped his fingertips together, then dropped his left hand to Kitten's hilt. "Our problem is to get the Magician alone, but too busy with what he is doing to notice Kitten scanning him. Our plan is to use the ceremony. We think that when a man is giving his oath, he will be too involved to notice Kitten probing him."

"That is all? Then what do you need from me?"

"Just that you make sure each of those five men stays with you long enough, and has his attention on you firmly enough."

"How long is that?"

"I have never seen a Swearing In, my Lord. How long does it take for each individual to speak his oath?"

The Overlord raised his hand, then mouthed the words of the Oath. When he finished, he dropped his hand. "That long."

"Kitten?"

That might be long enough, since I dare not go far in.

"Is there any way to extend it?"

Delfontes considered. "I usually make one comment to each man. I try to make it personal, so he knows that I know who he is."

Perica smiled. "Ask each one what his desired position in your demesne will be. One that is honestly here for duty will be intent on his desires. One who isn't will be intent on his lies."

"My daughter's expensive tutoring becomes more and more worthwhile."

"I actually got that from a romance I read when I was thirteen."

"Part of your education as well, my dear."

Ecmund glanced at each of them. "Is that it? Any other ideas?"

Lord Delfontes rubbed his hands along his thighs. "I am looking forward to solving this problem. It has been nagging at me too long. Ecmund, I gather the ladies have plans to discuss. Will you walk with me?"

Perica stood. "Yes, we have important things to deal with." She took the taller girl's arm. "Especially our friend's opinion of a certain Lord Tyrbrand Ostersund."

The two left, their argument already beginning. The Overlord shook his head and made for the opposite door.

Ecmund?

Yes, Kitten?

Could I go with Eirlin?

Go with her? We can't. Lord Delfontes has asked me to walk with him. Why do you want to go with her?

I want to hear what they are saying.

About Lord Ostersund?

165

Why are you laughing?

Listen, my friend. You are a Sword. We may call you 'she', but you are still a Sword, and I am your Hand. When the women start talking about other men, we want to be as far away as possible.

Why is that?

Because we might hear all sorts of things we would rather not.

Oh. What sorts of things?

I'm not actually sure. Probably the kind of things they say about us.

They will only say wonderful things about us. They love us.

Which just tells us how much you know about women.

Danger. Lord Ostersund.

Ecmund's eyes flicked both ways. There was no one in sight, but a moment later, Ostersund turned the corner ahead of them, his expression brightening as he saw them.

"Lord Delfontes. I have been looking for you."

"I thought you were hunting."

"My horse turned up lame, so I came back."

I wonder.

Yes, convenient, isn't it?

"You have found me."

"I was wondering if I might have a word."

Delfontes glanced at Ecmund then back to the other lord. "In private?"

Ostersund smiled briefly. "If Ecmund wouldn't mind. It won't take a moment."

Ecmund bowed slightly. "I can amuse myself with the scenery."

"Thank you."

He walked towards the window, and the two other men turned slightly aside.

?

Nothing.

Nothing at all?

Just the usual. He seems as powerful as you, not much more.

True to his word, the lord finished what he had to say, saluted Ecmund with one finger to his hat, and strode away. Delfontes joined the younger man, his lip twisted in a wry grin.

"So much for our plan."

"What is the problem?"

"Lord Ostersund informs me that because of 'conflicting loyalties' he does not find it appropriate that he swear fealty to me."

"So he won't be there at the ceremony."

"He'll be there, but you won't get your chance with his undivided attention."

166

"Oh, well. At least we can check all the others. If they are all clear, that leaves him, doesn't it?"

"I suppose."

"You don't think he knew, somehow?"

"I don't see how. He seemed very straightforward about the whole thing. When I reminded him that this would make it difficult for me to find him a position in my demesne, he assured me that he knew this, and that I had his undivided support, nevertheless."

"How can he give you his undivided support, when he has conflicting loyalties?"

"I'm thinking about that. The only way that can happen is if his other loyalty is to someone above me in the ranks."

"But the only one above an Overlord is the King."

"Precisely."

"Do you think he meant you to figure that out?"

"I don't know. I wish I knew what was going on in that blond head."

"So do I. Kitten got nothing from him. As usual. She admitted that he seemed a bit more powerful than me, which is something."

"It is?"

"Oh, yes. She is loyal to a fault. To concede that someone else is better means that he is quite a bit better."

Never!

"Kitten, you have to learn to be more precise. You can't let your emotions spoil your value."

I am a Sword. Emotions have no power over me.

That's something else you need to work on.

He turned to the Overlord. "Could we go down to the hall, and look at the way the ceremony will be set up? Kitten can sense the direction a thought is coming from, so I would like to stand in the place of best advantage."

They entered the main hall of the castle, where the servants were hanging bunting from the minstrels' balcony and giving the stone of the fireplace a polish.

"I sit in my usual chair, there. Everyone who is pledging stands down here, to my left. Families and others sit in the chairs and benches at the centre. As the ceremony starts, I stand. Each noble comes forward, says his oath facing me, his back to everyone else. Once I have given my acceptance, he goes down the other side of the dais, to my right, and back to his place."

Ecmund looked around. "I only need a spot where I have a clear line of sight, where nobody can get in my way." Suddenly he slapped his leg. "No, there's another problem. Lord Ostersund."

"Why is that?"

"If he is the Magician, he will be able to read Kitten when she probes the others," Ecmund paced around, sizing up angles, "unless the others are directly between us, of course. Then he won't be able to tell where the probe is coming from."

"So you need to be standing directly opposite him, with me between you."

"Can you arrange that?"

"Easily. He is not swearing, so I can ask him to be part of my honour guard. I will place him as far as I can to my right. You will not be swearing, so I will assign you the role of signalling each lord when he will proceed, which puts you as far as I can get you to my left."

"You can give me a role in the ceremony?"

"We don't want to draw too much attention to you. It's a minor role, but puts you close at hand. If anyone asks, which no one will dare, it's because you know everyone." He spun to face Ecmund, as a thought struck him. "You know everyone, and you know all the ranks, don't you? You know the precedences."

Ecmund shrugged. "In general. Everyone of the Blood of Inderjorne has some idea of our order. There are only a few of your Maridon retainers to fit in."

"Good. Come over here." He led the way to a table strewn with papers, pawed through them, finally came up with a list. "What do you think of that?"

Ecmund scanned the paper, glanced up at the Overlord, read it again. "Who made up this list?"

"I did. The lists that were left behind were very confusing, so I merged them, to make one clean list of my own. Why? Is there something wrong with it?"

Ecmund grinned. "It might be interesting."

"What might be interesting?"

"To set the order of precedence this way on Swearing Day, and see whether you have active rebellion before nightfall."

"You're joking! No you're not. What's wrong with it?"

Ecmund scanned the list again. "The way I see it, you must be missing the latest version. This one would be about twenty years out of date."

"So every change, every compromise, every deal that has been made in the last twenty years, would be overturned?"

"Something like that."

"By all the stars of the heavens. Are you serious?"

Ecmund shrugged. "I could be wrong on a few details – Eirlin would know better than me – but it's certainly no representation of the present situation."

"So Eirlin knows this better."

"Do you want me to ask her?"

The Overlord paced across the floor and back. "I am not going to let myself get rushed into anything. I have discovered a crucial error, but I must resist the urge to fix it quickly." He turned to Ecmund. "The question is not what the list should be. The question is who should have been asked, to make sure the list was correct."

Ecmund shook his head. "I don't understand. Where are all the aides who were supposed to help you take over this demesne? Surely there were people in the castle who knew what was going on?"

Delfontes shook his head. "I hate to admit it, Ecmund, but the charge you made on the day I threw you in gaol was completely justified; I just didn't realize it at that time. I was given all the information that anyone in Koningsholm had about this demesne. The largest gift, I think, was an incredible ignorance of what was really going on. Old Lord Salar kept everything very close, and his steward left when he died."

He sat down in his big chair, his feet spread before him. "You have no idea, Ecmund, how different life is out here, from the way we lived in Koningsholm. Back there, everything is organized and the rules are set. Out here, it's all improvisation and trial and error."

"It isn't, actually."

The Overlord raised his head. "Isn't it? It seems that way to me."

Ecmund grinned. "Well, for someone wandering around in a complete fog, I think you've done pretty well."

"Once again, the new officer gets the approbation of the grizzled sergeant. I feel so much better."

"I'm serious, my Lord. If it hadn't been for a Magician messing things around, this would have been a very smooth transition. It seems to me that you have taken command here, impressed the local people with your fairness, firmness, yet willingness to learn, and made great steps in understanding the complexity of the task you have taken on."

"If 'made great steps' means that I understand how absolutely impossible this is, then I have made giant strides!"

Ecmund regarded the Overlord for a moment. "So, when you got here, there was no one in the castle who could tell you how things worked, who was who, what your responsibilities were, what your rights were?"

Delfontes shook a finger. "Oh, no. We're not going to have that argument again. I'd just as likely send myself to the gaol afterwards, realizing how I must have sounded that day."

Ecmund grinned. "In other words, there was no one, and you've been trying to catch up ever since. I think you have managed on the practical level.

169

"The social complexities, on the other hand, you may never understand. I've lived here all my life, and I don't know what's going on half the time. Somebody is suddenly wildly insulted by something, and I don't know what it is, but some third party has to rush around and persuade everyone that nobody actually said what everybody knows they really did say, and then everything calms down again. Until the next time."

The Overlord wiped a hand across his face. "That was a good example of what I don't understand. What did you just say?"

Ecmund laughed aloud. "Don't worry about it. You're doing fine. Let's get back to the original question."

"Which was?"

"Who should be checking over this list, to make sure it is correct."

"Right. Who?"

"I don't know."

"A fine situation. The only one in the demesne willing to help me, and he doesn't know."

"Aha! But I know who knows."

"You do?"

"Yes. The women know."

"The women?"

"Yes. They're the ones who take care of the kinships and social obligations. If I take this list to Eirlin, she'll take it to...I don't know, whoever else knows the way it's supposed to be, and they'll fix it up."

"Will they? And they'll do it right?"

"Whether it's right or not doesn't really matter."

"But you've just told me..."

"It won't be right. Somebody will be sure to be upset."

"But...wait a moment. I see what you're getting at. What matters, is that the proper people made up the list. If anybody is upset, they can't come shouting at me."

"Exactly."

"I'm beginning to catch on. So will you do that? Give it to Eirlin?"

"It might take a few days."

"I hesitate to remind you that the Swearing is three days from now."

"I guess it will take three days, then."

"I suppose it will." Delfontes' face brightened. "And at the Swearing, you can read the list, and everyone will see it and see you reading it, and know..."

"I'd rather not, my Lord. I'll have other things on my mind."

"Oh. Right. What about Eirlin, then? If the women make up the list, one of them can take responsibility for it."

170

Ecmund wagged his head, left then right. "She will have a beautiful new dress…"

"Excellent. And if I know Eirlin, nobody will dare to argue."

"That will be an advantage." Ecmund bowed his head in an informal leave-taking. "I will let you know when the list is ready, my Lord."

Eirlin is wonderful. She can do anything.

Don't tell her. She hasn't realized it yet.

You are the Hand. I bow to your judgement.

Hmm.

Chapter 20

Ecmund looked askance at the scroll his sister was holding. "What are all the ribbons for?"

"Oh, Ecmund, you will never understand, will you?"

"I believe that is the reason one asks questions. Because one does not understand."

Eirlin swished the scroll past his face, the ribbons fluttering across his cheeks. "Don't be snippy. The ribbons are to give the scroll power, to make it more festive and important."

"And you do this because...?"

"...because nobody is really sure how accurate this list is. So we give it the power of ceremony, and nobody argues."

"That is truly devious and sneaky. I am beginning to agree with Jesco's analysis of women's logic."

"Go ahead. Just take advantage of it when it works."

He stood back, looked her up and down. "And that goes for the reader of the scroll as well, does it?"

"What do you mean?"

"Without a mirror, you'd never believe me."

"What? Ecmund, what are you talking about?"

He means you are beautiful, Eirlin.

"What did Kitten just say?"

He grinned. "I think you heard, and you just want me to say it as well. A brother is not supposed to notice things like that, but it...fits...you very nicely."

"There's nothing wrong with the fit of this dress. Wynna and I spent hours getting it right. Perica says this is the way all the women are dressing in Koningsholm."

"I'll believe that when I see what she wears today."

It was Eirlin's turn to look superior. "I think you'll be pleased."

Ecmund, I don't think you're supposed to think about Perica like that.

You know better.

I suppose.

"I probably will be, if it fits her like yours fits you."

She was saved from having to respond by the appearance of Uncle Aeldwig with his family. Jesco took one look at her and shook his head.

"I think she'd better bring the axe, Ecmund."

She frowned. "What do you mean?"

"I mean that Ecmund and I with our swords won't be enough to beat the suitors away."

Eirlin huffed and stepped forward, taking her uncle by the arm and towing him up the street.

Jesco grinned at his cousin. "At least we've got our family precedence right."

"You mean her striding ahead, towing your father, and the rest of us tagging along?"

"As usual."

"Your father looks good today."

"Maerwin persuaded him that this was important."

"Was he pleased with his position on the list?"

"Of course not."

"I was afraid of that."

"But he never said anything. Eirlin made up the list, consulted with the other women, and he had no room to argue."

"So he accepted it, then."

Jesco indicated his father, striding along beside Eirlin. "I think he's rather pleased that you and Eirlin have such influence with Lord Delfontes. Not that he'd ever tell you."

"You've got influence, too, Jesco. It's easy to be diplomatic when you have the power behind you."

His cousin nodded. "Good. That's the way it's supposed to work." Then he glanced across. "Ecmund, I was out of line the other day."

"You were."

"Sorry. You going to marry her?"

Ecmund grinned, shook his head. "Doesn't seem likely, does it?"

"Why not? Your lineage is as good as any Maridon aristocrat's."

Ecmund laid a hand on his cousin's shoulder. "The other day you were in a rage because I might marry her. Now you're steaming because I'm not?"

"But that's different..." he caught Ecmund's smile. "I know." Then he frowned. "I apologized. You don't get to tie me in knots as well."

"Fair enough. We can let it go, then."

"Fine. But if you get the chance, you marry her. It's more important to have the power than it is to keep the Blood pure."

"You believe that?"

Jesco shrugged. "I don't like it, but that's the way it goes. It's no good having pure Blood if you don't have the power to do what the Blood is supposed to do."

"It's good to hear you say that, but I won't be marrying anyone for her power."

"Why not? It's your duty."

"No, no Jesco. You're the Heir of the Blood. You're the one that has to marry properly. I'm just a poor relation."

"Hah! Me? Some chance."

"Don't worry. I'll just have a word with Eirlin. She'll start looking around."

"Ecmund!" Jesco's fingers were tight enough on his arm to cause pain. "You don't even joke about that. She would!"

"Who says I was joking?" He glanced pointedly at his arm.

Jesco released his grip with a sheepish smile. "All right, Ecmund. I know you were joking. But I'm not ready yet. You tell her that, Ecmund. You tell her I'm not ready yet."

Ecmund slapped his cousin's shoulder. "Don't worry, Jesco. She hasn't said anything, I won't bring up the subject, and if she does, I'll head her off."

"Thanks, Ecmund."

Ecmund glanced at his cousin again. "She's about the only thing in the world that you're afraid of, isn't she?"

"Aye. Strange isn't it. And she's the Healer."

They watched her striding ahead of them through the castle gate, tall and proud and, just for today, even beautiful.

You all love her. How could you be afraid?

"Nobody's afraid of Eirlin. What they are afraid of is that she won't think well of them."

"Truth, little cousin. Very simple truth."

The crowd of brightly dressed people slowed them as they crossed the bailey and entered the castle. Inside the main hall, they separated: Maerwin and Leofwina to their seats, Aeldwig and Jesco to their positions in the line, Ecmund and Eirlin to their posts on the Lord's left side.

This is rather nice.

Rather nice? Is that all?

I have seen other ceremonies that were... larger.

He suppressed his smile, leaned towards his sister. "Kitten doesn't think much of our simple country panoply."

"Small stuff, are we?"

"She said it was nice. Isn't it nice, Eirlin?"

She looked around. "I think it's glorious. I've never seen the castle so well decorated."

"Now it's your turn to be loyal." He held up a cautioning hand. "I think she did a wonderful job, too. Don't cause a disturbance. We have important official positions, and our demeanour reflects upon the dignity of our Overlord."

"Jesco is right. Your head really has been turned!"

"Don't you think I'd make a great court toady?"

174

"No, thank the Power of the Blood." She scanned the room. "When do we start?"

"Lord Delfontes will come out with Perica when he thinks everyone is here. Until then, we wait."

"Any word on...?"

He laid a hand on Kitten's hilt.

Nothing yet.

"Nothing."

There are many open minds here, Ecmund. It is very noisy.

All of the Blood are here, Kitten. It should help us.

He leaned over to Eirlin again. "Kitten says it's very noisy. All the Blood here, all excited."

"Isn't that better?"

"It will make it easier for Kitten to remain undetected. It might make it harder for her to search. We'll have to see."

"Can she practice?"

"I suppose."

Do you want to practice, Kitten?

On whom?

I don't know. Anyone, I suppose.

Should we?

I think it would be allowed if we were looking out for trouble.

Of course.

They spread their senses through the jumbled thoughts of the crowd.

Eirlin raised an eyebrow. "Anything?"

He shrugged. "It's like listening to all the conversations in a crowded room. We can get the feeling of the group, which is good. Generally excited and optimistic. We can pick up on individuals if we try hard. So far, the same response from anyone we've listened to. The darkest thoughts so far are from Uncle Aeldwig, and we know he isn't going to cause trouble."

They come.

The noise of the crowd stilled as the honour guard, led by Tyrbrand Ostersund, marched at a stately pace across the front of the fireplace and stationed themselves evenly along the wall. Then a page entered, proudly carrying a standard with the Delfontes crest, surmounted by the arms of the Falken demesne. He stopped beside the Overlord's chair and thumped the staff three times.

When the silence was complete, Lord Delfontes entered, followed by Perica. A suppressed sigh gusted through the ladies in their seats. Father and daughter were both dressed in forest green, the family colour, but there the resemblance ended. While his tunic was rough velvet, her dress was fine silk, fitted tight from the low neckline to the knee. From there it

175

split and widened, falling to the floor with a froth of lace in the vee. The bodice spread out below her bare shoulders, framing a gold and emerald torque that glowed on her dark skin. Matching earrings and comb completed the picture: no fancy coif, no noticeable maquillage.

She glided forward, and, at her father's courtly gesture, sat in her usual place. He smiled, and she returned the smile regally.

She is so proud!

Hmm.

We are proud of her.

Yes.

Pay attention, Ecmund!

I am.

To the ceremony, Ecmund.

The Overlord stood a moment, gazing out over his new subjects. Then, when the moment was right, he sat. There was a slight relaxation in the crowd, a settling on benches and chairs. Once again he waited for an appropriate interval, and then he spoke.

"Welcome to Falkengard Castle, people of the Demesne of the Falcon."

Ecmund exchanged a glance with his sister. "Demesne of the Falcon" was the name from the time of Old Inderjorne.

"In the name of King Vetrorrillo da Maridon, I come to formally take possession of this demesne. It is his majesty's will and my pleasure to receive today the pledges of the local families, and to return my assurance of the responsibilities of my position and the provisions of the Charter of Alcudo and the system of mutual homage that governs the realm of Inderjorne."

There was a definite easing of tension in the room. Delfontes had been listening.

The Overlord stood, looking to Eirlin. She raised the scroll and read the first Family name. Ecmund, not sure exactly what to do, bowed slightly to the Family Head, who stepped in front of the Overlord and spoke the words of the oath. Delfontes responded, and the man moved away. Eirlin read the next name, and Ecmund realized that he should be checking that the right person was ready.

Fortunately, the suspect Magicians were not at the top of the list, so he was able to get his duties settled before the first one came forward. It was Lord Ambroz de Genil, a stocky man, balding prematurely. As he strode forward, Ecmund set aside his doubts. This man hardly had the presence of a Magician, and his dark skin and hair marked him as a Maridon. Nonetheless...

Careful, now.

I am careful. He is anxious. This is very important to him. Money.

176

Money?

Money is on his mind, Ecmund. Desire to please. Oh!

What?

He is very happy. He wants to tell Lord Delfontes. He thinks he has a chance.

A chance at what?

I do not know. He is pleased.

The man strode down from the dais, his head higher than when he mounted.

No Magician?

Not likely.

Is the real Magician here?

Yes. He is searching, but quietly. I can read no more.

Wait for the next.

One by one, the local nobility made their pledges and moved on. One by one, the suspects approached the Overlord, and Kitten searched their minds while they were distracted.

Always, in the background, the true Magician's mind lurked, like an unidentified insect's buzz. Ever and again, Ecmund's eyes strayed to Lord Ostersund, who seemed to have fallen into that pleasant, half-aware state every courtier learns to get him through the long ceremonies.

Except once.

After the last suspected Magician had been tested and rejected, Ecmund happened to glance at Ostersund. To his surprise, the man seemed to be looking directly at him. The blond lord made an imperceptible bow, smiled slightly, then resumed his neutral expression. Confused, Ecmund glanced around...

...to see his sister's neck and shoulders, exposed by her dress, a rather bright shade of red. He glanced back at Ostersund, but received no response.

"Eirlin!"

Flustered, she held up the scroll, read the next name. Ecmund glared at her. She raised her hands in a helpless gesture.

What is wrong with Eirlin?

I think he smiled at her.

Who?

The man we think is the Magician.

Why did he smile at her?

Ecmund sighed. *Because of that confounded dress, is why. And everything else.*

Because she is beautiful?

We should have brought the axe.

She is happy, Ecmund. Confused but happy.

This is going to be wonderful.

Why are you not happy when your sister is?

We must do our duty here, Kitten. We'll talk about it later.

He turned to the next man in line, bowed, and ushered him forward.

Soon the rites were completed, and the new Lord Falken led his people into the courtyard. The weather was cooperating, and tables were spread in the shade of the curtain wall. A keg of ale was tapped, bottles of wine stood open, and a huge selection of meats and loaves lay enticingly on the white linen.

Perica, as hostess, guided the first of the nobles, still in order of precedence, towards the food. As plates began to fill, the formality began to ease, and soon the jovial air of a country feast took over. Children who had not been invited to the ceremony appeared from wherever they had been hidden. A band of local musicians – viols, hauteboys, and a harp – began to play. Two huge wolfhounds, escaped somehow from their kennels, begged so pleadingly for scraps that no one had the heart to send them away, and soon they lay, bellies distended, at the feet of their lord.

Ecmund took his courage in his hands. "You look stunning."

Perica glanced up at him, ran a hand down the side of her dress. "I had rather hoped I would be."

"Why?"

"Why? What kind of a question is that?"

"Just a question. Oh, I know every lady wants to look good. I just wondered why now, why here?"

She shrugged, to an intriguing effect in the shoulderless gown. "Because it's a special day."

"I suppose it is."

Suddenly her eyes were burning up into his. "I don't think you understand."

He made an open gesture with his hands. "If you say so. Make me."

She smiled. "All right." She glanced around to ascertain that she was not neglecting her duties, then turned and grasped his arm, her face serious. "Do you understand what a risk this was for Father and me? Leaving everything we knew behind, and coming all the way out here, where everything is so different and dangerous?"

"Oh. I see. This is the moment, then. This is the first big step in your success."

"I knew you would see." She stood taller, another interesting move, considering the dress. She gazed fondly at her father, mingling with his guests.

"Up until this day, my father's name was only Delfontes. Now, he is Sarza Delfontes da Falken. Before, he was only pretending. Up to now, he could have been ousted easily." Again, she turned earnestly toward

178

him. "I have learned that the people here believe strongly in their traditions. They have sworn their fealty to my father, and they meant it. I could feel the honesty. He is now their Overlord in truth as well as in name."

"That is true. I am glad that you recognize it. It contains great power and great responsibility."

Great honour and glory.

"I heard that!"

Kitten! Be careful!

She is so happy, Ecmund. They are all happy. Even the Magician is happy.

He is?

"Perica, touch Kitten's hilt. I want you to hear this. She says the Magician is happy."

"The Magician?"

Yes. He is happy.

"How do you know?"

How do you know anyone is happy? You can tell.

"Why is he happy?"

I don't know.

"Kitten, what kind of happy?"

What do you mean, Perica?

"Happy because some plan is working, or happy because people are happy?"

Some of both. Let me check.

Careful!

I am being careful. He is not looking. He is pleased with the ceremony, I think. He is pleased with Lord Sarza Delfontes da Falken. He is also pleased at something else. Something personal...

I am the froth of the beer from the keg. I am the feet of the dancers on stone.

"Did he spot you?"

I think he became suspicious. I'm sorry, Ecmund and Perica. I could not find out the other thing. It was too deep.

"Don't worry. As long as you don't get the feeling that he has anything nasty planned."

Nothing like that.

He turned to Perica. "I don't think you should let this spoil your special day. Kitten and I will keep watch. You go and enjoy yourself."

"Thank you, Ecmund, Thank you, Kitten." She scanned the party again. "Oh. I see some empty plates."

He stopped her, his hand on her arm. "Your father is very proud of you."

179

Her smile flashed wider. "And I'm very proud of him." Then she was away across the bailey.

Ecmund.

Ecmund!

"What?"

Are we not supposed to be watching?

"I was watching."

I don't think that is what you are supposed to be watching.

"Do you see the way that dress...No I suppose not." He gave himself a mental shake and began to check the crowd himself. He was not looking for empty plates.

As he strolled around, he realized what a successful ceremony it had been. Kitten fed him the feelings as he passed. All were happy: satisfied with their positions, satisfied with the new Overlord. Even Aeldwig was less unhappy than usual.

Eirlin.

"What?"

She is uncertain.

"Is she in trouble?"

No. Just uncertain. Excited, happy, wary, worried.

"Where is she?"

That way.

He began to stride through the crowd, then realized that no one was moving fast. He slowed, but kept going.

There.

Eirlin was standing against the bailey wall, talking to someone. As Ecmund approached, the man bent over her hand, then turned away.

What is she thinking?

I...I cannot say.

What?

I do not think Eirlin wants me to say what she thinks.

He strode forward. "Was that who I thought it was?"

"I suspect it was. Very interesting."

"Interesting? What did he want?"

She frowned. "If I didn't know otherwise, I'd say he was a young man wanting to make conversation with a pretty girl. If I thought I was a pretty girl."

"You are far more than a pretty girl and that's what has me worried. Kitten won't tell me what you were thinking."

Her hand came out and rubbed the pommel of the Sword gently. "Kitten is very wise."

"She is?"

"Yes. Do you see this large ruby in her hilt?"

180

"Yes, of course."

"Do you want ruby-sized dents all over your head?"

"No, but..."

"Because if you ever use Kitten to pry into my mind, I will beat you over the head with her hilt!"

"Oh."

I think she means it.

"Right and true I mean it. Kitten, we are going to have a talk."

Yes, Eirlin.

"But not now."

No, Eirlin. You are to enjoy the party, and Ecmund and I must watch.

"Oh, no, Ecmund. You have to enjoy yourself, too."

"I'm still not too pleased about the Magician. We didn't catch him, and Kitten says he's happy."

"Happy?"

"Yes. She couldn't figure out why."

She scratched her ear for a moment. "There are only two reasons why the Magician might be happy..."

"One being that he is really not against Lord Delfontes, so he is happy, as we all are, at his success..."

"...and the other being that he has some nefarious plan which is about to come to fruition."

"...and we don't know which." Ecmund shook his head. "So I think I'd still better stay on guard. You go and have a good time, Linna."

"I am having a good time, silly."

"In spite of Lord Magician Ostersund?"

"Maybe because of him. After all, maybe he was just a young man having a conversation with a pretty girl. You were the one who told me I should look around for an appropriate mate."

"But..."

Ecmund, don't be such a sap.

"What? Oh. You're joking, aren't you? Aren't you?"

She shrugged. "Maybe I am, and maybe I'm not, but Kitten isn't going to help you figure it out. Are you, dear?"

Not at all.

"I get the point."

"Fine. Now, the musicians just started a reel, and everyone is afraid to ask Perica to dance. Give me your Sword, and go ask her. I'll stay on guard."

"What? You can't sit here holding a sword."

"Of course I can. Better than an axe for keeping the young men away. Go!"

Reluctantly, he undid his sword belt. She snatched it from him, pushed him. "Hurry up. She's going to feel so bad if no one asks her. And you're going to feel so bad if someone else does."

He glanced back over his shoulder at her, but walked faster.

Leaning against the rough stone, the sword belt wrapped around her wrist, Eirlin watched her brother spin the tiny Maridon girl out onto the floor, guiding her weight easily with one hand. She saw Perica gasp at the speed, then grin and spin out even faster.

They are happy.

Of course. They are the future.

How can we make that future?

We don't have to, Kitten. They will.

But her father said...

Her father knows better than to meddle in something he has no control over.

Then he approves?

Of course he does. Ecmund just has to make sure that everyone else does.

He must win honour and glory.

He will. With you and me to help him, how can he not?

How can he not!

Back to work, Sword.

Yes, Lady. We are on guard.

Kitten sent her senses through the crowd, and Eirlin learned to follow, spreading their scan farther and farther as their minds became closer tuned.

There!

What?

The Magician. Feel him?

Careful! What is he doing?

Nothing. Watching the crowd. He is happy.

Yes, I see.

Danger! I am the music in the sky.

"I was about to ask you to dance, but you seem otherwise occupied."

She looked around, as if surprised. "I'm sorry, my Lord Ostersund. Ecmund asked me to mind his sword while he danced."

"You could leave it here. I'm sure it would be safe."

She looked into his eyes. Was there a slight mocking in that pleasant smile? "You don't know my brother and his sword."

She sent the faintest query to Kitten, but received no reply.

"An interesting sword. May I see it?"

"You really don't know my brother and his sword."

"I shall take that as a 'no' shall I?"

182

"You are perceptive, my Lord."

"Yes. I rarely make the same mistake twice." He smiled again, bowed, and faded away.

What did that mean?

He was saying two things, Kitten. First, he meant that he would not bother me about you again. The second meant that he would not make the mistake of talking to me again.

Why are you sad?

Because he is handsome, and intelligent, and in other circumstances I might find him interesting.

But he is the enemy!

Which is why I am not finding him interesting.

I see. Eirlin?

Yes, Kitten.

You said I am not allowed to tell Ecmund what you are thinking.

That's right.

Am I allowed to tell you what you are thinking?

Most definitely not!

All right.

What was I thinking?

I... couldn't say.

Hmm.

Chapter 21

"What do you know about the Leute, Ecmund?"

The Leute. A bitter memory flashed across Kitten's mind, hurriedly pushed away.

Ecmund took a deep breath, turned to look out the window at the cooling rain. It had been a hot summer. "The Leute. Is that why you asked me to visit?"

Delfontes tapped his fingers on the table. "The Leute. Surely you know something."

Ecmund shook his head. "It might be better to ask what you know about them. Anything?"

"I have to admit, not much. Of course, everyone knows that they are the native people of the northern mountains. When I realized that they were part of my new demesne, I asked around. Yes, Ecmund, I did do some basic research before I came here. It seems as though no one knows much about them."

Ecmund nodded. "How do I explain this? Let me see."

He sat on the windowsill, his brow knitted. "Look at it this way. You know of the problems Alcudo and the Maridons had taking Inderjorne from the Blood?"

"An old story."

"Here's the same story, older still. Many years ago, the Blood of Inderjorne had the same trouble with the Leute, and with the same result."

"You mean, they never did really subdue them, but just made treaties that acknowledged their traditional powers, in order to prevent continued warfare?"

"Close enough. And I'm not sure the Leute look at a treaty the same way we do. Why do you ask?" He glanced at the Overlord. "As if I don't already know."

Lord Delfontes nodded. "The Leute are part of my demesne, and they are starting to cause trouble. There has been little Maridon presence in their area lately, and they seem to be taking advantage. Their neighbours are getting fed up with the constant thefts, the insolence, the demands."

Ecmund nodded. "That would be expected. As far as I know, they are an independent people, and the rules they live by are very different from ours. They don't seem to understand ownership, especially of the land. If you told them that you own the ground they live on, they would look at you as if you had told them that you own the air they breathe. The idea just doesn't register."

"That jibes with my knowledge."

"I have to assume that you have brought me here for other reasons than to compare our ignorances."

The Overlord laughed aloud. "Ecmund, you have such a refreshing approach. I just picture a more tradition-minded Overlord near Koningsholm hearing that from one of his people. He would go apoplectic!"

"Why is that? Nothing I said was disrespectful."

"Perhaps not. Just take it from me; if you ever go anywhere near those people, you are going to have to mind your tongue very carefully."

"A piece of advice my family has been giving me for years. Didn't keep me out of your cells, did it?"

The Overlord chuckled. "Ecmund, I think you are incurable." He looked more serious. "And that makes you perfect for a small duty I have in mind."

"A 'small duty', my Lord? Like go and talk to a horde of the Leute, and persuade them to be good little citizens of Lord Delfontes' demesne?"

"Something like that."

"Sounds easy. Can I take about two hundred trained mountain fighters with me?"

"I was thinking rather of six or eight men."

Ecmund nodded glumly. "That sounds like the way my life usually goes. Sent out with a slingshot to kill a wild boar."

"How would you do that?"

Ecmund looked up. "What?"

"Hah! Got you! Now tell me. If I sent you out to kill a wild boar, a big one, and all you had was a slingshot, how would you go about it?"

Ecmund shrugged. "I'd use the slingshot to knock over a spearman, take his spear, and kill the boar."

The Lord's laugh rolled out. When he regained control of his breath, he shook his head, wiped his eyes, and sighed. "I don't know why I even try."

"Even try what, Father?"

"You do have a habit of entering in the middle of a conversation, Perica. To get a straight answer out of Ecmund."

"Oh. That's easy."

Her father shook his head. "Doesn't matter. If you get a straight answer, it won't be the one you want."

She sniffed. "If you already know the answer you want, you certainly don't ask Ecmund."

"My point exactly. Now, what would you like, my dear?"

She regarded him a moment, eyebrows raised. "I would like to learn everything I possibly can about diplomacy and the running of a large

185

demesne, so I can take over from you as early as possible, so you can retire and enjoy a well-earned dotage."

"I find it impossible to conceive what one would do to earn one's dotage. I'm not even sure what a dotage is."

"A sure sign you've entered it already. So, since it seems I will be taking over sooner than I thought, you'd better tell me what we are sending Ecmund out to do now."

"I'm sending him out to check on the Leute."

"Good idea. May I go?"

"No!"

"I thought not." She turned to Ecmund. "There is your objective, Ecmund. I find it objectionable that there is a portion of my demesne that I dare not visit. Fix it." She waved a hand dismissively.

"Yes, my Lady. Whatever my Lady wishes."

"I do like subservient servants."

"Then go find some."

"All right, children. Time to stop playing and get to work. Eight soldiers?"

"All very well to get me there, but useless for the main task."

"Why is that?"

"The Leute have little respect for the force of arms. Unless I take an army big enough to wipe them out, I might as well go alone."

"I think that option is well down the list of my priorities."

Perica mimed unrolling a long scroll. "Ah, yes. Here it is. Send an army and wipe out the Leute. That ranks just behind...clearing off the whole forest and planting a flower garden, and right in front of...buying your daughter a new ball gown."

"Neither of which is likely to be accomplished in the next few months, although miracles have happened."

"Then what is the plan?"

"That is what we are here to discuss. Ideas?"

Ecmund sat a moment, and Kitten could feel him thinking seriously. The Hand needed her help, and she could not refuse, much though her heart recoiled at the thought.

Fight them.

"Not now."

"Pardon me?"

"My Sword is suggesting that we fight them."

Perica's glance was the one she usually reserved for imbeciles who knew better. "So listen to her."

"Fight them? We've just decided that is impossible."

"I don't know what she means, but it probably isn't what you mean. Ask her."

186

He shrugged. "I suppose. What do you mean, 'fight them'? We can't."

Fight the champion. Beat him, they listen. Otherwise, you waste your time.

"What do you know about the Leute?"

I know them. She shuddered inwardly.

He turned to the Overlord. "She knows the Leute. She says the only way to get their attention is to fight their champion."

The Overlord spread his hands. "I have no idea."

"Nor have I, but if she says she knows them, then obviously it's worth considering."

"In my studies of primitive peoples, I ran across similar situations."

Ecmund turned a puzzled frown to Perica. "You have studied primitive peoples?"

Her head came up primly. "I have an education, you know."

"And I can't think of a better way for you to repay me for all the money I spent on those tutors." Her father's hand slapped the table. "Tell us what you learned."

"If you're sure it's important. I can recall certain sarcastic comments about my choice of subject."

The Overlord smiled slyly. "And you took them at face value didn't you?"

"Father! Are you telling me that you tricked me into throwing myself into my studies?"

He shrugged modestly. "You were young. The alternatives were not so agreeable."

She frowned, her eyes looking to the ceiling. "Would that have been about the time of Raoul?"

"I can scarcely remember. Perhaps."

"Then I don't feel so bad. Raoul had his uses as well."

"What? You mean...?"

"My Lord..."

Lord Delfontes turned to Ecmund. "I do apologize. Rehashing our family history is not helping you any." He turned back to his daughter. "Please give us the benefit of your extensive and valuable tutelage, my dear."

"With pleasure. It is a common device in primitive tribes, in order to avoid constant interpersonal conflict, to have a ritually appointed champion, who is acknowledged as the strongest fighter. This champion is considered the right hand of the chief or ruling group. Since he is known to be better than any other fighter, he is rarely challenged. The system functions very well, I gather."

"If you aren't the champion."

"Yes. I hadn't thought of that. There must be a replacement, sooner or later, mustn't there? Thank you, Ecmund. It seems my education continues."

"You suggest the Leute might have a similar structure."

Why all this discussion? I told you!

"My Sword finds this conversation a waste of time. She already told us this."

"My apologies to your Sword, Ecmund. Of course, she is right."

The Overlord smoothed his beard. "Does this Sword not have a name? It seems awkward to call her 'The Sword' all the time."

I suppose. Go ahead.

Ecmund laughed. "Do you think a Sword can sigh? I just got a distinct feeling of resignation. The name we use, the one that Eirlin gave her, is Kitten."

"Kitten? I presume she has claws, then?"

"Oh, yes."

A very perceptive man, this Overlord. I think I will like him.

I am sure he will be relieved to hear that.

"She approves of your perspicacity, my Lord."

"Fine. I approve of hers. What else does she know?"

When their champion is dead, they will listen.

"That's it? We just have to kill the champion?"

What do you want?

Ecmund sighed. "Her perspective is limited, my Lord. She is confident that we can win, and they will listen. She finds it hard to understand why we would need more information."

"I can see how she would. I heard the 'kill' part. Let us consider that as a final alternative."

"I can't help but agree. What else?"

The Overlord looked to his daughter.

"I'm with Kitten. Our sources agree."

"There you are, Ecmund. That's all we have."

"You have no others here with any knowledge?"

The Overlord grinned. "None who are willing to go to those extremes to achieve my good will."

"And I am?"

"You know better, Ecmund."

"Yes, my Lord. I do."

"I know better as well. I know how little my good will means to you."

"My Lord, that is not true!"

"Perhaps, but the rest of my courtiers would see it that way. Most of them are here because of the possibilities of advancement. The society at

188

Koningsholm is full of young men, trying to move upward, and there is nowhere for them to go. Hence the lure of this posting. However, an extended leave, even with a chance of great success, is too risky. They would rather take their chances here at the seat of power, where they can use the skills they have learned from birth."

"Wrangling, power mongering, and treachery?"

"Diplomacy."

"I think I just said that."

"Then we are agreed. In spite of the lack of information, or perhaps because of it, you are the best choice for my ambassador. Whom will you take with you?"

Ecmund considered. "My first thought is to take Jesco, but I'm not so sure. He is a fine swordsman, and I know I can trust him with my life. He is of the Blood. However, he would be the first to tell you that diplomacy is not his strong point."

"Can you control him?"

"I can usually persuade him to control himself."

The Overlord nodded. "Far better."

He turned to his daughter. "Do you have anything to add?"

She frowned thoughtfully. "As I say. I am in favour of the expedition, and while I think Ecmund is the best one to go, it would perhaps be an insult to his abilities to say I fear for him."

Ecmund began to grin, then sobered. "I am not insulted. I know the odds."

"When would you like to leave?"

"Is there a rush?"

"Not that I know of, although it would be unhappy to arrive the day after a crucial event."

"I understand, my Lord. I will be ready in two days. I will inform Jesco, and consult with him on the other six."

"You will want a cook, servants, grooms."

"No, my Lord. When I said eight, I meant eight."

The Overlord raised his eyebrows. "I suppose."

Ecmund grinned. "Don't worry. We won't suffer. The horses must graze several hours every night, and men cannot ride for that many hours a day. There is plenty of time to cook, eat, and clean up. Besides, on the road we will be staying with local landowners."

"Bivouac is not a condition I search out."

"My own experience, whenever I am away from the tender ministrations of my sister, leads me to agree."

"She does well for you?"

"Of course."

189

"Do not be concerned. With both you and Jesco away, I will take special care of your village and your sister."

"Thank you, my Lord. She will appreciate it. What about our little problem in the castle?"

The Overlord smiled thinly. "It is my duty to take command of this demesne. The King considers my skills equal to the task. Do you have another opinion?"

"I apologize, my Lord. Of course not. It is just the nature of the problem that bothers me. I can only assume that the King was unaware of it."

"That is true. Are you suggesting that I have your sister brought to the castle while you are away?"

Perica dropped her regal pose. "Oh, Father, that would be a marvellous idea! She could help me to learn how to use my talents, and no one would be the wiser, because they would all think that it was for her safety. Hah! More fools they will be!"

"What do you say, Ecmund?"

"I say nothing, my Lord. I am not the one to ask. I think it a good plan, but it is up to Eirlin."

"You will put the plan to her."

"Of course."

"Fine. If she will not, fine as well. Perica would be glad of her company, in any case. You might mention that."

"I will."

"Good. Let us set this all in motion. We will meet tomorrow, and discuss it further."

"I will talk to Jesco immediately."

The Overlord rose. "Until tomorrow then, my Lord."

"Until tomorrow, my Lord."

Jesco's reaction was about what Ecmund expected. "What? You are going on a mission for this Overlord? And you want me to tag along?"

Ecmund merely waited.

"You are leaving Eirlin alone again, after what happened? "

"The Overlord's daughter has invited her to stay at the castle for the duration of our trip. If she will go there."

"She will go. I'll make sure of that!"

"Thank you. I was wondering how to break it to her. Perhaps you will come home with me now, and we can face her together."

Jesco frowned, unsure whether he had just been taken in. "Right. Let's go, then."

As the two cousins strode through the village, Jesco looked up at Ecmund. "You seem to be moving up in station. Ambassador for the Overlord, no less."

"And you are worried about what I may be paying for this preference?"

"I might be."

Ecmund looked down at his cousin, then walked in silence for a few paces.

"Jesco, do you want to be King?"

"What?"

"Simple question. Do you want to be King? You're of the Blood, the heir of a ranking family. If things had worked out differently, you might have been King. What do you think of that?"

"Completely ludicrous. I'd be a terrible King. Diplomacy? Hah! I'd have half the kingdom at war with the other half, without even knowing what I said."

"Fine. Do you want me to be King?"

"You?" He thought a moment. "Aye, you'd make a good King."

"Seriously, Jesco."

"I am serious. You're smart, you're even-tempered, you have a stronger mind than I ever suspected. Yes, you'd make a good King."

"All right, but can you see what it would take for me to be King? If I led a rebellion against the present King and rallied all the Blood, would you be my general? Would you put me on the throne?"

Jesco shook his head. "These are completely crazy questions, Ecmund. In the first place, I have no idea if I'd be a decent general. Probably not. But can you imagine what a revolution like that would do to the country? All the destruction, the killing? I don't even want to think about it."

"That's good, Jesco, because neither do I."

"You don't?" Jesco frowned. "Then why all the questions? Are you testing me or something?"

"No. I'm just trying to make a point. Personally, I don't think it matters that much who is king, as long as he fulfils his duties properly. We are agreed that we have no interest in putting the realm through a war. So what's left? What can we do to make the lives of our people better? We are of the Blood. That's our duty. To our people."

"You're right, there, Ecmund. That is our duty. So what's your question?"

"I'm asking you to come up with the best way to serve our people, to make sure that they are treated with respect and fairness, that they have the best chance to prosper."

191

Jesco thought a moment, frowning in concentration. Finally he raised his head. "I see. I know where you're leading me. Why didn't you just say it?"

Ecmund smiled. "Because if I just said it, you wouldn't believe me. You have to walk the same path that I did, so you truly understand."

"I understand all right, though I don't like it. You're saying that we have to support this Overlord, make sure he's a success, so our people can live happy, prosperous, lives."

"Basically, yes. I'm also saying that I think we have a good chance with this Overlord. He's strong, he's fair, and he is depending on me to help him with some of his problems. This gives me a chance to influence him, now and in the future."

"And he has a beautiful daughter."

"I cannot allow that to influence my decision."

"You always were the one with the high mind, Ecmund." Jesco's head came around quickly. "Some will say you've joined the enemy."

"What enemy? The last battle was 187 years ago, Jesco. Don't you think it's time for us to accept that we got what we could out of the situation, and move ahead?"

"I suppose so."

"So do I."

"So I have to knuckle under to this Overlord, and play all sweet and courtly?"

Ecmund laughed. "I don't think anyone ever expects you to be sweet and courtly, Jesco. Just don't fight him. Do your duty. Protect the village. If the Overlord's soldiers attack again, kill as many of them as you can. I'll be right beside you."

"You will?"

"That's right. My main effort with this Overlord is to get him to deeply understand, and not just pay lip service to, the Charter, his duties, and the rights of our people."

"I can go with that, Ecmund. Hell, even my father will be happy to hear you're doing that."

"Well, if we can make your father happy, I think we can make this work."

Eirlin was a different matter.

"You two are expecting me to sit safe and warm up at the castle, playing games with the Overlord's daughter, while you go off into unknown danger?"

Jesco met Ecmund's eyes, shrugged, turned to her.

"Eirlin, listen to me. Have I ever done anything that was against your welfare?"

She gave him a level stare. "Not since I was nine years old, and you persuaded me that I could float on that log in the creek."

"You still remember that? Good. It was a lesson you needed."

"You didn't have to laugh so loudly. I was very proud of how well I had ironed that dress."

"Eirlin, I never thought you were one to bear a grudge."

"I don't bear a grudge, Jesco, but I have an excellent memory. It keeps me from repeating my mistakes."

"You're just trying to get me off topic. Ecmund and I are worried about you, out here exposed with both of us away. You were the target last time. What if they try harder next time? You might not be so lucky."

She had no answer.

"Besides that, the Overlord needs you."

"He does?"

"Yes. He needs help with this Magician that Ecmund senses. If Lord Delfontes is that ignorant of the Blood and our powers, he needs someone to tell him what's going on. Someone he trusts. You could do that."

"Why would he trust me?"

Jesco glanced at Ecmund.

Because I say so.

Eirlin nodded. "All right, then. Everybody seems to agree." Suddenly she grinned. "I've always wondered what it might be like to be nobility."

"Don't get used to it. I'll need my supper when I get back."

"How long will you be gone?"

"It's almost three days' travel to the nearest Leute village. A stay of two or three days, then a day on to the next. That may be enough, or we may have to go to another village. I can't see getting anything done in less than ten days."

"All right. I'll see to putting the horse out at the farm while we're away. When do you leave?"

"The day after tomorrow."

"Good enough. You two will take care of each other, I know."

They met eyes, and both nodded. It was as binding as an oath.

Lord Delfontes started their next meeting with a serious face. "We have a new wrinkle to our plans."

"What is that, my Lord?"

"You have a volunteer. One I didn't expect."

"Who?"

"Lord Ostersund."

"He could be more than a wrinkle."

"As the Magician? He does have the colouring of one of your Blood, and he was at the forest fire. Anything else?"

"Not much, just a feeling."

"What does Kitten say?"

"She hasn't been able to scan him, for fear of being detected."

The Overlord considered. "If you have him alone, you will be able to figure it out easily."

"That's right, but his chances of figuring us out go up accordingly. That will hamper my use of Kitten. She will have to work in a more subtle fashion when he is around."

"He seems to be a good man. Knowledgeable, thoughtful. He was specially recommended by his Majesty."

"He was very useful at the fire. If he is not our enemy, he might be an asset to our embassy."

"Exactly. Are you willing to risk it?"

"I think so. I just wish I knew what he was after."

"Believe me, so do I. But I must leave it up to you to decide. Does he go?"

Ecmund shrugged, grinned. "He has laid down the gauntlet. I think we must pick it up."

"Would you like to confront him?"

"If he is our enemy, our only advantage is that we know about him, and he doesn't know that. If he is a Magician and not our enemy, then perhaps he has good reason for what he does."

"Then we shall include him in the planning."

Ecmund raised a cautioning hand. "He rides alone like the rest of us. No retainers, no servants."

"Agreed. If he will go on those terms, more power to him."

"Agreed."

"I will send for him."

The blond lord appeared quickly, as if he had been waiting.

I am the stone of the wall.

Ecmund regarded the man carefully. For some reason, he looked smaller than Ecmund had remembered, and younger.

He is doing that.

What?

He does not want you to see him as a threat.

Thank you, Kitten.

"Lord Ostersund, you fought the forest fire with Ecmund Liutswin Falconric, one of the local Blood, a lord in his own right, and leader of this expedition. Ecmund, Tyrbrand Ostersund has offered his assistance in your embassy."

194

"I understand, my Lord." The older man turned the full force of his pale blue eyes on Ecmund. "I would be pleased to work with you again, my Lord."

"I will be pleased of your support in this venture, my Lord. Have you any knowledge of the Leute?"

"Only what I have gleaned from my family's lore. As you can see, I am of the Blood myself, but our lands are to the south, so we have had little to do with the northern natives."

"We will have time to talk along the way."

"I gather it is a fair ride?"

"It is two days' ride from here, and I have planned for ten days in total."

"Good enough. I will be ready tomorrow morning."

"You realize that we travel light, my Lord?"

"I am not unfamiliar with campaigning; I will be ready." He smiled. "I am a fair shot with a bow, and not unskilled at the preparation of my game."

"That would be of great use to us, my Lord. The less food we have to carry, the easier we can travel."

They spent some time discussing the details of their trip, and then Ecmund started home.

"What do you think, Kitten?"

Very strange. He is strong in the Blood, as you and Eirlin are, but he shows little other sign of power.

"Little?"

There is something, but I dare not push too hard to find it.

"Good. Leave it at that. You can talk to me easily, as long as you are at my side, without anyone knowing."

I will be very careful.

Chapter 22

They left the next morning, early enough to make good distance before the day warmed. Eirlin was there in the castle courtyard to see them off, towering, a bit uncomfortably, over her new friend. Ecmund went close enough for Kitten to talk with both of them.

"Take care, Ecmund. Kitten, you take care of him."

You worry too much. We will be fine.

"We always worry about those we love, Kitten."

Then all is correct. I know these people. We will have no trouble.

"I wish I knew what you know, Kitten."

I have told you.

Ecmund shared a helpless glance with the two women. Then Eirlin stepped forward to hug him fiercely, and Perica took a more formal adieu.

He mounted, rather proud to be leading his party away from the castle. He grinned as he watched Jesco, swinging past Eirlin to kiss her hand from his moving horse, and tipping his hat to Perica. As they lined out along the northward road, Lord Ostersund naturally moved up beside Ecmund, and Jesco, with a wry smile, was forced to slide back beside the sergeant in charge of the troops.

"A fine morning."

Ecmund glanced over. The lord was certainly ready for the trail. He was clad in worn leathers, and his only concession to rank was the badge in his hat. He was also well armed, with rapier and dagger at his belt, a worn hunting bow slung ahead of his right knee, arrows to the near side.

"The roads are good. It will not be a difficult day."

"We could go farther?"

"There is no point. Manors are spread out in this area. Lord Delfontes wishes us to make our presence known with the local nobility as well. We stay with Lord Quentar tonight, then make another easy day to stay with Lord Oliveres. He is the chief complainant, and from there the Leute camps are not far."

"Much too close for the comfort of Lord Oliveres, I expect."

"True. He has dealt with them for years with little trouble, but always backed by the Overlord's men. Recently he has had little help."

"It is not unusual, with a gap in the power structure, for factions to push for more."

"You have seen this before?"

The lord shrugged. "Not precisely the same, but it fits. History supports me."

Ecmund thought. "You mean the problems when King Barracon was killed, and Prince Mesio was only two years old?"

196

"Precisely. You don't think Lord Javier and Lord Tajarda would have dared to quarrel, with Barracon on the throne?"

"Not likely. Barracon had a firm hand, from all accounts."

As they filled out the miles, Ecmund found himself enjoying the other's company. Ostersund seemed to have lost the superior air that had bothered them, and his sardonic humour was directed at himself as often as at anyone else.

As her subject relaxed, Kitten listened closely, probing the emanations that seeped from what she began to realize was a far more powerful mind than she had ever experienced.

But Ecmund felt little suspicion, later in the afternoon, when the lord pulled up his horse. "Do we want to take a present to tonight's host?"

Ecmund followed Ostersund's eyes. A chubby, four-prong buck stood hidden in the leaves of a copse. As the lord strung his bow, the animal stepped away into the forest.

Kitten?

Eager to hunt.

That's all?

All I dare.

To Ostersund's questioning look, Ecmund nodded. He signalled his two bowmen, who had also prepared their weapons, to dismount and follow.

When the three had faded into the undergrowth, Ecmund motioned the rest to take a break. He strolled a bit away from the group, his hand on Kitten's hilt.

What do you think?

He is the Magician. I have been listening all day. He hides it very easily, but I have learned enough.

But Kitten, I'm beginning to like him.

He is very strong. It is possible that he hides it all, even from me.

You think he could be evil, but cunning and powerful enough to hide it completely from all of us?

It is not wise to underestimate the enemy.

I bow to your experience. So what do we do?

We look for evidence of malice, of trickery.

Do you see any of that now?

He did not conjure up that deer. I saw it before he showed you.

Maybe he took advantage of it.

To do what?

I don't know. Slip away to confer with his men?

Do you trust the two that hunt with him?

I've known them all their lives, never had reason to mistrust.

Then we will wait for their report.

197

Not much else we can do. Let's keep our senses alert, though.
Carefully.
Of course.

He strolled back to his men, accepted a chew of jerky from the sergeant, and patrolled the other way along the road.

Soon a whistle pierced the forest calm.

"Successful hunt."

And little time for anything else.

Three happy bowmen appeared through the forest, the buck slung on a pole. The two soldiers were full of the lord's excellent shot, but Ostersund refused their praise. "It is a calm day, and I had an excellent view." He slapped the bow affectionately as he slipped it back into its case. "She's a fine bow."

She?

No sign.

Just an expression, then.

Seems to be.

Once the deer was dressed out, they slung the carcass across the packhorse's load, and made their cheerful way towards the castle of Lord Quentar.

Ostersund grinned over at Ecmund. "I enjoyed that. It has been too long."

"Obviously you have hunted."

"When I was young and had fewer responsibilities. Now, I rarely get the chance." He frowned. "I hope we aren't treading on any toes, here."

"I think we are far enough from the castle that Quentar will not hunt here himself. A deer his own huntsmen would take is an appropriate gift."

"Good. I would not wish to create discord. I understand the delicacy of your mission."

"It shouldn't be too delicate here. Lord Quentar is an easy man to deal with, and has always been loyal. He is partly of the Blood, as well."

"That will help?"

Ecmund grinned. "For you and me, it will."

"Will it? Back at Koningsholm, they often discuss how the Old Blood is more important out here at the edge of the kingdom. With a great deal of gossip, and very little actual knowledge, I might add. I was interested, when I came here, to see what the reality is."

"And what have you discovered?"

"Not much. I saw more blond heads at the Swearing, I suppose. So far, you and your sister are the only evidence of strong leadership from the Blood."

"And that was why you came on this trip?"

198

"Partly. Also a chance to see more of the territory. I consider clinging to the presence of those in power to be an odious habit, which fosters poor leaders, acting on poorer information. I am of more use to myself and to my King when I go out into the realm and take action." He grinned over at Ecmund. "And I have more fun."

Ecmund couldn't help but return the smile.

They jogged on for a while longer, and the Magician seemed to be making a decision. He glanced at Ecmund several times before he spoke.

Ecmund had developed the habit of riding with his reins in his right hand, his left resting casually on his Sword hilt. It enabled very close communication.

Now he asks what he wanted to ask before.

"Do you find it odd that Lord Delfontes would send two of the Blood out on this mission?"

"He only sent me. You volunteered."

"True, but he did allow me to go."

"What is your question?"

"I am trying to see this from his point of view. He is new in power, is having the usual problems, and he chooses two possible problems for a very delicate mission. Not one of his own trusted people who came from Koningsholm with him, but two relative strangers. Why would he do that?"

Ecmund shrugged. "Why do you think?"

Ostersund shrugged in imitation. "On the surface, it seems a good move. One thing I do know is that our people have been dealing with the Leute since long before the Maridons came."

"Not too successfully."

"History suggests that this peace, tenuous though it is, could be considered great success."

"I suppose. So you think he sent the best men he could. On the surface."

"That could be it. However, I am a bit surprised that he was aware of the fact. He did not seem to me to be one who knows much of our Blood, or pays much heed to us. I can't help but wonder if there's something else."

He wants something.

I think I will give him something

Ecmund put on a wry smile. "Perhaps Lord Delfontes is acting like a prudent bowman, and hitting two targets with the same arrow."

He is very interested.

"What is the second target?"

"He might have decided that it was time for his daughter to spend less time in my presence."

The lord burst into laughter. "Ah! The indomitable Perica. And you?"

Ecmund shrugged, his slight discomfort not feigned.

Ostersund shook his head. "She would be a good catch. She is certainly beautiful."

Ecmund shot the man a glance. "Did you have ideas in that direction yourself?"

The lord chuckled. "No, you have no worries from me. Of course, I considered it. She is very beautiful, and intelligent as well. However, I don't think she likes me very much."

"Why not?"

"I'm not sure. Every time I look at her, she stares back fiercely, as if she would like to pin me to the nearest doorframe."

"I suppose you shouldn't look at her like that, then."

"Like what?"

"I don't know. You're the one doing it."

"What?" The lord stared at Ecmund. "She has mentioned it to you?"

"She says you stare."

"Hah! I'm losing my touch. I feel like an idiot. I shall have to go to her and apologize, the moment we return to the castle."

"Are you sure you dare go near her?"

The Magician laughed. "I shall abase myself, and throw my honour upon her mercy."

"And she will cut you into little pieces. Perica does not like people who play games like that."

"Hmm. You're right. And she isn't shy to let them know. I shall have to consider another approach."

"Why?"

"I don't know. Sort of a challenge, I suppose." He looked across at Ecmund, laughed. "Don't worry. I'm not going to try to take her from you."

"I don't think I have anything you could take."

"Well, I wish you good luck in any case."

He means it.

"Why?" Ecmund kept his voice light.

"I guess I'm a romantic. Besides, I like to think of one of the Blood allying with that kind of power. It can only help our realm and our people."

He means that, too.

"Well, I guess I should thank you for your good wishes. If they could do me any good."

"Yes, when it comes to the ladies, I wonder whether any of us really has any choice."

200

"Perhaps you have more experience in that area than I do."

Now the lord laughed out loud. "I certainly hope so!" His smile faded as they rode along, and finally he mused, almost to himself. "And not always the happiest."

He doesn't mean you to comment.

I didn't think so.

Ecmund glanced over at the Magician, who rode heedlessly, his eyes fixed on a spot between his horse's ears, seeming to see nothing.

He is very sad, Ecmund.

Or putting on a very good act.

I have no experience with a Magician powerful enough to make such an act, nor do I dare seek further.

Let it ride. We have made progress, and we have time.

After a few bowshots of silent travel, Ostersund seemed to come back to his surroundings. "But we stray from our topic."

Ecmund looked around, puzzled. "Lord Delfontes and this mission?"

"Yes. I still feel the two of us to be a strange choice. Would you not expect him to send at least one of his advisors, his friends who came with him?"

Ecmund pondered. Was there another meaning to this question? Perhaps not. "I see little evidence that he brought advisors from Koningsholm who could be called friends."

"I do find one thing strange, at least from my point of view. Since he has been here, I think he has done more consulting with you than any of us. Can you explain that?" Ostersund grinned. "No, not a good question. I probably have a better idea of the answer. Do you know the history of his progress here?"

"Perica has explained a lot of it."

"You understand that Lord Delfontes is a rather strange man. A bit of a loner. Not many allies in court. This, among other problems, sent him here. Last chance, the story goes. One final toss of the dice. As you noted, he brought few friends with him. Only his daughter. Once he got here, he picked you, and speaks little of import to anyone who came with him."

"Perhaps he doesn't trust them?"

"Why not?"

"Once again, a question you should be answering. You're the one who didn't swear to him."

"That wasn't possible, given the circumstances."

"I won't pry into your reasons, but it still doesn't look good. If you can't swear to the lord, I ask myself, why would you follow him here? What good is your presence to him?"

"Delfontes knows I am loyal to the King. The King sent him here, and sent me to help. That was enough for him. Is it not enough for you?"

Ecmund shrugged. "What if you were sent to cause trouble?"

Ostersund threw up his hands and laughed. "If the King sent him here, then sent me along to cause him trouble...well, the plots are so complicated that there is no use you or me discussing them."

He did not answer you.

"You are an honest man, my Lord, with a clever way of turning aside from the point before you are required to falsify an answer."

"When such evasion becomes obvious, it might be considered good manners to stop asking."

"Lord Ostersund, we are not talking about a game of cards. This is my demesne, where my people live, and if our safety is concerned, I will not be turned aside by a charge of rudeness."

That's it! That set him straight!

The lord glanced over at him, seemed to hold back a smile. "No, I suppose you would not."

It was not the kind of response that invited further discussion, so Ecmund did not continue. They rode in silence for a long time.

When they stopped for the noon meal, Jesco strolled beside Ecmund as he patrolled their perimeter. "A serious conversation, you and Lord Ostersund."

"I don't know what he was after, but I gave him something else."

The swordsman grinned. "How did he take that?"

Ecmund shrugged in irritation. "It didn't seem to bother him. In fact, he seemed a bit...amused."

"Do you think it's time I went and unamused him?"

"No, not yet. At the moment we still consider him an ally. And are you sure the word isn't 'disamused'?"

"Since I just made it up, I have no idea."

"Hmm. Making up words. You really are spending too much time thinking."

"Aye. Couldn't you find me a quick battle or something, put me back on my usual trail?"

Ecmund sobered. "Be careful what you wish for."

His cousin slapped him on the back. "Don't be taking responsibility for everyone's woes. Can't you get it straight that I really like fighting?"

"Not really. I can work with it, though."

"Good. What about Lord Blond-and-Handsome?"

"He knows where I stand."

"Good. And he knows I stand behind you."

"Oh, I don't imagine he missed that point." He grinned at his cousin, and they turned back towards their camp.

202

Chapter 23

Ecmund restrained himself from driving his fist into the post in front of him. He turned to use the force of his superior height against the old chieftain. "Then why can't we meet with your Council?"

The blanket-clad shoulders shrugged, the grey head moved to one side, then the other. "The proper conditions do not exist."

"Well, you and I are the ones to make them exist. You claim to represent your people; I represent mine. I have been here for two days, and you refuse to meet with me."

"I represent my people. You seem young for an ambassador."

"You have seen the letter. You have seen the Lord's seal. I have the full confidence of Lord Delfontes da Falken in this matter. There is a problem, and I have been sent to solve it."

Polvijarvi looked Ecmund slowly up and down. "You speak as one with a great deal of confidence, but when I look at you, I see no reason to believe it. What do you call that sort of person in your world?"

Ecmund looked the chieftain in the eye. "I think we would call that person a braggart."

"Ah. That is the word. I am not experienced in the rites of your people, but I think that I should not give you that name, here at the table of diplomacy."

"I have yet to see any table, any diplomacy."

"Then tell me, Ecmund of Falcon's Home. What have you to show me to tell me I would be wrong about you?"

"Among my people, it would not be necessary. I speak with the voice of the Overlord da Falken, who is responsible to the King for this territory. This is not a boast. It is fact."

"Ah, but my people have dealt with the armies of the Maridon King."

"Yes, and the armies of the Blood of Inderjorne before that. Each time, as our lore tells us, you decided that it would be better to make an agreement than to have your people torn apart by war. Have we come to a time when you must be forced to that decision again?"

"Have we come to the time when you will return to your Overlord, and tell him that your mission has failed?"

"Oh, no. That time is far from now. For example, I think that if I were to sit with your elders, and discuss our treaties, we could perhaps make them more relevant. Decide which parts are out-dated, which still hold. Why should we not have this conversation?"

"And now we are back at the start of the trail. I see no reason for my elders to sit with you. By the rules of my people, you have not earned the right."

"And there are ways to earn that right?"

"Of course. Our allies have that right. One who has done us a great service has that right."

"I see no opportunity for myself to become such a person."

"Then I see no reason to speak in council with you."

"None?"

"None that you could accomplish."

Ecmund bowed slightly. "I will discuss this with my advisors."

Polvijarvi grinned, showing broken teeth. "Your Magician and your soldiers? Such fine advisors your Overlord has given you."

"By my own choice, Polvijarvi. I am quite capable of handling this situation in my own way."

A faint frown crossed the wrinkled brow. "When you have consulted your 'advisors', if you have any more to say, we may speak again." Again the gap-toothed grin. "I find it entertaining."

"I am pleased to have pleased you." He spoke in a flat tone, not masking the sarcasm.

Again the chieftain sent him an assessing glance, then turned and strolled back to the group of his people who had been watching the exchange. As he met them, he made a loud comment, which caused immoderate laughter.

"If we could only speak their language. I'm sure that would help."

I speak their language.

Not yet, Kitten.

He knows Magicians.

Yes. Interesting.

He approached his own party. "Impasse. He will not have any official speech with us until we have earned the right. He seems quite happy to chat any time, but without a meeting of the elders, there will be no progress."

Ostersund frowned across the field. "I'd like to take the flat of my sword to his butt."

Ecmund smiled. "You're not going to get the opportunity, unless you beat his champion first. Are you up to it?"

The Lord shook his head. "I'm not that good a swordsman."

"I'm out of ideas."

Ostersund sighed. "I have heard the tales. It was ever thus. They are a very frustrating people to deal with."

"Do you have any suggestions?"

"The easy one would be to decide that we have done our best, and go back for the army."

Ecmund glanced sharply at the older man. "And is this what you advise?"

Ostersund shrugged. "Lord Delfontes cannot rule with this canker chafing his side. The problem must be solved, or it will get worse."

"Which leaves us with the last solution. The only way they are going to listen to us is if someone beats their champion in single combat."

Jesco was staring across at the muscular warrior hovering at the chieftain's elbow. "I can't see that it's going to be you, Ecmund..."

We could win.

Could we?

Probably.

Not good enough.

"...so it obviously has to be me."

Ecmund turned to face his cousin. "This is not why I brought you, Jesco."

"No. You never know exactly why you will need someone like me, until you need me." He grinned. "Then we all find out."

Ecmund looked at the sergeant. "Anything to add?"

"I'm with Jesco, sir. If you need fighting, that's what we're here for. Until that moment, the decisions are yours."

The side of Ecmund's mouth twisted. "Well, thanks for the vote of confidence. Does anyone know how we send the challenge? I somehow doubt that we get to slap a glove across his face, much though I would like to."

Ostersund shrugged again. "I am sorry to be of such little help, but the finer details of Leute etiquette were not part of my courtly education."

"Mine either. I guess we'll have to ask, much though I hate to."

Go to the fighting ground.

What?

The challenge is issued from the fighting ground.

Ecmund pretended to consider. "Perhaps we don't have to ask. If we're going to fight, let's go to that field over there, with the posts. It looks like a training space of some sort."

He led the way towards a flat, finely-gravelled area, with shoulder-high posts surrounding it.

Only you.

He stopped his people at the nearest post. "I think perhaps I should be the one to enter." Ecmund stepped three precise paces.

Stop. Face them.

His action had attracted a great deal of attention. The whole group of elders moved towards them and calls and queries echoed through the camp. The chieftain circled the field, entered at a point exactly opposite Ecmund.

Give nothing. Show strength.

As the old man approached, Ecmund planted his feet, crossed his arms on his chest, lowered his chin.

A slight shadow crossed the chieftain's face. "This is not a place for outsiders to wander, Ecmund of Falcon's Home."

"It seems as good a place as any for us to chat."

"My people do not consider this a place for chat. On this ground, we have other means of settling disputes."

"Good. Perhaps that will help solve our problem."

"You realize there are others in my tribe who are better able to dispute with you than I."

"You realize that there are others of my 'advisors' who may be more useful than you thought."

Kitten could feel the old memories stirring. She tried to hold them in check, but they boiled around her.

The beady old eyes flitted to Ecmund's party, then back to his face. "I believe you know what you are doing. I will have my champion prepare himself."

... to DIE.

The chieftain suddenly stiffened, as if someone had struck him. He shook his head slightly, frowning.

Easy, girl.

"As will I. Please inform us if you have any ritual requirements. We have no wish to offend."

"That is diplomatic of you."

"We have no wish to give you an excuse to sidestep the discussion which you know is coming, sooner or later, whether you want it or not."

He turned his back before the old man could react, and strode to the edge of the field.

Ostersund nodded. "I don't know what you said at the end there, but it set him back on his heels."

"It was meant to. I tire of his games, and I hope he realizes how far he has pushed them. Now a life is at stake. At least I think so. I have no idea of the rules."

Death is possible, serious injury normal.

Jesco pulled off his cloak and began stretching his arms. "You don't know whether I'm supposed to kill him or not?"

"If he dies, they can't call foul. This is a sword fight, not skittles."

"Fair enough. That's my kind of fight, anyway."

"I'm sorry it came to this, Jesco. I was always hoping..."

"I know, little cousin. You have your ways and I have mine. We agree that there is a time for each. You had your time, now my turn comes."

Ecmund frowned. "You like that idea, don't you?"

206

Jesco rolled his fingers together until the joints cracked, stretched them over his head. "There is a bit of satisfaction, I must admit."

Suddenly he stopped his warm-up, faced his cousin directly. "Don't you go worrying, if this goes wrong. You know it is what I trained for. Don't blame yourself. I won't blame you. You did your best, and I think it was enough. This is their way, and it's my way, and so I'm the one to deal with it."

His face softened. "If it does go wrong, do me a favour."

"Of course."

"You take care of that sister of yours. It's her way that works the best."

"It is?"

Jesco laughed and went back to his warm-up. "In case you didn't notice, she's got me, and you, and my father, all doing exactly what she wants, and all happy to be doing it. I'll tell you, Ecmund, if I had a kingdom to run, I'd put her in charge!"

Ecmund shook his head. "I know what you mean. I'll take care of her, no matter what. You know that."

"We're a good family, Ecmund, and I'm proud to be a part."

Ecmund's worry deepened. "Jesco, don't talk as if you're going to lose. What kind of attitude is that?"

"Ah, I'm just saying all these things so that after I win, you'll have a handle to pull me back to the ground."

Ecmund clapped his hand on his cousin's shoulder and turned to see what was happening on the other side of the square. The broad-shouldered one was also warming up, his face serious, despite the laughter and cheering from his people. He looked very competent.

Chapter 24

"Do you think you can beat him?"

"I have no idea. Doesn't really matter at this point, does it?"

"He looks very strong."

"I don't see how he could be otherwise."

Ecmund tried to find something that would help. "That's a big, heavy, sword. I have to assume he'll be slow to swing it."

Ecmund...

"Did you look at his arms? He's heavier in the shoulders than you are, Ecmund. He can probably swing it."

Ecmund grimaced. "I have no advice. You're the swordsman."

I will fight, Ecmund.

"Thank you, Ecmund. If you had advice, I'd probably listen, and it would probably mess me up."

Ecmund! She put all the strength she dared into the call, with the Magician so close.

"I do have one request, though, Jesco."

"One request?"

"Use my Sword."

Jesco looked down at the hilt his cousin offered.

"I don't think so, Ecmund. That's a heavier sword than I'm used to. We just decided that my speed is the best way to beat him."

"I think you'll find she's very light."

"It isn't a good idea, fighting an important battle with a sword I've never tried before. Why should I?"

Ecmund weighed the possibilities, then pulled his cousin out onto the fighting field, away from the others. "Jesco, do you trust me?"

"Of course."

"If I tell you that I know something that I can't tell anyone, even you, can you accept that?"

"Aye, politics again. I can accept that. I told you long ago; you stick to the politics, I'll do the fighting."

"Yes, but here's the moment when the politics interferes with the fighting. I'm asking you to fight with my Sword, Jesco, taking my word that you will be much happier if you do. I'm asking you to say nothing about it, now or later, no matter what happens."

"That's a lot to ask."

"It's important. The Overlord and I decided before we left on this mission that this was the way it might have to go. All you have to do is be a good soldier, Jesco."

"And die if I have to, for the good of my people."

"Yes, but I don't think that's likely."

"You don't think it likely."

Let me speak to him.

You will not.

"Here Jesco. Take a few passes with her. You'll like the feel."

His cousin frowned, shrugged. "If you say so, Ecmund."

Do not speak to him. Just fight.

Yes, Ecmund. I will fight very well.

Don't forget...

I will fight, Ecmund. It is what I do.

Jesco took the sword, fitted his hand inside the guard. Kitten nestled happily against familiar calluses. Another frown crossed his brow.

"Fits really well. I wouldn't have thought..."

He swung the sword, and a keen whistle pierced the air.

"Say..." He swung again, and the whistle, louder this time, seemed to linger in the light mountain air.

Heads came up all over the encampment. After a brief silence, a sudden burst of talking erupted from the cluster around the chieftain and his champion. Then the group broke open, and Polvijarvi was striding towards them. When he came close enough, Ecmund could see his eyes stray to Jesco.

"Ecmund of Falcon's Home. This is your champion?"

"Yes, this is Jesco, of my Blood. He fights for my right to speak."

The chieftain reached out a hand with studied casualness, and touched the hilt of the Sword. "It will be an honour for my champion to match his blade. A great honour."

Kitten could feel Polvijarvi's heart, and it did not rise with the words he spoke. In fact, a great sadness was settling on him. Her instinct was to send fear, but she held back. Somehow, it was not right. Deep down in his mind, a Name was resonating. It was not a Name she wanted to hear.

"Pardon us for a brief while, Ecmund of Falcon's Home. This makes a change. We must prepare the proper rites for the passing."

"What passing?"

"The passing of the champion."

"Why would the champion pass, and what does that mean?"

The chieftain looked at Ecmund as if he was unsure of the question. "The champion must die, of course. We were not aware, and we wish it were not so, but such is fate."

"Why should he die? They fight only to establish my right to speak."

The chieftain gestured with open hands. "Of course he will die. It has always been so."

"What if he doesn't die?"

The old man shrugged. "I would be very happy, but our lore says otherwise."

"I see. Then please make the proper rites."

The chieftain returned into the press of onlookers.

"Jesco. Give me the sword back, just for a moment."

Jesco looked surprised, but handed back the weapon without comment,

You have fought here before.

Yes.

And always you killed.

Yes.

Was that necessary?

It happened.

Can you fight and not kill?

Ask Eirlin.

Please do not kill unless you have to.

Will that be better?

Yes. Much better.

I will not kill unless Jesco feels he must.

Thank you, Kitten.

He handed the Sword back. "Jesco, the game has changed. Can you fight this man and not kill him?"

"That's a tough order, Ecmund. I'm not sure I can even beat him. It would be a big handicap."

"They're all certain you're going to win. He's over there taking his final rites, whatever they are. Will you see how it goes, and disarm or wound him if you can? I know it is not your style of fighting, but try. I suspect you won't find it hard. Think of it this way. It's a game of battle squares, and you just got promoted from Sword to Trooper."

"I did?"

"Maybe even General. They move differently from Swords. You must change as well."

"What happened? They were all uppity-ass and sure of themselves, and now they're thinking about death? I don't get it."

Kitten's mind ranged back through the faded years. She had been so young, so naïve. And then that Name! She cringed. *Please the Smith, do not let him hear that Name!*

Ecmund smiled grimly. "It all happened about the time you swung my sword for the first time. That whistle really caught them."

"You mean this?" He swung Kitten again, in a swift double eight, and she let the sound stretch out of her, reaching higher and higher, until only the dogs could hear it, and they set up an accompanying howl. Heads turned and shoulders hunched, as against the cold of winter.

Jesco shook his head. "There are many things afoot around here, and I don't know what they are, but you seem to, and that's enough for me. If I can possibly survive and keep from killing him, I will do that."

"Thank you, Jesco."

"I'll tell you that you're welcome after the fight. If I can."

During this conversation, a serious and moving ceremony had taken place. Several women, presumably relatives of the champion, were making brave but tearful farewells. A drink was passed, and a young man, almost the size of the champion, seemed to be preparing to take over the position. He did not look happy about it, either.

The only one showing no sorrow appeared to be the champion. He had a strange look, as if something wonderful was about to happen to him, but he wasn't sure what.

"Look at his face. Has he been drinking, or something?"

"Only what the others drank. I tell you, Jesco, this is part of their mythology. It isn't just a ritual. He is expecting to die. Nobody wants him to, but he will fight anyway, because it's expected of him."

"I can understand that."

"He'll fight as hard as he can, though. Harder perhaps, because he has nothing to lose. Keep that in mind."

"Right." Jesco seemed to be entering his own ritual, withdrawing into himself, his eyes piercing nearby objects, focused on the distance. He held the Sword before him, his hand weaving gently, as if rehearsing a defence. As he moved, Kitten responded. He frowned, and the scope of his motions increased. She could feel puzzlement, then a growing suspicion. Suddenly his brow cleared, and he met Ecmund's eyes, a faint smile creasing the corners of his mouth.

Kitten did not have to speak. Jesco was of the Blood. He had to know.

Then the ceremonies were over, and the two men stepped onto the field of battle.

Up until now, Kitten had been silent, feeling only enough through the skin contact to allow her to learn about this new mind. It was similar to Ecmund's, yet so much was different. She shuddered at the dark corners, and avoided them. For any Sword to take a soul like this would be a terrible mistake. Even to Join with it would be nightmare.

As the men slipped towards each other, the emotion of the crowd flowed around them, and she could risk opening herself more. She filled his arm with strength and his mind with clarity, and he responded enthusiastically. She remembered his style, and fed a fine thread of caution through it all, reassuring, gentling, calming.

211

Then the blades touched, and a shock ran through them, back and forth. This was no common sword either, though far from sentient. It was imbued with the strength of generations, the belief of a people.

This will truly be a memorable battle.

The speed with which the first passes occurred left no doubt as to the opponent's skill. He was quick and strong, and his sword responded like magic to his every move.

Like magic. Ha, ha. Nobody laughing this time. You want magic? Watch closely...

As Jesco was drawn into the fight, his mind opened more to her, and she increased her support. She had never fought this way before, never been held by a Hand with so much skill of his own. She did not control him, allowing him to take the fight as he would. She had no knowledge of his individual moves, only focused on the mind of the Hand, feeding him strength, agility, and her decades of fighting experience.

As the duel moved past the opening touches, she could feel the fierce determination, held in check by caution. Then the speed increased and the caution began to fade, replaced by confidence. She boosted that assurance, just enough, not too much, and set herself to observe.

The fight was very even at first, merely a back-and-forth testing of skills and patterns. Jesco could handle this easily, and she searched for a way to aid him more. She explored deeper, skirting the dark areas. She could sense something there, something wrong, but she couldn't tell what. Careful not to disturb the part of his mind that fought, she cast around further. There was a dark, twisted, corner, which oozed gloom, and she carefully approached: open, watching, listening. Then she pounced. It writhed and squirmed against her, and her mind was bombarded with images of incredible pain, of anger, of bloodshed. Grimly, she fought until she had it, read it, knew its meaning. As the understanding grew, she recoiled in dismay. A part of his mind was fighting, surging against restraints, eager to escape, to control. The urge was almost overwhelming, even as he fought with all his skill to survive.

At any moment, he might throw himself forward, attack without parry, die in order to win.

In desperate haste she pushed back, frantically tucking the edges of his sanity around the gap, urging the walls to grow firmer, compelling the terrible craving deeper inside. As she worked she could feel his strength join with hers. Some level of his consciousness wanted what she wanted; together they fought, inside and out, and finally the awful wound was safely closed.

Relieved, she turned her attention back to the battle.

Jesco was suddenly enjoying himself. She could feel a small part of his mind frowning in surprise, but the rest of him revelled in the contest.

The cut and thrust, turn and slide, the grit under his feet, the whistle of the sword, and the sharp rattle of parry and riposte, sent a glow through him, and he fought with an intense concentration bordering on ecstasy.

The Leute champion, too, seemed to have lost his fear, his determination, and everything other than the knowledge that he was fighting an epic contest. The sweat flew from his body as he lunged and dodged, avoiding Kitten's cuts and thrusts in a euphoric frenzy.

More confident, now, she allowed herself to be caught up in the ring of steel on steel, the minds of the opponents so involved in their dance that the two became one. Back and forth they strove, their feet tearing gouges in the gravel, their free hands grasping for balance, and all centred on the snick and clang of the edges. She fed joyfully on the waves pouring over her, carefully treading the line between control and rapture.

She began to see, by the shape of the battle, that the end was near. Jesco was completely in control now, stretching the game for the joy of the play. The Leute no longer carried any initiative, following her bright ripple like a puppet on a fine steel string. Then Jesco started a pattern that could have only one finish. A series of alternating outside attacks forced the opponent's arm farther and farther out of line, until his sword was swinging back and forth in front of him like a pendulum. As his arm passed across his face in a desperate backhand slash, Jesco circled under and lunged forward; Kitten caught the opposing sword at the hilt, trapping it in her quillion. Jesco gave a sharp twist in the direction of the blow, and the Leute champion literally threw his own sword across the field.

Jesco finished the move with a flourish, kicking the back of his opponent's leg to drop the man to his knees, head down, neck exposed to Kitten's edge.

Hold. Calm.

Jesco held, his hand rigid as the battle faded and reality oozed back into his mind. There was a pause, then he slowly raised the Sword. With a long, even, sweep, he brought her around in a salute, first to the Leute people, then to Ecmund. She hummed softly to herself, fed the pleasure through his hand, receiving an equal flow from him.

Then he flipped her over, catching her blade, hilt up. His other hand reached down to help the stunned Leute to his feet. The man's face began to work, as if he were returning from a trance. She used the skin contact to send joy to him as well, and a sudden burst of emotion surged back.

They stood there, stretching the moment, basking in the shared sensation. Then the cheering of the crowd came through to them, and their senses reached outward. A flow of Leute swept inwards, circling around as if afraid to come too near.

Jesco looked up into the Leute's eyes. "I have never had a battle like that! Never!"

"Not me either. I thought I was dead. I thought I fought the Battles of the Ancestors."

"Sorry, friend. You're still down here on earth. But I've never been so near heaven myself."

Me too. But she spoke so softly that neither man noticed.

Jesco stepped away, picked up the other sword from the gravel. "A fine sword. Hope there's no damage."

The champion took his weapon, ran a glance along the nicked blade. "Honourably gained."

Jesco nodded. "Honourably earned."

Then the champion was mobbed by his family, and Jesco turned back to his own small party.

As he approached, he could tell from Ecmund's anxious look that he was to say nothing. He grinned. "Nice Sword, cousin. A little heavy for my taste, but it helped against his arm."

Ecmund shook his head. "I have never seen such a fight, Jesco."

"Sure, but what do you know?" Still, his hand lingered as he passed Kitten over.

Ecmund caressed her blade, once, before he sheathed her. "I know a classic when I see one. Was he as good as you thought?"

"Better. Of course, when you think you're already dead, it lends a certain quality to your style."

"Sounds familiar."

"Um…yes. There was something else there, too…"

"We'll talk about it. Not now."

The soldiers had allowed the cousins a moment, but now they crowded around Jesco with their congratulations, and Ecmund allowed himself to be shouldered aside. A presence made him look around, and there was Ostersund at his shoulder.

"We rarely see such a fight."

Something about the man's superior smile irked Ecmund. "Do you think so? I have little experience with that sort of thing. They certainly looked evenly matched."

"I do have some experience, and it was not as evenly matched as you might have thought. Your cousin was enjoying himself a great deal."

"I told him not to kill if he could avoid it."

"Dangerous instructions."

"We are here as ambassadors, not conquerors."

"A laudable goal, and one which you seem to have accomplished."

He nodded towards the chieftain, who was striding towards them, beaming.

"A fine demonstration, Ecmund of Falcon's Home. You have truly honoured us today."

"Thank you, Polvijarvi. It was a pleasure to see your champion fight so well."

Polvijarvi grinned even wider. "You are kind. It was even more pleasure to see him on his feet at the end."

Ecmund refrained from further discussion. He didn't want the Magician to start thinking about the reason for the Leute's attitude.

"So, Polvijarvi. Has my kinsman earned us the right to speak?"

"Of course, of course. You must forgive us our small pride, see this situation our way. We had done nothing, changed nothing. Your Overlord was the new one. It was for him to come to us with the appropriate embassy, to assure us that he would follow the proper forms, give us our hereditary due. Now, everything has been done according to the traditions."

The chieftain slapped Ecmund on the back. "You have earned your right to talk. Almost."

"Almost?"

"Yes. There will be a meeting, never fear. But first, there will be a feast. Seldom do the legends come to life, and we must celebrate. Tomorrow, when our heads are clear again, we will speak the words that must be spoken. Tonight, we eat and drink, and whatever else might befall."

Ecmund smiled, and Polvijarvi strode away, renewed youth in his step, calling orders.

The soldiers began to grin, but their sergeant frowned. "There will be four of us on duty at all times and don't you forget it! There will be no trouble with the local females!"

They answered in an eager chorus, the gist being that the local women would find them no trouble at all, if they were given the chance.

I will guard.

Ecmund shook his head and grinned at the sergeant. "I agree with your caution, but I don't envy you your duty."

The old soldier waved a hand. "No problem, sir. There's three of them's married, and not likely to overdo it. We didn't bring novices on a serious mission like this."

Ecmund nodded, pleased to have one less worry. Then he gave himself over to the festivities.

When he woke the next morning, there was a vague blurring of his memory, but otherwise he felt clear-headed. Considering the amount of tribal hooch he had finished off, it was a wonder.

You were terrible.

"What?"

You were very hard to help. I felt quite strange.

"You helped? How?"

You know what I always do. I clear your mind.

"Did you? And how does that affect you?" He concentrated, and she could feel his mind searching into her. "Kitten! You got drunk, too!"

I did not.

"You didn't? I remember now. You were singing."

I merely hummed a bit. The chieftain liked it.

"Did he, now? And did our personal Magician like it as well?"

Neither of us was that drunk. He was otherwise occupied, and there was much singing and drinking, much emotion to hide me. Many of these people think as clearly as you, Ecmund. He could hear nothing, with all of these noisy minds around us.

"Well, until someone comes in with a different tale, I guess we managed to pass last night's test as well. Now I can get down to what I came to do."

A strong voice in council, a strong hand in war.

Ecmund shrugged ruefully. "So far, I haven't shown either."

You will speak well.

"Thank you. I'm sure you have great experience in these matters."

I have spent time in council.

Especially the years she had spent embedded in the centre of a certain conference table. It had been an instructive time, if mostly boring, and better left unmentioned.

Humans say the same things, over and over.

"I'm sure you'll remind me if I start repeating myself."

It is often necessary. When the swords are put away, the ears seem to stop working.

"And that is your opinion of diplomacy, is it?"

I am a Sword.

"And a very good one. We would not be here today, were it not for your skills."

Yesterday was a good day: both enjoyable and beneficial. It is not always thus.

"You can make good money betting on that." He swooped up her belt, buckling it on as he left his tent.

And now?

"Now, if we have any luck, they don't want to rehash too many of the treaty provisions. We get a day or two of boring talk, and then we go home."

Polvijarvi is not boring.

"That's too true to be funny."

Chapter *25*

Ecmund found Polvijarvi outside the meeting tent. The old man looked him up and down. "You look well, Ecmund of the Falcon Home."

"As do you, Chieftain Polvijarvi."

The old man grinned. "But you drank twice what I did last night. Ah, for young blood again."

Ecmund shrugged. "The trials we must undergo to serve."

"Ah, that is a truth."

"I came to ask if there is any ceremony we need to know about."

"Nothing your people would term ceremonial. We will line up, you will line up, you and I will enter the tent together, with our people following. Does your Magician wish recognition of his rank?"

"Lord Ostersund prefers not to flaunt his powers."

"Ah, yes. With the present monarch, the position of a Magician of the Blood is not so clear, is it?"

Ecmund looked at the old man. "You know more of our doings than one might expect."

"I did not learn your language by sticking my head down a woodchuck's hole. Nor does one get to be Chief of Clans of the Leute by sitting on the farthest mountain and staring into the infinity of the night sky. I had to work all my life for the post I hold."

"Your people are wise."

"How is it with you? How did you become a leader of your people?"

"I was born to the opportunity, then trained all my life. I lead as much as I deserve."

The chieftain shrugged. "So your people get the position first, and then work for it. It makes little difference in the end."

Ecmund set that aside for further thought, and signalled Jesco and Ostersund to follow towards the large meeting tent. It was not really a tent, more a circular earthen wall with a canvas cover over pole rafters. A lot of light came through the cloth, so it was full daylight inside. The elders sat around the rim, and there were places for Ecmund's party along one side.

As the chieftain said, there was little ritual. It could have been a meeting of the combined Village Councils. The main focus, of course, was the treaty itself.

With an air of ceremony, Polvijarvi bore the box containing the original manuscript to a table at the centre of the assembly. Trying for equal dignity, Ecmund brought his paper-written copy to lay beside it. Then he and Polvijarvi took turns reading from their documents, until all present agreed that both contained the same information.

217

Once that task was finished, the chieftain stood, gazing around at the company. "Does any man present desire any change to this treaty?"

There was silence.

The chieftain turned to each of the elders in turn, and asked the same question. In each case, the response was negative. Then he turned to Ecmund. "And you? Your credentials say that you speak for all, including your Overlord. Does he wish any changes?"

Ecmund glanced to Lord Ostersund, thought a moment. "No. We are quite happy with the treaty, if it is followed."

"Good." Polvijarvi turned the circle one more time, his glance carefully taking in every person present. "In that case, having heard agreement from all present, I declare this treaty lawful and binding upon my people and their descendants." He said something in his own language, then turned expectantly to Ecmund.

Ecmund rose. "I, too, declare this treaty lawful and binding upon my Overlord, his people, and all our descendants."

Polvijarvi translated. There was a satisfied nodding of heads, a dignified pause, and the elders began to rise and stroll out of the tent. Ecmund watched them go, a slight frown on his face. Finally he turned to Polvijarvi. "Is that it?"

"Is there more? You came to reaffirm the treaty. It is reaffirmed."

"But what about all the trouble? The infringements, the thefts?"

The chieftain slapped Ecmund on the shoulder. "Those were merely to get your Overlord's attention."

Lord Ostersund snorted. "More likely to see if anyone was paying attention at all."

"That might have been some part of it."

Ecmund nodded slowly. "So now that the treaty has been verified, everything will go back to the way it was?"

"That's right."

"I see."

As his own party left the tent, Ecmund paused. "Tell me, Polvijarvi, how many of your people can read that document?"

"Read and understand? About three."

"Then how do you follow it?"

Polvijarvi smiled and raised his voice. "Voice Onniemi, will you attend us?"

A scruffy little man limped over to them.

"We have need of your services. We must show our understanding."

"As we always must." A grin passed between the two old men.

Polvijarvi lifted the manuscript, indicated a heading. "Missing stock. Onniemi, what is the lore on missing stock?"

Without glancing at the treaty, the little man proceeded to recite the whole section, almost letter-perfect. At his leader's nod, he strolled away.

"You understand that this paper is in your language, because ours is not written. We have our own translation, of course."

"And your own interpretation, I assume?"

"Do you wish to hear the section on arbitration of mistranslations?"

Ecmund laughed. "No, I am impressed that it was included, and I'm sure it has functioned well, over the last several hundred years."

The chieftain shook his head. "That was only put in when the Maridons came. They are a people so fussy about words."

Ecmund nodded, and they left the tent. As his group moved towards their billet, he paused beside the old Leute.

"Polvijarvi, this has made valuable learning for me. Perhaps you would give me the benefit of your age and experience?"

"Of course."

"How do you suggest I approach the other clans? Will we have to fight our way into every council?"

"I suggest strongly that you do nothing of the sort. If you were to approach another clan, you would be stepping firmly on the toes of the Chief of Clans."

"Who is...you?"

"Of course. I will take care of this duty. With pleasure. Besides, you would spoil the fun for my heralds."

"Why is that?"

"Because a legend has returned, and they get to tell the story. In this case, since it was a rather unhappy legend and the new tale is much more agreeable, everyone will be very pleased to hear it. Oh, yes, my heralds will eat and drink their fill until their stomachs endanger their ability to perform their duties."

"The legend of the Sword. Perhaps you would like to tell me about that?"

You will say NOTHING! That Name does not exist.

The chieftain glanced down at her, winced, shook his head. "Every man has a time in his past which he would rather not spread to the world. Nations are no different. Your Sword took part in one of those times."

Even a Sword knows when there is too much killing.

You'll have to tell me later.

I think not. Everyone has a time in her past...

Mhmm.

"Now She has returned to us, but something has changed. Maybe it is the Sword. Maybe it is you, maybe us. Maybe it is the will of the Gods. It matters little. We have much to rejoice in, and our people will remember

219

that it began with the arrival of Overlord Delfontes. It will be good for all, I think."

Very satisfying.

"She expresses the same sentiment."

The chieftain placed two fingertips carefully on Kitten's pommel. "I am honoured."

She fed him a deep purr, but could not resist a tiny scratch.

He pulled his hand away sharply, then smiled. "I think I have just been prompted to remember her full abilities."

"She is like that."

"I do not envy you your life, Hand."

He shrugged. "It seems I was chosen. What can I do but make the best of it? Ouch!"

"I gather you have been reminded as well."

"I have."

The old man was silent for a moment, and Kitten could feel his mind seeking. She opened to him, just the first level. That Name hovered, ever ready to sound.

Some Names are best forgotten.

Finally he spoke. "I think it must be the Sword who has changed. I cannot reconcile the legend with what I feel from her now."

Neither can I.

"She agrees."

The old man's eyes took a faraway sheen. "I dreamed of the cat who lives high in the mountains to the west. Long hair of mottled white and grey, invisible on snow and shadow. Shy of man, but unafraid to tackle any prey, no matter how fierce. He who claims the Cloud Cat as his totem must be terrible in battle, ferocious in the hunt."

"Doesn't sound like me."

"Nonetheless."

He has given me a Name!

The old man brought himself back. "I have messengers to send, and I'm sure you want to get out of this barbarian encampment and return to the luxury of your castle."

Ecmund grinned. "Back in the world of luxury, I am a woodcutter, and I live in a cottage about the size of your tent."

The chieftain stared at Ecmund a moment. "Not for long, I suspect." Then he turned away and began to lay out orders to those who stood waiting for him.

A Name. A new Name. I am the Cloud Cat, invisible in snow and shadow!

"Do you want that spread around?"

It is not done thus. A Name grows within the hearts of the people.

"I see. Well, this one's likely to grow within the hearts of the Leute."

I am Cloud Cat of the Leute. It is a Name.

"As long as you're happy. You deserve it."

Of course I do. The Cloud Cat, afraid of none. I have a Name, here in the mountains. We must return when we have time to enjoy our visit.

"Under easier circumstances, I hope."

I have a Name.

"So you keep saying. Maybe we can go home now."

And I shall have a Name there as well. Soon.

"I'm sure you will."

Ecmund returned to his own party.

"What was that little meeting about? It seemed to go well."

Ecmund refrained from shooting Ostersund a suspicious look. "Just the usual, I guess. You do the ceremonies, follow the rituals, then you check afterwards to make sure that it really went like it sounded."

The Magician nodded. "A good precaution. What is our plan now?"

Ecmund smiled. "It turns out we don't have one. As we might have guessed, the first leader we met turns out to be the Chief of Clans. He will send the runners out to tell everybody to be good, and, if we are to believe him, they will."

"And do you believe him?"

"Within the usual range of human ability to get along, yes. I suspect life here will continue as it has for the past hundred years, maybe a bit more smoothly. Jesco's ability seems to have impressed them. They love the chance for a story, and that battle was a new tale altogether."

Jesco reddened, but said nothing.

"So when do we leave?"

"As soon as is polite. I think we should spread the message among our people quickly. It would be too bad if it was one of us who committed the next breach."

"I agree. You have done well here, Lord Falkenric."

Ecmund shot the man a glance. "That was rather formal."

For the first time, the Magician actually grinned. "There is a time for such a pronouncement."

Ecmund returned the smile. "Then I must thank you for your approbation, my Lord."

"Let's not get carried away."

"The language does sound rather strange, considering the setting."

They both looked around at the encampment: dirt-walled tents, outside cooking fires, skins stretched to dry.

"I'll be happy to get home."

"We can agree on that, as well."

221

Chapter 26

Ecmund stood in the stirrups and craned his neck back to Jesco. "Good to see familiar ground."

His cousin grinned. "You don't travel enough, Ecmund. I've been on familiar ground for hours."

"Only because you once took a fancy to that miller's daughter over in Sandhorst."

"Every man has his reasons for travelling."

"And every man is glad to get home after."

"There is truth in that."

They lifted their horses to a lope for a while, in recognition of the pleasant day and their desire to be home. Soon, however, good sense prevailed, and they returned to a fast walk.

Alert.

What?

Rider in a hurry.

Ecmund held up his hand. "Rider coming. Form up."

The soldiers reacted instantly. Gathering in a loose knot, hands on hilts, bows strung, they waited in the middle of a straight stretch of trail.

Soon a galloping horse appeared, its rider pulling up briefly at the sight of armed men, then spurring forward. "Ecmund!"

"It's Maer."

The lad skidded his horse to a halt, almost running into Ecmund in the process. "It's Eirlin! They've taken her!"

Ecmund reached out to grab the boy's arm. "Who took her?"

"Nobody knows. About fifteen men. They lured her out of the castle, ambushed her, and took her away. We lost three men trying to save her. They said it was that Tajar fellow."

"The one who attacked her before. Which way did they go?"

"Lady Perica sent out a tracking party. They'll contact us when they figure it out. I came to find you, because I'm lightest. We didn't know how far you'd be."

Ecmund turned to his party. "Stay together. This could be some kind of trick, but we have to go, and quickly. Thanks, Maer. Follow as well as you can."

He kicked his horse sharply in the ribs, and the animal burst into a gallop to the south.

Save the horse.

What do Swords know about horses?

I know horses.

Can you read him? How is he?

Eager to run. Caught in your emotion. He is having fun.

Good. We'll get there quickly.
Unless you have to chase them.
But they took Eirlin!
We will get her back.

He eased his mount down to a lope and the others, strung out along the road, gathered closer behind him.

They had not been riding long before another rider approached. This one started waving them to stop as soon as he saw them.

"What's going on, Aelf?"

"Turn back, Ecmund. Turn back!"

"Why?"

The man was panting almost as hard as his horse. "They've headed northwest. Burke says if they keep in that direction, they'll hit Bassen Road. When the trackers cross it, they'll leave a man to guide you."

Ecmund reined his horse around. "Perfect."

"What's going on?"

He signalled Lord Ostersund to ride beside him. "Our enemies have played into our hands. They are headed north, on a route parallel to ours. That road we just crossed will take us over, and we'll cut their trail."

"But aren't there fifteen of them?"

Jesco shouldered his horse ahead of the Magician's. "Too bad for them."

Ecmund grinned fiercely at him, and turned his attention to his riding.

They reached the crossroads and turned west, saving their horses now, sure of a final chase. It was only a short trot until they came upon another village lad, waving and pointing. "They went that way, Ecmund. Only a couple of hours ago. Burke and the soldiers are right behind them!"

"We're going to move faster. Catch up when you can."

The trail was easy to follow, with the trampling of the soldiers to mangle the undergrowth. Travelling at their best speed, they soon overtook the trackers. It was a group of castle regulars, but all were locals, and all knew the woods. As Ecmund rode up they split apart, gathered around him.

"Good to see you here, Burke. What's the tale?"

The older man who answered was well known in the area as a poacher, but he had hired on with the Overlord to get the cash to pay off some obscure debt his family had contracted.

"They were here late this morning, Ecmund. They have wounded. I doubt they went far. They were pushing their horses hard, and there's not much fodder ahead. Rocky ground. They'll have to stop for the night before the mountains."

"Then let's go carefully. Point guards out."

"Long as they stay off the track."

Ecmund nodded, and two men headed out to either side ahead. The rest settled down to follow the old tracker, who was having little trouble. "They're tryin' hard, Ecmund, but somebody keeps messin' up the track. Havin' trouble with his horse. It shies and spins, and the tracks go deeper. Easy to spot, hard to cover."

Ecmund grinned. "Or *her* horse."

The older man nodded. "Kind of thing Eirlin'd do, all right. Girl's got spunk."

"I hope they don't catch on."

Heads nodded soberly, and the march continued.

"Hold!"

Everyone stopped at Burke's call, eyes and ears alert.

"I smell smoke."

Nothing yet, Ecmund.

After a long, searching moment, the tracker shook his head. "Errant breeze. They must have stopped, but maybe they moved on. Go slow, lads."

They slipped forward more carefully, all senses attuned.

Eirlin!

Ecmund raised a hand, and everyone froze again.

Where?

Ahead. Very faint.

They waited, Ecmund's hand holding them.

Not moving.

He spoke low. "They aren't moving."

"You jest."

"No."

"The fools."

"Anyone who thought he could steal my sister is a fool."

Smiles answered, and they were not pleasant.

"Dismount. Jesco and I will go ahead, check the terrain. Someone take care of the horses; move them back out of hearing. The rest spread out, not too far apart, and wait for a signal. If you hear fighting, come ahead anyway."

Ecmund and his cousin moved forward, silent as woodsmen can be, through a thinning band of trees. Ahead they could see bare rock, where the mountain rose abruptly out of the forest.

Anything? We've come a long way since you sensed her.

I can hear Eirlin from a long way, Ecmund.

I suppose.

"They're still farther on, Jesco. Should we go back and bring the others ahead?"

"We're not out of shouting. Let's give it a hundred paces more."

Ecmund nodded and they moved on.

Sentry.

Ecmund raised a hand, and Jesco immediately stilled.

Where?

Up to the left.

One?

One.

Ecmund's eyes searched, and Jesco followed his lead.

There!

The two men's eyes met. Jesco made an enclosing gesture with both hands, and Ecmund nodded. He cut right of the trail, and the swordsman went left.

We are the wind in the leaves, Ecmund. They will not hear.

"Keep it up, Kitten. We're going to find her." His whisper carried the force of a shout.

We have found her. She is not unhappy. She knows we are coming. She is here...

She laid out a hazy image of the campsite.

Eirlin is there, in that niche. Jesco will come down to the left. He is ahead. She will come... there. See that gap in the rocks?

"I will be there."

Time to hurry. Jesco is... There he goes!

There was a sudden shout ahead, and many voices answered. Ecmund abandoned stealth, leaping from rock to rock. Kitten guided his feet, strengthened his muscles, and they flew ahead.

There!

I see her!

Eirlin! This way!

Coming, Kitten!

Danger!

"Hey! Hold on there, lady. You ain't goin' nowhere!"

"Yes she is!"

"There's only one."

"It's the guy with the Sword, Menas!"

"Oh, shit!" The two enemy spun and sprinted away.

"Let's go, Eirlin."

Let's go, Eirlin.

"Good idea."

"Our men are that way."

225

They scuttled back through the rocks, trying to make speed without noise.

Jesco.

"What?"

Trouble.

"How much?"

Fifteen to one. He is Jesco, but his sword is only steel. Oops! Fourteen... thirteen. BEHIND YOU, JESCO! They have him, Ecmund!

"Eirlin, our men are just down there. Will you be all right?"

Twelve. Two more. Another!

A sudden wash of pain cramped them.

"JESCO!"

Go, Ecmund! This way! Hold on, Jesco, we come!

Ecmund burst out from behind a rock, skidded to a stop.

Jesco was semi-sitting, propped against a boulder, his sword wavering between the men who confronted him. In spite of their superiority, they seemed reluctant to attack.

Now it is our turn.

Ecmund stepped forward. "Your plan seems to be going wrong."

The bandit leader turned sharply, then took time to look around. "I see no reason for concern." He raised his sword.

There was a weak laugh from the ground. "Now you have to face the family Sword, Tajar, and you're not going to like it."

"What's he mumbling about?" The bandit peered closer at Kitten.

"You're about to find out." Ecmund slid forward again, rapped at the enemy's sword.

Flawed sword! Strike!

Without thought, Ecmund swung back and aimed a hard overhand at the bandit's head. The man had no choice but a direct block, and Kitten dove unerringly for the slight flaw she could sense in the forte of his blade. It snapped cleanly, and she jumped to the man's throat.

"Are you getting the picture now?"

Kitten fed the fear through the point, but the man sneered in desperation. "I have ten men to kill you if you harm me."

"Nine. Not long ago they were fifteen."

Soon to be less. This feels right. She couldn't help it, the hum just floated out of her, laying a carpet of sound around the rocks, echoing from the cliffs. *Come, Ecmund, let me have a few!*

The bandit went cross-eyed, staring at her edge. "I tell you what. You take your sister and go. I never harmed her. She fixed up our wounds, in spite of what we did."

The others are backing up, Ecmund.

226

She could feel the tension in Ecmund's jaw as he spoke through gritted teeth. "I tell you what, Tajar. You take your men and go. I will stay and tend to my cousin. If he dies, I will start after you immediately. You have as long as he has."

"You'd better get moving, Tajar." Jesco coughed again, and his voice came weaker. "I don't think I've got much time left."

"If he doesn't die, you'll be lucky. I'll take him back to the castle, and then I'll come after you. I suggest you find the nearest trail out of this kingdom, and don't stop until far past the border."

He stamped a foot and lunged. The bandit started backward, caught his heel, half fell, and scrambled away.

Kitten hurled fear after him, and the whole pack turned tail. The sound of their flight clattered faintly away over the rocks.

Ecmund knelt by his cousin. "How does it feel, Jesco?"

"It was a pretty good fight, but they finally figured out how to attack all at once."

Ecmund glanced at the still forms around. "It looks like you did all right until then."

"It wasn't half so much fun with my regular weapon. I think your Sword has spoiled me. Not that it's going to matter now, but tell her that, will you? Fighting with her was so much better. One fight like that, and a man can die happy."

I can hear you, swordsman, but you're talking nonsense.

"Hey, I heard that. She spoke to me! Is that because I'm going to die, and it doesn't matter any more? Is she going to take my soul, now?"

No you are not! And I don't want your soul anyway. It's ugly!

His voice faded. "You may be magic, sweetheart, but you're not very smart. I've seen wounds before, and this doesn't look good, especially not from where I stand. I mean sit."

EIRLIN!

She could feel an answering call, faint and far away.

She's coming.

"I have great respect for my cousin's abilities, Sword, but I don't think..."

My name is Kitten, and I am not stupid.

He almost laughed, coughed instead. "Kitten? No wonder Ecmund never told me he had named you."

Careful, Swordsman. You aren't in any condition for a fight!

"I soon won't be in any condition for anything."

Yes, you will.

Ecmund. He needs me. I must be close.

227

"Of course. Here." Ecmund laid her along his cousin's body, nearest to the worst of the wounds, low on the ribs of his right side. She snuggled closer, searching for a way to aid him.

Healing isn't really my forte. Get it? Forte? Hahaha?

Jesco seemed to rally. "A sword with a sense of humour is trouble, Kitten. A sword with a bad sense of humour is much worse."

Another one with no taste.

"I don't seem to have much else, either. I can't really feel my body, and my arms are all prickles."

I'm slowing the blood flow. Better if you sleep, Jesco. I will calm your heart so you don't bleed so much. Then Eirlin will come and all will be well.

"She'd better come pretty quick."

She will. Sleep.

"Is he...?"

Help Eirlin. Get that Magician as well. He might be good for something.

"Good idea, if he'll help."

IF?

"He doesn't have a choice?"

Humans talk too much. Get Eirlin. I will keep Jesco here.

Without a word, he scrambled away.

Kitten moved back into the unconscious mind of her patient, then scanned down his body. His life oozed out in many places, but everything was slack and loose and the heart barely beat. She channelled the blood up to the mind, squeezing off the flow to the wounded lung. She could feel dirt and blight beginning its work, but had no idea how to stop it. She set her grasp firmly, and held on for his life.

Soon there was a scrabbling of footsteps and Eirlin burst upon them, her clothing torn, hair flying. "Where is he? Oh!"

Heedless of the rocks, she dropped to her knees at her cousin's side, a hand on his forehead. "He's barely alive, Ecmund."

"Kitten put him to sleep."

"Good. Where's the worst wound?"

"In his side. I think they got a lung."

She winced. "I don't know what I can do about that. What have you done, Kitten?"

Slowed him down. Shut off blood to wounds.

"You can do that?"

I have done it.

"Can you start him Healing?"

I don't know how.

228

She grasped Kitten's hilt firmly. "I do. I've just never been able to work from the inside. Show me."

Kitten expanded her senses, showing Eirlin what she needed to know. Together they assessed damage, calculated loss.

"That chest wound is the problem. He's got blood in the lung, and not much left to pump around. Let's start the Healing, close up everything we can."

Do so. I find this fascinating.

"I am not doing it for your entertainment."

I am sorry, Eirlin. Sometimes I do not know what to say.

They combined forces again, working as swiftly as possible, but the slow blood seeped through the bandages as quickly as Eirlin put them on.

"Kitten, is he slipping away? I can't feel him like I could."

We are doing what we can.

"I don't think it is enough. He is failing."

We need more Power, to work faster.

"I don't have any more, Kitten. I'm working as fast as possible!"

Something had been itching at the edge of her senses. She withdrew from her task, and it crashed in on her.

Look up, Eirlin. Can you not feel him?

"What? Oh. You!"

Lord Ostersund and Ecmund stood looking on helplessly. Eirlin beckoned to the Magician.

"Come over here!"

He stepped forward hesitantly. "What can I do? I have little knowledge of Healing."

"I have all the knowledge I want. I need Power, Magician. Lay your hand on the blade."

"Mag...Oh. Yes, of course."

He knelt down, reached out, grasped. Power flowed.

That is much better. Look, Eirlin, now I can move things! What do I do here? Like that? Right. What are those white things? They're all cut. Should I...of course I should. There. Look! The energy is flowing through them again. Magician, follow that energy to his mind. That's what you can do. Find what tells his heart to beat, and keep it going.

"This is fascina..."

Shut up. We're not doing this for your entertainment. Eirlin is trying to concentrate. What next? Ah. The lung. I can stop that. Look, I just tighten up the ends and the blood stops. Now we need to close the cut, right? I can't move it enough. Oh. The muscles. If I tense those, and relax those...

"Look, it's closing!"

229

Of course. We are getting much better. I like this. It is almost as much fun as fighting. Come on, Eirlin, we need to work on his leg. Eirlin! Come on! Magician! Help Eirlin. She does not have your strength. There, that's better.

You can relax, now. The other wounds are smaller, and we can work slower. What is that? I think it should be attached over there. Can you press on the outside; just push it… that's right… There. Good as new. At least, it will be.

She searched one more time, all the way through.

That is all. You may rest, Eirlin. His body has been repaired.

They all relaxed, looking at each other in hope. Kitten waited, then glided deeper into Jesco's mind. There was a tinge of warning. She moved into his brain, delved further. Something was not right. Everything was working properly, but still he slipped further away.

Why is he not responding? He is repaired!

It is in his mind.

But Magician, his mind is not injured.

The mind is where a Magician works best. I sense a deep hurt.

A hurt in the mind? Of course. Follow me. I know.

You do?

Yes. It is another kind of wound.

She pulled the Magician swiftly through the layers, deep into the shadows.

There!

I see. The scar has opened.

Yes. I fixed it, but somehow…

You did not remove the injury, only healed it over. The harm remained.

I did not know!

Do not be sorry. We can do this now. Help me. Eirlin, can you mend this?

Yes. Give me more. What about that?

That, I know how to handle.

Yes, Magician. Be careful. He is dear to Eirlin.

I will be careful, little one. Watch and learn.

Little one? Who do you think… Oh! That is good. Very good. It is all coming out. What a ghastly colour! Like rust at night. Where will it go?

He has the natural ability to remove old pains. Slowly over time, if they are not too strong. Now that they are spread about, we can Heal the wound, leaving it empty of danger.

Good. You are very good at what you do.

Thank you. I have never done this before.

What?

Without you and Eirlin, I would not have the Power.

We work well together. There. It is Healed. It's not very neat, is it?

There will be a scar. It will always be part of him, but now it will not destroy him.

That is good. I think we should leave now. Eirlin is very tired.

Do you have extra?

For Eirlin? Of course!

Shall we?

Oh, yes. Yes, she needs that so much. Open wide, Eirlin... there. Shall we stop now?

Yes, we must.

I like this.

That is one reason we must stop.

Yes, I can see. Thank you, Magician.

Thank you, Sword. Thank you, Eirlin.

The man took his hand away, and a cold shiver ran through them all. Then Eirlin withdrew as well, leaving Kitten lying against the bandages.

Ecmund rested a warm hand along her blade.

May I stay here for a while, Ecmund?

"I think you should. He is still very weak. He is hardly breathing."

He is fine. It will take time and rest. He will be more than fine! We were wonderful. By the Forge and the Fire, we were superb!

Ecmund laughed. "For once, I'm not going to disagree." He turned to the other two. "What do we do now?"

Eirlin ran a hand over her brow. "I should be worn out, but I feel strong."

"That is the Power of the Sword, my Lady. She feeds off emotion, but she can give it back as well. The Sword and I gave you a little boost, at the end there."

"Oh. Thank you. We can't move Jesco now, can we?"

"You're the Healer."

"I've never Healed like that, but I think we should stay here and see how he feels when he wakes up."

"Good enough."

Ecmund nodded. "Lord Ostersund, please ask the soldiers to set up camp right here. These rocks are easily defended."

"Right." The Magician strode away. Then he turned back. "And then we must speak."

Ecmund shook his head. "No, we must not. You have business with my Lord Delfontes. It is not for me to discuss it."

The Magician nodded. "I suppose that would be best."

"That's right. Now, let's get a shelter up, and move Jesco onto something more comfortable."

Chapter 27

Soon they had a tent pitched over Jesco, and a pot of soup over the fire.

"Smells good."

Eirlin glanced down in surprise. "You're awake!"

"I can't breathe. Can I sit up a bit?"

"Of course."

They propped him in the most comfortable position for his wounds, padded with blankets. He smiled wanly at Eirlin. "Now I want to hear your story."

"You're not well enough!"

"My ears are fine. I know you're going to tell it. Think of all the fretting I'll do if I can't hear."

Ecmund grinned and signalled the others to crowd in. Eirlin sat on a rock by Jesco's head, and began her tale.

"I was in the kitchen, talking to the cook, when a maid came looking for me. She said they got a message that Perica was in trouble. That she had fallen in the rocks above the castle and hurt her leg. Lord Delfontes was out, and the maid said they had requested a Healer. So I went."

"Of course you did."

"I recognized the man who came to escort me as a soldier from the castle, so I thought nothing of it. When I got up into the rocks, there were five men waiting, maybe more. They jumped out from either side of the trail, slapped a blanket around my head, threw me on a horse, and rode me away. I have to say it was very quickly done. I had no chance to defend myself."

Jesco frowned. "I don't see how you could have."

"But they didn't get away completely. Someone stopped them. I don't know who it was, but the voices sounded familiar. Then there was a fight." She shuddered. "Swords clanking, men crying out. It was terrible. Then there was silence, and then we rode on."

Burke's face was grim. "Three of the castle guard saw you go. They followed."

"And?"

"One dead. The others will be all right."

"I am so sorry."

Jesco snorted, coughed. "Why? It was no fault of yours. What happened next?"

"Be calm. I will tell you. We rode forever, it seemed. I got better at riding without being able to see. It's different, but I was getting used to it. Finally we stopped, and they untied the blanket. The first one I saw was one of the men who attacked me at the village: Tajar. He helped me down, said they needed my services. He had a slash along his arm, quite deep. Four others were wounded as well. Two badly.

"I told them I needed hot water, so they built a small fire. We stayed there while I patched them up. Tajar was quite nasty at first, but..."

Ecmund began to smile for the first time. "...but he let you work on him."

"That's right. He was the one I hit in our cottage. I took extra care with his wound, and that gave me time to work on his mind as well. I have to thank Kitten for that, actually."

"Why?"

Me?

Of course, you.

Of course, me. Why?

"Until I met her, I hadn't realized what I could do. I found I could tend to the mind as well as the body. He had many awful feelings inside him, and I smoothed them over as I worked."

"You Healed the man who abducted you."

"It was the second time I had Healed him, so I had an advantage. Familiar terrain, so to speak. There is a sense of decency in everyone, Ecmund. I find it useful to foster that sense. People tend to treat others better if I do."

Jesco chuckled, but said nothing.

"And did he treat you better?"

"Oh, yes. I could tell the difference. When he first helped me off the horse, it was all fake gallantry, with an implied threat. It was quite frightening, really, all that kind talk, with a sneer behind it. Once I had Healed him and his men, he changed. He spoke the same way, but the sneer was gone. He told me that I would not be harmed, that I was just to be held for ransom, and when the Overlord paid, I could go home."

"You believed this?"

She smiled wanly. "At the time he said it, he believed it. That was progress, I thought."

"Certainly. What happened next?"

"We mounted and rode again, but the wounded men couldn't gallop or trot, and we weren't making good time. They didn't put the blanket back on me so I was fine, except I don't ride that much, so I got sore after a while.

"The leader was worried, I could tell. We rode until well after dark, and when it became obvious that we were stumbling around wasting our energy, he decided to camp for the night. They had some liquor. They drank, not much, but they were tired, and it put them to sleep.

"This morning I woke up before they did, and I broadcast a sort of soothing, and they kept sleeping. I thought I could maybe slip away, but

233

then they woke up. I offered to make breakfast, and of course they said I could. Men are so predictable. Then I tended the wounded. I took as long as I could at that, working on their minds again as I did."

"And they never caught on that you were slowing them down?"

"Tajar started to get worried again, and I had to stop messing around. Then we got ahorse, and on we went." She smiled. "They were a pretty sorry troop: bruised, wounded, tired. I was beginning to think I was one of the happier ones.

"They had one man with them who knew some clever ways to cover their tracks. I did what I could to leave a trail, but I didn't want to get caught and destroy the good feeling I had created."

"You kept having trouble with your horse."

"They weren't happy with my riding skills, but what can you do?" She sobered. "I didn't like to be mean to the horse, but I thought it might help. I considered dropping something, but there were too many of them. Someone would have noticed."

She shrugged. "We rode all day to the north, and Tajar started to look less worried. He was so proud of his strategy, he just had to tell me. He was coming north because he knew you were coming down the same way, on the parallel road, and we'd ride right past you, and you'd have to go all the way to the castle before you started after us."

"Didn't he think about the soldiers from the castle?"

She shook her head. "He wasn't worried about them. Just you."

"But that's just stupid. Surely he thought…"

"I never got the impression he was very smart, Ecmund, and he was really worried about you and 'that Sword', as he kept calling her. Anyway, by this afternoon he thought they were safe, so we camped up in those rocks where you found us. They set out sentries, very military-like this time, and put me in a crevice where I couldn't get free without crossing the whole camp. I made sure they never thought to tie me up.

"I heard them arguing. The men were angry with Tajar because of the problems, and the fight. His excuse was that the plan was rushed because Ecmund was returning. The others had to accept that, because they all have some idea of Kitten's powers. Some were sceptical, but Tajar persuaded them otherwise."

She smiled at Ecmund. "As things turned out later, it was a big mistake to make his men so afraid of Kitten.

"They had sent a scout back along their trail, but were not planning on moving. When the scout came into camp and said that there were five soldiers coming, they got their weapons and prepared a defence. That's when I heard Kitten, telling me to go east when the noise came from the west. I tried to give her a picture of what the camp looked like, but she was faint and far away, so I don't know if she heard me."

I heard, Eirlin. It helped.

"Oh, good. Anyway, they all started shouting. I looked up, and there was Jesco, right above me, high on the rocks. They all forgot about me, so I ran, and Ecmund found me. He brought me to safety, and went back to help Jesco. Then everything went silent. We were just starting to move forward when I heard Kitten call again, in real distress. So I ran. When I got here, I saw Jesco down, and…well, you were all there for the rest of it."

Ecmund nodded, turned to the trackers. "What happened at the castle, Burke?"

The old soldier shrugged. "It was Lady Perica who set the plan. She sent Maer up the North Road to find you, and the rest of us to trail the outlaws. As soon as we realized that they were headed north on the Old Road, we sent Aelf out to cut you off. He had to go cross-country, but I guess he made it."

"He did, and we got here in good time. If Jesco hadn't jumped in so quickly, we could have organized a proper attack, and taken them easily."

Jesco shook his head, weakly, but with conviction. "I was there, you were in position, it looked as if they might leave. So I attacked. It all worked out fine, didn't it?"

Eirlin glared at him. "No thanks to you! What good is it if one of us gets killed to save another? There's no sense in that!"

He shook his head, only once. "Eirlin, some people are more important than others. If it was wartime, maybe I'd be the important one. This is peace, and you are more important than even the best soldier. Don't argue. It might be bad for my healing."

She frowned, but had no answer. He smiled, closed his eyes and lay back comfortably. "I don't often get to beat her in an argument. The truth must have been on my side."

"You're taking advantage, Jesco Coenfri, and I will not forget."

"Neither will I."

"Eirlin, if you're finished badgering the patient, can we finish?"

"I am not…! Oh. I'm sorry. Go ahead."

"Don't worry. It's due to you he's alive to badger."

Jesco spoke with exaggerated weakness. "Yes, go ahead, Eirlin, badger away."

"Oh, shut up, the two of you. I can't stand men when they're so pleased with themselves."

Ecmund became serious. "Is that it?"

They looked at each other. "Any word that there were orders coming from somewhere else? A higher authority?"

235

She shook her head. "From the argument, it looked as if it was all that Tajar fellow."

Ecmund glanced at Ostersund, then away.

Normal reaction, Ecmund.

But Kitten, he can't be the leader.

But he is the Magician.

There is no doubt! He is very powerful, Ecmund.

We'll keep that in mind.

"So, what now?"

Eirlin laid a hand on her cousin's brow. "Now you sleep. We'll see how you feel in the morning."

"Whatever you say, Healer."

She reached over to touch Kitten, sending drowsiness to the injured man. "That's right, Jesco. Whatever I say."

His eyes closed.

"Now, the rest of you can go about your duties. I will sleep here tonight, and I don't see a bed."

The men all bustled about, moving with exaggerated quiet. Night fell, and soon everyone except the sentry was asleep.

Eirlin awoke regularly to check on her patient, but he slept deeply, the Sword clutched against his chest.

"Is that purring I hear?"

He seems to like it. I will wake you if there is trouble.

"Thanks, Kitten." She rolled back into her blankets, and the Sword eased her into sleep as well.

Chapter 28

Jesco's recovery was amazing to everyone except those who had participated in the Healing. And the victim himself. He awoke the following morning complaining loudly.

"Eirlin! I am so thirsty my tongue is sticking to my teeth! What's for breakfast?"

"Drink this broth, Jesco, and we will see."

He started to sit up, winced, then moved more slowly. "I feel like twenty horses stomped over me." He shot Eirlin a glance. "And I seem to remember a few more stomping around in my head. What happened?"

"The Magician was able to use Kitten to aid me in Healing you."

"Oh, yes. The Kitten with the claws." He patted the blankets. "Here she is." He picked her up by the blade, regarded her closely. "I gather I have you to thank for my life."

You're welcome.

"She talked to me again!"

Eirlin shrugged. "She does that at times."

"And she can hear me all the time?"

Ecmund stuck his head into the tent. "From farther away than you would like to think."

"Hey, Ecmund. I remember you putting that bunch to flight. It was as satisfying as we could manage at the time." He looked thoughtful. "Not quite as satisfying as waking up alive this morning. Now, about that breakfast. I smell pan bread!"

"I'm not sure you should eat heavily so soon, Jesco."

"No steel got anywhere near my stomach, girl. I need my strength. Can I have more of that broth?"

She handed it over, smiling, and went out to get bread from the fire.

Once he had eaten, he rested awhile, but was soon twitching again. "When are we leaving?

"We're leaving when you're ready to travel."

"Then let's go."

"We'll see. Lord Ostersund, will you help again?"

Once again Kitten lay against Jesco's ribs, and the Magician and Healer combined their powers over him. It did not take long.

There was the same cold wrench, and Kitten was alone again. The two looked at each other.

"Amazing recovery."

"Yes. It looks like the healing of days. Weeks even."

"Fine. Let's go. Get me a horse."

Eirlin grinned at him. "As you dream. I have a special ride for you."

237

Jesco stopped swearing fairly soon after the party started down over the rocks, the wounded man slung in an improvised stretcher lengthways between two horses.

"Having second thoughts?"

He craned his neck back to look up at Eirlin, riding behind him. "It's very pleasant, swinging away here."

"And you aren't quite as strong as you thought."

He muttered something about women's logic, and lay back.

It was a slow, two-day trip back to the castle, and Jesco complained most of the way. By the end, Eirlin was ready to admit that he really was well enough to ride, but refused to allow him to.

That's right, Eirlin. Don't let him get away with it.

"It isn't that, Kitten. I think the Healing we did could be too much for him at the moment, but he's so happy, he doesn't realize it."

This is happy?

"Of course. He's happy to be alive enough to complain!"

Humans.

They were greeted outside the castle by a mob of villagers, peering curiously at Jesco, calling out questions, congratulations.

Perica managed to wait until they were inside the gate, but her anxious cry cut through the hubbub. "Eirlin! Are you all right?"

Eirlin swung down, stumbling slightly. "Except for the effects of four days on a horse, yes."

Perica took her arm, looked deep into her eyes. "I mean, really all right."

"Yes, Perica, I was not harmed in any way."

"I was so worried."

"I wasn't so happy about it myself at the beginning."

"Just the beginning?"

Eirlin smiled. "I worked things around."

"Did you? I can't wait for the whole tale."

Eirlin glanced up at the Overlord, striding down the stairs towards them. "I think you'll get it fairly soon."

Once he was sure everyone was healthy, Lord Delfontes bundled them all into his private audience chamber and sat them down. Then he looked around at the group. "So. What happened?"

They exchanged glances, and Eirlin nodded. "I suppose I should start." She narrated her experience.

"And you were able to influence those men not to harm you."

She frowned under Delfontes's close regard. "I know what you are thinking, my Lord. You are wrong. I have no control over people, except to help them to heal what they want to heal. If you had a flaw, deep in

238

your soul, that you did not want to deal with, I could do nothing about it. I hope you understand that."

"I see. But you knew what I was thinking."

She threw up her hands. "It was apparent to everyone in the room, my Lord, Powers or no!"

"So now, Ecmund, we need to hear your part in the action."

Our part.

"Our part, my Lord." Ecmund caressed her pommel. "As you know, Burke and I tracked them, with some help from Eirlin. When we got near, Jesco and I were supposed to reconnoitre. He got a bit ahead of the plan, and you know the rest."

"Why did you not take the Magician with you? It seems his skills would have been useful."

"We were still unsure if it was his plan, my Lord. Kitten and I managed quite well."

"Yes, you seem to have. I think it is time to speak to this Magician, and we have the right people here to do so."

He called the guard. "You may send Lord Ostersund in."

Chapter 29

The Magician stepped in, bowing to the ladies and Delfontes. The Overlord nodded and regarded him for a moment. "You have not been exactly forthright with me since your arrival."

The Magician looked slightly guilty. "It was advisable, my Lord."

"It seems to me that, in my demesne, I should be the one to make that decision. Now we come to the point. What do you say to the charge that you are a Magician?"

"I find that a rather strange charge, my Lord. It is like charging you that you are Maridon, or Eirlin that she is one of the Blood."

"You are fast approaching a charge of sophistry as well, my Lord. Are you, or are you not, a Magician?"

"I am a Magician."

"That wasn't so hard, now, was it? Now I must decide what to do with you."

"Do not concern yourself, my Lord. My task here is complete, and I plan to leave."

"Your task is completed? But we have foiled all your plots."

"Not at all, my Lord. You have exceeded my expectations."

"There is something here that I do not understand."

I understand. This Magician is much too proud.

"Not unusual, since I have spent considerable effort to make sure that you did not."

"Can you give me a good reason why I should not have you locked in irons?"

"...and tied to a tree in the middle of the forest, where there are no minds you can influence."

And then I can talk to him. That will be fun.

Don't speak like that, Kitten, Eirlin might hear.

Sorry, Eirlin.

It's all right. I didn't hear.

The Magician glanced at Ecmund, smiled, and looked back to the Overlord. "Once again, your ally proves his value. Would you have thought of removing me from other people?"

"Since I have only learned of your existence in this kingdom in the past three weeks, and known of your presence in my demesne in the past three hours, I have hardly had time to devise a defence."

"My point exactly. But you have a friend who has the knowledge."

The knowledge, yes, and the power. You had better tread softly around my Hand, my Lord Magician. He is wise and judicious, even without my help. Together, we are formidable. If you cross us, I am capable of flaying the skin from your bones. I have a Name, and I am powerful. I am...

"You are an exceptionally rude and talkative young Sword, with a lot of learning to do before you can achieve any sort of reputation."

I am WHAT? She could feel her steel redden... *I am?*

"You are. How many of us are you speaking to at this moment?"

Swords can't count.

To everyone's surprise, the Magician let go a burst of laughter. "And now she's going to pout! Oh, Ecmund, she is such a treasure."

"You know her?"

"Of course I do. I've known her since the first time you entered the castle gate." He looked thoughtful. "Not as well as I'd like, though. She seems to fade in and out. Very elusive. Do you know anything about that?"

A lady may have her little secrets.

"Fair enough." The Magician turned to Ecmund, his smile fading. "And now I may officially recognize the Hand who wields the Sword."

"I suppose."

"And a worthy Hand, there is no doubt. Used properly, she can be of great benefit to the realm. Held by a hero, she could be a crucial force in an emergency."

"But my Lord, what kind of hero am I? I have never lifted my Sword in battle."

The Magician frowned. "Never? You have never fought with her?"

"Just the one blow which broke Tajar's sword. I was ready to fight, and sometimes it looked as if I would have to, but it always seemed that there was another way that would work better."

The blond man nodded. "Hmm. Very good. Perhaps your Kitten is more mature than I thought."

How did you know my name?

"Your name, little one, is written all over you. It is blazoned through the mind of your Hand, and shouts itself from your friends."

What do you mean, written all over me?

"I mean that every word you speak has an undertone of your name. It is thus with all of us. Eirlin, here, calls her name by breathing. Even those with no Blood know her and respond. But also, little Kitten, I mean it literally. May I see your Blade, Ecmund?"

Frowning uncertainly, the Hand proffered his Sword. The Magician reached out and his fingers closed firmly around the hilt. This was not the gentle aid of the Healing. This was a grasp that carried its own steel within.

241

OH! Her mind was seized in the same strong grip, held, turned, observed from all angles. She knew that he could delve inside just as easily, but refrained.

I am sorry, my Lord. I had no idea...

Gently now, little one, I will do you no harm. Of course you did not know.

The Magician relaxed his hold. "Yes, a young one. A hundred years or so. That restricts the possibilities."

He held the Sword to the light, peered along the blade. "Show us your heritage, Sword."

Yes, my Lord. May I reveal in full?

"No, little one. Save your powers for when they are needed. Enough for all to see will be sufficient."

Kitten allowed her pride to show, and the letters fairly leapt out along her blade.

"Hmm. There we have it. Oh, my. See that swirl? That is the sigil of Hunflaed. He made some of the best weapons I have ever seen. She must have been one of his last. That would follow. Light, supple, with great finesse."

"And her name?"

"This part. Those symbols are her full name. The first one, here? With the hooked claw? That means Kitten, more or less."

More or less? I think it is more. Much more!

"I will leave you to discover that on your own, my Lady. It will be an interesting process."

He reluctantly handed the Sword back to her Hand. "You are a lucky man, Ecmund, with a great responsibility. She is young, and has received a very strange upbringing. For some reason she was lost to her hereditary owner, and has perhaps passed through some...questionable Joinings. It is lucky that she came to you when she did, before serious damage was done. The myths of rogue Swords who revel in destruction and the stealing of souls are not completely fiction."

I am not a rogue!

"Only in your own small way, Kitten. Speaking to several people is quite irregular."

I will not stop! I like them... May I not stop? Please, my Lord Magician? I love them!

"Yes, little one. I'm afraid the damage has already been done. It is too late to go back now."

What damage?

He laughed, reached out to touch her hilt gently. "Do you not understand, Kitten? They have stolen your soul."

Stolen my soul? But... Oh. I suppose they have... it's all right, isn't it?

"I don't know if it's all right. You will have to find out, won't you? I suspect there wasn't much theft involved. More of a gift."

He turned to the three young people. "You understand your responsibility, here? You have all been gifted with the trust of a new being. It is up to you to guide her into maturity, you and your descendents."

Ecmund frowned. "Our descendents?"

"Oh, yes. You don't think one human lifetime is enough to mature a Sword who will live a thousand years?"

"I see. But what about the hereditary owner you talked about? What if he comes back and claims her?"

The Magician chuckled. "Since he's probably been dead for fifty or a hundred years, it's doubtful. For his heirs, if we could find them, it is too late. She is Joined to you." He raised open hands. "For all we know, you may be one of them. The families of the Blood are small in number."

The Overlord cleared his throat, and all eyes turned to him. "It is good to have the Sword, or shall I say Kitten, settled. I have a broader interest. Perhaps you would like to explain your position here, Lord Ostersund."

"Of course. I owe you that. You understand, Lord Delfontes, that the King was rightfully concerned that you take your place here quickly and firmly. With respect, Ecmund, there is an especially active strain of the Blood in this demesne, and it is not out of the question that one of you might take advantage."

"You mean start a rebellion?"

"There are always those with old memories and new ambitions."

Ecmund shook his head. "The situation remains the same as it was two hundred years ago. Any attempt at power would result in civil war and destruction. For a responsible leader, the welfare of his people is more important than his own power."

"I am interested in the way you speak. Has anyone else picked up what I hear?"

Perica frowned. "He's talking as if he is still the leader of his people."

Ecmund matched her look. "I am. That is what being of the Blood means. Whoever is King on the throne at Koningsholm, whoever sits in that chair in the main hall out there. It does not excuse me from my responsibilities."

The Magician spread his hands. "You now understand what this means to any who wish to rule here. If Ecmund and the other Blood did not approve of you, where would you be?"

"Sitting here all alone in a castle with half my soldiers sympathetic to the other side. A leader at war with his own people is like a man at war with his own hand." The Overlord glanced at Ostersund. "It is an old saying of the country people here."

"So you see the King's problem."

"I do." Lord Delfontes frowned. "I just don't see how he is trying to solve it. I have never heard him speak of it, have been told no policies, no gossip, even."

"The King's method is the same as yours."

"Mine?"

"Yes. He has carefully chosen some of the Blood who think like Ecmund. He uses us to make sure that problems of this sort are dealt with quietly, by those who are best suited to solve them."

Ecmund's lips turned down. "You are his secret wardens. I don't exactly like that idea."

"Not completely secret. Like you, we are well known to be his supporters. Like you, we usually do not reveal the extent of our powers. You have discovered that this usually makes it easier to deal with others."

"And sometimes, as in your case, it does not."

The Magician smiled again. "In what way?"

Ecmund looked to the others for support. "All these troubles. All the misunderstanding. If you had come out honestly to Lord Delfontes at the very first..."

"What could have been avoided?"

"Well...what about the raid on the village?"

"There was nothing I could do about that, because I had no idea it was going to happen. Tajar is a troublemaker, and always has been. As you may suspect, he had his own motive in starting the whole thing."

"You mean he created that whole situation as a way to get at Eirlin?" Ecmund's hand sought the Sword's hilt. "I have an appointment with him. I told him that once Jesco was delivered to the castle, I would be on his trail. He will be dealt with!"

Yes, Ecmund. We will deal with him in our own sweet time.

His hand jumped from her hilt. "No, Kitten, we will not. This is the kind of thing the law must handle. Private revenge is not a good thing. Do you understand?"

I understand. Although, in this case, maybe a little...

"No, Kitten. That is final. We will let the King's law deal with him."

Yes, Ecmund.

The Magician's laugh was louder this time. "An unforeseen effect!"

Having missed the exchange, the Overlord was looking at the two of them, puzzled.

Ecmund smiled sheepishly. "Now I'm going to be more careful than ever in the use of my Sword, in case I give her the wrong ideas. I will allow the King's men to take care of him. If they catch him."

The Magician nodded. "As you should."

"All right. But what about Perica's horse? What caused it to run away?"

"I have no idea. I scanned the area, but my powers, like yours, work in present time. There was nothing."

"So it must have been a snake, a stick that she stepped on, even a rabbit."

"Horses are known to shy, without any help from those with nefarious purposes."

Lord Delfontes frowned. "So you are saying that there was no plot, no enemy? All our problems were created by our own imaginations?"

"I am saying nothing of the sort. You have had the usual problems of a new Overlord: missed communications, those who would take advantage of an uncertain situation, lack of knowledge of your new demesne, even plain old bad luck. It seems to me that events have worked out much smoother than the King supposed, when he sent me. If it had not been for the discovery of the Kitten, here, I would gladly go back to His Majesty and tell him that my time was wasted."

I am pleased to have been of service.

Perica tossed her hands up. "But what about all the time and effort we wasted, chasing you around? Wasn't that a risk? It could have taken our eyes off more important problems."

"I did not see it that way. I knew you were looking for me. The fear of an internal enemy led to extra vigilance in general, which allowed you to solve several problems before they occurred."

"Then why didn't you tell us about Tajar? We could have stopped him."

The Magician shrugged. "You begin to see the limits on my powers. I cannot say, 'This man is going to cause trouble, arrest him.' Think what that would lead to."

"I suppose, but what about the rest of our problems? I am still not convinced that your silence was any help."

"If you hadn't been sure I was causing a disturbance, Ecmund, would you have spent so much effort helping Lord Delfontes?"

"I suppose not. I only came because I knew it was a problem he couldn't handle. He doesn't feel a thing from Kitten. Of course you knew that."

The Magician turned to Delfontes. "So, as you see, my Lord, there was no reason for me to break the King's instructions."

"If you truly are the King's agent, and I have no reason to believe otherwise, I cannot argue."

The Magician nodded, as if to himself, thinking. Then he bowed to the Overlord. "So, my Lord, having ascertained that you have firmly established your line here, and have, in accordance with the King's wishes, enlisted the able assistance of the local Blood, I feel my mission is accomplished. With your permission, I will leave for Koningsholm in the next few days. It has been an entertaining holiday, but there are places where my talents are more seriously required."

"Of course you have my permission. I suspect Ecmund would like some time with you before you go, but otherwise...unless his Majesty has any other messages for me?"

"Then I am sure he will use more conventional means to send them."

Say it, Ecmund. Strike. Now is the time. Lunge!

"My Lord Ostersund?"

"Yes, Ecmund?"

"Am I to take it that the King thoroughly approves the support of those of the Blood for the ruling families?"

"Exactly. In his majesty's opinion, there can be no better combination to create a firm, fair system of governance."

Yes! Yes!

Calm down. We aren't through yet.

"Thank you, my Lord." He turned to Lord Delfontes. "Does this change your opinion on a topic we spoke of recently?"

The Overlord smiled. "I cannot argue with my sovereign, can I?"

"Thank you, my Lord. May I proceed, then?"

"I gather you have considered seriously what you are about to do to your life, and are willing to take responsibility for the consequences."

"I am, my Lord. Your conscience can be clear."

"Thank you. I wish you all the luck you will need."

"What is this all about?" Perica's frown was deepening. "Why is Kitten bouncing?"

I am not bouncing. I am perfectly dignified and still. Perhaps I will hum quietly, but that is all.

Ecmund smiled at her, bland and formal. "If my Lady would care to take a short walk, there is a matter I would discuss with her, and I require a forest in which to do so."

Her mouth became a straight line, and she looked to her father, who regarded her with a benevolent smile. "All right. I'll get my cloak." With a backward glance at Ecmund, she left the room.

He turned to the Magician. "I wish to ensure our privacy. Can you tell if the forest to the north of the castle is safe?"

The Magician reached out. "Join my hand on the hilt of your Sword. I will lend you Power."

As their hands touched her, Kitten felt a glow of strength. Suddenly her perceptions sharpened, widening through the castle as if it were gauze. She could see bright sparks where the people went about their daily work. Farther out, to the north, the dull green glow of plant life stretched away into the distance. At a nudge from the Magician, she centred on the path north from the castle. Specks of life indicated the smaller animals, but no one walked there. She raised her thoughts to look farther.

Time to come back, little one.

But I want to see…

So do I, but there are dangers. Always watch behind you. If you stretch too far, you can be cut off. You too, Ecmund.

I see.

I see.

Good. We will return now.

There was a wrench as the Magician's hand broke contact. The two men stood a moment, eyes locked.

The Magician looked puzzled. "You have done that before."

"Yes, but never like that. That was wonderful!"

"It was. I do not often get the chance to experience such ability."

"You don't?"

"Oh, no. It is forbidden for a Magician to own a Sword."

"Why?"

"Isn't it obvious? With a Sword such as Kitten, I could become twice as powerful, perhaps more. More than any man could resist. That is why it is forbidden. Also to the King or Overlord."

"What about me?"

"You are strong in the Blood, but you have a fraction of my natural Powers, and are untrained as well. With experience, and as Kitten matures, you will become as powerful as any man should be. By that time, you will be worthy of it."

"I hope so."

"You understand why I must not train you?"

"Yes. No man should have that much power."

"Well spoken." The Magician turned to the Overlord. "There is one who should receive training, though."

"Eirlin?"

"Yes. She has a great deal of talent, and unique experience. I suggest that she travel to Koningsholm with me. She would be very welcome in certain circles."

"Do you think it safe?"

"I think I can take care of her."

Ecmund turned to his sister, surprised to see a faint blush on her cheek. "What do you think, Eirlin?"

He could not help but notice that her eyes shot to Lord Ostersund before she answered.

That is not your business, Ecmund.

Yes it is! She's my sister!

She is her own woman, and she is lonely. He is rather handsome.

Kitten!

Listen. She speaks.

Eirlin looked thoughtful. "I think it would be a good idea. I feel Power that I cannot use because of lack of knowledge. If there is somewhere I could learn…"

"…and teach, my Lady."

She blushed deeper. "If you think so, my Lord."

"Then I can delay my departure until you are prepared."

"You can? Oh, thank, you." She had a sudden thought, and her eyes shot back to Ecmund. He smiled, shook his head, shrugged silently. Her smile suddenly blossomed.

Very good, Ecmund.

Diplomacy is knowing when to shut up.

You have your own problems at the moment.

A dark head appeared around the doorjamb. "I'm ready. What are you doing, jabbering?"

His head rose a fraction. "I was just checking the forest to see if there was any danger."

"Oh. Is there?"

He caught a look from her father and sighed. "Yes, but only to me."

Epilogue

The two children, one stocky and blond, one slim and dark, stood in the banquet room of the castle, staring up at the mantle of the huge fireplace.

The boy pointed. "That one is Grandpa's Sword. When I'm Overlord, it will be mine."

His sister was unimpressed. "No, she won't."

"Why not?"

"It isn't allowed. She will be mine and we will support your rule, and do glorious deeds together."

He glared across at her. "Great-Aunt Eirlin once fought three men with that Sword."

"I know. They almost killed one, but they stopped in time."

"How do you know that?"

"She told me."

"When?"

"Yesterday."

"She couldn't have. She's been in Koningsholm all summer, working at the big hospital."

"Her name's Kitten."

"What? Her name's Eirlin, you silly girl."

"Not her. Her." The pudgy hand pointed.

"Grandpa's Sword?"

"Yes."

"Grandpa's Sword is named Kitten? That's just dumb."

"That's her name. She told me."

The boy looked at his sister. "Why would a Sword want to be named Kitten?"

Because Kitten is my Name.

About the Author

Brought up in a logging camp with no electricity, Gordon Long learned his storytelling in the traditional way: at his father's knee. After a few university degrees, 40 years of theatre work, 30 years of teaching, and 20 years of writing, he feels he is ready to publish his first novel.

Gordon lives in Tsawwassen, British Columbia, with his wife, Linda, and their new puppy, Josh, who just might provide material for a sequel.